ETERNAL LOVE

Without warning, he turned his head slightly and quickly lowered his mouth to hers. It started as an angry, frustrated kiss, a means to quiet her, but somewhere in the heat of emotions, the anger turned to passion and the frustration to surprising longing, as Jenna melted under the remarkable softness of Morgan's lips.

She couldn't believe that this was happening to her, that she was actually responding to Morgan Trahern. Surely her joy in being alive and not wounded or worse was causing the unexpected tingling in her stomach.

As his lips reluctantly left hers, he looked deep into her blue-gray eyes. From there, he searched her face. He looked beyond the sweat, dirt, smudged makeup, and tears and saw how lovely she was, with her lips swollen from his kiss. Leaving them, Morgan again scrutinized her fantastic eyes.

Breathing deeply, he asked, "Who are you really, Jenna Weldon?" as he let go of her hands. . . .

BOOK YOUR PLACE ON OUR WEBSITE AND MAKE THE READING CONNECTION!

We've created a customized website just for our very special readers, where you can get the inside scoop on everything that's going on with Zebra, Pinnacle and Kensington books.

When you come online, you'll have the exciting opportunity to:

- View covers of upcoming books
- Read sample chapters
- Learn about our future publishing schedule (listed by publication month *and author*)
- Find out when your favorite authors will be visiting a city near you
- Search for and order backlist books from our online catalog
- Check out author bios and background information
- Send e-mail to your favorite authors
- Meet the Kensington staff online
- Join us in weekly chats with authors, readers and other guests
- Get writing guidelines
- AND MUCH MORE!

**Visit our website at
http://www.zebrabooks.com**

CONSTANCE O'DAY-FLANNERY

TIMESWEPT LOVERS

Zebra Books
Kensington Publishing Corp.

http://www.zebrabooks.com

ZEBRA BOOKS

are published by

Kensington Publishing Corp.
850 Third Avenue
New York, NY 10022

Copyright © 1987 by Constance O'Day-Flannery

Fifth printing: August, 1993

Printed in the United States of America
10 9 8 7 6

TO MY CHILDREN, KRISTEN AND RYAN—for their love, for their patience, and their wonderful ability to adjust.

And

ANNA BRENNAN—great-grandmother to my children . . . for sharing 94 years of memories with me.

ACKNOWLEDGMENT AND SPECIAL THANKS

Suzanne Hendrie—who knows the reason why.

Linda Cajio and Anne Beltz—two talented writers whose feedback and encouragement was invaluable.

Kathie and Larry Clinesmith—for providing me with priceless research and never objecting to the late night calls. It was their love of their home state that led me to write about Nevada.

Rick Sorensen—publicist for Harrah's Reno, for unselfishly giving of his time.

Hilari Cohen, my editor—for taking all the pressure off my shoulders and transferring it to hers. And for allowing me freedom by telling me to "have fun"—I did.

Prologue

"Take your time, Cassie . . . you can do it!" Jenna yelled across the baseball diamond. She didn't take her eyes off the young girl crouching nervously in the batter's box. Jenna Weldon's heart went out to her. Why her? she silently anguished. Was it always to be her fate that she would be up to bat at a crucial time? With two of her teammates already on base? Jenna inhaled deeply as the opposing pitcher eyeballed Cassie before straightening. As the taller girl brought back her arm, Jenna held her breath.

"Strike one!"

Cassie's face crumbled at the loud shout from the umpire behind her. "Good swing, Cassie," Jenna lied. She didn't care what anybody thought; Cassie needed this hit. Not for the game, and certainly not for her teammates who had teased her throughout the last month for not getting a single hit. She needed something positive in her life. She'd had enough disappointments.

Jenna looked at the short, blond girl and smiled reassuringly. Cassie, the only child of her mother's gardner and handyman, lived with her father in the old gatekeeper's house on the Weldon Estate. Jake, defeated and hurt by his wife's departure two years ago, saw to Cassie's education and little else. It was Jenna who recognized her isolation and took the girl under her wing. It was also her idea that Cassie sign up for softball. When Jake mumbled that he didn't think he could find the time, Jenna had volunteered to take his daughter to practices and games. What she hadn't counted on was being third base coach: that was something else she volunteered to do after finding that Cassie's team had none. Upon hearing it, her mother had shaken her head gracefully, demanding to know where Jenna hoped to find the time for this new cause.

Jenna didn't resent her mother's attitude; in fact, she loved her dearly. She just knew that at the time of her conception, Keene Weldon's genes had been stronger than Claire's carefully structured ones. Her mother's family had been outraged when their lovely daughter fell in love, and then ignored them by marrying the tall, handsome half Irish, half German stranger whose only assets were tied up in a fledgling manufacturing company—building railroad cars, no less.

Jenna smiled as she watched Cassie return to her batting stance. How she wished her maternal grand-parents had lived longer, to see her father's company grow and expand. His had outlasted every other. Weldon Transit was now the only manufacturer of railcars in the United States. The last of a dying breed in this country.

"C'mon, Cassie . . . shorten up on the bat!" Jenna resisted crossing her fingers, not wanting Marcia, Cassie's teammate, to see her partiality.

"She'll never hit it," Marcia sneered. "I don't know why she even plays."

Jenna looked down at the twelve-year-old whose left

foot was firmly attached to the smudged white square of canvas that constituted third base. She felt a flash of guilt for disliking the child, but quickly overcame it. Marcia was her mother's clone. Both mother and daughter were snobs, competitive ones. Jenna had grown up with girls like Marcia in private schools, girls who knew the difference between real pearls and cultured ones by ten years of age. To Jenna, it never mattered.

"Strike two!"

Jenna cringed. "See, I told you," Marcia snidely remarked. Coming back to third base, she looked at the tall, slender woman whose long, dark blond hair was pulled back into a ponytail. As she eyed Jenna's black Ocean Pacific sweatsuit, she said casually, "My mother says she never sees you at the club anymore. She said you'll lose your wrist if you just stop playing racketball."

Jenna tried to smile at the child. Maybe, she should have her steal home on the next pitch. Of course, she'd be tagged out, but at least Jenna would be rid of her, and Cassie would be saved from striking out. It was only a fleeting thought, one which Jenna knew came from her father. Her dad had insisted she play sports in school, and she had varsity letters in field hockey, lacrosse, and track, but it was horseback riding she loved—and baseball. This had been her father's game. It was something he couldn't share with Claire, but found an avid fan in his daughter. The two of them had spent countless hours each spring and summer discussing the strategy of the game as they sat in box seats watching the professionals.

Please, Keene, she silently prayed, as she focused in on Cassie, work some magic with this child. "Just like we practiced, Cassie. You can do it!" This time she

11

put her hands into the large center pocket of her top and crossed her slender fingers. Both hands.

The crack was distinct as the white ball connected with the wooden bat. Jenna's mouth dropped open as she watched the small sphere soar over the heads of the infield. It landed in the gap in the opposing team's outfield.

Remembering her job, she turned to the shocked Marcia and said quickly and a little forcefully, "Go!"

She didn't even watch Marcia run home. Her eyes were glued to Cassie's small, uniformed body as she crossed first base. Cassie watched her for instructions, and Jenna gladly gave her the sign to keep on running. She glanced to the outfield and saw the fielder had fumbled the play. Almost frantically, Jenna motioned for Cassie to keep going, and she had to restrain herself from opening her arms to catch the child who was pushing for third base.

"I did it, Jenna! I did it!" Cassie gulped for air as she stood right on top of third base, unconsciously showing her proud ownership of the small bag.

Jenna's smile was so wide, her cheeks began to hurt. "You sure did. I'd kiss you, except you'd probably die of embarrassment." Jenna shook her head in amazement and, as her own blue eyes caught the joy in Cassie's, she muttered, "What the heck, you'll get over it," and bent her head. As she placed her lips to Cassie's forehead, damp with exertion, she closed her eyes briefly and thanked her father, or whoever, for this moment.

Raising her head, she said happily, "You and I, young lady, are going to hit the Big Dipper on the way home and celebrate. I knew you could do it."

Jenna watched in silence as Cassie finished off her

12

Rocky Road sundae. Both of them had exhausted the conversation concerning Cassie's great hit and, sighing, Jenna sipped her coffee as she approached the subject of her business trip.

"Cassie, do you remember me telling you about my father? And his business?"

Cassie's tongue darted out to lick at the corner of her mouth. Quickly capturing the ice cream before it fell onto the table, she nodded. "Sure. You even took me through the factory and showed me how they made trains and stuff. I remember, Jenna. Why? You have to go back to work? No problem, I'll go with you."

Jenna laughed before continuing. "No, Cass, I don't have to go back to work, not tonight. But, part of my work is trying to get new contracts, new agreements or orders, to keep the plant busy. I told you how important that is, right?"

"Right. You're making trains for Egypt now. Everything's great." Cassie dug her spoon back into the frozen cream.

Jenna knew she was being a coward, not telling her right off, but she wanted Cassie to understand. "That takes care of work through 1987. I have to go out and look for more." Deciding not to skirt the issue any longer, she said, "Look, Cassie, there's a mass transit show, a convention, in Sacramento, and I have to go. I'm leaving tomorrow afternoon."

She watched as Cassie's face fell, and her old guarded look returned. "Okay," she said nonchalantly, as if Jenna's leaving meant nothing at all.

Wanting to break through to her, needing to for her sake as much as Cassie's, Jenna tried to make her understand. "I know you're disappointed," she said softly. "I am, too. Tom Freeman was supposed to go, but his wife was admitted to the hospital today—"

"What's wrong with her? Is she going to die?"

Cassie interrupted.

Taken back by her sudden, unusual question, Jenna shook her head. "No, I'm sure she'll be fine. Tom mentioned her gall bladder. Something about tests. Listen, Cassie . . . I know you think I'm deserting you, especially since I was the one to push you into playing softball, but I've talked to your dad. He says he'll take you, and he'll even coach third base until I come back. It'll all work out . . . you'll see."

Cassie's eyes narrowed. "My dad? I didn't even know he knew how to play ball. He never said anything to me."

Jenna had the feeling there was a lot of things Jake had never discussed with his daughter, and the least important of them was baseball.

Jenna really wanted a cigarette, but she promised herself to cut back to five a day. She'd already had three, and she wanted to save her last two for later tonight. Instead, she sipped on the cooled coffee, trying to overcome the urge.

"I asked him not to say anything. I wanted to tell you," she said softly. "I know it's been tough, Cassie, but be patient with him, okay?"

Cassie looked at the near empty, fluted-glass dish. She studied the melting ice cream for a few moments before looking up, then slowly nodded. "Okay," she said with what first sounded like resignation but perhaps was the wisdom of someone far more advanced than her twelve years. "How long will you be gone?" she asked shyly.

Jenna smiled. "Less than a week. I should be back before the seventh. Cassie, you know why I have to go, don't you?"

Cassie's eyes closed briefly before she attacked the remaining ice cream. "I know . . . your dad. You want to keep his company going."

Now Jenna really wanted the cigarette. "It's so important to me. Just because he's gone doesn't mean I can let everything go, or have someone else do it. I have to find more work for the company. If I don't . . ." She let the sentence hang. Even she didn't want to think about the disastrous consequences.

Cassie's hand reached across the formica table and patted Jenna's. "Don't worry, Jenna," she said reassuringly and smiled. "You can do it. That's what you always tell me."

Claire Weldon stood at the doorway to her daughter's room and quietly sighed as she watched Jenna pack for her trip. She was so much like her father that, at times, Claire didn't feel quite so lonely, knowing that such a strong part of Keene lived on.

She watched her daughter's swift, efficient movements, but also noticed the strain in her face. Such a lovely face, too, Claire admitted. Even if she weren't the mother of the attractive woman across the room, she would think the same: clear, blue-gray eyes, so much like her father's, showed an inherent intelligence above high cheekbones, a small, pert nose, and a quick, ready smile. Claire could only lay claim to Jenna's coloring: fair skin that tended to freckle and burn in the hot sun and thick, tawny hair. Jenna's always shone when the light hit it, and Claire tended to think of it as an outward sign of her personality.

Jenna had always been a happy, sunny child who excelled in school, but pushed further—for her father. Claire, though at times bemused, had never resented the special bond between the two. She knew the importance of a father in a girl's life. She and Jenna had their own special relationship, and through the years it had grown beyond the bounds of mother-daughter; it was better now. They were friends.

Pushing back a lock of pale, blond hair that she refused to let go gray, she entered the room. "Can I help, Jenna?" she asked softly, as she placed an aging hand on her child's firm, young adult back.

Her daughter turned quickly and presented her with a tired smile. "Thanks, Mom. Would you bring me my underwear? I've laid it out on top of the dresser."

Claire walked over to the antique cherry furniture and stared at the filmy underclothes neatly piled on its top. Reaching out, she fingered the delicate French panties, bras, and slips and shook her head. She smiled as she gathered them up, along with five wispy nightgowns that left little to the imagination.

"Who do you wear these for, Jenna?" she asked with a slight catch of laughter in her voice. It was hard to imagine her businesslike daughter, with her collection of Harvé Benard suits, wearing such tantalizing underwear beneath them.

Jenna turned her head away from her luggage, lying open on the bed. "For myself, Claire. Who do you think?"

Her mother placed the silky garments on the white satin comforter. "I was only teasing, Jenna," her mother said in a soothing voice. She pulled at the hem of her long, cream-colored robe and sat on the edge of Jenna's bed.

Her head down, concentrating on arranging her clothes with the least chance of wrinkling, Jenna glanced up at her mother. "You're not going to start, Claire, are you?" she asked with a certain amount of intimidation in her voice.

Her mother appeared to be the picture of innocence. "I'm afraid I don't know what you mean, dear."

16

Jenna couldn't help but laugh. "Please . . . I'll save you the lecture. I know I'm twenty-eight years old. Have never been married, although that doesn't imply complete naivete of a heterosexual relationship." She paused and looked at her mother for some reaction to her last statement. Admiring Claire's composure, she continued. "And yes, someday I would like to settle down and have a family . . . give you the grandchildren you seem to crave so desperately."

Claire pursed her carefully painted lips. "Unfair, Jenna," she stated simply. "I only want your happiness."

She looked at her mother's face and seemed to notice, for the first time, the lines, not quite invisible under the light application of makeup. When had her mother aged so? She always thought of Claire as young, ageless—the sophisticated half of her parents. But that had been before her father died. Since then, Claire didn't shine quite so often, nor laugh as easily as she remembered.

Wanting to again hear that sound from her mother's lips, Jenna raised her eyebrows impishly. "You know that after the convention I plan to go on to San Francisco, to see Laurie. I could always find someone suitable there, some virile stud of a man, and come home pregnant. Would that make you happy?"

Claire's shocked expression quickly turned to amusement as she laughed, a little embarrassed by her daughter's suggestion. "From what I've heard, you might have to look very hard to find such a man in that city," she said slyly.

"Mother!" It was Jenna's turn to be shocked before bursting into laughter.

"Well, I do read, Jenna. I think you could fare far better right here."

"You are going to persist in nagging, aren't you?"

Jenna asked with affection.

Claire raised her chin. "It isn't nagging. I'm concerned. If it isn't business, it's some cause you've taken up. All of it admirable, Jenna, but you've let your personal life flounder. I had hoped Lee and—"

"Lee and I are friends. That's it," Jenna finished her mother's sentence. As she placed the remaining articles in her suitcase, she added, "Mother, Lee and I have dated occasionally for over a year, and nothing serious has come out of it. Nothing ever will. I enjoy being with him. He's sensitive, charming, fun to be with, but no sparks fly. Besides," she said, as she snapped the first lock on her case shut, "he hasn't any business sense, none at all. If his uncle didn't manage his money, Lee's only income would be replacing the tennis pro at the club."

Claire held out her hand and glanced at her lacquered nails. Raising her eyebrows, she again sighed, this time audibly. "I should have fought harder when you and your father insisted that you major in business management. It's all you ever have on your mind. That, and your causes."

Jenna walked behind her mother and placed her arms about her shoulders. She leaned into the older woman and rested her chin on her mother's soft hair. "I'm glad I did," she said quietly. "I need every advantage I can get now. You know the trouble we're having at the plant. Once this Egypt job is done, we are, too, unless . . . I'm also glad Tom couldn't go to Sacramento. I have to do this. Weldon Transit is ours, and it's up to us to save it. If I fail," Jenna said looking out to her room, unseeing, "that means a battle with the union, wage cuts, reduced benefits, even possible layoffs. God, I don't want to do that."

Claire patted her daughter's hand. "I've seen you charm city officials, mayors . . . even an Arab sheik into accepting a bid from Weldon Transit. And, Jenna," she added with more than a little pride, "you are your father's daughter."

As she leaned back against the soft upholstery of the seat, Jenna closed her eyes and breathed deeply. After two and one half hours on the company's Lear, she needed the rest if she was to arrive in Sacramento fresh. Although she already knew what they would contain, she had glanced over Tom Freeman's extensive notes on the plane. Weldon Transit's financial future looked bleak, to say the least; and to avoid takeover or bankruptcy, it was imperative to convince those city officials attending the convention to buy American-made railcars.

She opened her eyes and looked about the railroad car as it sped across northern Nevada. It was a Weldon: stainless steel on the outside and plush within. It wasn't called the Rolls Royce of trains for nothing. Her father had built a quality car, and she had continued, never wanting less.

Jenna's eyes scanned the car, and she was pleased. Her men knew how to build a train. It was as comfortable and as structurally sound as any first-class carrier, either on the ground or in the air. Now, to compete with the foreign market, she was being asked to make inferior cars—to cut back on quality. So far, Jenna refused to do it. It rubbed her raw that Weldon had been beat out of every single new contract this past year. The United States was buying Japanese, French, German—cheaper, yes, but where did they come to fix the inferior cars, once delivered but unable to run? She refused to turn her father's once thriving business into a service company. She would not be defeated easily, and Sacramento was just the beginning.

It had been Tom Freeman's idea to come into the convention city aboard one of their own trains. Tom wanted to take the original transcontinental route into Sacramento. Not having any advance notice that she would be replacing Tom, Jenna had flown to Reno and picked up the train there for the last leg of the journey. Tom, as director of Corporate Affairs, was a wonderful publicity man. Jenna was sure she would be dealing with the press when she arrived in Sacramento, for right before she had left Philadelphia, Tom had winked and made a point of reminding Jenna that she had always been able to handle surprises. Since he refused to elaborate, she had left the Northeast prepared for anything. Now, tired and a little bedraggled from the all-day trip, she could only hope Tom, a whiz at manipulating the media, had used a little caution this time.

Glancing at her black-enameled watch, she decided she could afford to have a cigarette. She was trying and had cut back considerably, but when she was nervous, she found herself craving one. She'd given speeches before. It was this speech, this convention, that could make or break Weldon. She simply had to convince city government that they needed her cars. And she'd use quality, their delivery records, patriotism, anything—anything at all to accomplish it.

Knowing she was in for a tough four days, Jenna stood up and smoothed her deep-green gabardine split skirt back in place. As she walked back to the smoking car, she took in everything around her. These were her cars, and she was proud of them. From the plush, wide seats to the even suspension beneath the high heels of her leather boots—everything spoke of quality. She wished she could have a trainload of city planners with her right now so she could show them what that word meant.

At the last cab, she turned a brass knob, aware of a chilling rush of wind, and entered what she thought was the smoking car. As she crossed the threshold, the train unexpectedly lurched, as if the brakes were suddenly applied, and the heavy door slammed behind her. Fighting to keep her balance, she quickly glanced over her shoulder to make sure nothing had been broken. Blinking a few times in disbelief, she slowly turned her head back to the interior of the car. Where had Tom unearthed this? she mused, as she looked about her. It had to be over a hundred years old. One word stuck in her mind: opulence.

As she entered the door, she stood in front of six beautiful sofas, three on each side of the car, all upholstered in a gorgeous tapestry. Beyond them were compartments. One had tables, where two strangely dressed men were playing cards. Another was some sort of bar, and the last, behind an elaborately carved partition, looked to be a barber shop, where a gray-haired man had a towel wrapped across his face.

She took in all the brass and mahogany and the high frescoed ceiling while remembering Tom's advice about "surprises." Well, he'd outdone himself this time. It was a great publicity stunt, arriving in Sacramento with this car. She'd definitely invite the press in here. It should get Weldon terrific coverage and remind the tight-fisted mayors of the twenty cities attending that even a hundred years ago, America had insisted on first class.

Jenna raised her head and noticed the strange stares and actual frowns on the five men inside the car. The two playing cards, in the second section, had stopped and were scowling in her direction. Beyond them, the stout barber rearranged a white towel over the seated man's face, almost as if he were shielding

21

the man from her. She resisted shrugging her shoulders at their actions and noticed the remaining man, seated closest to her on one of the beautiful sofas that was bolted to the floor.

He was obviously part of this troupe of actors, but decidedly different. Whereas the others had dark, tailored suits, some with velvet lapels on either side of elaborately winged tip collars and dark, thick ties, this man was dressed like a cowboy.

A large Stetson hung absently from his crossed knee as this cowboy tried to bury his face behind a newspaper whose heading was *The Transcontinental*. Jenna had already caught a brief glance at his face. Beneath jet-black hair, his expression registered shock when she first entered, before a slight smirk curled his full lips and softened his smile beneath a dark mustache. She never got to see his eyes, but she had the distinct impression they would show laughter if he hadn't hurried to bring the newspaper up in front of them.

Feeling a little self-conscious at the stares of the other men, Jenna decided to take a seat next to the man so engrossed in the old newspaper. As she seated herself on the antique sofa, she placed her briefcase across her lap and opened her leather purse.

As neat as she was about her appearance, her purse was an outright disaster. She'd once heard that viewing the inside of a woman's purse was a major clue to her character and, as she rummaged through hers, Jenna only hoped the saying wasn't true. It wasn't that she encouraged chaos; it was just that she was always in too much of a hurry and found herself stuffing necessary articles inside the current bag she was using. Her briefcase, on the other hand, would make Felix Unger envious. There, she was a stickler on neatness.

Finding her cigarettes, she withdrew one and held it

in her hand as she retrieved her lighter. Jenna settled back and held the cigarette to her mouth. She pressed down on the silver lighter a few times, but could produce nothing more than sparks. Suppressing a groan, she refrained from throwing it back and merely dropped it into the clutter of her purse.

She turned her head sideways and looked at the lean legs encased in tight-fitting jeans. As her gaze lowered, she wasn't surprised to find worn cowboy boots, one of which was very close to her own crossed leg.

Feeling she wasn't being too bold, she asked in a polite voice, "I'm sorry, would you happen to have a light?"

The paper slowly lowered, and Jenna Weldon, head of a large manufacturing company, known for her cool objectivity and understated sophistication, found herself immobilized as she stared into the deep-blue eyes of the original Marlboro man.

Chapter One

"I beg your pardon?" he asked in a curious, polite voice.

Jenna felt foolish. Of course, he was great looking—aren't most actors? His deep, polished voice seemed to rumble up from behind a navy-blue cotton shirt that fit snugly to his chest and emphasized his hard leanness.

She tore her eyes away from his and glanced to the slope of his hairline. His hair was too long to suit her, and his sideburns had gone out in the seventies, but she found her eyes returning to the nape of his neck where thick black hair was starting to curl up. She swallowed the ridiculous urge to place her finger there to turn it back under.

Jenna mentally shook herself. Her mother was right. She was spending too much time engrossed in her work. What other reason could there be for her to act like a teenager? Even Cassie could manage this better.

Pulling together her corporate look, she smiled slightly and repeated her request. "Would you happen to have a light?"

The man's eyes widened, making them seem bluer than she had originally thought. "A light?" he asked, glancing at her hand.

She held up the cigarette. "Please."

She watched the way he caught the inside of his right cheek between his jaws, as if he were holding back laughter, then reached inside his pocket to produce a single, long, wooden match. Without a word, she watched, fascinated by his casual movements. Holding the match between his fingers, he brought it to his foot, the one so close to hers, and flicked it against the heel of his boot. Almost immediately, Jenna smelled the acrid odor of sulphur as the match caught.

Cupping the long flame in his tanned hand, he brought it close to her. She placed the cigarette to her mouth and inhaled deeply. No sooner had the cowboy shaken out the flame when she heard another male voice, this one blatantly shocked.

"Now, see here!"

Before she had a chance to thank the cowboy, she was drawn to the tone of the other actor's voice. She glanced up to see one of the card players frowning his disapproval. Jenna didn't want to get defensive—didn't feel she had to explain that she had cut back from a pack and a half a day to five cigarettes. She knew everything negative about smoking and recognized that she must stop. She *was* trying, but she wasn't going to explain it all to a stranger. Ignoring the man, she turned back to her cowboy.

"Thank you," she said in a soft voice to hide her annoyance.

This time he looked at her, really looked, and Jenna found herself growing warm under his close scrutiny. His gaze wasn't insolent, but rather openly curious as he took in her stylish boots and calf-length split skirt. As his eyes rose to her white crepe blouse with its shoulder pads and tiny tucks that started at her shoulder and ended in soft folds at her breasts, she decided to end his now embarrassing perusal.

"Are you going on to Sacramento?" she asked pointedly.

Her voice seemed to stop his thoughts, and he looked back into her face. Folding the newspaper in his hands, he answered with a short, "Yes, ma'am."

Well, Jenna thought, he wasn't much on words, and she would have ended the conversation right there if the card player hadn't continued to stare as he watched her smoke.

She wanted to ask what his problem was, but didn't want to start a discussion on the evils of smoking. This *was* the smoking car, wasn't it? And, after all, if these men were hired by Tom, then they were working for her. Deciding to make sure of her facts before she took on the rude one, she turned back to the man she thought of as the cowboy.

"What are your instructions, once you reach Sacramento? Is there some plan I should be aware of?"

She wasn't prepared for his sharp look. His eyes, the ones she thought of as magnetic just moments ago, turned ice blue as they bore into hers. "I'm afraid I don't understand, madam," he said while watching her face. "I have no plans."

Deciding it was time to reveal herself, Jenna smiled at his reluctance to state his purpose and said, "I should have introduced myself earlier. I'm Jenna Weldon. If you were to report to Tom Freeman, I'm afraid it will have to be me. Tom isn't coming on this trip."

The cowboy took his hat off his crossed knee and played with its leather band as he held it front of him.

26

"Ma'am, you're talking to the wrong person," he stated in a definite voice.

Jenna always believed you could tell a lot by a person's body language, and this one was telling her to back off—that he was uncomfortable with her words.

"I'm sorry," she said. "I thought you were hired by Tom Freeman to play a cowboy. In fact, I'm sure these other gentlemen are actors. It's a great publicity stunt. This car . . . everyone dressed in nineteenth century clothes . . . it's terrific. I'm sure we'll get a lot of play out of it."

For some reason, she wanted to make an impression on him and looked down to the paper in his hands. "Like this paper," she pointed out. "See, *The Transcontinental*. Look at the date . . . June 10, 1870. I really have to give Tom credit. He thought of everything. Imagine! Copies of a hundred seventeen-year-old newspaper."

The cowboy slowly turned his head in her direction. "You think this paper is a hundred and seventeen years old?"

Jenna exhaled and smiled. "I don't know where Tom unearthed it, but it's great copy. Could I see it?"

His dark eyebrows almost met as a look of confusion came over him. "Sure, here." He handed the folded paper to her and sat back on the sofa. Again, she felt his eyes on her as she glanced over the headlines.

"And you think those men are actors?" He interrupted her reading.

She glanced up to the men who continued to stare at her as if she were less than human. Not wanting to assert herself and perhaps provoke an argument when they were so close to Sacramento, and especially not wanting to jeopardize Tom's work, she again ignored them and said in a whisper, "Some people are touchy about smoking. I know they're right, and I have no defense, so I make it a habit of not getting into a discussion with them."

"If you'll pardon me for saying so, ma'am, those men are not actors. I just don't believe they've seen a woman quite like you before." And with that statement, he placed the wide black hat on his head, tilted the brim so it reached his nose, and closed his eyes.

Jenna sat in the chair, obviously dismissed. She continued to look at the man seated next to her. The hat couldn't hide his rugged good looks, the square jaw that looked in need of a shave, the slightly flared nostrils as he breathed; the way the very tip of his hat touched his straight nose; the thick mustache, trimmed to the corners of his mouth, and his full lower lip that dropped slightly to reveal straight, white teeth.

Jenna felt more than foolish for staring. She had always firmly believed that an expertly tailored, three-piece suit was a turn-on, but this man was so casually masculine—so male—that she found herself growing warm again as she watched him ignoring her.

Embarrassed by the unexpected turn of events, she ran a long-fingered hand through thick, blond hair, which she had parted on the side and held back with a thin, tortoiseshell clip, the rest falling straight to just below her shoulders. Jenna had been ignored before, but never in so forthright a manner. Perhaps she had been too pushy. Yes, she thought, that was it—telling him about being a Weldon and how these men were working for her.

The whole encounter couldn't have taken more than five minutes, but right then, to Jenna, it seemed like more than an hour had passed since she entered this strange car.

Thinking she wasn't about to accomplish anything with these men, Jenna stood and resisted telling them what great company they had been as she looked for a place to dispose of her cigarette. Spying a brass spittoon by the door, Jenna walked to it with her head held high. Not daring to look into the large urn, she delicately dropped her cigarette and, placing her hand on the door, she turned back to them.

She wouldn't tell them they were actually working for her—she'd save that for the station, and it wouldn't hurt to see them squirm when they discovered that she was the one who pulled the money strings at Weldon. Instead, knowing it would annoy them further, she cocked her head and gave them her sexiest wink and smile, saying in a sultry voice, "See you in Sacramento, guys."

She turned and opened the heavy door to leave, but not before she heard their quick gasp of outrage, and then caught sight of the cowboy's lower lip turn up in a half smile under the shield of his hat.

As she tried to manage the open vestibule in order to get into the next car, she couldn't help but wonder who the cowboy really was. And as she unwillingly shouldered the door open, she thought about his great eyes and his confused smile. It was too bad she'd never see him again—at least he had a sense of humor.

Thinking of his smile, she entered the next car, and the upward curve of her lips froze as she looked into the faces of a whole carload of actors. Men, women, even children were sitting on straight leather seats—all of them dressed in old-fashioned clothes. The smooth ride from the modern suspension she had taken pride in, less than fifteen minutes ago, had disappeared as she held onto the door behind her for balance. Faces, most tired looking, stared up at her as the door slammed. Her mind registered first their shock in seeing her, then the leering looks of some poorly dressed men, coupled with haughty glances and lips pursed in disapproval from most of the women.

Squaring her shoulders, she tried to make her way down the center aisle by holding onto the backs of each seat as she passed. Where had *this* car come from? she worried, as she tried to ignore the more obvious glances and listened to the *harrumphs* and *tsks* coming from the passengers as she passed. I know I didn't come through this car, Jenna thought uneasily. I wouldn't have forgotten this kind of hazing. Absently, she thought about the talk she would have with Tom. The five in the smoking car were brilliant, but this? How much was it going to cost to pay for a whole car of actors?

Deciding enough was enough, she stopped her awkward movement and touched the shoulder of one very overweight woman, dressed entirely in black from her stout shoes to the heavy, long dress and plain bonnet that was tied under her third chin.

"Excuse me, could you tell me—" she began.

"You will remove your harlot's hand. How *dare* you!"

Jenna pulled back her fingers, as if burned, and stared into the thin, pinched face of the man seated next to the large woman. She could feel her heart begin pounding behind her rib cage, as her own fury started to mount. She noticed the woman had shifted her cumbersome body closer to the man, as if Jenna's touch had been contaminated.

Jenna felt the color rise to her face. She hated scenes, and everyone on the train had heard the words uttered by the little man with the fanatical eyes.

"I only wanted to know where the rest of the train was," she explained in a deceptively soft voice. "The modern part."

"Where is your shame, woman?" the man said in a voice meant to stir the rest of the passengers. Jenna quickly glanced around her and could see the man's tactic had worked. She almost cringed from the leering and disgust she saw reflected there.

She couldn't help but pick up the loud whispers coming from all around her. "Look at her face!" "See, she even paints her nails!" "Doesn't possess a shred of decency . . . prancing about with her skirt a foot off the ground!" "I thought the Central Pacific was reputable. I didn't think we'd be subjected to *this*!"

Something in Jenna made her raise her shoulders and lift her chin. Call it breeding, or just plain class— Jenna Weldon would not get into a cat fight. These were actors for goodness sake!

When the name calling began in earnest, Jenna started backing up. She didn't like the look in the little man's eyes or his wife, who called her harlot for at least the tenth time and brought up her huge fist, brandishing a thick, black umbrella.

What the hell is wrong with these people? Jenna thought as the blood in her veins started to pulse faster. If she didn't get out of here, she was going to find herself in the middle of a riot. Already, others were beginning to join the crazed couple.

Clutching her purse and briefcase in front of her, holding them to her chest, almost as a shield, Jenna reached behind her for the door handle.

Morgan Trahern found himself silently chuckling as he thought back to the incredible woman. When she had first entered the car, he'd been as shocked as the rest. For him, it was because he hadn't expected to

31

find such a beauty, paint and all, entering this strictly male domain.

He could still hear them talking about her as he waited for a shave and a much needed haircut. Perhaps he had been foolish to risk coming into this car without permission, but he wanted to arrive in Sacramento, minus the extra growth of hair on his head and face.

Now that his mission was over, he was anxious to relay his information and get on with his life. What had started as a favor had turned into a three month investigation. He had accumulated such volatile evidence that the entire country was going to be shaken when it was revealed.

Morgan shifted in his seat. He never thought, those months ago, when he was first approached by Frank Adams to investigate the railroad, that he would have unearthed anything of this magnitude. Damn! He'd expected to uncover some graft, but not this—nothing like this. Hell, how was he to report that almost half the members of the U.S. Congress and even as high as Grant's cabinet, were in on the biggest hoax this country had ever experienced?

The Credit Moblier: such a fancy name to disguise the Pacific Railroad ring. Its members were the most powerful of politicians. Bribery, in the form of stocks, ran rampant. It was just like Adams had said those months ago, only then he hadn't wanted to believe it, had refused, until Frank challenged him to find out for himself.

He'd thought his days of spying were over, left behind in his past, with the end of the war. He was wealthy in his own right now and didn't need the adventure any longer. At least, that was what he told himself until that night in early March when Frank had come for a visit. He should have known his former superior wouldn't have wasted a trip East for mere social reasons. Frank Adams had a purpose behind every action, and that night in Morgan's study had proved to be the most infuriating. Grant had specifically requested Morgan's assistance, and Adams had used every trick in the book, including their friendship, to make him take up his old profession.

Now, all he wanted was to hand over the president's requested information to his contact in Sacramento and take the returning train back East. He'd left his import business too long in the hands of hired help, and he wanted to resume his quiet, patterned life.

During the last month, too many unexpected, half hidden memories came creeping in from his subconscious. Memories that, since the war, he had tried to bury. He knew now that they were always there. Waiting.

The first month he enjoyed the resumption of his old life, trading in his tailored suits for the more inconspicuous garb of a drifter. Between Omaha and Salt Lake City, he'd worked in more than eight camps, gathering information by any means, legal or otherwise. When he realized the extent of corruption and who was involved, he'd lost the taste for the hunt. It was over and, like any stalker of game, he yearned to return to civilization—to a more orderly way of life. He planned to spend three days in Sacramento, and then he was going home—back to Baltimore.

Morgan raised his hand and lifted the tip of his hat back a few inches. He glanced toward the barber to see how much longer he'd have to wait. Damn! All he needed was for the conductor to catch him here. He'd already had one encounter with the burly, bad-tempered man, who considered himself appointed by the Almighty to rule this train with a heavy hand. Not wanting to confront the man again, especially when he was so close to completing this assignment, Morgan was about to hurry the barber along when the door opened and the tall woman with the great smile returned. Only this time she wasn't smiling.

Chapter Two

Jenna looked around at the men inside the smoking car and saw little to reassure her in their faces. They again looked outraged, and one older man looked ready to pull the right side of his mustache off as he yanked at it in an obvious attempt to control his anger. Her eyes unconsciously sought the cowboy's. His were questioning, but she didn't see annoyance and was relieved. Returning to the seat next to him, Jenna asked in a breathless voice, "What's going on in the next car? Those people are crazy!"

She watched the dark eyebrows come together and noticed that the tiny lines at the corners of his eyes deepened. "Had some trouble, did you?"

"Trouble? You should have heard them! All I asked was, where's the modern part of the train . . . the cars I was traveling on earlier. One of them looked ready to attack me. And the things he said!" She let the air in her lungs escape through clenched teeth and took a deep breath in an effort to calm down. "Talk about method acting!" she said, shaking her head.

The cowboy's lips came together, and she saw he was again amused. "Why are you insisting that everyone on this train is an actor?" he asked with a grin

35

creeping up the corners of his mouth.

The smile, which had been endearing when she first saw it, became annoying as she sensed him condescending to her. "And what am I supposed to think?" she asked in a tight voice, unable to keep her growing irritation from showing. "That all of you are dressed like this because you enjoy it?"

She looked at the other men. "What are all of you, if you aren't actors?" she demanded in a loud voice.

A gray-haired man pulled at the stiff collar at his neck and stood, facing her. "Now, look here, madam. When you invaded this car the first time, it was bad enough. Now, you've returned and demand to know our professions, as if it's any of your business. I think we've all had quite enough. You and your companion had better leave before we call the conductor."

Jenna watched the others nod their approval of the way the man handled her. As she rose, she sensed the cowboy also come to his feet. "I'm not going anywhere until I get some answers. And he's not my companion, he's just—"

Jenna's words were cut off by the rush of air coming from the door. She turned and saw a husky, dark-haired man outfitted in an old-fashioned conductor's uniform. Following him was the fanatical man and his red-faced wife.

"What's going on in here?" the conductor demanded. Without waiting for an answer, he turned to the couple behind him. "She's the one?" he asked, and Jenna saw the two nod in her direction.

"That's the strumpet—parading herself up and down the aisles, in front of decent men and women. She actually put her hands on my wife. I want something done about this. You're the conductor . . . do something!"

36

Jenna could feel the heat rise from her throat and cover her face. She began to breathe quickly and deeply as her own anger was renewed.

"Now wait just one minute," she said in a clipped voice. "I have something to say about this. I merely asked the woman a question. If I touched her shoulder, I apologize, but I certainly didn't deserve to be verbally attacked. I have as much right to be here as anyone, and now *I* would like some answers."

The conductor lifted his dark round eyes to her, and Jenna unconsciously swallowed when she read the cynicism and cruelty written there. "Just when did you get on this train, missy? I don't remember you being here before."

Something about the man frightened her, and she quickly reached inside her purse for her ticket. As she handed it to him, she said, "I boarded in Reno. And I'm going through to Sacramento."

Thick fingers, reminding Jenna of sausages, took the ticket from her hand. She watched the man read it, then gasped as he turned it sideways and ripped it in half. "I don't honor no bogus tickets for some railroad called, *Amtrak*. You got money for a proper ticket?"

Foolishly, Jenna lost her patience. "That *was* a proper ticket, you . . . you jackass! I'll see that the next time you work for a railroad will be to clean out the men's rooms! I've had it with this whole stunt! It's gotten out of hand."

Everyone started shouting at once, and Jenna's ears hurt from the calliope of angry voices. The conductor's hand reached out to grab her upper arm, and she pulled back, right into the silent cowboy behind her.

"Look," the voice behind her finally sounded. "I'll pay for her ticket. There's no need for this."

Jenna started to turn around to tell him there was no need for him to pay for her when the ham-fisted conductor took hold of her arm. "What're you doing in here?" he directed to the cowboy. "Didn't I tell you to keep to your seat?"

"He's her fancy man. Why else would he want to pay for her?" the heavy woman, who'd been silent up till then, stated. "I say we put them both off the train. They don't belong with decent people."

Her small husband seemed inspired with his wife's words. Suddenly, he raised his hands to the ceiling of the car and closed his eyes. In a loud, strident voice, he cried, "I have been instructed by the Lord to banish evil in this wicked land. He has seen fit to place these two wantons before me, and I see it as my duty to Him, and to you, my Christian brothers, to start them on the path to reconciliation."

Jenna couldn't help it. She started to laugh. It was perfect comic relief. Still clutching her handbag and briefcase, she said between giggles, "Don't tell me . . . you're supposed to be the traveling preacher, right?"

The fanatic's eyes burned into hers. "You will always remember the name of the Reverend Nathaniel Hobart as the servant of the Lord who put an end to your wickedness." He turned to the conductor. *"The Lord demands this train be stopped!"*

Jenna had heard about it, contagious hysteria, but had never seen it in action before. She didn't know how all of it happened so fast, but she found herself and the astonished cowboy held at gunpoint by one of the men she had seen playing cards. The conductor had left, and she stared at the group of people around her.

"Have you all lost your minds?" she demanded.

38

"This is 1987. You can't do this to people and get away with it! I certainly hope none of you expect to be paid when we reach Sacramento. This is outrageous!"

Everyone stared at her as if she had lost her reasoning, and she turned to the cowboy next to her. "Why don't you say something? Tell them we don't know each other."

The cowboy's face was devoid of any emotion. Jenna sensed he was barely controlling his temper. A round muscle moved slowly at his jaw, by his ear, as if he were clenching his back teeth, and the top of his thick mustache moved slightly as he exhaled more strongly than normal. "Lady, you seem to be doing all the talking. I might suggest that you keep your mouth closed from here on in. They'll go easier on you if you don't continue to antagonize them."

"Antagonize *them*? You and I are being held here like prisoners, waiting for God knows what—"

"Blasphemy! You heard her, brothers. She uses the Lord's name. We're right in what we are about to do." The crazed preacher shook his head at Jenna and the cowboy as if they were doomed, while his wife's face held a look of supreme satisfaction.

Jenna was about to tell the old cow what she could do with her smirk, when the train screeched and suddenly lurched forward. Everyone but Jenna seemed to be prepared for it, and she started to fall. Almost immediately, she felt strong hands on her, one at her shoulder and another at her waist.

She looked up into the blue eyes of the cowboy and, despite the ridiculous position she was in, she felt the strange stirring of something in her thighs: a crazy, out-of-place tingling that settled in her stomach. Feeling foolish, she stumbled to her feet, mumbling a hoarse "thank you," and watched the bear of a conductor reenter the car. He came directly to them and asked shortly, "You got anything in the luggage car? Hand me the numbers now or you'll never see it again."

Jenna watched the cowboy reach into the top pocket of his shirt and bring out a small plate, numbered and embossed with the name, Sacramento. He reluctantly handed it over, then looked at her. "No luggage," he asked skeptically. "No trunk? Nothing?"

She saw the doubting look in his eyes. "I . . . I had a suitcase when I came on in Reno. I don't know . . ." She let the words trail. She wasn't about to give the paper luggage claim to the conductor and have him destroy it. She wanted it with her when she arrived in Sacramento and straightened out this mess.

"All right! Missy, here, has no luggage. Find this one and bring it back." Impatiently, the burly conductor handed over the cowboy's metal claim to a younger version of himself and then turned back to them.

"You two got one choice . . . one choice only. I got a schedule to stick to, so you listen real close to the preacher here." He nodded to the small man, who produced a worn Bible from inside his long frock coat.

Even when he turned his crazed eyes to the conductor and said, "I'll need two witnesses," Jenna still didn't grasp what was about to happen.

She found herself ushered outside. Standing in the blazing heat, the sun pounding on her unsheltered head, she continued holding her purse and briefcase in front of her, as if the two articles could protect her from the lunatics standing on all sides. She looked over their heads to the train. It was old, *real* old. Or, more accurately, it was an antique version of an old train. She watched the steam that hissed out from under the frame and wondered how she could have found herself on it. *What happened back there, outside Reno?* The windows of the passenger cars were open, and she could clearly see the faces of the people inside, as they pressed close to the opening to see the spectacle taking place outside.

"Look, you threw us off. That's enough! You can't do this!"

Jenna heard the angry voice of the cowboy protesting something the conductor said, but she had been busy watching the preacher's wife trying to maneuver her wide girth down from the train and had missed the man's words. She continued to watch the woman as she made her way to them, and it was only then that Jenna looked back to the people surrounding her.

Her mouth dropped open, and she gasped as she took in the bizarre scene before her. The cowboy stood rigidly straight and stared over the train and into the sky. His lips were pulled back in a tight, grim line, and his nostrils, again, flared out as he expelled breath that she could actually hear. The reason for his frustrated anger was a pistol, held to the side of his temple by the gloating conductor.

"Now, we're gonna do this all legal like," the man said calmly, as he continued to hold the revolver with a steady hand. "Let's get on with the wedding, Reverend. I take on fuel and water at Verdi, in twenty-six minutes."

"Wedding?" Jenna said the word softly, refusing to believe the insinuation. "Who's getting married?"

"*We are*," the cowboy growled from the corner of his mouth. "Haven't you been listening? It was the good Reverend Hobart's idea that we start our new life as husband and wife. Our friendly conductor and his persuasive pistol, here, are to be our witnesses."

"This has to be done right," the heavy woman puffed out as she came to the front of the small gathering. "I shall also stand as witness."

The cowboy gave her a cynical smile. "Thank you, ma'am," he said with exaggerated politeness. "Now, perhaps your friend won't mind removing his gun. I'd hate to deprive this lady of her wedding night."

As the woman gasped, the preacher opened his Bible and began reading. Jenna didn't listen to him, but turned to the man next to her. "Are they serious? They can't do this. This is America, for Christ's sake!"

The cowboy didn't have a chance to answer her as the reverend shouted, "You take the Lord's name in vain once more and I'll have you gagged! Where is your shame?"

Jenna studied the eyes of her adversaries. They showed anger, determination, satisfaction, and glee. She started nodding as she scanned their faces. "I know," she said, as if she finally figured out what had happened. "This is one of those T.V. shows, isn't it? Practical jokes? You're going to show this at the convention and get a good laugh, right?"

The conductor's round eyes became slits as he squinted at her. When they slid to the cowboy, he said, "Sounds like you're marrying a real loon. Should have listened to me and stayed where you belong, drifter." And, cocking his head, he indicated his impatience. "Get to the important parts, Reverend."

The reverend cleared his throat before continuing. "Do you . . . what is your name, son?" he asked the cowboy.

When the tall man beside her didn't answer, the conductor pushed the pistol further into the cowboy's dark hair.

"Morgan Trahern . . . and I'm not your son."

"Do you, Morgan Trahern, take this woman to be your lawful wife?"

Silence.

Jenna's eyes widened as she heard a deadly click from the hammer being pulled back. She watched Trahern close his eyes and lift his chin. Even though she knew it was part of a joke, she was relieved when he nodded, glad that now the conductor would remove the gun.

"You must say the word, Morgan Trahern," the preacher advised. "Do you take this woman to be your lawful wife?"

"Oh, go ahead," Jenna said lightly, now that she was sure it was all some bizarre practical joke. Even though she was furious, fuming inside, she wasn't about to let the unseen camera catch her at it. She'd play right along with them and have the last laugh in Sacramento—and would also fire Tom Freeman the moment she reached a phone.

Standing next to the furious Trahern, she stretched her neck out and turned her head to see him better. Lifting one hand to shield her eyes from the hot sun, she looked into his angry, dark-blue ones and smiled. "Ah, Morgan," she said his name caressingly. "You'll be getting quite a woman."

She could tell he caught the humor in her voice, and the anger of his eyes turned to confusion. "*You are a loon*," he breathed softly.

"Well, what's it to be, Trahern? A bullet to the head or a crazy wife? I'm pulling this train out in three minutes."

Ignoring the conductor, Morgan continued to look at her. Didn't she realize these people were serious? Or *was* she really crazy? As he looked deeper into her

43

blue-gray eyes, he could tell she was laughing at them, like she had some trick up her sleeve. This farce couldn't be legal, and anyway, he liked the way she said his name.

"Yes. I do."

The reverend looked pleased. He turned to Jenna. "And you . . . your name?"

Jenna smiled at him sweetly. "Jenna Weldon. And don't bother reading it. We all know what a hurry the conductor is in, so I'll save you the time. I do, too."

The preacher's eyes shifted nervously. "I think we'll skip the part about anyone having any objection. By the power invested in me by the state of Nevada, I hereby pronounce you husband and wife.'

Everyone seemed satisfied, though no one offered their congratulations, and they hurried back to the train. She was left standing next to the man, Morgan Trahern, as she watched them all disappear into the red cars.

"What? No ring? No rice? What a disappointment," she called after them and, finally dropping her purse and briefcase to the ground, she linked her arm through her cowboy's and waved to the spectators, one of whom she was sure was holding a camera.

When the conductor reappeared, the train was starting to move slowly, and great clouds of steam rose from the high, black chimney stack. "Tell me, sir," Jenna yelled over the noise of the train. "What is the name of our witness? For the family records?"

The hulking man laughed, as he threw out a cloth satchel and a large leather saddle. Doffing his black cap, he yelled back, "Harry Bullmason. Name your first son after me!"

Jenna continued to smile as she waved. "Oh, Harry," she said under her breath, "I'll never forget you, but you'll live to regret this day. I promise."

Morgan untangled himself from her arm and turned away from the moving train to face her. "What's the matter with you?" he demanded. *"Are you really crazy?"*

Chapter Three

"C'mon, Trahern. Lighten up. I'll see you get paid," she said as she watched the train slowly disappear. He began walking past her to where Bullmason had thrown his gear, and she talked to his retreating back. "Look, I went along, didn't I? All of you had me fooled, right up till the end. But, it's over." And, wiping her damp forehead, she asked, "When does the car come? It's *hot* out here!"

She watched him heave the heavy saddle over his shoulder and bend to pick up the bag. When he turned back to her, she thought what a perfect picture of the West he made, outlined against the distant snowcapped mountains. As he came closer, she was able to distinguish that he was again working his jaw, a sure sign of his anger, and that his blue eyes took on a menacing appearance as they turned ice blue.

"You just saw the last of any cars," he nearly yelled. "There won't be another for three days. Why don't you grow up, Miss Weldon? Do you really think everything that just happened was for your amusement?"

She felt the skin on her face tighten as he shouted at her. "Why are you angry with me?" she demanded hotly. "I didn't set this up."

He walked past her her, dropping the cloth satchel and throwing the large saddle at her feet. "Because of you and your mouth, I'm going to miss an important meeting. But, maybe that's something you wouldn't care about . . . other people's lives."

Jenna watched the lines on either side of his mouth deepen as his anger increased. She guessed his age to be anywhere from thirty to thirty-five, and she wondered, not for the first time, where Tom had found him and the others. Probably some agency on the West Coast—all of them, out-of-work actors willing to make a few extra dollars. And, now the high and mighty Mr. Trahern is upset because he's about to miss a—a casting call?

Well, she did care about people. That was what the whole damn trip was about. Jenna looked into his face and forced a smile.

"We're having our first fight, aren't we?" she asked sweetly. She watched as he closed his eyes in frustration, then continued. "Look, if I miss out on this convention, a lot of people's lives are going to be affected. My company's whole future is riding on my getting to Sacramento. You have business in the city, and so do I. Whatever Tom is paying you, I'll double it if you help me get there."

He opened his eyes and stared down at her. The annoyance in his voice was only slightly less when he asked, "Why do you talk like that? You haven't made any sense since the first time you walked into the smoking car."

"Me?"

"Yes, you. You are the most exasperating, irrational woman I have ever met." Picking up his saddle and bag, he said, "I'm going back to Reno."

She stared at his broad back and trim hips and

called after him, "Why Reno? Bullmason said this Verdi was twenty-six minutes away. Anyway, I've heard it's best to stay where you are. That way they'll be able to find us. I'm sure we could find some sort of shelter from the sun."

He stopped walking and just stood, immobile, and she was treated to the way his right hip swung out to balance the dark brown saddle at his shoulder. When he moved, it was as if in slow motion. He lazily turned back to her and stared. He didn't say anything for a few moments—just continued to look at her, as though examining her face for some clue.

"Lady." He dragged the word out. "Have you even bothered to look around you?"

Jenna turned her head away from him and did, indeed, look at her surroundings. Huge gray-white boulders were strewn between tall, straight pine trees. The isolation and silence seemed deafening, and she turned back to him, looking in the direction the train had gone. In the far distance was a long chain of mountains.

"No one's picking us up?" she asked in disbelief.

They stared at each other for a few tense-filled seconds, Jenna trying to cope with the flood of emotions that swept through her.

"No one," he stated simply.

Pushing down the panic, she said with a contrived attempt at authority, "I say we go on to Verdi. I promise, if you can get me near civilization, as soon as I get to a phone . . . you'll get your money."

She watched him close the ten feet separating them, and something about his expression made her nervous. To avoid his face for a few seconds, she bent and picked up her purse and briefcase. When she was again upright, Trahern was standing directly in front of her.

"He said twenty minutes *by train*," he hissed from beneath his mustache. "Not by foot. And what's a phone?"

Jenna's light-brown eyebrows came together, and her mouth opened slightly as she stared into his angry eyes. "You know, a telephone," she said, as if talking to a child and brought an invisible one up to her ear.

"You mean a telegraph."

"No. I meant a telephone, but if you can get me to a telegraph, that'll do the job, too."

"What job!" The frustration was clear in his voice.

Jenna felt he was intentionally being obtuse, and the heat and her anger were quickly reaching the same high degree. "To get you your money! Isn't that what we're talking about? Of course . . ." She couldn't help but add a trifle sarcastically, "As an additional minor benefit, I can have someone come and help us get the hell out of here!"

Ever since she had assumed her position at Weldon Transit, she had been involved in one power confrontation after another. Sometimes, it was merely the fact that she was a woman that made others doubt her ability and tenacity to work her way through a problem. At any rate, the position she now found herself in was not new to her. She'd had men angry with her before, glaring at her like the cowboy, hoping to intimidate her into subjection. It hadn't worked then, and it wouldn't work now.

Seeing his neck muscles cord, as he again worked his jaw, she hoped to throw him off balance with her next words. "Anyone ever tell you, you're beautiful when you're angry?" she asked innocently.

Jenna watched him catch his breath and knew her comment had interrupted his chain of fierce thoughts. It was exactly what she intended with her inane remark.

Before she could add anything else, Trahern regained his composure. "I'm sorry I can't say the same," he said unemotionally, then added, "I'm not going to stand out in the middle of nowhere arguing with you about it, or anything else."

"Why are you so defensive? Men have used that tactic against women for ages. Or don't you like being called beautiful? I thought you had to be part egotist to be an actor."

"I am not an actor!"

She watched it—the complete unraveling of a person's patience—and couldn't suppress a giggle. It was a terrible, terrible habit she had. When nervous, in a totally unfamiliar situation, Jenna unintentionally resorted to laughter.

She bit her bottom lip as his blue eyes turned to steel, and she tried valiantly to stop the rush of air from her nostrils and to control her stomach muscles as he turned away from her and let out a low growl of rage. When he threw his hat to the ground and stormed away from her, she was hopelessly overcome with a fit of giggles.

"I'm sorry," she said, then laughed again. Looking at his stiff back as he stared at the ground and tried to bring his breathing under control, Jenna tried again. "No. Really, I'm sorry. I can't help it."

She picked up his hat and brushed the soft suede before walking to his side. Handing it to him, she said, "Here's your hat. I . . . I am really sorry for laughing. It wasn't directed at you. It's just a nervous habit."

He quickly brought his eyes up from the ground. "Just get away from me," he said quietly, too quietly.

Jenna's shoulders slumped when she realized he didn't accept her apology. She tilted her head and met his icy glare. Trying again, she said, "Please, I apologize. I know it's annoying. I just can't help it. Instead of fighting, why don't we try to figure some way out of this?"

He continued to stare at her, but she could sense some of his anger had left him. Without removing his eyes from hers, he asked, "Who *are* you?"

Surprised by his question, she answered truthfully. "Jenna Weldon, I told you that."

"*What* are you?"

"What do you mean, *what am I*?" she asked, feeling her defenses come back to the surface. "I head Weldon Transit, a railcar manufacturing company. Look, Trahern, this is the 1980s. Don't get macho on me. Thank God, that went out in the seventies."

She thought this time she had truly put him in his place for he didn't answer. In fact, he didn't do anything except stare at her, openmouthed.

Unconsciously, she put her hand out to him in a gesture of truce. "I don't want to argue with you. I know what happened on that train wasn't your fault, any more than it was mine. If it makes you feel any better, I intend to fire the man who arranged it. But that doesn't change the fact that we're stranded out here. Can't we try and get along, at least until we reach this Verdi?"

Almost as if he hadn't heard a word she'd just said, he asked her, "What year is it?"

"What year?" she asked, not able to connect the question with anything pertinent to their situation. "Nineteen eighty-seven. What year do *you* think it is?"

He blinked a few times, his face expressionless, then said slowly, "I don't think—I know. It's June 10, 1870."

Jenna knew he was watching her face for her reaction, and she didn't know what to do. Should she laugh at him? Or try pacification? Either way, she was in trouble.

Trying to remain calm, she again offered him his hat and said, "I'm going to Verdi. I suppose if I just follow the railroad tracks, I'll eventually get there."

Without saying a word, he accepted the black hat, but as she brushed past him, he reached out and grabbed hold of her upper arm. "You'd better keep this," he said, studying her face while placing the too large hat on her head. "I think you've already been out in the sun too long."

Jenna's eyes narrowed. "Very funny," she said sarcastically. "But thanks for the hat. I will use it."

She pulled her arm free and walked back to her briefcase. Picking it and her purse up, she started to follow the uneven wooden planks that made up the track.

"Do you realize that you're walking right in the middle of Indian territory?" she heard from behind her.

"Never met an Indian I didn't like," she threw over her shoulder and, without looking back, she widened the distance between them.

Morgan watched her walk away from him. His mind was racing with a whirlwind of jumbled questions: Who was she? What was she doing on that train? Why does she continue to think the whole episode was some practical joke? Was she really crazy? Could it be that someone had caught onto him? Had he made a mistake, a slipup? Was the whole thing planned to detain him, making his connection in Sacramento impossible? Who the hell was she? Was he supposed to be sidetracked by her slim, graceful body, which she did little to cover with her unusual attire? And why, in spite of everything, did he find himself moved by her? It was the last question that irritated him most.

"I'm hungry. Aren't you hungry?" Jenna asked the silent man in front of her. When she received no answer, she again studied the cowboy's back, a sight that was becoming annoyingly familiar. Why did he continue to ignore her, as if she were to blame for the whole thing? She was the one who should be angry. Here she was, in the middle of nowhere, following a man who claimed to be living a hundred and seventeen years ago, missing the opening of the convention and developing excruciating blisters on the insides of both heels. She'd already rolled the sleeves up on her blouse and tucked her long hair into the cowboy's large hat. It had helped, somewhat, to cool off, but she was afraid that nothing could be done about her feet until they stopped.

With that thought in mind, and the insistant rumbling of her stomach in her ears, Jenna stumbled away from the tracks and made for the shade of a tree.

"I'm stopping," she called out, and did just that as she neared the base of a large pine tree. Letting her arms fall, she watched in disinterest as her briefcase fell to the ground, and her purse slowly slid down her arm to join it. She remained upright for less than five seconds before weariness overcame her, and she sank down to her knees. Kneeling in front of the tree, she didn't even bother to turn back to see if Trahern had stopped. Instead, she raised her head as a rare breeze brought a faint, delicious aroma wafting past her nostrils. Licking her dry lips, her eyes searched the immediate area for its source. Not seeing anything, she crawled closer to the trunk of the tree and inhaled deeply.

It was the heat, that was it, she thought desperately. Why else would an intelligent woman be sniffing around, ready to tear off a piece of bark and chew it?

"Are you all right?"

Jenna quickly turned her head. Embarrassed to be found on all fours, sniffing the tree like a dog with a full bladder, she tried to regain her composure. "Come here," she motioned with her hand. "Do you smell something sweet?"

He dropped his gear and slowly walked up to her. Lowering his head, he inhaled deeply, and Jenna couldn't help but notice the way the dark-blue material at his chest strained as he filled his lungs. She knew he could detect something and watched as his eyes darted back and forth while he tried to identify it.

Slowly, he reached out and broke off a chunk of bark from the large, plated trunk. Holding the orange, brownish piece to his nose, he smiled. "Here," he said, as he handed it to her. "Jeffrey pine . . . smells like vanilla."

Jenna took it and brought it to her nose. Waving it back and forth in a small arc, she shook her head. "No," she stated emphatically, "it's more like pineapple. Can we eat it?"

He laughed. He actually laughed, and Jenna found herself extremely pleased that she had broken through his tough exterior. Bringing himself down to her level, he rested the back of his thighs on his heels and asked with a grin, "Are you really that hungry?"

Jenna returned his smile and tried to keep the sarcasm out of her voice as she answered, "No, I always hunt bark. Of course, I'm hungry. I skipped lunch. Aren't you . . . hungry?"

He really smiled at her then, and Jenna felt her chest muscles tighten as she saw a dimple appear on

54

his right cheek—just one. One lousy dimple, and she forgot about her hunger. He had a wonderful, genuine smile, and she thought it was a shame he didn't use it more often, but then, since she met him, he scarcely had the chance.

Still thinking of his smile, she watched as he reached into his saddle and brought out a cloth. Unwrapping it, he said, "Here, this might help until we can find something better." He handed her a stiff, dark-brown object.

"What is it?" she asked suspiciously.

"Jerky . . . You've never had it?"

Jenna shook her head. "What do you do with it? Besides keeping it for a weapon?" she asked, as she unsuccessfully tried to break it.

"Put it in your mouth until it softens, and you can bite a piece off. Then just keep it there. Like this." He showed her how to work off a chunk.

The smoked flavor was too strong for Jenna, but she refrained from saying so. Besides, it had to be better than the tree bark she found, though it certainly didn't smell better. This was no leisure snack. She found you really had to work at it, like eating taffy. Ignoring her sore jaws, she removed Trahern's hat and waved it in front of her in a feeble effort to create a cooling breeze.

"Know what I would love?" she asked between jaw workouts. Not waiting for an answer, she said dreamily, "A steak . . . nothing fancy. Just a plain old steak . . . with a baked potato, big salad. Mmm . . ." She closed her eyes and smiled. "Of course, right now I'd scarf down a Big Mac just as quickly."

"Big Mac?"

She opened her eyes and studied his confused expression. "You know . . . two all beef patties, special sauce, et cetera. McDonalds."

He seemed to understand. "A favorite restaurant of yours?" he asked seriously. Before she could answer him, he continued. "I may not be able to provide you with a McDonald's steak, but I can offer you something equally delicious."

He reached over to his gear and brought back a canteen. "Water," he stated simply. "You have to be thirsty."

Jenna chewed the jerky a few times, trying hard not to openly salivate. "You mean, all this time you've had water?" she asked in disbelief.

"We have to conserve it," he stated matter-of-factly. "Remember, it was your idea to travel further to Verdi, instead of going back to Reno."

"All this time I'm trekking through mountains, and you had water?" she again demanded.

He ignored her question and unscrewed the lid. Handing the canteen to her, he said patiently, "These are not mountains. Just rolling hills."

"Some of these rocks are as big as hills. I've seen mountains before, Trahern, and we're on one." She threw his hat to the ground and took the canteen from him. Tilting her head back, she took a sip and grimaced. It tasted like the leather container, but she would not complain again. She knew they were lucky Bullmason had thrown it out with the rest of Trahern's things.

She handed it back and thanked him. He nodded once then lifted it to his lips, and Jenna studied him as he drank. She watched the way his Adam's apple moved as he swallowed, the way a few tiny drops clung to his mustache when he removed the canteen from his mouth. When he replaced the cap, her eyes unwillingly traveled from his chest to his waist, and she was startled to find a brown leather holster and a gun resting there.

"When did you start wearing *that*?" she asked as she tried to keep the concern out of her voice.

His eyes followed the direction of hers, and he answered nonchalantly, "They were in my bag. I didn't wear them on the train, if that's what you mean."

Her eyes seemed glued to the dark-gray metal. "Is it loaded?" she couldn't help but ask.

"Of course. What would be the point of wearing it if I couldn't use it?"

Jenna's mouth went dry, and no amount of water could restore its moisture. "You don't plan to use it, do you? I mean . . . why are you wearing a gun now?"

"Miss Weldon, they are for your protection, as much as mine. I have no intention of harming you, if that's what you're worried about."

Jenna had never been around a gun before. She didn't like the uneasy feeling and shook her head. "Just be careful, please."

Trahern continued to stare at her for a few more seconds, then stood and rubbed the tops of his thighs as he looked around them. "It might be best to rest for a little while. This is the hottest part of the day. We'll start up again in about forty-five minutes. Why don't you try and relax until then?"

Jenna watched as he moved over to his saddle. Lying down, he rested his head against it and closed his eyes. Since he was facing away from her, she took that opportunity to remove the wad of stringy meat from her mouth and throw it around the other side of the tree. Knowing she would never relax while she was stranded with an armed man, obviously suffering from delusions of living in the past, Jenna opened her briefcase and searched through its contents.

Not wanting to disturb Trahern, she turned down

the volume of her recorder and slipped in the micro tape. Within seconds, the faint sounds of Tina Turner could be heard. Jenna held the recorder in both hands, her thumb remaining on the small round wheel that controlled its volume when, without warning, Trahern rolled over onto his stomach and, in a lightning flash of speed, he produced a gun and pointed it directly at her stomach!

Frightened by his unexpected actions, her thumb, resting on the volume control, slipped, and Jenna Weldon and Morgan Trahern found themselves staring wide eyed at each other while Tina rasped out in a loud, agonized voice, *"What's love go to do with it? Got to do with it?"*

Quickly, Jenna turned the volume down. When she found her voice, she wasn't surprised to hear the frightened, nervous squeak as she asked, "You don't like Tina Turner? I'm sorry. Why don't you put the gun away? See, it's off," she said, and showed him the now silent recorder, as if reasoning with a child.

He continued to stare at her, his eyes searching her face and body for some clue. His breathing was heavy and irregular as he fought with his intellect, but he couldn't stop his lips from forming the words, "What *are* you," he breathed. *"A witch?"*

58

Jenna stared at the long thin barrel, still pointed at her. Desperately, she tried to clear her throat and speak. "I . . . ah, I suppose I've been called that at some time in my life, but if you mean am I really a witch—spells and such, well, then the answer is no. I don't believe they exist. *Do you*?"

His eyes burned into hers, barely blinking as a steady hand held the revolver in an unswerving line. "Then, what are you?" he asked in a grim, determined voice. "I want some answers. What the hell is that thing in your hand?" He motioned with the gun.

Jenna looked down to her fingers, still tightly clutching the micro cassette player. "A tape recorder and cassette player. I keep it in my briefcase. Don't tell me you've never heard one?"

He ignored her question and asked her another. "Where did you get it?"

Tiny lines appeared between Jenna's eyebrows as they came closer together. The man's curiosity was out of place. Where had he been living, not to have heard of a tape recorder? Very slowly, she showed him what she was doing as she removed the small music cassette and replaced it with a blank one. "Where are you from, Trahern?" she asked as casually as possible, wanting him to talk.

"Baltimore. What difference does that make? Where did you get that box?"

"It isn't a box. I told you, it's a tape recorder. Are you really a drifter, like Bullmason says? Do you have another profession?"

She could tell that was not the right question to ask by the hard look on his face.

"And why is it that you're so interested in what I do, or do not do? Who are *you*, Jenna Weldon? Who sent you?"

Jenna felt something strange at the back of her neck. What was wrong with the man? "I've already told you who I am. No one sent me, Trahern, not after you anyway. Listen, if you'll put that gun away, I'll show you something that will explain it all. Okay?"

His eyes didn't leave hers for more than a few seconds before coming to the decision that she and the box were harmless. He holstered the long pistol, his curiosity proving to be stronger than his suspicions. "What is it?"

There was no way to hide the relief that washed over her as she watched him replace the gun. She thought he looked dangerous with the leather holster hanging low on his jeaned hip, the handle of the gun in such close proximity to his fingers, but now that the moisture had returned to her mouth, she gulped away her anxiety and smiled weakly. "I'd like you to just listen."

Jenna rewound the tape and pressed the tiny button that said Play. Within seconds, her voice came through the small machine:

"Where are you from, Trahern?"

"Baltimore. What difference does that make?

Where did you get that box?"

When his reasoning returned, it took every ounce of willpower to stand before her and not run into the woods. She was a witch. There was no doubt about it. She had captured his voice within that small metal box and, if he were not careful, she would take his soul as well. Every shred of intellect was telling him such a thing was not possible. Witches were the imaginings made up to scare young children into behaving. But, how else had she done it? *It was his voice!*

He listened to himself ask, *"What is it?"* and to her answer, *"I'd like you to just listen."* Then, the machine went as silent as their conversation.

"Well?" she asked, a very pleased expression on her face.

He answered her carefully, not exactly sure what had happened. "You're very powerful," he said softly. He couldn't help but wipe his damp palms on his upper thighs while saying, "I'll take you into Verdi, but we should leave soon or we won't make it before nightfall."

Jenna gave a small incredulous laugh. "Powerful? I didn't do anything but press a button. This is a *tape recorder*. *It* records your voice—I don't. It's a machine, Trahern. Why haven't you ever seen one? Where have you been living?"

Her derisive tone of voice made him forget his childish fears, and he came closer, until he was standing right in front of where she was sitting. "What else is in your briefcase?" he asked suspiciously.

Jenna shrugged. "Just papers, and things . . . information I'll need for the convention. Why?"

His face was expressionless as he asked politely, "May I see one?"

Again Jenna shrugged. "Sure. Why not? Here,"

she said, handing him an office directive.

She watched him read it, but was unprepared for his next statement when he lifted a serious face from the page of typewritten words. "It seems one of us, Miss Weldon, is in the wrong century and, judging from the train we left earlier, I would have to say it isn't me."

She couldn't stop the short, unladylike snort. "Wrong century! Come off it, Trahern. What happened on the train and afterwards was staged, and both you and I know it."

"You're wrong, Jenna."

She didn't know if it was the use of her first name or the deadly serious look on his face that threw her most. Whichever, she refused to entertain the possibility that such a thing could occur. "What are you suggesting?" she asked with a falsely calm voice.

He smoothed the sides of his mustache down with his thumb and index finger. "One of three things: You're someone of extraordinary powers, which I'm less inclined to believe than previously, or perhaps you're unbalanced; or maybe you've gone through a great deal of trouble to keep me from reaching Sacramento. If I had to pick one, right now I'd take the last."

Jenna quickly stood and closed her briefcase. "What a monumental ego you have! I suppose it hasn't occurred to you that *I* might be telling the truth? That *you* might be the unbalanced one here? By God, Trahern, you act like some member of a long-lost tribe, thinking I'm a witch because you hear your voice on a damn tape recorder. Now, I ask you— who's the crazy one? Me, or you?"

Putting her purse strap back on her shoulder, she added, "And why would I want to detain you? I don't care what Bullmason said. You're no drifter, Trahern.

You ask too many questions, and you're in just as much of a hurry to reach Sacramento as I am. But, I'm the one who gets grilled. You won't answer a single question. Who are *you*, Morgan Trahern? And just what kind of game are you planning?"

Gathering his gear, he said, "I'm not playing any games. I've told you . . . it's June 10, 1870."

Angry with him, the situation, but mostly him, she said in a clipped voice, "Read my lips, Trahern. It's May 2, 1987."

Hoisting the saddle to his shoulder, he handed her the hat. "Put this on," he directed in an exasperated tone. "You seem to conveniently forget about the other people on the train. Can you remember one single person dressed like you? And don't say they're all actors. Even you can't believe that now."

Deciding there was no use in discussing the matter further, she turned away from him. "Keep your lousy hat. It was too big anyway." She left the shade of the tree and returned to the tracks.

God, her feet were killing her! She'd never figured to go mountain climbing. Rolling hills? What the hell qualified as a mountain out here, if not this? And how was she expected to make Sacramento today? Thinking of the convention brought the image of Tom Freeman to mind. Firing was too good for him. She'd taken a course in self-defense once and found herself grinning as she thought about the bone-crunching moves she'd been taught. Even if she couldn't do it, she'd love to hire someone to make sure Tom occupied the bed next to his wife in the hospital. Beating was too good for him, too. He deserved something more for this trick. She had certainly been a poor judge of character in hiring him two years ago. She would never guess he possessed such a sick sense of humor. And now she found herself trying to explain modern technology to a cave dweller! What else could explain his almost hermitlike lack of knowledge?

Jenna lifted her one free arm and wiped her forehead on her sleeve. She looked with distaste at the soiled spot on her expensive blouse and again silently cursed the position she was in. Never had she been so frustrated or more miserable. She was used to modern living, not this type of enforced march back to civilization.

Trahern was crazy. Eighteen seventy! But why did the middle of her chest feel like a solid rock when she thought about the train? There, he was right. Ever since she'd entered that smoking car, she hadn't seen one single person dressed in modern clothes. And what the hell had happened to the rest of the train, the one she had traveled on leaving Reno, the one with her luggage? There had been no stop to disconnect. Her mind searched for possibilities, but could find none. She didn't know how it had taken place, how she found herself surrounded by people acting and dressing as if they were living in the last century, but she was sure once she reached a town, a community of people, it would all straighten out.

But what if it didn't? No, she silently denied the insane possibility that Trahern could be right. It was the heat, that's all, and the heavy feeling in her chest was brought about by hunger. Something the hard, leather-type meat had done little to satisfy.

Daydreaming about soaking in a cool bath, then feasting on a huge meal, she was startled, and jumped when she heard the voice behind her.

"You're limping. Did you hurt your foot?"

She turned halfway around and looked at the man. Too bad he was nuts, she thought surprisingly. At any other time, his rugged good looks would have made her look twice in appreciation. It was an overused term—rugged good looks—but Jenna could think of no other phrase to describe him. He certainly wasn't sophisticated. He was ruggedly handsome, with his worn jeans that fit snugly around trim hips, his dark, thin shirt that strained against corded muscles as he balanced the large saddle against a broad shoulder. She looked into his face and felt an unexpected twinge of regret that they had started out so poorly. His face was handsome; but more than that, it was compelling, and sometimes, when he thought you weren't looking, it held a strange sadness, making his eyes look older than his years.

Mentally shaking herself, Jenna asked him to repeat his question.

"I asked if you'd hurt your foot. I couldn't help but notice you limping."

Jenna looked down to her feet. Lifting one heeled boot, she grinned wryly. "If I knew I was going to get kicked off a train, I'd have worn more suitable shoes." Looking back into his face, she remarked, "It's just blisters. How much further do you think this town is?"

Trahern tilted his head to one side, then shifted the saddle a little higher on his shoulder. "I don't think we've come more than a mile." He looked into her face and lifted his eyebrows questioningly. "We're not making very good time, are we?" he asked.

Jenna couldn't help the tiny laugh. "I don't see how we can," she stated simply. "What, with my feet and you lugging around that saddle. Why don't you just leave it? Once we get to Verdi, you can come back and get it."

He looked at her in disbelief. "Leave it?"

Jenna thought it was the sensible thing to do. "Sure. Who's going to take it out here?" She looked around at the deserted woods.

He shook his head in a way that reminded her of her father when she had said something very naive. "Indians. Remember, you're walking through their land. Or any miner that comes wandering out of the Sierras, making their way to Reno or Virginia City. Besides, it'll be worth something when we reach Verdi. I don't know about you, but I'm not carrying much money."

Jenna put a hand on her purse. Thinking of the soft leather billfold within it, she replied, "I have very little cash, but I told you . . . I have the Gold card and some traveler's checks. Once we reach this town I'll have money wired to you, so leave the saddle."

"You don't mind if I bring it along for insurance?" he said as he looked over her head and into the woods.

"You don't believe me, do you, Trahern?"

He looked down at her. Seeing the stubborn tilt to her chin, he resisted the urge to brush it with his finger. "Jenna, so far I don't believe a word you've said."

She wouldn't say it. Her mind screamed it, but she refused to utter aloud that foulest of profanities. Instead, thinking about her burning skin, her feet, the incredible weariness and misery she'd been forced to endure, she looked at the man she felt was largely responsible for it and spat, "Go to hell, Trahern. If I'm such a liar, why do you keep following me? I don't need you, you know. I can make it on my own."

"Lady, alone you couldn't make it an hour out here. You have no food, no water . . . you don't even know where you're going, or how far it is." And, seeing the growing dislike on her face, he smiled smugly and added, "Besides, you're my wife. Remember?"

"Like hell! That ceremony wasn't real and you know it!"

"Are you sure those people on the train weren't

right? You have one of the worst mouths I've ever heard on a woman. I'm sure the reverend would approve of a beating, if you keep it up."

Lifting her chin higher, she could feel a heat on her face that had nothing to do with the strong sun. Breathing heavily, she said in a low, threatening voice, "You'll hear far worse if you attempt to lay a finger on me. Why don't you and your primitive mind go back to Reno, or whatever cave you crawled out of?"

What was the point of arguing with a lobotomized version of Tom Selleck? she thought. The old saying was right: Beauty is only skin deep. Somewhere along the line intellect has got to enter into it, and the man in front of her hadn't progressed that far.

Turning away, she headed for the woods. If she kept the tracks in sight, she wouldn't get lost, and at least she'd be out of the sun. She didn't bother to turn around to see if he was following, though her eyes shifted over her shoulder once or twice a little nervously.

Trying to keep her feet moving, Jenna swallowed back tears. She would *not* cry. If the lunatic was behind her, she wouldn't give him the satisfaction of knowing he was wearing her down. Tightening her face, she was willing the dampness at her eyelids to evaporate when a loud explosion sounded in back of her. Her heart fluttered, and the heat of fear quickly spread over her chest as she let out a frightened scream and slowly toppled to the ground.

She was shot! My God, she thought as her face met the grass. *Trahern shot her!*

Chapter Five

She waited for the pain. She was sure there should be pain, terrible agonizing pain, like in the movies. All she could feel was the fast, heavy beat of her heart as it thundered against the ground under her. Turning her head at the sound of his hurried approach, she stared through the tall grass at Trahern's scuffed brown boots as she heard him exclaim, "Are you all right? I would have called out a warning, but I didn't want to scare it away."

Slowly, Jenna raised her eyes past his boots to his jeans. From there she gazed to his left. Hanging from his hand was a long, skinny rabbit that he held by the hind legs.

Watching it swing lifelessly, its long ears nearly touching the ground beside her, she lost all reason. With a low growl of rage, she stumbled to her feet and charged his stomach. Having the force of her anger behind her, her shoulder connected with his solar plexus, and she managed to knock him off his feet. As they fell to the ground, she started punching him anywhere. It didn't matter where her blows landed.

She was like a woman possessed.

"You stupid, stupid, son of a bitch!" she sobbed out between tears of relief and rage.

She was gasping for breath when he caught both her wrists, rendering her hands useless. When she tried to hit him with one of her elbows, he quickly dodged it and muttered a curse of his own before rolling her over onto her back.

Feeling trapped with the ground behind her and the man on top, she started crying again. "What kind of person does that?" she demanded in a sobbing, hoarse voice. Not waiting for an answer, she shouted, *"I'll tell you . . . a crazy person! A crazy, stupid son of a bitch!"*

Breathing heavily, he swallowed as he stared into her face. "I've told you about your mouth, Jenna," he said, in between ragged gasps of air. "I've listened to you insult my mother just once too often."

Without warning, he turned his head slightly and quickly lowered his mouth to hers. It started as an angry, frustrated kiss, a means to quiet her, but somewhere in the heat of emotions, the anger turned to passion and the frustration to surprising longing, as Jenna melted under the remarkable softness of his lips.

She couldn't believe this was happening to her, that she was actually responding to Morgan Trahern. Surely, her joy of being alive and not wounded, or worse, was causing the unexpected tingling in her stomach and the hardness of her breasts as they ached into his chest. Not wanting to feel the liquid fire, as it spread through her veins, making her extremities feel heavy with longing, Jenna pushed at his shoulders with her elbows.

As his lips reluctantly left hers, he looked deep into her blue-gray eyes. From there, he searched her face.

He looked beyond the sweat, dirt, smudged makeup, and tears and saw how lovely she was, with her lips swollen from his kiss. Leaving them, he again scrutinized her fantastic eyes.

Breathing deeply, he asked, "Who are you really, Jenna Weldon?" as he let go of her hands.

Jenna was too aware of his body, the lean contours and the hardness of his thighs as they pressed into hers, to answer. "Please," she said in a small voice. "Please, let me go."

Slowly, he moved away from her, and Jenna sat up next to him. She pulled her legs toward her and, leaning her arms across them, she buried her face.

Morgan, thinking she was crying, tried to apologize. "Look, I'm sorry. I didn't mean to frighten you. You did say you were hungry."

Jenna's face immediately popped up from the shelter of her arms. What was he apologizing for? For scaring her half to death? Or for the breathtaking kiss that made her dormant senses come alive? And was the statement about being hungry meant as a double entendre? Damn, her mother was right. She'd spent too little time tending her personal life if this Neanderthal could cause such a violent emotion one minute then create such sweet longing in the next. What was wrong with her?

Angry that she had allowed him such power, she pushed the tangled strands of hair away from her face and snapped back at him. "Keep your apologies, Trahern. All I want from you is to be left alone."

Seeing the near hate that marred her lovely face of only moments ago, he responded in like manner. "You got it, lady." He stood, leaving her sitting in the tall grass.

She turned away from his retreating back, her eyes glazed, not seeing the magnificent landscape around her, but only picturing in her mind the two of them grinding their mouths together, as if starved for the other.

Her acute embarrassment lasted less than a minute. It was replaced by a far more familiar emotion when Trahern came back to her. Dropping the dead rabbit at her feet, he produced a knife and expertly threw it next to the carcass. It landed not two inches from the rabbit, and Jenna stared at its black carved handle as she heard him say, "I'm going to look for fresh water. When I come back we'll build a fire. See if you can manage to have it dressed by the time I return."

He didn't wait for her to answer. He left so quickly, Jenna thought she must have imagined him giving her that order. Was he kidding? What was she supposed to do—skin it or something?

Reluctantly, her eyes slid over to the furry animal, and she involuntarily shuddered. She'd never done anything like this before and didn't know the first thing to do. Unable to stop the shudder of horror, she went over to her purse and brought out a fine cotton handkerchief, trimmed in crocheted lace. Coming back to the rabbit, she placed it gently over the top half of its body. As she straightened, she walked over to her briefcase and laid it flat on the ground, about four feet away.

She sat down on top of it, pulling her legs to her chest and leaning back against the trunk of another pine tree. With her right hand, she reached into her purse and brought out her pack of cigarettes. She only had three left. She should save them for the rest of the way into Verdi, but she needed one now, right now! Finding her lighter that refused to work on the train, but did now, she lit one. Inhaling deeply, she let out her first contented sigh since this morning and stared at the smoke, as it disappeared into the woods.

She switched the cigarette to her left hand and crossed her arms over her knees. Gingerly, she rested her head on her sunburned forearms and again sighed—this time with exhaustion. Unwillingly, she let her eyes stray back to the rabbit. Closing them tightly, she knew without a doubt, no matter how hungry she was, no matter how bad the pains were in her stomach, she would not be able to consume the poor creature. Trahern must be the product of a deprived childhood. Hadn't he ever laughed at, and then loved, Bugs Bunny?

He could almost smell it. Strange how all the dormant instincts for survival had come rushing back in the last few months, he thought, and within moments Morgan pushed aside a low-hanging branch to view a small, clear stream of water. Unconsciously, he licked his dry lips in anticipation as he closed the short distance between him and the inviting sight.

God, there was nothing like it, he realized, as he cupped his hands and greedily drank the second time. He returned his hands to the water and this time splashed his face and hair, letting cooling droplets fall down the collar of his shirt. The urge to rip his clothes from his body was overwhelming, and his right hand immediately moved to the small white buttons at his chest.

In less than a minute, he was sitting in the shallow stream relaxing for the first time in months, letting the rippling water wash over him. He closed his eyes and inhaled deeply, a smile starting under his mustache, at the corners of his mouth. Water: the most primitive need of man, yet the most satisfying. His eyes slowly opened, and he stared at the rapidly moving current.

Well, maybe not the most satisfying, but a damn close runner-up, especially when you've had to do without. And do without, he had—the luxury of unlimited water use had been almost nonexistent since he'd begun this assignment. And though self-imposed, the luxury of women had been just as scarce—until today.

He'd had his opportunities in the last three months, but didn't want any complications in his guise of a drifter. The last thing he needed was to get into some fight over a woman, and that, too, he'd successfully avoided—until now.

What was it about Jenna Weldon that made him lose his reason and his temper? Almost convinced now that she was a railroad agent, sent to prevent him from making contact in Sacramento, Morgan knew the way to get information about her was not through kissing her. And, without thinking, he shook his head as he thought about the last scene between them.

She was gutsy, he'd give her that. Not too many could have caught him by surprise and knocked him off his feet. And she had a mouth on her. God, did she have a mouth! If she wasn't spewing ridicule or curses at him, she could use it to kiss like a fifty dollar whore.

No, he reassessed his thoughts. She didn't kiss like a whore—more like a woman who'd done without for a long time. Maybe that's why the kiss had been so damn good. They both had been denied for too long.

He thought about the woman then, really thought about her, and cursed his own stupidity for falling for her charms. She might not have planned for him to kiss her, but she had damn well planned to get him thrown off the train; that much he knew, and he intended to find out just who was paying her.

Thinking about Jenna, he couldn't help the smile

from creeping across his lips. Whoever planned this had gone to a hell of a lot of trouble. He still wanted to know how she had captured his voice in that little box. It must be some sort of new invention that worked like the delay of an echo. She had controlled it, timing it exactly to repeat their conversation. He didn't understand how it worked, but he would find out.

Feeling foolish at being duped by the woman, Morgan left the water and reached for his clothes. There wasn't any way the two of them could make Verdi before nightfall and, as he buttoned his denims, he vowed that tonight he would find out all the answers to his questions.

Jenna's eyes felt scratchy, as if someone had thrown sand into them, so she quickly shut them again. Her throat was dry, and her nose tickled. Running the side of her finger across it, she resisted opening her eyes and tried to return to sleep. Her neck felt sore, and she jerked her head up from her shoulder just as a delicious aroma entered her nostrils and settled at the back of her palate, making her taste buds tingle in her mouth.

She forced her eyes to open and, for a moment, thought she was dreaming as she looked into the reddish yellow haze of a forest at dusk. It took her a few moments more to realize she was awake. As she tried to straighten, she gasped from a sharp pain at the small of her back. Turning her stiff neck, she faced the trunk of a large tree.

"Anyone ever told you, you snore?"

Her head swung back too quickly at the sound of a man's voice. She blinked once in pain then blinked again as she stared at the man kneeling before a small fire. Above the flames, on a makeshift spit, was the small browned body of the rabbit, minus fur, head, and paws.

Holding the sides of her neck, Jenna tightened her face to keep from crying. It hadn't been a dream! My God, it was a nightmare! And it was real—he was real!

She watched him turn the rabbit, without saying a word. Still trying to organize her frantic thoughts, Jenna rubbed the grit from her eyes. She knew she should say something, anything, but her voice stuck in her throat.

"Don't be embarrassed. Most people snore when they are exhausted. Feel better now that you've slept?"

Quickly, Jenna remembered how thoroughly obnoxious Morgan Trahern could be. "I do not snore," she stated emphatically. "I have never snored in my life."

She watched him curl his lower lip under that damn mustache as he smiled indulgently at her words. "Whatever you say, Jenna. It must have been some animal I've been listening to for the past half hour."

Jenna tried stretching her cramped limbs. She never should have fallen asleep sitting up. Listening to his words, she screwed up her mouth in disgust. "Very funny, Trahern. The sound you heard very possibly came from that immense void located between your ears, a recurring echo of nothingness."

"You come back pretty quick, lady, especially after just waking up." Again turning the animal above the flames, he added, "Who would have thought I'd marry such a nag?"

Jenna closed her eyes, trying to bring her temper back under control. Why did she even wake up? She should have just slept until a rescue party located them. She was too tired to trade barbs with this idiot.

But she knew what had intruded into her deep

slumber. It was the smell of food, cooked food. Opening her eyes, she saw Trahern cut off a slice of meat from the animal and gingerly test it with his mouth. She could tell it was hot by the expression on his face, but was unprepared to see him walk in her direction.

Holding the knife out to her, with the meat skewered to its sharp tip, Trahern said, "Here, I think it's done. Watch your tongue. It's hot."

Jenna's mind battled with her empty stomach. She looked at the hunk of meat and immediately pictured the poor lifeless rabbit. Just as quickly she pictured herself starving in the Sierras for days, while Trahern remained as content as a fat cat, consuming all the protein himself.

Hating herself, hating him, but mostly herself for lowering her standards to his, Jenna reached out a filthy hand to accept the meat.

She almost gagged as her front teeth bit into the soft flesh of the rabbit. Never would she be able to forget this. No wonder why so many people became vegetarians. Every one of them probably made their decision while camping.

She forced the chewed mass down her throat, telling herself it was for survival, not that she was actually enjoying eating real food again.

She glanced back to the fire and watched Trahern slice a piece for himself. Bringing the canteen with him, he settled himself at her feet. "Want some water to wash that down?" he asked.

Grateful for anything that would make this dinner easier to consume, Jenna reached out her hand for the leather canteen. He unscrewed the cap and left it dangling by a thin chain as he handed it to her. Jenna lifted it to her lips and, remembering his lecture on the scarcity of water, merely sipped briefly.

"It's fresh!" She couldn't stop the words from escaping from her mouth. No longer did it taste of leather. It was wonderfully cool water. "Where did you get it?" she demanded with a catch of joy in her voice.

He smiled at her then, another of his real smiles that had previously disarmed her. She reminded herself not to relax her guard as she listened to him. "While you were sleeping, I found a small stream. It was so inviting, I couldn't resist a quick bath. Don't worry, Jenna, the water you were drinking came from further upstream."

"Then there's more?" When he nodded, she returned the canteen to her mouth and drank greedily. She didn't even care that it ran down her chin and spotted her blouse. What did it matter, she thought, as she wiped at her lower jaw with her hand. Looking at the back of her hand, she lifted the corner of her upper lip in distaste. Where the water had hit it, her skin showed through the dirt, while the rest looked almost muddy. She was filthy. She hadn't been this dirty since she was a child.

"After you've eaten I could show you where it is," he offered.

Because of the way she imagined she looked, she asked quietly and a little self-consciously, "Do you think we have time? I mean, it's already getting dark. Don't you think we should push on to Verdi?"

He finished chewing, then said casually, "We're not going to make Verdi today. If we're lucky and get an early start, we might make it before noon tomorrow."

"What do you mean? We have to spend the night out here? Alone?"

He stood up and walked back to the food. "I've told you before, Jenna. You're perfectly safe with me."

She refused to answer him, afraid of what might

come out of her mouth. Safe? He called what happened between them safe?

"Here," he said as he handed her another piece of meat. "I know you're hungry."

Still shocked by his announcement that they would be spending the night together, Jenna's hand automatically reached up and took the meat. Without thinking, she put it into her mouth and began chewing. He really was crazy if he thought she believed him. She knew she wouldn't be safe until she reached Verdi.

"C'mon, Jenna. Hurry up. It's almost too dark to find our way back to camp. What're you doing there?"

Shut up, Trahern, she thought. Just shut up and let me finish dressing. She struggled with her clothes, trying to pull her split skirt back into place over her wet body. "I'll be right there," she shouted back at him. Damn, when he'd taken his bath, he didn't have to put up with her impatience. Forgetting that she had been asleep at the time, she silently cursed the hidden figure of Trahern.

"Jenna?" She heard her name called again, this time a little menacingly.

Damn! All she wanted was to take a bath, to wash the grime from her skin. Could she help it if she had to go the bathroom, too? Bathroom, ha! What she had just endured made the term roughing it laughable. And what about Trahern? What was he, superman? Wasn't he human? Didn't he ever give into the needs of his body? Pulling her damp blouse away from her breasts, she thought to herself: Forget his needs. Don't even think about his body. She pushed the long, wet tendrils of hair away from her face and straightened her shoulders, preparing herself to face him, while she called out, "Keep your pants on, Trahern. I'm coming!" Then she winced at the careless slip of the tongue.

He watched her across the firelight, unable to tear his eyes away. Damn! Why did she have to be so beautiful? Even wet? He knew she was aware of him as he watched her nervously pull slender fingers through her long, tangled wet hair. His hot gaze lowered to her chest, and he swallowed deeply to contain the groan from escaping his lips. He didn't know if it was him or the invigorating water she'd bathed in that had caused her nipples to stand out so invitingly beneath her thin blouse. He only knew that whatever caused her arousal, he had her matched. He just thanked God that his was well hidden at the moment.

Morgan continued to watch her, until the pain in his groin became almost unbearable. Quickly, he rose to his feet and walked to his gear. Coming back, he tossed something into her lap, then seated himself away from her. "There, use that," he gruffly mumbled as he turned his back to her.

Jenna picked up the comb in one hand and lightly ran her thumb across its wide teeth. "You don't mind?" she asked innocently.

"Please!" he almost groaned. "Feel free to use it." Shrugging her shoulders, Jenna lifted it to her hair and worked with the snarls. She wondered why he was so touchy. It wasn't as though she were staring at him, making him uncomfortable, was it? Watching him look off into the surrounding woods, she noticed the tight clenching of his jaw, the way his chest muscles would expand with each frustrated breath, his clean profile, his— Mentally shaking herself, she blinked a few times, looked back to the dancing flames that separated them, and concentrated on her hair. God, but she couldn't wait to get back to civilization, and to civil men!

Chapter Six

Jenna tried to ignore her screaming muscles and straighten her aching body as she made her way back to the small camp. Ten minutes ago, when she first woke up, she would have sworn she was crippled for life from sleeping on the ground. Now, pushing aside a branch and leaving nature's lavatory far behind her, she congratulated herself on surviving as she watched Trahern gather his belongings.

"I'm back," she quietly announced to him. He didn't even acknowledge her return.

Okay, so she'd acted a little crazy last night. That still didn't give him the right to totally ignore her. Jenna could feel the years mentally slipping away as she looked across the small camp to Mr. Morgan Trahern, a classic case of a paranoid hermit, if there was such a thing. She resisted sticking her tongue out in the direction of his back and, instead, picked up her briefcase and purse as she watched him kick dirt onto the already dead ashes of last night's fire.

"You ready?" he asked tersely, without even turning back to her.

Watching him pick up his saddle and gear, she ignored her grumbling stomach and mumbled, "Sure.

Why not?" She was glad now that she hadn't asked about breakfast. He was in such a lousy mood, he might have produced leftover rabbit from last night, and Jenna didn't think she could manage to even look at it, let alone eat it again.

She fell in behind Trahern as they made their way back to the railroad tracks. Looking at his gun, nestled co close to his thigh, Jenna turned her face away and inhaled deeply the fresh morning smell of the forest. It was so clean, and it had truly been lovely this morning before she had tried to move, not at all like last night. Oh God, she thought, as she winced in memory, nothing at all like last night. . .

"Who sent you?"

Jenna gave him a look of impatience, annoyed that since her hurried bath, he'd kept hammering at her. "I told you, Trahern. No one."

Grabbing his comb from her hands, he demanded, "Then why were you on that train? Why did you have me thrown off with you? Was it to keep me from reaching Sacramento?"

She couldn't help it. She laughed. "You really are crazy, cowboy. Why would I care whether or not you reached Sacramento? And it was only a matter of being in the wrong place at the wrong time . . . for both of us . . . that got us thrown off that train."

Sitting back down, he glared at her across the fire. "I think you're lying."

She could feel her muscles tighten in anger. "And I think you're insane."

He didn't say anything, just worked the muscle in his jaw. Finally, he seemed to dismiss her last statement and, instead, changed the subject. "What about the echo box? Where did you get it?"

She closed her eyes and wearily ran her fingers across her temple. Not again! "I *told* you. I bought it."

"How does it work? It is an echo chamber, isn't it?"

Exhaustion had brought all her emotions close to the surface, and she knew it was useless to try and stop the giggles. Shaking her head, she reached into her briefcase and held up the tape recorder. "It's got buttons, Trahern, that control it. Everything is recorded on a thin little tape inside it."

He stood up and came around the fire. "May I see it?"

Foolishly, she handed it over. She watched as he turned it around in his hands and laughed when he talked into it, and then held it up to his ear as if expecting the tape to answer him. "Not like that," she said and held up her hand. "Here, give it to me and I'll show you."

It was as if he didn't hear her. He continued to shake it, tried opening it with his nail and would have pulled the tape, itself, out of the recorder if she didn't jump to her feet to save the expensive equipment.

He held it above her reach. "Now, wait. I only want to know how it works," he teased.

Grabbing for it, she called him another name. "Give it back, you . . . you mindless *baboon*! You haven't got the brains you were born with!"

He was grinning. "Anyone ever tell you you were beautiful when you get angry?" he asked in a teasing voice, and laughed when he saw she remembered saying the exact same thing to him earlier.

He released the recorder in her hands and smiled. "Shut up, Trahern. Just shut up . . ."

She should have remembered that his eyes only darkened when he got angry, but by then she'd had enough of him and his nagging. They continued to argue for almost half an hour, until she noticed that Trahern was almost enjoying it, baiting her, waiting to see what would come out of her mouth. She knew, then that the way to really put him in his place was to not respond at all. She left him then. Going back to the tree where she had slept the afternoon away, she rummaged through her briefcase for a few moments, before closing her eyes. She didn't fall asleep quickly. How could she when she was at such odds with Trahern, and him with that damn gun? She spent some time wondering why no one was searching for them; why she hadn't heard helicopters or seen any signs of a rescue party. Surely, she was missed. Someone must have contacted Weldon to see why she hadn't arrived in Sacramento. Why had no one taken action?

Her thoughts were confused as she half sat, half lay under the tree. She kept her eyes closed but soon sensed Trahern coming closer to her. She dared to open one eye, and her breath caught in back of her throat as she viewed the man slowly, quietly, approaching with a blanket held out in front of him.

Instinct told her he meant to harm her, maybe smother her with the thing and, without waiting to find out, she brought her right hand up and let him have it. In the palm of her hand, she kept her automatic umbrella. Just as his face was about ten inches away from hers, she whipped it out from her side and pushed down the release button.

As the black umbrella instantly opened in his face, Trahern called out in shock, then pulled back from her so quickly he landed flat on his rear.

"Damn you, woman! What the *hell* was that!"

As she lowered the protective umbrella and peered over its edge, she burst out in unrestrained laughter at the sight of him sprawled in the grass. That had only brought about a resumption of arguing.

"I'm glad you think it's amusing. What else do you have in your bag of tricks?" he asked, standing up and brushing off the leaves from his pants. "No poison snakes? No witch's cauldron? Where do you keep your broom, madam?"

She stopped laughing. "Very funny, Trahern. You can knock off the sarcasm. I was only protecting myself."

He looked around the camp. "From *whom*?"

She looked him straight in the eye. "From you."

He held her gaze a moment before chuckling and picking up the blanket. "Since you have rebuffed my kindness in letting you use the horse blanket, I'll keep myself warm with it."

She shrugged her shoulders and closed the umbrella. "Suit yourself. Just stay on the other side of the fire."

He startled her by laughing. "Hell, *Miss* Weldon, you have too high an opinion of yourself if you think I'd ever be attracted to a shrewish, old maid."

She'd wanted to shout at him as he'd turned away from her, ask him what he'd thought he'd been doing earlier—first, when he'd kissed her, then, after her bath? What the hell was all that staring about? But she didn't say anything, just crossed her arms in anger and returned to her sleeping position. She'd had more than a few regrets during the night for not keeping the blanket as the temperature dropped, but eventually found that exhaustion, even cold exhaustion couldn't be denied.

Now, walking again behind him, Jenna silently prayed that they reach this Verdi before noon. She didn't think she could stand to be around Trahern another full day. Shrewish, old maid! Well, what was he but a horny old hermit! He acted like he'd never even heard about modern technology, the advancement of women, and that you could be twenty-eight and unmarried and not be considered an old maid. *Old maid?* Who even talked like that anymore?

A half hour later, the blisters on Jenna's heels were rubbed raw, and she was having trouble maneuvering even the slightest inclines, let alone the boulders Trahern was climbing over, dragging that saddle of his with him like it weighed almost nothing. If he wanted to brood and not speak to her, that was just fine. She would not ask him to stop. Her pride prevented her from begging for relief, though it seemed her feet were screaming up at her not to be so stubborn.

Looking up, she bit her bottom lip to keep from crying as she viewed another rocky hill. How the heck had they managed to build a railroad through this? she wondered, and reached out with her hand to find some sort of leverage to help pull herself up yet another huge boulder.

She had developed a set pattern when she encountered such an obstacle. First, she'd throw her briefcase, either over it if were small enough, or on top, if it were larger, as the one in front of her was. Then she would take her purse and use the long leather strap as a headband of sorts, letting the bulk of the bag rest on her neck and upper back, thus keeping it out of the way and letting her have the full use of her arms.

Trahern had gone over the large rock with ease, and Jenna had everything in place and was congratulating herself on her ingenuity when, suddenly, she heard a loud animal roar on the other side, like something out of a zoo. At the frightening sound, her head jerked up, and the strap at her forehead slipped to her neck, cutting off her air. She knew in that flash second of fear that if she let go to remove it, she would surely fall back, landing on the smaller, but sharp jutting rocks behind her.

Without hesitation, she clawed at the large gray stone, not caring that she broke nails, only mindful of reaching the top and removing the heavy weight from her throat. She was gasping for breath when she reached the peak, the sound of her own breathing roaring in her ears, so that when she ripped the purse away from her head, she didn't at first, connect the continued roaring as not being hers.

Slowly, she brought her head up, but nothing in her life prepared her for the scene unfolding before her eyes.

"Morgan!"

His name ripped out of her throat in a terrorized scream as she watched man and animal roll over on the ground, over and over again, wrestling with each other. A huge cat continued to growl while Morgan grunted, his hands buried in the cat's thick neck fur, desperately trying to hold it back from burying its teeth into his body, while at the same time avoiding its sharp, powerful claws.

Jenna came quickly to life. Her high heels moved down from the rock as if it were soft carpeting. She ran to him, stopping about ten feet away from the battle. "My God, Morgan! Tell me what to do!" she shouted in dismay. Never, never in her life had she felt so helpless!

"The gun . . ." he gasped out, just before the cat's right paw connected with his shoulder. Jenna screamed for him before terror released a fraction of its tight hold, and she tried to think clearly.

The gun! Damn, didn't he have it? Frantically, she searched the ground. She didn't realize when she brought her hand up to brush away the liquid at her eyes that it was tears. She only knew she was fighting down panic. "Where *is* it?" she begged stupidly. "Dear God, please help me find it! Please!"

When Jenna's eyes finally connected with the long gray barrel of the gun, she felt as blessed as the saints she had read about when she was a child. Grabbing for it, she straightened and looked up to the struggle taking place before her.

It was hard to tell where the animal left off and Morgan began, they were so entangled. Sobbing, when she sighted blood on Morgan's neck, she pulled the hammer back and brought the pistol up.

She'd never used a gun before, and her hand was shaking so badly she brought her other up to join it. Holding the pistol with both hands, she stretched out her arms and tried to aim it. Dammit! How could she do this?

In the end, all she needed was hearing Morgan cry out in pain as the cat again clawed him. Aiming as best she could, Jenna swallowed down as much panic as possible and squeezed the trigger.

Not braced for the powerful recoil, she stumbled backward and fell to the ground. When she looked up, it was to see the cat taking off into the woods and Morgan turning over to his side, trying to roll into a defensive ball.

She dropped the gun and half crawled, half ran to him.

"Oh my God! My God, Morgan! What should I do?" Horrified, she knelt next to him, pulling nervously at her fingers.

Morgan's pale face was beaded in perspiration, and his eyes were tightly closed, his lips pulled back in a grimace of pain. Jenna's eyes quickly scanned his body, forcing herself to look at the wounds at his neck, shoulder, and thigh.

"Oh, no!" she muttered aloud. "You're bleeding!"

She hadn't expected an answer, too preoccupied with trying to imagine what she had that would stop the bleeding, but if she were surprised by his answering, it was nothing compared to her shock at listening to his words.

"You . . . you shot me . . ." he gasped out, holding his right shoulder with a bloodied left hand.

"What? I shot you?" Jenna's hands came up to cover her mouth, horrified that she had actually shot the man lying in front of her. "Oh my God! I didn't mean it! You know I didn't mean it, don't you? Oh God, Morgan, tell me you know I didn't mean it!" she sobbed out from behind her hands.

"I know . . . I know," his voice rasped out. "Don't cry. Go to my bag. Try to find something to stop the bleeding, Jenna. Hurry . . ."

She saw his lower jaw go slack as he gasped again in pain. It was all she needed to stop her tears. Jenna hurried back to the boulder they had crossed and grabbed his satchel. She fought with the lock for a few seconds, until she realized she couldn't open it without a key. Bringing it with her, she returned to Morgan's side.

"It's locked. Where's the key, Morgan? Please, is it in one of your pockets?"

He was breathing deeply now, no longer thrashing from side to side as before. "My pants pocket," he whispered, keeping his eyes closed.

Jenna didn't even hesitate before slipping her hand inside the soft denim at his hip. She was forced to search with her fingers and apologized when she heard Morgan again gasp. "I'm sorry. I'm trying to be gentle. Here! I think I've got it!"

Morgan let out his breath. "Thank God!"

Jenna quickly rummaged through the small case until she found a white cotton shirt. "This should do," she said to herself and brought the material up before her. Using all her strength, she ripped it in half down the back. Bringing the canteen with her, she hurried back to Morgan.

"This might hurt, but I have to clean your wounds. Do you think you can move?"

He nodded, and Jenna bit her bottom lip as she tried to help him. He managed to bring himself up on his left elbow but the effort was too much, and he quickly returned to the ground. "You'll have to do it . . . I can't. Use my knife. Cut the cloth away to get at them."

Jenna broke out into a cold sweat. "The knife! Right! Where is it?"

He groaned again in pain as he touched his right shoulder. "In my boot. Couldn't get to it. Damn mountain lion . . . must have come too close . . ."

She held the knife in front of her, poised between them. When she looked down into his eyes, she had to swallow back a fresh flood of tears. She'd never seen a person in such pain, yet he didn't scream. When their eyes connected, she didn't see accusation, just the pain.

"You all right, Jenna? Calm down. Just cut it away so you can get to the bullet hole."

Oh God, she thought. A bullet hole . . . and I've put it there! She took several deep breaths to steady her hand and then gingerly cut away the material at his shoulder.

"Ohhh . . ." She couldn't stop the sound from coming out of her mouth. It was horrible! She, too, was breathing deeply, feeling as if she had run a mile just to get to this point and staring at the bleeding puncture, seeing where the bullet had entered, she also gasped for breath, trying not to scream.

In between three oozing scratches was a small hole, blood streaming in a steady rivulet down the side of his arm to join a puddle that was already staining the ground beneath him.

"Jenna." He said her name while biting his lower lip. "I think the bullet passed through . . . the back of my shoulder . . . it feels like it's on fire. Help me roll over."

She did as he asked while gulping down hysteria. Using the knife, she completely took off the sleeve of his shirt.

"Oh God, Morgan! It's worse in back!"

His eyes remained closed and his breath came in short pants, while he tried to speak. "The . . . the exit hole is always bigger. At least the bullet isn't in me. Wrap it . . . as best as you can. Don't . . . don't use too much water. We need it to get out of here."

Seeing how just speaking had weakened him, Jenna ordered, "Shut up. And I don't give a damn about the water. We'll use the whole thing, if we have to. Just tell me what to do."

He tried to look over his shoulder at her, but winced when he moved. Unbelievably, he smiled. "Listen . . . *Dead Eye* . . . one of us had better be able to get help. I don't know if I can make it."

He was teasing her! She'd just shot him and he was again teasing! Didn't anything stop the man? "Now you listen to me, Trahern. We're *both* getting out of here. You hear me? I'm not leaving without you."

She didn't wait for an answer. She picked up the canteen and poured a small amount of water over the wound at the back of his shoulder. The blood cleared for a second before it pooled again, and Jenna quickly slipped the folded material over the shredded skin. After his initial gasp when the water hit him, Morgan sensed her nervousness and remained quiet, though he almost bit through his bottom lip when she wrapped his shoulder with the cotton shirt.

"The least you can do now is use my . . . first name."

Jenna couldn't help the smile. She had the strangest feeling he was trying to put her at ease. Her! Without thinking, she reached out and gently brushed his thick hair back from his forehead. She felt the dampness brought about by trying to control the pain, and her heart constricted with remorse. "God, you have to know how sorry I am. I tried to hit the cat. Even if we fought, Morgan, I wouldn't purposely hurt you. You do believe that, don't you?"

"Not even for calling you shrewish?" he managed to get out, though Jenna could see what speaking was costing him.

Again, her long fingers entered his raven hair and slowly, gently she stroked him. "I didn't care about the shrewish part. It was being called an old maid that got to me. I'm not old, you know. Just twenty-eight."

"And a bad shot," he said softly. He opened his eyes and stared into hers. Trying to smile, he said, "A twenty-eight year old *desperada*. What else will I learn about you, Jenna?"

She couldn't stand to see the pain in his blue eyes and shifted the focus of their attention elsewhere. "Nothing, and you're too weak to interrogate me again. Listen, we haven't even seen to your leg yet. I'd better . . . Wait! Wait!" Without explaining, she left his side and ran back to the boulder.

When she came back he saw she had her leather purse. She stopped in front of him and rummaged through it while sitting back down next to him. Several times she removed articles from the bag and laid them on the ground. Without looking at him, she tried explaining what she was doing.

"I didn't switch purses last night. I was planning to do that in Sacramento. I know it's in here, just . . . Here! Thank God, my bags are always a mess." Jenna brought a small container up into view. "First aid kit! The bandages are too small to be of any use, except for the scratches, but here's a disinfectant."

She looked at him seriously. "I'm going to have to remove the shirt, Morgan, and spray this on the . . . well, the wound. Okay?"

He seemed to gather his strength. "Jenna, just leave it alone. I've already been subject to your bag of tricks."

She pursed her lips together. "Read it yourself. It's disinfectant. Now, don't be such a baby. Would you rather it became infected?"

"Hell, woman, those scratches from the cat are more likely to be trouble. Leave the bullet wound . . . alone. Please."

She refused to be affected by his voice. She had to do it. "Listen, Trahern, you're in no condition to fight me on this. It has to be done. C'mon."

She didn't wait for his permission. As much as she dreaded looking at his shoulder again, she untied the clumsy bandage and quickly sprayed his wound. As she tried to fashion the shirt into a bandage again, she could see it was hopeless. She needed something stronger, more elastic to keep it in place. Her brain searched for the solution. Suddenly, she knew just what would work, and it would also serve as a sling of sorts. Without any hesitation, she took off her boots and stood. Not seeing Morgan's eyes on her, she unzipped her skirt and slipped it down her body. Stepping out of it, she shocked him further by hiking up her slip and rolling down the strangest looking hose he'd ever seen.

"Here!" she stated triumphantly as she held them out. "This is going to do the trick." Clad only in her thin blouse and the tiniest, white lace underwear Morgan had ever seen—before her short slip came back to fall at her knees—Jenna knelt down beside him again.

As she picked up the knife and started hacking away at her panty hose, Jenna barely heard him as he lifted his left hand to his forehead and muttered, "Lord! The fever must be starting already. I'm hallucinating!"

Chapter Seven

Nestled within a lush green meadow, it appeared to Jenna like a set for a western movie. Old-fashioned buildings that didn't look quite weathered bordered a small community of homes. There were no paved roads, no visible signs of anything modern. Even from the hill overlooking the town, Jenna could not see a single car, just tiny horse-drawn wagons. And the sound that had led Jenna to the town was intense, even though she still had not yet left the woods. It was all around her, the loud whining screech of a saw.

She had only stopped to catch her breath and could not afford to waste time pondering the noisy town. At that moment Verdi looked better than a Club Med resort, for there she would find help for Morgan. Just thinking about leaving him alone made her hurry.

He had tried to walk and had, with her help, succeeded for about a mile. After that, Jenna had felt his weight on her shoulder increase, and she knew he was weakening. When they stopped to rest, Morgan looked into her eyes, and Jenna knew he could not continue. She'd been close to tears when she left him lying with his back against a large rock. She'd picked a spot out of the sun and had left him the water, but she would never forget the sight of him. He was weak from the loss of blood and the enforced march. His once healthy, tanned face looked sallow behind the black hair of his mustache and the short growth of whiskers. Even though his eyes seemed glazed with pain, his lips still managed to smile, and his voice still held a teasing note as he called her his *desperada*. That was when she had left him, at his insistence. He'd waved her off, holding his gun in one hand, as if he would have the strength to use it.

As Jenna entered the town, she found herself walking on a dirt road, with the railroad tracks on one side and buildings on the other. She stood facing a huge establishment on the corner. Looking up and down both streets for any sign of a doctor's office, she decided to enter the building which seemed to be the center of town and ask for directions.

Jenna raised her face to the immense sign painted in red and blue over the front of the building: Four Mile Saloon, Stan Tearle, Proprietor. Once again she quickly scanned both streets. People were too far away, and she needed immediate help. Squaring her shoulders, she lifted her aching feet to the wooden sidewalk and, within moments, entered the bar.

Her eyes took a number of seconds adjusting to the dim interior after she walked for so long in the blazing sun. When her pupils had dilated sufficiently to allow more definition, Jenna could see three men at the long wooden bar, two of them huge, and another tall man bartending. All four seemed to turn as one, as if in slow motion, and look at her.

She shook the eerie feeling away. Coming further into the bar, Jenna adjusted the strap of her purse at her shoulder and cleared her throat. "Please . . . tell me where the doctor is! I left a man in the woods. He's been hurt. Please."

The men came to life. One of the tall ones, a muscular blonde, reached her first. "What happened?" he asked in a deep, slightly accented voice.

For some reason, her eyes seemed glued to the man's muscled arms. His plaid shirt was rolled up above his elbows, and his thick forearms were covered in a mat of blond fuzz. She forced her eyes to his face, and in that moment the hair at the back of her neck rose of its own accord. Frightened by what was happening to her body, Jenna looked to the bar. Behind the long length of mahogany, nestled in between glasses and bottles of liquor, was a calendar. Her eyebrows came together as she strained to read it. Big black X's marked off the days under the month of June. There were eleven of them. And above it all were the large numbers one-eight-seven-zero. June 11, 1870!

How could they be part of Tom Freeman's hoax?! A hundred questions shot through her mind, none of which seemed to have a logical answer. This couldn't be real! *It simply could not have happened. It was May 3, 1987. Nineteen eighty-seven!*

The man in front of her repeated his question. "What happened to the man? How was he hurt?"

Jenna tore her eyes away from the calendar and faced the man. "There was a cat," she began hesitantly, "a mountain lion, or something. It attacked and . . ." Her words trailed off. What should she say? What would these people do when she said she'd shot Morgan? She didn't do it intentionally. Surely they would understand.

"Your man hurt bad?" Another, this one shorter and balding, asked urgently.

Jenna nodded. "He's lost so much blood. He couldn't walk any further. I had to leave him about a mile up the railroad track. Where's the doctor? He needs a doctor! Please!" she begged.

The four men looked at each other, a silent conversation going on with their eyes. Finally, the tall, blond one turned back to her. "Doc Marshall, he's out past Crystal Peak, tending Ted Newlins and then moving on up north of that. Don't expect him back until tomorrow."

Oh God, Jenna's already parched mouth went drier. "We have to do something!" Even she recognized the hysteria coming into her voice. "He could die! He's been shot!"

"*Shot!* Thought you said a cat got him?" This time it was the bartender who spoke up.

Jenna looked down to the blonde's heavy work shoes and then the bare wooden floor. "I did it," she said in a voice full of remorse. Quickly, her eyes flew to the man's in front of her. "I didn't mean for him to get hurt. I was aiming for the mountain lion!" Her eyes begged him to believe her.

"I'll take her to get her man."

Jenna quickly turned when she heard the low-sounding voice behind her. It belonged to a short, dark-haired young man. He looked to be no more than fifteen or sixteen, yet stood almost defiantly, looking at the other men present while tightly holding the wooden handle of a broom.

"You ain't got no fit wagon, Jace, not to make it up them hills," the bartender said. "You leave it to Swede here. He'll get the lady's husband down."

Jenna caught the dislike in the boy's eyes as he looked at the other men, but she had no time to be diplomatic. She tried to smile at the young man, but found it was forced and, without hesitation, she turned back to the man named Swede.

Knowing she didn't have any time to waste she asked urgently, "Don't any of you have cars? Something quicker than a wagon?"

Disbelief showed on their faces. "Ma'am, lumbering may be big business here, but ain't nobody rich enough to own their own car. Verdi don't sport no Charlie Crocker or Mark Hopkins. We ain't no railroad barons, but we'll bring him down to you." The man, Swede, finished his mug of beer and slammed it on the surface of the bar. "Let's go, boys!" he bellowed to his drinking partners.

"Wait! I'm coming with you," Jenna announced immediately. "I'll show you where I left him."

Swede stopped in his tracks and turned back to her. "What's your husband's name?"

"He's not—" Something about the men made her stop just short of revealing that she wasn't married. "Morgan. Morgan Trahern. But you don't know where he is. He might be unconscious and not hear you. I have to come."

The tall handsome man's mouth broke into a that spread across his lower face. "Ma'am, we're woods men, and these are our woods. If we can't find him, he ain't there."

He led her to a table by the double swinging doors and called over his shoulder. "Stan, get her something . . . a lemonade." Then smiling again at her, he said softly, "You look like you've had a bad time of it, yourself. Stay here and get rested."

"But—" Jenna didn't want to give up so easily.

"Your man's gonna need you, little lady, when we bring him back." Without another word, Swede and the two others with him disappeared out the saloon doors.

Slowly, Jenna sank onto the wooden chair. She rested her elbows on the table in front of her and raised her hands to her forehead. Deliberately, she pushed back the damp strands of hair that seemed glued to her skin.

"This ought to make you feel a little bit better."

Jenna raised her head and looked at the bartender placing a tall glass of lemonade on the table. She gave him a tired smile. "Thanks," she said, while reaching for her purse. "How much is it?"

The man seemed offended. "Ain't no charge for helping out. Looks like you might be staying here for a spell, with your husband hurt and all. Maybe sometime I'll be passing you on a hot day and need a cool drink. You pay me back then."

Jenna nodded. She didn't see any reason for telling the man she wasn't Morgan's wife, nor that they wouldn't be staying in town for any length of time. She brought the glass to her lips and took a long drink. Her thirst seemed to have a mind of its own. Rudely, she finished the entire contents without stopping. Only when it was empty, did she realize she had drank the whole thing. She was too tired to be embarrassed and, looking at the kindly man, she said, "That was delicious. I'll have another. And this time I insist on paying."

Stan Tearle looked down at the dirty, tired woman and smiled before going back to the bar. He didn't think she had the money to pay for much of anything, even a lemonade. She was even wearing a skirt that she'd grown out of years ago. Being a smart businessman, he'd taken in her strange attire, but also picked up her underlying beauty. Stan figured once she was cleaned up she'd make one pretty woman. Too bad she was married. Eligible females were scarce in this booming lumber town. And he had a business upstairs that could use a fresh face. Lord knows, Gertie and the girls were wearing thin with the men of Verdi.

Placing the second glass of lemonade in front of her, he smiled first before saying, "Five cents, if you got it," more out of curiosity to see if she had any money.

Jenna opened her purse and brought out a dollar bill. "Surely, lemonade costs more than a nickel." She held her breath as she watched him look at the money. He turned it over more than once before he raised his head and looked at her.

Handing it back, he informed her, "Don't rightly know what this'll buy you. You have any other kind of money?"

Jenna's heart pounded against her rib cage. She tried to keep the anxiety out of her voice when she asked, "What about American Express?"

He shook his head each time she mentioned one of the credit cards in her wallet. "Never heard of 'em, not a one. Them banks of yours? Maybe Bill Drayton, down at the bank, can help there." He looked into her stricken face and was moved to say, "Don't worry. I don't do much of a business this early. You can wait here, unless you'd be more comfortable at the inn or hotel."

Jenna only shook her head. Her voice was lost somewhere in the tightened muscles of her neck. She didn't even watch the bartender walk away, but just stared at the condensation building up on the outside of the glass. *This could not have happened! She could not be transported back in time! She couldn't!* Yet the logical side of her brain demanded that she examine what had happened to her since she entered that damn smoking car. It had all started there. *Something* had happened. When the door had slammed shut behind her, the train had lurched, and since that time she hadn't seen one single, modern thing. Morgan had insisted that it was 1870, and she had laughed at him. Now, sitting in the dim saloon, she had a terrible feeling in the pit of her stomach that he might be right. She was afraid, too frightened to even touch the glass in front of her. Nothing seemed right anymore. Even Tom couldn't have arranged a joke of this magnitude. What was wrong with these people? What was wrong with her? *Dear God, what had happened on that train?*

Like a monster out of a child's book, the pain reached out its fiery tentacles to grasp his back and chest. He had long ago given up trying to control it. It controlled him now, and he thought to embrace it, to let it have its way. Like any wild thing, it had a mind of its own, but perhaps he could overcome it by not fighting. Morgan attempted to relax, not centering his thoughts on the pain. He tried to think of other things, his business, his assignment, his home, his *desperada*, but the effort was enormous and soon, behind his sweating forehead, his brain would again return him to the beast.

"Don't fight it, Billy . . ." he whispered to the young boy in front of him. He was dreaming again and he knew it, yet this time it seemed so real, as if he could feel the young soldier's pain.

"You . . . you'll write and tell her I was brave, won't ya, major? She . . . they're gonna take this hard."

"You tell her yourself. We're going to get out of this. I won't leave you, Bill."

"Oh God! Help me . . . I can hear 'em. Get out . . . Get out!"

Startled, he woke to his name being called.

"Trahern? Morgan Trahern?"

Morgan blinked at the tall blond giant kneeling in

102

front of him. His eyes slid past the man to see two others with him of almost equal height. Waiting for his head to clear, he finally nodded.

The blonde smiled. "Didn't think there could be two up here in this bad of shape. Name's Nils Jensen. Everybody calls me Swede. Your missus told us where to find you."

Morgan closed his eyes again briefly in confusion. "Missus? You mean Jenna?"

"Ya, she's waiting for you in town. Put up a fight, too. Wanted to come with us. You had any water?"

Morgan opened his eyes and looked at the canteen by his side. "Some. Didn't know how long I'd be out here."

Swede saw the flash of pain cross the man's face as he tried to sit up straighter, and he held his hand up to one of the men behind him as he talked to Morgan. "Well . . . Ned, here, has somethin' you might appreciate a bit more." Unscrewing the top of a bottle, he announced, "Whiskey. That ought to take the edge off till we get you into town."

Morgan's frustration was great when he found himself too weak to hold the bottle. Instead, he suffered having it brought to his mouth like a helpless child. He took a long swig and coughed, spilling some of the liquor down his chest. Looking up to Swede he smiled weakly. "Thanks. A little more of that and I'll be ready to . . . to find the damn cat that did this."

Swede looked at Ned and Max and nodded. Without asking for permission, they bent down and lifted Morgan. Feeling himself borne through the air in the arms of the strong men, Morgan thought to say, "My saddle . . . Jenna left it a couple of miles back."

Max, the shortest of the men, grunted as they reached the wagon. "Let's take care of you first. Don't worry about your saddle." They put Morgan in the back of a flatbed wagon. Ned took the reins, and Max and Swede remained in back with the pale, injured man. As Swede brought the bottle once more to Morgan's lips, he smiled good-naturedly and said, "You better hope the whiskey knocks you out. When that pretty woman of yours takes one whiff of you, she's gonna give us all hell for getting you drunk."

Morgan tried to smile at Swede's worlds. Even this giant wouldn't stand much of a chance against Jenna once she got going. And thinking about her, he felt his body grow warm. He attributed it to the drink, or perhaps the fever that he knew was growing higher with each hour. As the alcohol permeated his system, the pain actually lessened, and his thoughs returned to Jenna. He closed his eyes and saw her as she'd left him. It hadn't been easy persuading her to go on alone, but he'd been aware of his growing weakness and knew he would never make it. She was his only hope. And she'd come through, just like he knew she would. His woman, Swede called her. His missus. He pictured her sad blue-gray eyes when she promised to find help; her full luscious mouth that could melt your heart when she wasn't angry; the stubborn tilt of her chin when she was defiant. He remembered his brief glimpse of her body when she stripped off her hose. He wished she was his woman. Hell, he thought, it must be the fever to make him want her. But then, maybe it was time for a woman of his own.

Jenna knew the young man was quietly standing next to her, waiting for her to look at him. She again examined the scratches on the wooden table in front of her, not wanting to answer his question. She didn't feel capable of forming the words. What should she tell him? That yes, if this was the twentieth century, then she'd certainly have the money for a place to stay? Or would her answer be negative? If what she thought happened, had actually occurred, then no, she was without funds or the means to attain them. How long would Mr. Stan Tearle let her sit in this dark corner of his saloon? Where were she and Morgan going to find shelter, until she figured out what to do?

"Ma'am, if you don't have much money and are lookin' for a place to stay, I might be able to help you." He repeated his statement, thinking she hadn't heard him the first time. Jace wished she would answer him. Not only did he want to hear her voice again, but Stan was going to come out of the back room any minute now and catch him trying to speak to her.

This time Jenna did look at him. He was young, and he looked nervous, but sincere. His long, straight black hair, dark eyes, and copper skin reminded her of an Indian. Not the tall, regal, high-cheekboned Indians who were so often displayed in pictures. This one was short and robustly built.

Seeing him glance once more in the direction of the back of the bar, she remembered he was the one who had first volunteered to bring Morgan here. For some reason she had known it had taken courage for him to speak up in front of the other men, and she smiled before asking, "You think you might know of an inexpensive place my . . . my husband and I might be able to afford?"

He returned her smile, and his whole appearance changed. He looked boyishly handsome as he spoke. "I live just outside of town with my mother. Since my father died, we have both been trying to earn extra." He indicated the bar with his head. "I would rather see my mother stay in her home," he said in a lower voice tinged with pride, "instead of helping the Chinese man with his laundry. We have room for you and your man."

"I . . . well, we don't have much money," Jenna informed him. She didn't even know how much Morgan had. She just remembered his telling her he was carrying very little cash. Thinking of that conversation, she hurried to add. "My . . . my man has a saddle that he wanted to sell. I had to leave it, but if you'll help me get it off the mountain, then, yes . . . we'll stay at your home."

He nodded his head sharply in agreement. "I will be fair. Each week you will pay two dollars to my mother. You will tell me where you left the saddle, and I will leave now to tell my mother to prepare for you. Once your husband is here, I will bring back your saddle. You agree to this?"

Jenna made the decision for both Morgan and herself. "Yes." She wouldn't argue that two dollars a week was an outrageously small sum of money for lodging. In this town, at this time, she didn't have two good dollar bills to her name.

"Jace, you leave that lady be. Don't you have work?"

Jace squared his shoulders and looked at his boss who had just reappeared. "Mr. Teale, this lady and her man are going to be boarding at my place. I'm going to have to leave now and tell my mother. I'll make up the time tonight and tomorrow."

"Your place?" Stan Teale came closer to them. He looked at Jenna and said, "Lady, you sure about this?"

She observed both men. Jace lifted his chin as if insulted while his boss seemed disdainful of her decision. "Yes, Mr. Teale, I am. When they bring my husband, I'm going to take him to Jace's." Jenna

106

watched Stan shrug his shoulders and return to the bar, while Jace nodded in her direction before disappearing out the front doors.

Settling back in her wooden chair, she picked up the warm lemonade and sipped it with all the grace that had been bred into her. She couldn't help the small smile from creeping up the corners of her mouth. Strange how easily lying was coming to her. Why she hadn't even hesitated that last time when referring to Morgan as her husband. But thinking of him, her smile disappeared. Dear God, where were they? She knew she should have gone along. What if they haven't found him? What if he was still lying there, bleeding to death? She closed her eyes and silently offered a small prayer for Morgan, for herself, and for guidance. Only divine intervention was going to help her out of this. That, and using her head.

Chapter Eight

She studied the man lying on the bed. She'd only known him for little over twenty-four hours, yet Jenna felt closer to Morgan than most men she'd known for years. She reached out her hand to his forehead, covered in a slick sheen of sweat. The heat radiated up from him and, instinctively, Jenna lowered her face to his and brought her lips to his temple. It was something her mother had always done to her when she was sick. Jenna didn't know if it was her mother's private gauge, but it had always made her feel better.

Even though she had never cared for a sick person before, she knew Morgan would be unaware that her cool lips had touched his feverish skin. Since he'd been unconscious when Swede brought him into town, Jenna never had a chance to talk to him, to ask him if she'd made the right decisions.

Looking around her, she knew she'd made the only one possible, considering their situation. She and Morgan occupied a tiny room, attached to a deserted barn. When Swede and his friends carried Morgan into this place, Jenna had to bite down a protest. Although clean, it consisted only of a narrow bed, a single chair, and a small black stove, its chimney venting outside through one wall.

She straightened and her eyes returned to Morgan. Lying on his side, he barely moved. His breathing was shallow, and his coloring was flushed from the fever. Jenna knew she had to do something. She couldn't wait until the doctor returned tomorrow. Morgan had lost too much blood. He needed immediate attention.

She had always prided herself in calmly reacting to an emergency. Of course, those emergencies were in business, nothing like this. Taking a deep breath, she realized her first priority was getting Morgan out of those filthy clothes. Starting with his boots, she tugged at one, then the other, and found her lips curling upward when she viewed his red, woolen socks. She removed them and stared at his feet. There was something so personal about looking at a stranger's feet. Morgan's were like the rest of him, long and lean. She mentally pushed the ridiculous thought from her mind while rolling the socks together and throwing them at the bottom of the bed. Slowly, she moved to his chest. Removing what little remained of his shirt by the conventional method was out of the question. She went to her purse and brought out the knife. Within less than a minute, its sharp edge had sliced through the cotton material, and Jenna was able to remove it without causing any more discomfort to Morgan. Laying the knife on the bed, she stared at him, clad only in his makeshift bandages and jeans. Like the hair on his head and at his upper lip, the damp mat of curling hair that covered his chest was jet black. Jenna could feel the heat coming from his body and, without hesitation, she reached for the first button at the top of his denims. Just as she pushed the button through its matching hole, a soft knock sounded on the other side of the wooden door, and Jenna quickly brought her hands back to her chest, as if guilty of some unpardonable sin.

It took her a few seconds until she found her voice. "Yes. Come in."

The weathered pine door slowly opened, and Jenna stared at a dark-haired woman, wearing a long dress and apron and carrying blankets, sheets, and two small bowls in her sturdy brown arms. "Jason Eberly is my son," she stated in a soft, low voice.

"Of course," Jenna quickly added. "Thank you for taking us in, Mrs. Eberly. Can I help you with those?" Jenna reached out her hands to take the blanket and sheets.

Willow Eberly felt surprised, but let the white woman take them from her. She watched her put them on the bottom of the bed, then bring a hand up to brush back her long yellow hair from her face. She then looked to her man briefly before turning those startling blue eyes back to her.

"Jason tells me your man has been shot. I can see the fever has come to him. The blanket and sheets will help. You have already seen to his wounds?"

Jenna was uncomfortable with everyone calling Morgan her man, yet she said nothing to correct it. "No, not really. I did the best I could after it happened. I was hoping to find a doctor here, who could help him."

Willow came closer to the bed. "Dr. Clinton Marshall is a man of great talent," she said almost absently, while eyeing the white man's back.

Jenna watched her watching Morgan. "I was told the doctor is away. He won't be back until tomorrow."

"Your man cannot wait for him."

Dark-brown, practical eyes connected with frightened blue ones. "Can you help me?" Jenna pleaded, very close to erupting into a fresh flood of tears.

Like her son, she stared at Jenna briefly before

110

abruptly nodding. "First, we must continue to remove his clothing. Then we shall see to his wound. What is your man's name?"

"Morgan. Morgan Trahern," she said gratefully. She quickly thought to add, "I'm Jenna, and thank you, Mrs. Eberly, you and your son have been very kind."

As much as she was pleased to have the white woman show her respect, for not many had done so, she was not comfortable being called by her dead husband's name. "I am called Willow," she stated simply, as she put the two small bowls she'd been holding on the bed, next to the knife. "You will finish what you were doing and cover him with the sheet. If you wish, I will leave until you are done."

Not wanting the quiet, self-assured woman to leave her, Jenna said in an embarrassed rush, "I don't see why. I don't think modesty is a matter of great concern right now, do you?" And without waiting for an answer, she reached for Morgan's second button.

Willow Eberly was an efficient nurse. If she noticed Jenna's shocked expression when Morgan's body was completely exposed, she hid it well. Bringing the sheet up to his waist, she looked to Jenna. "You will remove the cloth from his shoulder while I make a poultice. If it does not come away easily, pour water on it until the dried blood softens."

Jenna blinked a few times at the woman. Willow said it in her soft voice. It wasn't an order. She just took for granted Jenna would want to do it. Swallowing apprehension, Jenna came to Morgan's side. She watched Willow pick up one of the bowls and go to the stove. From her apron pocket, the woman brought out a small, thick wooden spoon and started grinding whatever was in front of her.

Jenna reached out to Morgan. Gingerly, she untied

111

pieces of her panty hose. When she reached the cloth under them, it was soaked through with dried, brown blood, and she knew, without trying, that she would not be able to remove it. She walked over to the windowsill and brought back a pitcher of water and the large bowl it rested in. Placing the bowl on the bed, next to Morgan's back, Jenna poured cool water onto the stiff bandage.

Instinctively, Morgan jerked as the water made contact with his wound. Although unconscious, his muscles reacted without thought, and Jenna cried out, thinking she had once more hurt him.

Willow had come up quietly behind her. "Your man was strong, and he is brave to have fought with the mountain lion. My son seems to think you are also brave. You must now be that for your man."

Jenna looked at the back of Morgan's head. Yes, she thought, resisting touching his curling back hair, he is brave. She pictured him on the train, standing up for her against the crowd of fanatics, wrestling with the large cat, never crying out as she tried to patch him up, never complaining on the long, agonizing walk afterward, sending her off alone with a smile, calling her his *desperada*. Without hesitation, she squared her shoulders and started to pick away the now soft layers of bandaging.

Minutes later, Jenna's bravery wavered as she stood behind Willow. "What are you doing?" she asked with concern, as the other woman brought out a long needle and thread.

"Now that it is clean, we must close his torn skin. You will go around to the other side of the bed and hold his arms out straight. He will fight you, but you must be stronger. Do you understand?" She looked over her shoulder at Jenna, waiting for an answer.

Jenna's eyes moved from Willow's dark, patient

ones to the needle and thread. My God, she thought, how can we do this? Without a doctor? Just as quickly, her eyes fastened on Morgan's bleeding back. She had done this to him, and she would try anything, anything at all, to repair the damage she had done.

Quickly, Jenna moved to the opposite side of the bed. Before she took his arms, she bent her head and kissed his hot cheek. "I'm sorry, Morgan," she whispered. "I'm sorry." Straightening, she reached out her hands and tightly held his forearms and, taking a deep breath, nodded to the woman in back of him.

Within seconds Morgan let out an anguished groan and, involuntarily, he grabbed her arms, digging his fingers into her skin. Again and again, Jenna saw the needle dip downward to pierce his raw flesh. Each time his body jerked, Jenna fought to keep him from rolling back onto his open wound. Her eyes blurred and she furiously blinked, causing the salty moisture to slowly run down her cheeks. After what seemed like an eternity, Willow finally spoke, "You may let him go. It is done."

Slowly, her hands released Morgan. She was so emotionally drained, she wanted to collapse next to him. But there was more to be done and, widening her eyes while tightening her facial muscles, she willed the tears to stop.

Standing once again in back of Willow, Jenna watched her pour a powdery substance over the jagged scars. "What is it?" she asked hesitantly.

The smaller woman once more looked over her shoulder and smiled at Jenna for the first time. "Clinton Marshall and I have traded secrets many times. This curse is his. Ergot . . . powerful medicine Clinton tells me comes from the grain of a grass." Turning back to Morgan, she added, "It is used to stop bleeding."

Jenna watched as she applied the poultice and tightly wrapped his shoulder in clean white linen. When she finished, Willow stood and wiped her hands on the front of her apron. "I will bring more water while you see to the rest of his wounds. He will need to be bathed often to bring down the fever."

Jenna stepped out of her way, murmuring a quiet "thank you" as the woman silently left. As she took her place behind Morgan, she picked up the bowl containing the dark fungus and brought it to the other side of the bed. Without too much trouble, she took care of the scratches that started at Morgan's neck and stopped at his shoulder bone. All that was left were the ones on his right thigh. Wanting to be done before Willow returned, Jenna lifted the muslin to expose his leg.

She made sure she kept the sheet over his abdomen so that everything lower than that was covered. Putting herself in Morgan's position, unconscious and unaware of what was being done, she knew she would want the same. As she worked on him, she tried to maintain an impersonal touch, but found she had to stop her fingers from becoming soft and caressing as she wound the bandage around his dark-haired, muscled thigh. She found it strange that she should feel so moved by a man she detested yesterday, and couldn't entirely blame it on the fact that she had put him in this condition.

Of course, caring for him had taken her mind off her own problems—like being caught in the last century. Jenna tightened the bandage. She would not think about it, at least, not yet. Standing back, she viewed her handiwork and shook her head in dismay. Whereas Willow's bandage looked neat and supportive, Jenna felt she had made Morgan look like one of the extras in the "Thriller" video. Ah well, she

114

thought, as she unzipped her boots, at least everything that was supposed to be bandaged was taken care of, although she wasn't sure about using this ergot as a medicine. Why had everything gone wrong since she had entered that smoking car? And now to have finally reached a town, to find everyone living as though in the last century, and the doctor gone? Using a *fungus* on a gunshot wound? Dear God, it could only get better from here. It had no place to go, but up.

"Morgan, please. Please lay still!"

Although he had yet to wake up, he'd begun to moan and thrash around on the bed about three hours ago. Jenna had no idea what time it was. She had forgotten to wind her watch yesterday and it had stopped, just as the world she was familiar with had ceased to exist.

As she placed herself across his chest, hoping to keep him immobile, he kicked the sheets completely off him. Jenna was beyond embarrassment, beyond exhaustion, and she railed at him. "Go ahead, Trahern, expose yourself. See if I care." But within seconds, she found the energy to turn her head and let her eyes travel the length of his body.

Jenna felt a surprising sensation build up at the tops of her thighs and settle uncomfortably where they were joined together. Just lying there, he was so male. Unconscious, he was no threat to her, yet she turned her eyes away as an unwelcomed warmth spread quickly over her body. What was wrong with her? She stepped away from the bed and brought her hands up to her flushed face. She was acting like some teenaged virgin, getting her first look at a man!

Not wanting to analyze the reason behind what was

happening to her, Jenna efficiently brought the sheet up to Morgan's waist and again dipped the cotton rag into the basin of water. She worked diligently, sponging him off, talking to him, covering him when he would kick the sheet away. His body fought the fever and so did Jenna. She made up her mind that she wouldn't stop until Morgan was resting comfortably. She had done this to him, and it was up to her to see him through.

"You did not hear me knock, Jenna. I have brought you food and a change of clothes." Willow Eberly slowly came into the room and placed a large bowl on the stove. As she turned around to Jenna, she smiled shyly. "I could not help but notice you have no clothing. You will accept this?" she asked hesitantly as she held out a plain cotton nightgown.

Jenna looked down to her soiled clothes. Her once white blouse looked almost brown from dirt and dried blood. It hung crookedly outside her skirt and, looking past the filthy gabardine, she couldn't help but curl her bare toes under in embarrassment. She brought her hand up to her neck, humiliated by her appearance. "I must look terrible," she muttered under her breath.

"You look like a woman who is working hard for her man's life. Come, I know you are tired. Put on the gown and then eat. I will take your place." Willow took Jenna's left hand and placed the nightgown in it. She waited until Jenna raised her eyes to hers and then nodded reassuringly. "Rest. You have many more hours of work ahead of you before your Morgan is out of danger."

Jenna looked at the Indian woman in front of her and felt like crying, but knew it would be wasted energy. She admitted to herself that she had been running on adrenaline and, if she were to continue to nurse Morgan, then she must also take care of herself. Jenna covered Willow's hand with her shaking one. "You're a wise woman," she said in a small voice. "Thank you."

Jace's mother seemed embarrassed by the compliment and withdrew her hand, leaving the nightgown in Jenna's. Turning her back, she murmured, "We will add vinegar to the water, and perhaps that will help to bring the fever down."

Jenna saw her begin to attend to Morgan, and she brought her hand up to the buttons on her blouse. As she removed it, she couldn't help but let her eyes travel to where Willow had placed the food. Inhaling the pungent aroma of the stew, her fingers worked quickly to shed her twentieth century garments, and replace them with the soft, white cotton of the nightgown.

As with every day since the beginning, the strong rays of daylight were replaced by the quiet blanket of darkness. In northwest Nevada, a lone teenaged boy stood under the starlit sky and cursed the white men who had raped his mother's people's land. Jace knew the story well, and he repeated it over and over to himself, never wanting to forget how the white man had robbed the Washo and Paiute of their hunting grounds. Being half Washo and resembling his mother's people, he felt the rage of his grandfather. First it was gold that had brought the trespassers as they made their way to California. Then years later, silver was discovered east of the big lake, at Virginia City, and the eastern slope of the fertile Sierras began to fill up with mining camps, boomtowns crawling with the earth's scavengers. Cattle and sheep took over and roamed the Indian's best wildseed lands and brush slopes. Then the newcomers preempted game and fish and started cutting pinyon and pine trees for fuel.

Ten years ago the Paiutes fought back against the invader. Even though the Washo accepted their fate bravely and managed to exist without retaliation against the white man, they were punished along with the Paiutes. Eventually, to survive, they were forced to work for the trespassers. But memories are long, on both sides, and Jace felt the extent of hidden resentment when his father died.

Michael Eberly was a teamster and, since the demand for wood was insatiable, he made a good living for his Indian wife and son by delivering lumber to build, first the railroad, then the silver mines. It was the railroad that had killed his father, and Jason hated it even more than the those white men who first changed the Washo land. It had taken his father's business away, and Michael Eberly had to work harder and longer just to survive. In an accident, two years ago, his white father had lost his wagon, his team—and his life.

Jason was torn between love of his father's memory and a nagging resentment against being a part of them: those who considered him less than their equal. It was to his shame that his only means of employment was to sweep Stan Tearle's barroom floor and clean up after Gertie and the three women who occupied the floor upstairs from the saloon. At fifteen, he was a man and yearned to be treated as one. Today, he had again attempted to show them he was no longer a child, but they had not listened. He could have brought the man out of the hills, but they would not let him. He had shown them, though. The woman and her injured man were living in his old room in the barn, and he had found her man's saddle and brought it to the livery. He could not wait until morning so he could give her the thirty dollars Joseph Finney had reluctantly paid for it. And he admitted in his young heart that he could also not wait to hear her voice, gaze at her lovely face, and once again see her beautiful yellow hair.

As he looked across the yard to the single lamp that continued to burn in the barn, Jason Eberly felt, for the first time, longing—and pride.

Chapter Nine

"Sweat, dammit!"

Morgan's body refused to give up its moisture, and Jenna found herself in a battle. No matter how many blankets she put on him, no matter how many times she bathed him, Morgan's skin remained flushed and dry. It had started at dusk, the retention of fluids, and Jenna had been unrelenting in trying to break the fever. But the unseen forces of his body worked against her, causing his skin to turn an alarming shade of pink and give off a frightening degree of heat. She was at a loss and didn't know what more she could do.

"Please, Morgan," she begged, as she again dripped water into the inside of his cheek, massaging his throat in an effort to make him swallow, "please try. You have to get better! I'm all alone here. You're the only person I know. Fight this damn fever! Do you hear me?"

She couldn't stop the moan of frustration as she watched the water slide out the corner of his mouth and run in a thin line down his jaw. Picking up the rag she'd been using to bathe him, Jenna patted at it. She was too tired to cry and too frightened to admit defeat.

"I know you can hear me, Trahern," she said while pulling her perspiration-soaked nightgown away from her body. "Somewhere, in your subconscious, you can hear me, so listen. I was wrong about you. It's me . . . not you, that's crazy. If this isn't some bizarre dream I'm living, then somehow I'm in the wrong century. I need you. Do you hear me? You have to get better. I don't know what I'm doing here . . ." She put the heels of her palms against her eyes and tried to take a steadying breath. What's the use? she thought. I'm only kidding myself. He can't hear me, and if the doctor can't help him tomorrow, well then—she would be a murderer. Who knows what these people would do? So far—

"Get down! Goddamn, can't you see them?"

The yell tore out of Morgan's throat, and Jenna was so shocked she could only stare. Morgan's glazed eyes were wide open and fixed on the door across the room. So realistic were his words that Jenna turned her head to see if there really was cause for concern. Quickly, she turned back and bent over him. "Morgan, thank God! It's me . . . Jenna!"

She had no more time to speak as his arms came up and grabbed her shoulders. With a strength she would not have thought him capable of, he brought her to his chest and held her there.

"Don't open your mouth . . . let them pass. Oh God . . . oh no . . . no . . . no . . ." Behind the intense heat of his chest, Jenna could hear his heart pounding furiously.

She tried to raise her head. "Morgan, look at me. It's Jenna."

His eyes were frantic, searching the opposite wall for something or someone. Jenna felt chills erupt over her body. He was delirious!

121

A look of pain emerged on his face. "We could have taken them without a fight. Had to be a goddamn hero, didn't you, Billy? Don't cry. I'll get you help. I promise! Don't die on me. Don't!"

He loosened his tight grip, and Jenna was able to straighten. As her eyes slowly moved to his face, she saw his were once again closed and his face was in repose. But, unbelievably, perspiration had burst out over his entire body. Jenna, at first, watched it in fascination, seeing tiny beads of sweat grow larger and collect until they ran from his forehead, his neck, shoulders, chest, legs, everywhere. Dipping her rag once more into the water, she let the tears freely come. This time they were a release. He was going to survive.

Once more, Jenna was in the throes of another struggle—this one against the shattering chills that held Morgan prisoner. She threw herself next to him, covering them both with the scratchy woolen blanket, giving of herself, her body heat, anything that would stop his teeth from chattering. Tucking the cover around his face, she listened to his angry, delirious words: "Goddamn, money-hungry thieves! Never satisfied . . . Credit Moblier . . . Congress . . . Lousy politicians, sons of bitches ruin everything they touch . . . Tell the president . . . Keep him out of it. Never should have taken this one on . . . Grant doesn't know . . . Bribery . . ."

He stopped mumbling and Jenna tried to make sense out of his words. Tell the president? Grant doesn't know? President Grant? What the hell was he talking about? Congress, the Credit Moblier ruining everything? *Who was Morgan Trahern?*

An hour later, Jenna left Morgan sleeping quietly and walked to the outhouse Willow had shown her earlier. She was too tired to care about its primitive condition. When she emerged, she lifted her weary head and looked up to the dark sky. Studded with jewel-like stars, it appeared just like the one she had left in Pennsylvania. But this one's different, she thought as she made her way back to the room. This night is a hundred years younger. It was Morgan who had convinced her. She'd spent too much time with him to know that he wasn't acting. In his delirium, he had spoken the words of truth. Morgan Trahern was living in 1870; so was everyone she had met—and now, so was she.

As she closed the wooden door behind her, she knew she was too exhausted to deal with it tonight. She had just finished fighting Morgan's battle with him, and soon—he might help her find her way back. That she would return was never a doubt, she just didn't know how. And, looking at the bare pine floor, the straight, uncomfortable chair, she moved closer to the bed.

Turning the lamp down, which cast a faint yellow glow around the room, Jenna lifted the heavy cover and slid in beside the quietly sleeping man. She closed her eyes, but flashes of the past thirty-six hours crossed her mind. Instinctively moving closer, she turned her face toward him and placed a small kiss on his cooled cheek. "Good night, Morgan," she whispered, feeling, somehow, that after tonight, in some small way he belonged to her—and she to him.

In the early morning, just after dawn, Jenna brought the blanket up to her chin and snuggled closer to the source of warmth behind her. She wriggled her bottom against the hard, warm flesh and sighed exhaustedly, her body not yet ready to give up the wonderful peace found in sleep. Not more than seconds slipped by before her eyelids snapped open, and her body became rigid. Hard, warm flesh?

Jenna Weldon's eyes remained fixed on the rough-planked wall across the small room as she tried to orient herself. Within seconds, the nightmare returned and, lifting her head, she glanced over her shoulder. Seeing Morgan's peaceful face confirmed that it was all real. She was still in the past. Immediately, she thought of her mother, Cassie, her friends, her company—everything she had left behind. What were they doing now? Were they searching frantically for her? How could she ever hope to find them again? She closed her eyes and let her head return to the mattress. She wouldn't think about them now. Not now—not when there wasn't any way of reaching them.

Despite the too few hours of sleep, she was fully awake, and Jenna slowly lifted the blanket and slipped out of bed. Standing barefoot in the middle of the small room, she looked around her. It really was primitive, little more than a shack, yet it was her and Morgan's only refuge. Shaking her head at her surroundings, Jenna slowly walked to the pitcher of water. Pouring a small amount in her one hand, she quickly brought it up to her face. Damn, the water was freezing! And now she was more fully awake.

She picked up her clothes and grimaced. They were filthy. Yet, having nothing else, she hurried to remove Willow's nightgown and replace it with her own clothing. She had hoped once she was dressed in modern clothes, they would make her feel better, but that wasn't the case. She felt grimy and itchy and yearned for a refreshing shower. Knowing that, at the moment, she couldn't even find a decent bath, Jenna gave up the idea of cleaning herself and searched for her boots. Finding them under the bed, she refrained from groaning out loud. How she hated the thought of putting them back on!

Dragging her boots with her, Jenna sat in the chair and looked at her feet. They were a mess. Hell, she was a mess! Her poor feet had taken quite a beating. Besides being filthy, like the rest of her, her feet were a mass of blisters, most already broken and raw. Funny, that during last night's crisis, she hadn't even noticed, or even felt any pain, but this morning was a different story. She reached over and took a dried rag. Dipping it into the nearby basin of water, she gently bathed her feet, hissing with a quick intake of breath at the stinging, burning results. Knowing she had no other choice, she wrapped two thin cotton cloths around her heels and attempted to place her sore feet into the once fashionable, but now totally impractical, high-heeled boots. Standing proved painful, but soon she was able to move around the room. The end of her short awkward journey was the window. Looking out, she held her breath for a moment. It was beautiful. The sun was creeping up over the tips of the distant mountains, and the birds melodiously joined together as they paid it a cheerful tribute. Her eyes scanned the unfamilar landscape as the strange world in which she found herself started to awake to another day.

Reluctant to leave the window, Jenna nevertheless turned back to the man she had slept with during the wee hours of the morning. She watched as Morgan continued to breathe deeply. Through a dense growth of whiskers, his skin appeared pale. She came closer to the bed and watched his thin nostrils constrict with each breath. Under his thick mustache, his dry lips opened slightly as he expelled the air. Her eyes traveled up to his eyelids. Also pale, they showed infrequent eye movements behind them, while Jenna envied the thick curling hair at their tips.

She was proud of him and of herself. Together, they had managed to survive. Jenna felt very protective toward him, having nursed him through the nightmare of yesterday, and promised herself that she would continue to take care of Morgan until he was as strong as when she had met him. It wasn't just that she felt obliged, though she took full responsibility for inflicting the more serious of his wounds. It was more than that. Morgan Trahern was the only link to her past, and she found herself regarding him as almost family, like a brother or a cousin.

Looking down the long length of his body and remembering running her fingers across it when she'd bathed him, she had to reevaluate her feelings. No. Even if she'd had a brother, she wouldn't have felt anything like those breathtaking emotions as when she'd touched Morgan, and no cousin could evoke such provocative thoughts as those which overwhelmed her yesterday. No. In the quiet of the morning, Jenna had to admit that she found Morgan Trahern a very attractive man. Of course, she thought, her eyes once again wandering to his sleeping face, once his destestable sideburns were gone he would prove devastating. She wondered if she dared. To remove them would make him seem more modern, and probably more attractive. Knowing that the doctor would come sometime today, Jenna immediately resolved to clean her patient up—and that meant a shave. She could hardly wait.

She had met Jace at the water pump down behind the house. After speaking with him for a few minutes, she almost skipped back to the barn. Her aching feet felt almost light as she hurried to the small room. Jenna had to slow down several times so as to not spill all the fresh water in her bucket. She had money! She held in her free hand the wonderful sum of thirty dollars!

As she entered the room, she saw Morgan had yet to awake. Knowing he would probably sleep through most of the morning, she poured over half of the water into the huge cast-iron pot Willow had given her and set the bucket on the floor. Using matches she had found in Morgan's bag, she opened the firebox and lit the kindling Jace had thoughtfully put inside it.

Waiting for the small stove to heat up, Jenna thought over the best use of the money. She would need clothes. The ones she wore were obviously ruined, and she stood out like a sore thumb in them. Morgan's also needed to be replaced. Jenna figured if a room cost two dollars, then clothes couldn't be that expensive. After she paid Willow for their first week's rent, and then, the doctor, she decided she would walk into town and take a look around. She hadn't really bothered while she was waiting for Morgan yesterday, but today it would be necessary to scout the area and look for work. It never occurred to her that she wouldn't support Morgan while he was recuperating. Jenna reasoned it wouldn't be too hard. Surely, the chief executive officer of a large manufacturing company should be able to secure some type of employment before the day was out.

Testing the water and finding it warm, she left the stove and picked up Morgan's satchel. Inside, she found a leather shaving kit, another pair of socks, a set of long johns, and extra bullets for his gun. Taking out the shaving kit, she opened it and, although she shouldn't have been, considering the time she was in, she was surprised. Her fingers withdrew a folded metal object that, when opened, produced a long, straight-edge razor. Just looking at it, Jenna knew it was sharp enough. There would be no need for the long leather strap, which, she assumed, was used to

127

hone its fine edge. Holding the razor in one hand she took out a thin shaving brush. Well, she mused, she had everything she needed—except the courage. Looking over her shoulder to Morgan's quietly sleeping form, Jenna decided it was worth a try.

He stirred when she lathered his face and neck, and jerked when she accidentally nicked him under his left ear, but when it was over and Jenna wiped his face with the towel she had placed across his chest, she was extremely pleased with herself—and with him. She hadn't dared touch his mustache, but without those thick, furry sideburns, Morgan Trahern was one very handsome man. Who was she kidding? Even sick, he was the best-looking man Jenna had ever shot.

She and Willow watched nervously as Dr. Marshall looked at their work. He said little as he fingered Willow's bandage, but turned to them when he saw the others. "Seeing as how Willow treated the gunshot wound, I'm not even going to remove it to take a look. No sense taking a chance on starting it bleeding again. But these others . . ." He indicated Jenna's work. "Looks like they're coming off already. Might as well have a look-see."

Jenna observed the short, stocky man as he bent over Morgan's leg. He looked like the typical country doctor: disheveled, wearing a rumpled black suit, and pushing his graying hair back in an impatient gesture, as if thinking about all the other house calls that he was expected to make in a single day. "Don't even think he needs these bandages. Those scratches are healing fine. Might be good to let the air get at them for a time. You say he tangled with a mountain lion?"

Jenna nodded, before saying, "It just attacked him. He held it off until I could find the gun. I'm afraid

I'm not a very good shot," she mumbled sheepishly.

The doctor smiled. "That you're not, Mrs. Trahern. But when your husband wakes up, he'll be mighty grateful that you're such a good nurse."

"But it was Willow who showed me everything. I wouldn't have known what to do without her," Jenna admitted truthfully.

"Then you've had a very good teacher, Mrs. Trahern," Clinton Marshall said with a smile.

Willow turned to gaze out the window, but not before Jenna had caught the pleased look on her face, while Dr. Marshall surreptitiously cast his eyes in the direction of the Indian woman's back more than once.

Finished with his examination, the doctor straightened and looked to Jenna. "Not too much I can do here. Your husband's doing fine. He's going to be mighty weak for some time yet, so don't let him push too much too soon. I'll come back tomorrow morning and check on him."

So relieved by his words, Jenna smiled broadly as she asked, "How much do we owe you, Doctor?" She was very willing to pay for the good news.

Clinton Marshall picked up his small, black leather bag. "Can't see as I did anything to deserve payment," he stated matter-of-factly. "If you need me for any reason tonight, Willow knows where I'll be."

Putting on his hat, he again looked toward the Indian woman's back. "I think the least my best competitor can do is walk me outside, don't you, Mrs. Trahern?"

Willow never gave Jenna a chance to form an answer. Delicately lifting the hem of her long skirt, she moved to exit the room. As Jace's mother held the door open, Jenna could hear her remark to the smiling, older man, "You are a very cautious man of medicine, Dr. Marshall. It is a shame you can not also be that with your words."

As if not hearing her rebuke of him, Clinton Marshall continued to smile. Tipping his hat, after Jenna thanked him for coming, he followed the small, dark-skinned woman out of the room.

Thoughtfully, Jenna turned back to her patient. He was still sleeping peacefully. If she hurried, she might be able to get into town, buy some clothes and take a quick look around. She certainly couldn't do anything more while Morgan slept, so why should she just sit around and wait for him to wake up? They'd also need food. One look around the small farm early this morning told her that Willow and Jace had little enough as it was and could not afford to be charitable.

Her mind made up, Jenna took Morgan's shredded clothes and wrapped them into a ball. Holding them in one hand, she checked her purse to make sure she had the thirty dollars from the saddle and the twelve she'd found earlier in the back pocket of Morgan's jeans. After she paid Willow their first week's rent, they would have forty dollars. Not exactly a sum to inspire security, she thought and, casting one quick look over her shoulder as she left, she worried over how long, even in 1870, that could possibly last.

The thin dirt road from the Eberlys' gradually widened until Jenna could see the small town of Verdi. From the direction she entered, the first building she passed was a home with a sign out front saying, Shragen's Undertaking And Funeral Parlor. Jenna shuddered when she thought of how close last night she'd come to paying the establishment a visit. Looking away from the rough shingled house, she saw the Chinese laundry where Willow must have worked, and from there a wooden sidewalk started in front of a line of stores. Ascending the planked walk, she saw two men standing in front of a large building. As she looked up, she saw it was a hotel of sorts, called the Union House. The men, both old and dressed in typical work clothes, took off their worn hats and held them to their chests.

Jenna smiled. "Good morning. Could either of you possibly tell me where there's a clothing store?" she asked politely.

One of the men ran a hand over his weathered, whiskered face, as if embarrassed by his appearance, while the other spoke up without the slightest hesitation. "Sure enough, Miz Trahern. Go on past the law office, next door, and you'll find the place. Miz Amanda, she'll take good care of you," he added, eager to be of help.

"You know my name?" Jenna asked, unable to keep the surprised tone out of her question.

" 'Spect most of the town's heard of you and your husband by now. Doc Marshall says he's goin' to pull through. Me'n Nate was just talkin' about him. Was it bobcat or cougar that got him?"

Taken back, Jenna answered honestly, "I'm afraid I don't know the difference, Mr. . . ."

The more talkative one slapped his hat against his chest. "I'm called Len Crowley, and this here's Nate Shorter," he said, while indicating with his head the silent man next to him who continued to stare.

Jenna held out her hand, and Len Crowley gaped at it for a few seconds before wiping his on his hip and placing his right one in hers. "It was a pleasure to meet you Mr. Crowley. Mr. Shorter?" she added, including the shocked older man with her eyes. "Thank you for the directions. Perhaps, when my husband is up to it, he can tell you more about the animal that attacked him."

She smiled at them once more before she moved on. Jenna wasn't more than two feet away before Len Crowley turned to his companion. "You ever had a woman come up and shake your hand like that, Nate? Sure is a strange thing. Only happened to me once before," he said knowingly. With a grin he added, "And she weren't half as pretty as Miz Trahern!"

Two pairs of old, yet curious eyes watched Jenna stop in front of Miss Amanda Jenks's store. Age had lessened their vision, thus Len and Nate were unable to see Jenna's shoulders move up and down in silent laughter. One very old-fashioned, very proper, gray dress was displayed in the shop window. It was not, however, what had caused Jenna's fit of giggles. Painted over the door and on the glass windowpane was the name of the place: Esme—Emporium For Today's Discriminating Woman.

Opening the white-painted door, she heard an overhead bell announce her entrance and, as she surveyed the small shop, she thought of her wallet full of credit cards. She had to stop herself from groaning at the long, heavy clothing displayed. Ah well, she thought wistfully, as she closed the door behind her: good-bye, Bergdorfs, hello, Esme.

Chapter Ten

Jenna couldn't understand one word the Chinese man in front of her was saying, but she could tell by the way he shook his head, causing his long braid to swing back and forth, and by the frantic tone of his impassioned speech that she was once more being turned down for employment. She couldn't believe it. She'd been to every single store on Center Street seeking work and all she had done was spend money, precious money. Although sympathetic, no one needed her, nor could she think of a single service she could provide that would earn any money. The laundry had been her last hope.

Shifting her purchases to her hip, she eyed the Indian woman who had beat her out of the job. I should have come here first, she thought, angry with herself for thinking she was too good to wash clothes for a living. Now, her pride had cost her the only available job in town—for a woman, that is. If she were a man, she would have no trouble finding employment at one of the five saw mills in Verdi. She didn't even want to think about how they had almost laughed at her when she'd applied there for a position. No one cared about her accounting background, or believed her, for that matter. They only hired men, big, strong men who could work twelve hours a day, she was told.

Looking back to the small Chinese man who continued to harangue her, she held up her hand. "All right! I get the message. Thanks anyway," Jenna said, trying to placate him. Obviously, he had as much trouble with English as she had with Chinese, for now that he was on a roll, it seemed as though he couldn't stop. Shaking her head at his gesturing and singsong, rapid words, Jenna exited his tiny shop and left the town of Verdi behind her.

Discouragement was too mild a word to describe how Jenna felt when she sighted the Eberlys' farm. Her arms ached from carrying the clothes and food she had purchased. Her legs were still sore, even though she had managed to have the high heels of her boots replaced with smaller, more practical ones at Albert Clemens's shoe store. But it was her head that was the most painful. From the disappointing attempts to find employment, combined with too few hours of sleep, she had developed a colossal headache. Opening the door to the small room, Jenna felt like she was suffering from a hangover. All she wanted was a little peace and quiet, just a few hours of sleep before she again had to face the ever present problems of survival.

Morgan was still sleeping, and she put the food on the cooled stove before dropping the packages to the floor. Wearily, she walked to the chair and sank to its seat. Before she removed her boots, Jenna glanced up at her patient. He looked so different with his sideburns removed. Although exhausted, she was still capable of finding him attractive, and she sighed loudly before returning her eyes to her aching feet. How was she ever going to support them both? she worried, as she unzipped her boot.

"You're back."

It was a simple statement, spoken in a hoarse voice, yet Jenna's ears picked up each whispered word. Jerking her head up, she stared into Morgan's tired blue eyes.

"Morgan!" she said his name in awe, before smiling broadly and standing up. Coming the few feet to the bed, she looked down into his pale face. "How do you feel?" she asked quietly.

He closed his eyes briefly before attempting to smile. "Like I was just hit by a freight train. Where are we? Last thing I remember was some Swedish giant giving me whiskey."

Jenna didn't stop the small laugh. "That was Swede. He and his friends brought you into town." She felt his forehead and found it cool. Almost naturally, she let her fingers wander to his hair. Running them through his dark strands, she informed him, "We're renting this room from the Eberlys. They live right outside Verdi. Willow and her son, Jace, have been wonderful. She was the one who took care of your shoulder. How is it?"

Morgan raised his chin. "If I think about it, it hurts like hell. Is Willow an Indian?"

"Yes."

"Thought I was dreaming. She came in a while ago, puttered around for a bit and then left. I thought she brought water. Could you get me a drink?" He ran his tongue over his bottom lip. "I swear my mouth feels like Sherman just marched through it."

Jenna moved quickly. Supporting the back of his neck with one hand, she held a half full tin cup to his lips with the other. When he emptied the cup of water, she slowly lowered his head to the pillow and patted his moist chin with the edge of the sheet. "There. Feel better?" It was an automatic question, and she didn't wait for an answer. "I went shopping this morning," she informed him cheerfully. "We both have new clothes, and I'm about to make you my famous chicken soup."

Morgan smiled weakly. "You're famous for your chicken soup?"

Shrugging her shoulders, Jenna tucked the sheet back around him. "Well, no. Actually, Hildy, my mother's cook, showed me how to make it. I used to sit in the kitchen and watch her work. If it wasn't for Hildy, I wouldn't know a thing about cooking." Unconsciously mimicking her old cook, she curled her fingers into her palms and placed her knuckles on her hips. Looking down into his face, Jenna cocked her head to one side and smiled before saying, "Okay, you forced the truth from me. I'm about to make you Hildy's famous chicken soup. All right?"

Morgan's eyelids slowly moved as he tried to keep them open, while again, under his mustache, his full bottom lip curved upward in a half smile. "I can hardly wait," he mumbled sleepily.

"I don't think you'll have any trouble waiting. Go back to sleep, Morgan. It's the best thing for you. I'll impress you with my cooking when you wake up." Smiling at his already closed eyes, she reached out and gently touched his clean-shaven cheek.

Instinctively, she quickly pulled her hand back to her waist and turned around. What's wrong with me? she mentally questioned. Why am I always touching him? What's worse, why does it seem so right? So natural? Confused, she picked up the food and began unwrapping the ingredients for the soup.

"You don't have to . . ."

At his thick words, Jenna looked over her shoulder at him. His eyes remained closed, yet she didn't have

136

to wait long for him to continue.

On the edge of sleep, he managed to haltingly finish his sentence. "You've already . . . impressed me."

Turning back to the stove, Jenna had to bite the tip of her bottom lip to keep the pleased smile under control.

Oh, the joy of it! She didn't care that she was sitting in a round wooden tub, in the middle of the deserted barn, bathing with well water and using soap made from a suspicious substance. She was clean! Rinsing her shoulder-length hair again, Jenna reveled in the most sensuous feeling of the water as it ran down her back. She knew she shouldn't linger in the cool bath. Morgan might wake up. Her soup might boil away to nothing, but what caused her to self-consciously stand up was the knowledge that, at any moment, some stranger might open one of the barn doors and find her naked. After squeezing the excess moisture from her hair, Jenna reached out for the pieces of rags she'd brought with her. Hastily, she blotted the droplets of water from her skin, then picked up the strange pantalets and camisole she'd bought this morning.

Not able to afford the softer silk that Miss Amanda Jenks had put in her hand, Jenna had settled on the thicker, yet more practical, cotton underwear. She stepped into the pants and was surprised to find them comfortable. Quickly, she tied a knot at her waist, and they adjusted to her size. Next, she donned the white camisole, with its small ruffle that started at her waist and ended right above her hips. Again, she had to pull a ribbon, this time at the top, above her breasts. As she gathered the material and tied a small bow, Jenna thought how utterly feminine she felt in the foreign garments.

Before she dressed any further, she threw her soiled clothes into the water. Morgan's only salvageable article of clothing were his red socks and, bending down, she picked them up and quickly tossed them into the wooden tub. Letting her small load of wash soak, Jenna turned to the folded dry clothes she'd brought into the barn with her.

She had purposefully picked out a light-weight skirt. It was dark brown and buttoned at her side. After she finished fastening her new plain white blouse, Jenna rolled the sleeves up past her elbows and knelt before the tub. It amazed her that she had taken so many things for granted—like the pleasure of a clean enameled bathtub and the modern wonders of an automatic washer. Vigorously rubbing soap into one of Morgan's socks, she thought with a self-deprecating smile that the Chinese man didn't know what he had passed up. She may not know what she was doing, but she was a hard worker.

"I'm sure it's delicious, Jenna, but I think I can feed myself."

"Nonsense. Dr. Marshall said you weren't to push yourself. Now, open up." She held a cloth under the spoonful of steaming chicken broth and brought it closer to his lips.

Reluctantly, Morgan opened his mouth, and Jenna quickly placed the spoon inside it. After he swallowed the hot liquid, his eyes started to water and he spoke more forcefully than he intended. "I can't eat like this! I may be weak, but I won't be spoon fed, like a helpless child. I'm not an invalid."

Jenna gritted her teeth together, trying to be patient. "You may not be an invalid, but you're acting like a cranky child." She rose from the edge of the bed where she was sitting and held the bowl out to him. "Since you're so stubborn, feed yourself. See if you can use that arm, but I'm warning you right now; if you spill it I'm not washing that sheet. I've done all the laundry I'm going to do for one day."

Propped up against the two pillows, Morgan eyed her scowling face before reaching for the hot bowl. With his uninjured left hand, he carefully brought it to his lap, and Jenna watched as he struggled with his right. Several times he tried to pick up the wooden spoon and failed.

Knowing he would never admit defeat in front of her, Jenna made an impatient noise with her mouth and again took possession of the bowl. "You know those stitches are tight. What are you trying to do? Rip them out? Believe me, Morgan, I don't think either one of us is up to repeating that scene again. Now, will you let me feed you?"

Frustrated, Morgan let his head sink into the pillows behind him. He closed his eyes briefly and nodded. "You're not exactly a sympathetic nurse, you know," he grumbled, looking into her determined blue eyes.

"Oh, shut up, Morgan," Jenna scolded, as she took up her position on the edge of the bed. Putting another spoonful of soup into his mouth, she smugly informed him, "I'll have you know Dr. Marshall happens to think I'm a wonderful nurse. He said so yesterday."

In between spoonfuls, Morgan muttered, "He probably says that to every woman."

Jenna's eyes narrowed and she repeatedly shoved the wooden spoon into his mouth, thus preventing him from speaking further.

Within moments, he brought his left hand up to her

wrist in order to halt, in midair, her repeated invasion of his mouth. "Hold on there. What're you trying to do, drown me in chicken soup?"

They both looked to the sheet, where he had made her spill the broth. Breathing deeply, Jenna's chin quivered as she said in a deceptively quiet voice, "I'm not cleaning that up. I have better things to do than play nursemaid to an ungrateful . . . cowboy." She stood up and placed the bowl on the wooden night table. "When you decide to be civil, I'll continue to feed you."

He watched her straight back as she walked away from him. Confused, he asked, "What did I say? Look, Jenna, I am grateful. You saved my life. I'm just not used to being a patient."

Standing over the stove, she stirred the chicken soup and tried to hold back the tears that she could feel gathering at her eyes. Taking a deep breath, she continued to look into the pot before her while she answered him. "Well, I'm not used to being a nurse, so I guess we're even. But don't worry, Morgan. I fully intend to take care of you until you're back on your feet."

From behind her, she heard his voice. "I'm sorry if I said something to offend you, but listen to me . . . Jenna, you don't have to take care of me. I mean, you're not obligated. I can—"

She spun around and stared at him. "Not obligated? I *shot* you! You wouldn't be here if it wasn't for me. *I'm* the one who got you thrown off that train. You would have been safely in Sacramento, not on some damn mountain. God, don't you think I feel bad enough? Don't you understand yet, Morgan? Something happened to me on that train. In my world, *my world*," she cried, hitting the side of the stove in frustration. "It's 1987! I don't know what happened.

140

Maybe it was an accident of time, a freak occurrence, some kind of crazy testing they're doing in Nevada. I don't know. I just know I don't belong here!" Turning away as the embarrassing tears rolled down her cheeks, she sobbed out once more with a mixture of self-pity and frustration, *"I don't belong here!"*

A crushing wave of loneliness overwhelmed her and Jenna knew she had to leave, just get out and get away, before she completely broke down in front of him. Knowing her tight, aching throat wasn't capable of speech, she ran out the door without saying a word.

Morgan stared at the opened wooden door. What the hell had just happened? All he'd wanted was for her to slow down before he choked on the soup. Seeing that stain on the sheet had completely unnerved her, until she started rambling on about being from the future again. He didn't know what to think. If she were acting, then she just gave one hell of a performance. If she wasn't? . . .

Ignoring the throbbing in his shoulder, Morgan tried to get up from the mattress. He slid one leg, then the other, over the side of the bed. Using his good hand, he grabbed a handful of sheet with him as he attempted to stand. Immediately, he was assaulted by a nauseating wave of dizziness. Holding on to the bed, Morgan closed his eyes, waiting for it to pass, and he fought the frustrating weakness with a singular determination. He would not fall back—he wouldn't. Soon, gathering his strength with one concentrated effort, he slowly straightened.

Standing, Morgan wiped away the annoying perspiration on his face with his good hand before clumsily gathering the sheet around him. Remembering Jenna's agonized face, he very carefully put one shaking foot in front of the other. By the time he reached the door, he felt as if he'd walked a hundred yards, and he had to grab hold of the rough wall next to it for support. Putting his forehead against the unfinished wood, Morgan breathed deeply, silently cursing his weakness.

"What are you doing out of bed?"

Jenna threw the dried clothes in her arms onto the chair and hurried to his side. "Damn you, Morgan. What do you think you're doing? If you've reinjured your shoulder, this time you won't be unconscious when Willow sews it back together."

He looked down into her angry, blue eyes. "I wanted to find you, Jenna."

She read his confusion, his concern, and Jenna couldn't pull her eyes away from his. Peripheral vision showed her that the sheet he had wrapped around himself had slipped down his back to reveal the tops of his buttocks. Her anger quickly disappeared, only to be replaced by a far more uncomfortable emotion. Just knowing he was nude, a thin sheet the only barrier between them, made Jenna's breasts ache into arousal. She thought herself perverted that she could be so affected by a man—a sick man, on top of that—yet she couldn't tear her eyes away from him. He was so damn handsome, with his black hair falling over his forehead. Even in his weakness, he was so masculine. Jenna already was familiar with his body. She had seen every inch of it when she'd nursed him, but now he was awake; and awake he inspired ridiculously provocative thoughts.

Without saying a word, Morgan reached out with his good arm and brought her close to his chest. She didn't resist. She didn't want to resist, for it felt right, perfectly natural. She let her cheek rest against the thick, curling hair on his chest and inhaled. Her nostrils were filled with the heady scent of him, and Jenna's knees felt weak with an unexplained longing.

142

Almost of their own accord, her arms lifted to his back and she held him, reveling in the feeling of belonging.

Morgan let most of his weight rest against the wall behind him. Damn, he had only meant to comfort her. When he'd stared into her red-rimmed eyes, his heart had constricted with remorse for somehow causing her pain. Now, feeling the hard points of her breasts pushing against him, his body tensed and his thoughts started swimming against a hot current of desire. He knew if she moved closer, let the lower half of her body come in contact with his, he would lose control. For a crazed moment, he considered pulling her into him, giving way to the frenzied hunger that coursed through him, but he knew when sanity returned that he was too weak. In truth, he didn't want her this soon, and not like this. He knew now that, despite her protests, her mask of independence, Jenna was similarly affected.

Above her soft, blond hair, he quietly spoke. "I think you were right. I'd better get back to bed."

Immediately, Jenna moved away from him, though as she lifted her head from his chest, her break was not complete. Fine strands of blond caught and twirled with crisp black. Embarrassed, she quickly separated them, silently cursing the static electricity in her hair. "Here," she said, in an effort to cover her confusion as she reached for his good arm, "put your arm around my shoulder and rest on me. I'll help you."

"Jenna, if I so much as move, this sheet is going to fall to the ground. It's already halfway there."

Unwittingly, her eyes traveled down his body. He was right. He held the white muslin only by pressing the corner of the sheet between his right elbow and his waist. Swallowing once, at the sight of his lean contours, Jenna hurried to gather it once more around him. When he was covered, she made sure he would remain so by holding it together herself as she led him back to the bed.

Jenna played the role of efficient nurse, tucking the covers over him and under the mattress. She tried not to admit that she had come very close to making a supreme fool of herself. Her juvenile reaction to his touch was humiliating, and she refused to dwell on the subject. She promised herself to be more careful, for she could not afford to become emotionally involved now, not now when all her energy should be channeled into getting Morgan well and finding a way back to the future.

Standing near the bottom of the bed, Jenna surveyed her patient. She knew he had been watching her as she'd briskly adjusted the bed linens around him, and once more, he held her with his eyes.

"You know we have to talk, don't you?" he asked slowly, almost gently.

Chapter Eleven

"Talk?"

Nervously, Jenna reached for the clothes she had thrown onto the chair. As she began folding them, she could feel his eyes burning into her back. "About what?" she asked in a disinterested voice as she rolled his red socks together.

"I think you know."

Picking up her blouse, which two days ago had been white, but would never be restored to that color, she stared at the limp, dingy material. Dear God, she thought, I have already been through so much. I can't bear this humiliation, too. He's not stupid. Morgan knows I . . . I'm attracted to him. How can I discuss it? I can't even understand it!

"Jenna?"

She forced herself to turn around and face him. "Not tonight, Morgan. Please. You're not up to it, and neither am I. We'll talk tomorrow."

He would not be put off. It was too important. "I'm not too tired, or too weak, for a discussion. We'll talk now."

Uncomfortable with what she knew was coming, Jenna sought to hide her embarrassment by assuming

145

a defensive position. "Fine. Just what is it you have to say, Morgan?" She turned away and continued to fold the rest of her clothes. She would not let him see how mortified she was to have a man tell her that she must keep her hands to herself.

"Why do you keep insisting it's 1987?" he asked in a quiet voice. "Surely, now that you've been in a town, you must know how ridiculous that sounds. Don't you think it's time for the truth?"

Her shoulders sagged in relief. Thank God, she thought. He doesn't want to talk about their strange embrace, only her emotional outburst before she ran out. "I've always told you the truth," she murmured, not yet ready to trust her voice.

Tired of talking to her back, he asked a bit impatiently, "Then tell me again. Where are you really from?"

Jenna dropped the clothes from her hands and wiped her palms on her skirt before slowly turning around. Holding his questioning blue eyes with her own, she said it as simply and truthfully as she knew how. "The future."

Morgan's lower jaw dropped, and he continued to stare at her. Silent moments passed as he tried to read whether there was any sanity at all in her eyes.

"I won't accept that," he finally stated.

Now that she knew this discussion would not prove embarrassing, difficult maybe, but certainly not the humiliation she had feared, Jenna was confident enough to smile. "I'm afraid you're going to have to accept it, Morgan. It is the truth."

"Jenna, do you have any idea how crazy that sounds?" Running his hand through his hair, Morgan worried over how to reach her. "What you're saying is impossible. People cannot travel through time and appear in another century. Think about what you're asking me to believe!"

"You want answers, and I can't give them. You ask for proof and I can't provide it." Frustrated by her instability, Jenna impulsively picked up a piece of clothing from the chair and held it up for his inspection. "What do you think this is? I can bet you've never seen anything like it. You know why, Morgan?" she asked, as she threw her lacy bra onto the bottom of the bed. Ignoring his startled expression as he continued to stare at the end of the mattress, she added, "I'll tell you why. Because it hasn't been invented yet! Neither has this." She picked up her matching French-cut panties and dropped them on top of the bra. "Nor this . . ." Jenna reached for her split gabardine skirt, but before adding it to her underwear, she stopped and looked at it. "Damn!"

Holding the shrunken dark green material out in front of her, she cursed again. "Great . . . look at this! Now I have a pair of short pants! How am I supposed to live with only one skirt?" She didn't really want an answer and, annoyed with her own ineptitude, she threw the skirt back onto the chair.

"I don't see what clothes, and . . . and underthings, have to do with your claim of being from the future. It doesn't prove anything, except that you dress strangely . . . to say the least." Morgan adjusted the bandage at his shoulder, trying to take his mind off the pieces of silk that lay on the covers above his feet.

Jenna willed the damning flush to stop creeping up her neck, but she could feel it spreading upward to her face. She only hoped her sunburn would camouflage it. What was wrong with her? Why, in heaven's name, did she wave her pants and bra at him like some mindless bullfighter? What was she subconsciously hoping to do? It certainly didn't make him believe

147

her. It had only made him uneasy, and it made her want to pry up a few floorboards and crawl under them.

Needing something to do with her hands, Jenna bent down and picked up one of her boots. "Well, what about this?" she asked.

Holding the dark leather boot closer to him, she placed her fingers on the small flap that ran down the inside and revealed its zipper. Slowly, she opened and closed the side of her boot. "Do you know what this is?"

Morgan watched the two rows of interlocking teeth separate, then close as Jenna pulled on a small, sliding device. It was a curious thing, yet he didn't want to appear lacking, and he felt he must provide some answer. "Of course. It's a fastener of some sort. What do you call it?"

Jenna had to bite the inside of her cheek to keep from smiling. Now, she was on a better footing. She'd made a mistake with the underwear, letting her emotions rule her, but this was different. This was technical, and Morgan had no idea what he was looking at.

"It's called a zipper. A very handy, little invention that's used on almost every piece of clothing in the twentieth century. Want to try it?" She held the boot out to him, and he took it with his good hand. He placed it on his lap, and Jenna watched for a few seconds as Morgan slid the zipper up and down, before standing. When she returned to him, she had her purse.

"You made fun of me when I showed you the tape recorder. Let's see what other goodies I might have in here." Opening her purse, Jenna rooted through it and, when her fingers touched the small, thin object attached to her keys, she had to swallow a giggle.

"Don't be alarmed, Morgan," she said, as she

148

reached for the lamp. Turning the tiny handle that controlled the amount of light, she lowered the wick and the room was bathed in a faint, soft, yellow glow.

"What are you doing?" he groaned, watching her carefully.

Holding the keys in her left hand, Jenna took the boot from him and let the giggle come. "You'll see. Now, close your eyes."

Morgan tried to rise higher in the bed. "Close my eyes? You must be kidding!"

"Trust me, Morgan."

"Trust you? After that laugh? I'm afraid of you. You have me at a disadvantage. How can I defend myself against whatever you're planning when I'm like this?" He quickly looked to his bandage and then back at her. "And what does this have to do with your claim of being from the future?"

Jenna's eyes widened and she grinned down at him. "Everything . . ." she said dramatically, letting the word trail for effect. "Now close your eyes. If I'd wanted to harm you, I had plenty of opportunity in the last three days. I think I deserve some trust." Again, she grinned. "You'll be sorry if you miss this," she whispered teasingly.

Morgan's eyes narrowed and, even in the dim light, she could make out the clenched muscle in his cheek. "I don't know why I'm going along with this," he grumbled.

"Because you can't help being curious." Jenna wanted to erase the tension in his face with her fingers, but she didn't dare touch him. "Just close your eyes, Morgan, please."

He gave her one last look of distrust before sighing loudly and lowering his eyelids. What kind of game was she playing now? he thought. And why does she make it so mysterious? He felt like a child, waiting to

149

be frightened.

"Okay. You can open them."

Almost hesitantly, Morgan opened his eyes, then gasped as he looked at the woman before him. Jenna was holding a thin, sheltered candle, and she appeared to him like an angel, her face surrounded in a celestial light. He was in awe as he drank in her breathtaking eyes, the soft sculpture of her high cheekbones, the provocative smile that played at her full, defined lips. "You're beautiful, Jenna," he whispered, while his heart pounded furiously behind his rib cage.

At his words, her hands shook. "Morgan, it's a flashlight, that's all. Look, I'll turn it off." Jenna switched the tiny pen light off and looked back at him. "I . . . I only wanted to prove something to you. I didn't mean . . ."

Slowly, his hand came up. When he captured her arm, she stopped speaking and watched his eyes as he pulled her down to him. Sitting on the bed, she listened to his soft voice. "What is it you wanted to prove, Jenna? Something we both already know?"

He continued to hold her arm, letting her thumb make light, circular movements on the inside of her elbow, and Jenna found it hard to speak as delightful shivers ran up her arm. "Don't you . . . I mean, aren't you even curious about the flashlight?" she asked, in an almost pleading voice. Didn't he know what he was doing to her?

"I'm sure you'll tell me later. Right now, I'm curious about something else." It had been building, this tense need, since he held her earlier, and seeing her moments ago had only triggered it throughout his body. He wanted her, honestly, without anger or regret, and gloried in the natural instincts of man. Although weak, he could feel himself growing hard

150

with an all consuming hunger.

Slowly, almost reverently, Morgan touched the side of her neck, letting his fingers curl around its nape while his thumb gently teased her earlobe. He continued to hold her eyes with his until he felt her breathing quicken. Then, using the slightest pressure, he brought her to him.

It started out sweetly, the mere grazing of lips. It was warm and tender, and very quickly—not enough. The hot urgency of Morgan's mouth increased, driving Jenna into a frenzy of need as his tongue explored, teased and finally dueled with her own. Her fingers ached to touch him, to silently communicate her deep yearning for further contact, yet her hands remained pressed against the mattress.

When he pulled his head back and stared into her eyes, Jenna couldn't help but gulp for air, so successful was he in wreaking havoc with her senses.

He looked at her flushed face, her swollen lips and said it simply, honestly. "I want you, Jenna."

She could feel her heartbeat hammering away in her ears. "But your shoulder . . . your fever . . ." She was too confused to know what she was saying. Her brain could think of nothing but the intense longing of her body.

Morgan smiled at her words. "It may not be the way I want it. I won't be able to properly seduce you with only one hand, and you might have to help at times, but . . ." His fingers moved to the buttons on her blouse. "God knows, I do want you, Jenna."

She stared at his tanned hand as it struggled with the small white buttons and, instinctively, she brought hers up to join it. Within moments, she had parted her blouse and slowly let it slide down her arms. She could feel his eyes watching her as she touched the ribbon of her chemise. Pulling one white strand, she loosened the garment and brought her eyes up to his.

Morgan's frustration was great at not being able to undress her. He knew she was uncertain by the trembling in her hands, and he wondered if he could have possibly misread her passion. "Jenna, I'm not asking you to do something you'd rather not, am I?"

It took courage for her to stand, but her body was being directed by an inner force that refused to be denied. She smiled at him and hoped he could read the answer in her eyes for she didn't trust her voice. With an agonizing slowness, she carefully removed the cotton chemise and, deliberately, she let it fall to the floor. It was soon followed by her skirt and pantalets. When she finally looked up to his shocked face, she reached for the barrettes that held her hair back and released them.

He drank in the perfection of her body, and his voice was hoarse, barely recognizable when he managed to speak. "I'm afraid to touch you, afraid you'll disappear as quickly as you came."

Jenna thrilled at his words. They gave her the courage to take the initiative. Her limbs felt heavy, filled with a hot restlessness, as she moved closer to the bed, yet she knew here was where she wanted to be. Every fiber of her being was shouting at her to continue, and delicately, she reached for the sheet that covered him. Once it was removed, she didn't trust herself to look at him, and there really was no need for his image was indelibly burned into her brain. Gracefully, she moved over him and, straddling his hips, she gasped as her sensitive woman's flesh made contact with his hard, pulsing manhood. Both were jolted by nature's contrast.

Morgan found his breath coming in short, ragged gasps, and his body reacted to her touch by stiffening involuntarily, as a roaring flame ignited within him.

"I *am* real, Morgan," she murmured, and brought his hand up to her breast. As his warm fingers cupped the satiny underside, his thumb enticed her nipple to a hard, excited peak. She, in turn, touched the curling black hair on his chest, letting her fingers sweep up his neck and wander over the handsome planes of his face. She traced each feature, committing to memory the shape of his nose, the depth of blue in his eyes, the soft texture of his mustache.

As if they had been lovers for years, knowing the other's needs and movements, they blended together. Jenna's hands left his face and she braced herself on the pillow, on either side of his head, while Morgan brought his upper body closer to her, enabling him to have freer access to her body. He felt starved for her and, moaning, Morgan plundered her breasts. With an agonizing slowness, he licked the fullness of her, drawing unchartered patterns with his tongue, yet always, always, he avoided the center of each mound.

Jenna's eyelids fluttered as her nerve endings seemed to erupt through her skin. Everywhere his tongue grazed became wet heat, and she quivered with a need for something more. She felt weightless, floating above him, and her mind didn't register the tiny, whimpering pleas that were coming from her throat.

His patience paid off as Morgan heard her soft cries and the repeated whispers of his name. Eagerly, not able to wait any more himself, Morgan devoured first one nipple, then the other. He paid each homage, gently nipping with this teeth, then laving with his tongue the tiny diamond hard points.

Without thought, she moved against him, feeling her femininity flower open. She was hot, moist, and throbbing with an overwhelming need. The feel of him against her was not enough. She wanted him.

153

"Oh God, Morgan . . . please!"

When Jenna's soft, white hips raised instinctively, Morgan needed no other sign. He positioned himself and thought if he had to wait any longer he would explode, either from the roaring in his ears or the furious pounding of his heart as it slammed against his ribs; but mostly from the exquisite pleasure-pain that Jenna's soft, pliant body brought to a boiling apex. Tightly holding her hip, he entered her with one steady, hungry stroke.

Throwing her head back, Jenna closed her eyes and let her breath out. Inhaling deeply, she let the thrilling sensations overtake her. It wasn't supposed to be this good. Nothing was supposed to be this good and, opening her eyes, she looked into his face. "Morgan . . ." She could only breathe his name as he began to move.

Staring into her desire-filled eyes, his jaw went slack as she started to move with him. His hand left her hip and traveled upward to her breasts, her face, her hair. She gripped his left shoulder, digging her nails into him and, with her other hand, covered his roving fingers with her own. In his life, he knew he had been with women more beautiful, yet at this moment, he couldn't think of one who could rival her. And it wasn't lust that made her appear superior, nor her astonishing silkiness that seared him, surrounded him, first pulling, then housing him with such tender warmth that he wanted to stay there forever. It was something else that made Jenna different, special, and he was afraid to name it.

Jenna bit her bottom lip to keep from crying out loud as their feverish pace increased. She leaned against his chest and cradled his head to her breasts, kissing his hair, his forehead. Throwing her head back while he whispered against her throat, encouraging her, telling her of his own need, she felt it swiftly build: that intense cluster of passion that could not be stopped. Quickly, mercifully, she was soaring, crying out to him, begging him to fly with her as hot, delicious currents hurled her higher and higher. Needing an anchor, she grabbed hold of his legs behind her while his strong hand sank into the soft flesh of her back, urgently pulling her into the hard wall of his chest. His body went rigid, and he seemed to grow even larger, filling every space, every fragile muscle within her, while he bathed her with his warmth. Jenna gasped for breath and held it as wild, continuing tremors traveled from her body to his, and then back again. Astonished, she slowly let the air escape her lungs. She wouldn't have believed such joy was possible, not until he raised his head. Looking at her with an unguarded tenderness, Morgan breathed her name into her mouth.

"Jenna. . . ."

Chapter Twelve

He pulled the damp blond strands of hair away from her forehead. In a voice filled with emotion, Morgan gently asked, "Did I hurt you? Are you all right?"

Jenna opened her eyes and stared down into his flushed face. She was overcome by the look of tender concern in his deep, blue eyes. "I'm fine," she murmured as she lightly kissed his temple. "Better than fine. I'm . . ." Her head jerked up, and her body went rigid before she quickly removed her weight and knelt next to him on the mattress.

"Are *you* all right? My God, Morgan, I'm sorry!" Her eyes were like scanners as they frantically roamed over him, waiting to pick up any damage. Seeing that his bandage had slid higher on his shoulder, she brought her hand up to cover her mouth. "What have I done?" she whispered against her fingers, horrified that she might have set back his recovery.

Morgan took her hand away from her mouth and brought it to his own. Lightly kissing her fingertips, he said, "What you've done, *desperada*, is make me very, very happy. Now, stop worrying and come back here."

Hearing him call her *desperada* again, she almost relented. Quickly, she regained her self-control and slipped her fingers from his. "If I've hurt you, I'll never forgive myself. Now turn over. I want to check your shoulder."

"Jenna, I'm fine. There's a little pinching, but that might be because the stitches are too tight. Can't you just relax? Lay with me, Jenna. I want to hold you."

"Not until I've checked your shoulder."

As he watched her step into her underwear, he grumbled, "You certainly have a way of ruining a mood. Don't you think I'd tell you if I was in unbearable pain?"

Buttoning her blouse, she walked around the bed. Standing at the side of his injured shoulder, Jenna looked at him and smiled. "I'm sorry, Morgan. It *was* beautiful. I just want to make sure I didn't hurt you."

"Jenna, how can making love hurt me?"

Lifting her chin, she ignored his question. "Turn over, Morgan."

Recognizing the stubborn tilt of her jaw and the determination in her eyes, he sighed loudly in resignation before exposing the back of his shoulder. "Well?"

Not hearing a response, Morgan stretched his neck to see behind him. Seeing the horrified expression on her face, he sought her attention. "Jenna?"

She looked up from his shoulder, held his eyes for a few seconds, then nervously bit her bottom lip. "It's bleeding again," she whispered. "There's blood on the bandage! Dear God, what have I done to you?"

Morgan lay down, thus preventing her from seeing his back. "Stop it, Jenna. I probably did it while getting out of bed." Though, now that his breathing was normal and his thoughts had stopping racing, his shoulder did throb like hell.

"What're you doing?" he asked, as he watched her

scramble into her skirt. "You're not going out now, are you?"

Dropping to her knees, she didn't answer as she searched under the bed for her boots. Finding them, Jenna sat in the chair and thrust first one foot then the other into them. Zipping them up, she looked at him. "I'm going to get Willow. She'll know what to do. If she can't help, then I'll find the doctor."

Bringing the sheet up over him, Morgan stared into her frightened eyes. "I'm sure it'll stop. Besides, it's too late. I don't want you wandering around out there in the dark."

"I'm a big girl," she stated, while tucking her blouse into her skirt. She briefly ran her fingers through her hair as she hurried to the door. Opening it, she ordered, "Don't you dare move until I get back!"

It was colder than she would have imagined, and she hugged herself to ward off the biting wind. Almost running across the darkened yard, Jenna used the glow from the window of Willow's small house to guide her. Breathless, she bounded up the three steps and knocked loudly. Nervous and impatient, she knocked again.

The door opened to reveal Jason. Even in the faint light, she could see he was surprised. "I'm sorry to come over so late. I need your mother. Is she here?" she asked, while over his shoulder, she searched the interior of the house.

He stared at her with astonishment, and Jenna was about to repeat her question when a feminine hand reached out from behind him and touched his arm. Jason suddenly reacted, giving Jenna an embarrassed look before stepping aside to reveal Willow. Realizing Jason had been shielding his mother all along, she apologized again. "I'm sorry if I frightened you both,

158

but, Willow, I need you. He's bleeding again."

The small, serene woman only nodded before turning back to her room. When she returned to the doorway, Jenna could see Willow had wrapped a blanket around her shoulders and, once again, she had her bowls and the small, little cloth envelope that contained the dreaded needle and thread.

"With your permission, my son will come with us. If I am not able to help your husband, Jason will find Dr. Marshall before he returns to Mr. Tearle's."

Jenna looked from mother to son, and then back again. "Certainly he can come, only, let's hurry . . . please!" Willow closed the door, and the three of them silently crossed the yard. As they entered the barn, she turned to her son. "Wait here. I will soon know whether you must find the doctor."

Jason nodded respectfully and, even though she was in a hurry, Jenna caught the look of pride and love in Willow's eyes. She smiled at the young boy before turning back to Jenna. "Come. I know you are worried about your husband."

Willow waited for Jenna to enter the room first, then she quietly followed, shutting the door behind her.

"Morgan, this is Mrs. Eberly. She's going to examine your shoulder." Jenna looked at Morgan and begged him with her eyes not to be difficult. She had already noticed that in her absence, he had used the comb on the night table, and the sheet was now neatly covering his long body.

He smiled at Willow. "From what Jenna has told me, I am in your debt, madam."

Willow looked embarrassed, and her eyes quickly sought the floor. "Your wife was very worried. I am glad to help."

As Willow said *your wife*, Morgan's eyes flew to

Jenna's, and a look of surprise and devilment came into them. He smiled at her broadly and, in doing so, the single dimple appeared on his cheek. Looking back at Willow, he said almost happily, "Well, I'm afraid, Mrs. Eberly, we need your help again. You see, I was trying to please my wife, but I'm afraid I overdid it. You did warn me though, dear, didn't you?"

Jenna's mouth opened in shock. "He got out of bed," she hurried to explain, aiming imaginary daggers at Morgan with her eyes. "Why don't we let Willow have a look at your shoulder, *dear*?"

He smiled at her anger. "Whatever you say, Jenna," Morgan murmured with mock obedience, then looked toward the Indian woman as she approached his side. "You see, Mrs. Eberly, we haven't been married very long. I'm afraid I tried to impress my new bride. Jenna realized, before I, that my strength had yet to return, and she came to my rescue. She did a very thorough job of easing my pain. Are all wives that attentive?"

Unaware that Jenna had just been rendered speechless, Willow placed her bowls on the night table. "Your wife has been very concerned, Mr. Trahern." Looking into his eyes, she asked, "May I remove your bandage?"

Morgan smiled and sat up straighter, making sure that he avoided Jenna's withering looks. "I'm in your hands, Mrs. Eberly."

Within minutes, the long, thin strip of bandaging was lying on the bed. Cautiously, Jenna moved closer as she tried to read Willow's face. It was impossible. The Indian woman's lovely features remained impassive. Unable to stand the suspense any longer, she asked, "What is it? He ripped it open, didn't he?"

Willow looked up from Morgan's back and smiled.

"Only one stitch, Jenna. I don't think we have to bother Dr. Marshall." Seeing a look of horror on the white woman's face, she added, "If you will tell Jason, I'll tend to your husband."

Jenna looked at Morgan, then back to Willow. They don't want me here, she realized. A feeling of hurt was immediately followed by relief. Let them handle it, she thought, as she nodded and turned to leave the room.

"Please remind Jason to wear a heavier coat," Willow softly called after her.

Knowing it was a subtle hint for her to also protect herself from the blustery wind, Jenna picked up the worn blanket from the chair and left the two of them to their grisly work.

Shutting the door behind her, she leaned against it and closed her eyes. A wave of exhaustion washed over her as she released a heavy sigh. Though her mind was tired, her conscience would not be put to rest. It was her fault. How *could* she? How could she have made love to an injured man? She should have had more sense and not listened to him. She would never have done anything like that if she were in her own time. It was frightening. She had an image, and principles, and—dammit, nothing was like before, nothing was recognizable, not even her!

"Should I get Dr. Marshall?"

Jenna nearly jumped out of her skin as Jason whispered to her.

Even in the dark, he could sense her panic. "I'm sorry. I didn't mean to frighten you."

Walking away from the door, she waited for the trip-hammer in her heart to slow down before answering him. "No. Your . . . your mother said she could handle it. Are you always that quiet?" she couldn't help asking.

161

She made out the white of his teeth as he smiled. "I learned to have patience while hunting with my grandfather." When she didn't speak to him, he feared he had angered her and thought to add, "I'm glad your man isn't worse."

Jenna wrapped the blanket tighter around her shoulders. "I don't know what I would have done without your mother. She's a remarkable woman." She stopped at the barn door and faced him. "Thanks for bringing us here, Jason. I hope, someday, I can repay you both."

His heart started to beat faster, and there didn't seem enough room in his chest to contain the immense yearning that accompanied it when he looked at her. Hoping his young voice wouldn't fail him, Jason managed to say, "But you are paying us. And because of that, my mother can remain in her home . . . instead of washing the white man's clothes." As soon as the words escaped his lips, he regretted them. Ashamed that he had verbalized his resentment of her race, he quickly looked out to the dark yard.

Sensing that he was troubled, Jenna changed the subject. "Do you always work this late? You must put in a lot of hours."

He didn't answer her right away, just continued to stare out into the night. Finally, the words came slowly. "I come home to eat and to check on my mother. The Four Mile Saloon is busy at night, and I have to wait until Gert—until everybody is done for the night before I can clean up and come home."

Thoughtfully, she let her eyes wander over the boy before turning her head and looking outside. "It seems awfully long hours. Have you tried to get work at the saw mills? I would think the pay is better, even if the hours might be just as long."

Jason laughed bitterly. "The white man doesn't

162

trust an Indian around machinery. I could go into the mountains and work the log flume, or follow the river and drive the logs down, but that would mean leaving my mother alone. I won't leave her."

"What about the railroad? Can you find work there?"

"I hate the railroad!"

"You hate it? Why?"

He turned his head and, through the darkness, his eyes seemed to rivet her to the ground. "First it steals the Indian land, then it scars it with its ugly tracks. It brings more and more people who buy the Indian's land from the railroad. Not from the Washoe, who have watched over it since the first elders' memories began. From the railroad! These people, these settlers, they bring their cattle. And even those animals are given more respect than the Indian. Years ago, coyotes were killing cattle, so ranchers put poison in the carcasses and dragged them out to the range as bait. Unfortunately, because they had lost their harvesting lands, the Washoe were quicker than the coyotes. Nobody is sure how many died."

Jenna inhaled in horror. "My God!"

"I hate the railroad because of its greed. Because it killed my father."

Jenna was stunned. "I'm sorry. I don't know what to say." In her need to express her sympathy, she reached out and touched his arm.

The young boy stiffened at her light touch. "I'm late already. I must get back to work." He walked about four feet away from her when she stopped him with her voice.

"Your mother wanted me to remind you to wear a heavy coat."

Turning around, his quiet voice carried over the wind. "Sometimes, my mother forgets I am a man."

For a few moments, neither spoke, only listened to the sound of the air as it rushed passed them, causing the pine trees to bend their heavy limbs.

Just before he turned and walked toward his house, Jason called out to her, "I'm glad you're here, Jenna." He didn't wait for her to answer, was half afraid of what it might be, and hurried to get his coat.

Closing the door behind Willow, Jenna turned around and looked at Morgan. He was paler than when she had left, but his eyes sparkled with mischief as he patted a spot on the mattress.

"Come here, Mrs. Trahern. I'm in need of some wifely attention."

Jenna ran her fingers through her hair. "Knock it off, Morgan. I've just had the most disturbing discussion with Jason."

"Willow's son?"

Nodding, she began pacing the short length of the room. "They're really poor, you know that? Two dollars a week is just not enough for what they've done for us. I have to come up with something to earn more money."

"Jenna, you don't have to . . ."

"Yes, I do. There has to be *something* this town needs that I can provide. I need more money. *They* need more money. I just have to think." She continued to pace as a thoughtful frown appeared on her face.

"Jenna, you don't understand. I have money."

"No, you don't."

"I don't?"

She stopped walking and faced him. "I took the twelve dollars out of your pants," she admitted. "And I also sold your saddle. After paying Willow our first week's rent and buying clothes and food, we have

164

twenty-seven dollars left. It isn't going to last long, Morgan. I have to get some money, somewhere."

Morgan shook his head. "If you would just listen to me. We can live off what remains until I get back on my feet, and then I can—"

"Forget it! You're staying right where you are. The last thing I need is for you to start getting chauvinistic on me. I put you in that bed and I'll support you until the doctor says you're able to work."

He only wanted to tell her that he could wire his bank in Baltimore for money. "Am I to be a kept man then?" he asked with a grin on his face. The more he thought about it, the more it appealed to him. He could get the doctor, or Swede, somebody to wire the bank, making sure that before Jenna had to ask for credit, it would already be established. Maybe she just had to work this burning need for attrition out of her system. And while she was busy cleansing her soul, he made up his mind to enjoy every moment of it.

"Think, Morgan. What can I do?"

"You could always be a barber," he remarked, touching the place where his right sideburn had been.

Jenna stopped dead in her tracks and stared at him. "You noticed?"

"Of course I noticed. A man doesn't have sideburns for three months and not notice that while he's been sleeping they've mysteriously disappeared. Did you have something against them?"

Feeling foolish, Jenna played with the button on her skirt. "No. I . . . well, I just thought you'd look better . . . cleaner, without them."

"And do I?"

She looked into his eyes and, instantly, her mind was filled with vivid pictures of the two of them making love.

Seeing the hot flush staining her neck, Morgan said

softly, "Come back to bed, Jenna. It's late. Your pursuit of money can wait until tomorrow morning."

Oh, how she wanted to lie with him—just to be held—but no, it wouldn't stop there, and they both knew it. What had happened between them was too electric, too magnetic, and it had gone way beyond attraction. He was the positive force, believing that everything would work out, while she was the negative, overcome by so many problems whose answers seemed just beyond her reach.

Jenna had felt the beginnings of panic ever since she had seen the blood on his bandage and had known she was to blame. She had tried swallowing it the past few days, immersing herself in nursing Morgan and trying to survive, but it was too close to the surface now. The hard facts hit her like a tidal wave, rendering her immobile, letting her float between two worlds, one of which wasn't hers. She had to face it. She was stranded in time! Her mother, her friends, her company, and all who depended on her and Weldon Transit for their livelihood, didn't even exist yet. For days, she had realized what she'd left behind, but in order to keep on going, she'd pushed it to the back of her mind. Now it resurfaced with a frightening, confusing jolt. How do you deal with being in the wrong century? *Just how the hell do you do it?* her brain screamed.

"Jenna, what's wrong?"

She looked at him and felt all her resolve melting away. Didn't she deserve the security of knowing she belonged somewhere? Would it be so wrong to retreat into his arms? That part of her that needed a refuge from all the unanswerable questions directed her body.

She lowered the wick completely, and the room was immediately cast into darkness. Surprisingly, she wasn't nervous, just tired, as her hands undid her buttons. As her own eyes became adjusted to the dark, she could make out his silent form and knew he was watching her.

"I'm sleeping on top of the sheet," she said, slipping into Willow's large cotton nightgown. Bringing the blanket with her, she lay down next to him. She felt his breath at her hair as he continued to look into her face.

"Don't say anything, Morgan. Just hold me. I want to belong *somewhere*."

He brought her close to his chest and kissed the top of her head. "You are where you belong," he whispered, his voice soft and warm, filled with understanding. "You're with me."

At his words, her throat ached, her eyes burned, and she could no longer stop the hot tears from streaming down her cheeks. Jenna didn't know about tomorrow, didn't even want to think about the problems she would have to face when morning came. At the moment, he was her refuge, her immunity from the past and the future. Kissing his chest, she tasted her tears and gratefully accepted the sanctuary of Morgan's arms.

Jenna's eyes snapped open. She'd been dreaming about her home and about Hildy. It had come to her then—what she had that Verdi had never seen—or tasted. Excited, she carefully left the bed and picked up her purse. Even though it was dark, she knew every inch of the room and quietly, secretively, she opened the door and entered the cold barn.

Taking out her tiny flashlight from her purse, she found a small notebook and ballpoint pen. It would work! It had to. She'd try it out on Willow and Jace.

If she passed that test, she decided the next best person to try was Stan Tearle. Feeling much better about herself and her future, Jenna Weldon, former head of Weldon Transit, wrote from memory the recipe for her new venture.

She was about to enter the business of introducing, producing, and marketing her own version of *soft pretzels*! Nevada would never be the same.

Chapter Thirteen

"Jenna . . . would you come here, please?"

Dear God! Not again! Looking toward the room she shared with Morgan, Jenna's eyes showed her impatience. "I'll be with you in a minute, Morgan," she yelled from the barn. The huge mass of dough she'd been kneading hadn't lost its stickiness, and Jenna's hands and forearms were covered with it. It was as if Morgan had radar, detecting the most awkward moment to demand attention.

Men make the worst patients, she thought with annoyance as she started to peel the dough from her arms. And the man lying beyond the wooden door was a prime example. He always needed something or was just plain bored and wanted to be entertained. She'd even taken to working in the barn, only using the stove in the room to bake the pretzels, but it hadn't worked. Morgan persisted in using every opportunity to interrupt her.

Wrapping a towel around her hands, Jenna pushed open the door. "Yes, Morgan, what is it?" she asked with barely concealed impatience, as she watched him swallow a piece of pretzel.

He brushed the edges of his mustache. "I know I've

said it before, but these bread pretzels are really delicious. Do you think I could have a few more?"

Jenna bit her bottom lip to stop the angry words from forming. How could one man consume so much food? "Honestly, Morgan! You're eating away any profits I might possibly make . . . if I could ever get away from the stove. I've told you how much money I used for the ingredients. I not only have to make that back, it would also be nice if I could make a little extra to pay for rent, food—those little necessities for survival."

He looked sheepish. "I'm sorry, Jenna. It's just that these things you call pretzels are so good. I don't mean to keep interrupting you, but I couldn't reach them myself. You did give me strict orders not to get up too often."

He was right. After the night that Willow had repaired his shoulder, Jenna had insisted he not get up, except, with her help, to use the outhouse. "Okay, Here's another two," she said, giving up more of her precious inventory. Walking back to the door, she threw over her shoulder, "I swear, Morgan, how you can eat all day long and still inhale three meals a day is beyond me. Either you have an overactive metabolism, or you're going to weigh over three hundred pounds before you're up and about." Without looking back, she shut the door behind her and quickly walked back to her waiting vat of dough.

As the door clicked shut, Morgan allowed himself to smile and, throwing back the sheets, he slowly rose from the bed. He'd been up and about for two days now, gradually regaining his strength and familiarizing himself with his surroundings. Walking to the open window, he couldn't help groaning as he looked at the two pretzels in his hand. He never thought he'd be so sick of looking, smelling and eating the damn things!

For two days, ever since she'd burst into the room and announced her plans for going into the pretzel business, he'd been watching her constantly bake. First, she listened to Willow's and Jace's praise, and that had given her the confidence to take her little prizes into town. Even he was surprised when she came back and announced that Stan Tearle, the saloon owner, had placed a trial order for two dozen. Since then, she was working day and night to keep up with her growing orders. To make it worse, she was planning to increase her stock and had every intention of selling them at the train depot tomorrow. She thought they would be an ideal novelty for hungry passengers who stretched their legs while the train refueled. She was probably right, he thought, not able to contain a soft belch. Of course, they hadn't tried to dispose of eighteen in the last twenty-four hours.

Well, he was sick to death of them. The coarse salt she had so liberally sprinkled over them had given him a constant thirst. No wonder Stan Tearle was thrilled. Since Jenna's pretzels, his bar business must have tripled.

Four pretzels ago, Morgan had vowed another would not pass his lips and, standing at the window, he started shredding the two in his hands, Within seconds, his new friends, the birds, started to gather as he threw tiny pieces to the ground. He kept glancing toward the outside door of the barn, hoping Jenna wouldn't catch him. He could just imagine her rage.

Jenna Weldon was a new breed of woman for him. He'd never met anyone like her before and didn't think he would again. She could be argumentative, giving back as good as she got; infuriating, with her insistence that she came from the future, although

171

recently, he was beginning to believe that there was definitely something very different about her. One minute she was showing him a brilliant new invention, something he hadn't even known existed, and in the next, she would lose her defiance and become warm and exciting, a woman every man dreams about but never really expects to find.

Well, he had found her, and he wasn't about to let her go. She was still too much of a mystery. He wanted to know her better, yet since the pretzels, he'd hardly had the chance. She lived and breathed the little devils. She worked herself into exhaustion and when, finally, she came to bed, only her light snoring told him he was lying in the dark, whispering to himself. But it was seeing the violet smudges under her eyes that had convinced him to undermine her business. It was foolish, anyway. She would have to make and sell two hundred pretzels, just to pay their rent. If she refused to listen to him about money, he made up his mind to stop her before she got in too deep. He was surprised she hadn't given up already. Her temper and frustration were clear indicators that she had second thoughts about this venture. He just had never come up against such a strong sense of independence in a woman before.

Brushing the crumbs off his hands, he smiled inwardly as he watched the birds carry away the last traces of his deception. Soon he would have her back where he wanted her, where he could get to know her better. Because of his enforced abstinence, he felt like a young boy, pulling out and going over in his mind each detail of when she had made love to him. It was frustrating, he thought as he returned to the bed, but he knew his patience would soon pay off. And then he would make love to her. It was what filled his waking thoughts: appreciating her the way she deserved, loving her the way he wanted. And God knows, he admitted, as he felt the heavy congestion in his groin grow stronger, he *wanted*.

She forced herself to smile at the well-dressed passengers. They stepped off the train as if hesitant to venture out among the uncivilized, rough settlers who flanked the depot. Jenna was as inquisitive as the rest of Verdi, as she stared at the handsomely dressed men and the gorgeous creations worn by the women. They're the beautiful people of this era, she realized, the well fed, privileged few who looked to the rest of the world as a necessary, but not embraceable, curiosity.

Always having hated condescencion, Jenna broke the silence as those who had stared at those who didn't.

"Pretzel! Pretzels! A penny apiece!" She moved forth, carrying her heavy basket up to the wary passengers. Soon, one brave man approached her, and she placed her burden down on the wooden platform.

"You say these are pretzels?" he asked in a cultured, eastern voice. "I don't believe I've ever seen anything quite like them before."

"I'm not surprised," Jenna said, trying not to laugh.

"I'll take two."

Jenna pocketed the money and watched as the man walked away. Soon, she was doing a brisk business and was down to her last two dozen or so, when she heard a light southern accent.

"I beg your pardon, madam. Might I buy one of your pretzels that everyone seems to be raving about?"

Pleased, Jenna picked up one from her basket and lifted her head to thank the tall man in front of her.

173

Whatever words she had intended to say remained in her throat as she looked at the handsome, distinguished man.

He was older, exuding a quiet power and, although they were completely different, she couldn't help comparing him to Morgan.

"They are for sale, aren't they?" he asked kindly, and she found herself to be the recipient of a fantastic smile that automatically extended to his eyes.

Jenna regained her voice. "Yes . . . of course. I'm sorry."

After he'd paid her, she continued to watch him as he made his way back to a small, attractive woman. Dressed in a fashionable rust and cream-striped outfit, the dainty woman accepted Jenna's pretzel. The woman seemed overly excited by the small snack, and Jenna continued to watch the couple as they talked. Soon, both heads were turned toward her, and the small woman smiled before walking in her direction.

Embarrassed to be caught staring, Jenna quickly picked up her basket and was about to walk away when she was stopped by a feminine voice.

"Excuse me. I was wondering what you call these?"

Close up, it was no great puzzle why the handsome man seemed enraptured by the tiny woman. Although Jenna guessed her age to be somewhere in her late thirties, she was exquisite. Curling auburn hair was pulled back and up under a small, stylish hat while dark-green, intelligent eyes held an almost pleading look. Jenna felt dowdy next to her, yet the woman's unusual eyes weren't patronizing. They just continued to search hers.

Neither woman was aware of exactly how much time they spent staring, yet both knew something was passing between them. They heard the man clear his throat, and immediately the two looked away.

"I . . . ah, I just call them pretzels. I hope you like them." Jenna felt foolish for wanting to know her better, and she could see the small woman was disappointed by her answer.

"What is your name?" the woman whispered, in a voice that didn't sound southern at all.

For some reason, she wasn't surprised by the intensity of the question. "Jenna. Jenna Weldon."

The woman took a deep breath, as if regaining her composure. "Well, Jenna. I'll take ten of your pretzels."

Still shaken by whatever had just transpired, Jenna looked to her basket. "I . . . I'm afraid I don't have anything to wrap them in."

Opening her cloth purse, the woman handed her a large, cotton handkerchief. The edges were worked in a delicate lace and embroidered with the initials B.Q.B.

Jenna stared at the initials for a few seconds and then looked back to the woman.

"I should apologize for being so rude. Here, I've asked for your name and withheld my own. It stands for Brianne Quinlan Barrington."

Ryan looked at his wife and smiled. It had taken fourteen years, three children, a civil war, and years of rebuilding before she would consent to taking their long-postponed honeymoon. Always one for adventure, he had suggested they take the new transcontinental route to San Francisco, and Brianne had readily agreed. Now, selfishly, he wanted her all to himself.

"Brianne, I think we should let this young woman go about her business. We've already taken up a great deal of her time."

The attractive man handed her a silver coin as she

gave the woman the pretzels. Looking down at her hand, Jenna said, "I'm sorry. I don't think I have change for a dollar."

The woman named Brianne smiled at her and said warmly, "We don't want the change, Jenna. Thank you."

Linking her arm through her husband's, she turned with him, and Jenna's heart tugged as she read the love in the man's eyes. He smiled down to the small woman and tenderly asked, "Nostalgia, little one?"

The woman affectionately squeezed the tall man's upper arm, and Jenna had to strain to hear her answer. "Why, Ryan, it's been positively . . . *years* since I've had a Philly soft pretzel!"

Throwing back his head in laughter, Ryan gathered Brianne closer, and together they disappeared into the crowd.

Philly soft pretzel?

When the words finally registered in her brain, Jenna's lower jaw dropped in shock. Did they have Philadelphia soft pretzels in 1870? Did they call Philadelphia "Philly"? No, she was certain both were modern terms. How could the woman know them? Frantically, she searched for a glimpse of the couple. She had to find them! That woman knew! Jenna could tell by her eyes, by her words.

They had disappeared, probably into the train. Wasting no time, Jenna walked by the windows of the cars, hoping to find them. She ignored the requests for more pretzels as she peered into each window.

"Well, what'a we have here?"

Jenna looked down to the huge hand on her arm, restraining her from moving. Her eyes took in the dark uniform before moving upward. She couldn't help the gasp as her mouth again widened in disbelief. Damn! It was Bullmason!

"What we have here," Jenna said in a deceptively calm voice, "is a woman who is going to scream bloody murder if you don't take your hand away. This isn't the middle of nowhere, Bullmason. You have no power here."

Harry Bullmason reluctantly removed his hand and stared down at her with an evil smile. "How's the husband, missy?" he asked, a lewd expression flashing across his face.

Jenna wanted to slap it. Just the way he looked at her made her feel cheap, as if she were beneath him. Jenna knew his type: power-hungry little men who could never achieve greatness on their own so they abused what small amount of authority they had. She'd dealt with men like him before, and the trick was to never back down.

Giving him a withering look, she said, "Don't you have something important to do . . . like take tickets? Surely, one of your passengers must be in need of your services. Isn't that essentially what your job is? An overgrown nanny for the railroad?"

It did her heart good to see his face turn crimson as his skin became mottled with a barely controlled anger.

He pulled the brim of his small cap down as he glared at her. "Listen, you little bitch," he hissed between yellowed teeth, "that crazy preacher was right about you. You're nothin' but trash. Now, get the hell away from my train!" He looked her up and down. "You ain't fit to mix with decent folks. Go do your peddling somewheres else."

Jenna held the basket tight to her stomach, glad that it took both of her hands to keep it from falling. She was itching to slap him. "You're not including

177

yourself when you say decent folks, I hope. I had you figured out when I first saw you, Bullmason, and my opinion hasn't changed. You're still a pretentious bastard!"

She saw his large fists clenching and unclenching and feared he might attack her. Foregoing her intended parting shot of offering him a pretzel and then telling him what to do with it, Jenna merely smiled at him with false sweetness and said, "See ya' around, Harry," and walked away.

She kept her shoulders straight and didn't stop or acknowledge his loud words. "You can be sure of that, missy! You can be damn well sure you ain't seen the last of Harry Bullmason!"

Mentally muttering a barnyard curse, she left the platform and continued walking past the windows of the train.

"Miss! Miss! You sellin' food?"

She was too furious to bother stopping. What did it matter anyway? Morgan was right. This was a dumb idea.

"Please! Wait!"

Jenna couldn't ignore the plaintive cry. Turning around, she faced a tired-looking woman. Her face looked too old to go with her young body. Within seconds, Jenna took in her drab appearance, her dull, sparrowlike dress with its matching brown kerchief and shawl.

Coming closer, the woman asked in a hesitant voice, "How much?"

Jenna continued to stare at her.

"I got three boys ain't had nothin' since last night. How much for them things in your basket?"

Jenna seemed to come to life. "Here," she said, shoving the basket at the woman, "take what you want."

Worn hands instinctively grabbed hold of the straw handles. "I don't ask for charity," the woman said, mustering up her dignity, though she put the basket down and took off her kerchief.

Jenna watched as she carefully laid out her scarf on the ground. Before she could reach into the basket, Jenna picked it up and dumped the whole thing onto the thin brown material lying in the dirt.

At the woman's look of astonishment, Jenna announced, "It's not charity. I just went out of the pretzel business!"

Three hours later, Jenna stood in the front office of the Cheney Lumber Company. Taking a deep breath, she looked around at the four men who stared at her and repeated her request. "I asked you, Mr. Cheney, approximately how long it took you to do your books each week."

Her eyes finally settled on the heavyset, balding man seated behind his desk. "I don't know what business it is of yours, Mrs. Trahern, but I probably spend an hour each day."

"I could do it faster."

Marcus Cheney leaned back in his chair. Rolling a fat cigar between his fingers, he smiled indulgently. "If I hire a bookkeeper, it won't be a woman."

"I can do it in fifteen minutes."

The men standing around the office laughed or turned their faces away so she wouldn't see their derisive smirks.

Holding back his own laughter, Marcus stood up. "I'm afraid you didn't hear me. I'm not hiring a woman." He smiled at one of the men.

"What takes you an hour, I can do in fifteen minutes, maybe even less."

This time, they didn't even bother to hold back the short chuckles of amusement. The graying lumber mill owner rolled his tongue over his bottom lip. "You challenging me to a contest, Mrs. Trahern?" he asked the pretty woman who stood before him.

Jenna let her smile include all the men in the small room. "That I am, Mr. Cheney." She didn't mind their laughter now that she had the small man exactly where she wanted him.

She watched as he came around the desk and sat on its edge. Crossing his arms over his chest, he again looked to the other men and bit the inside of his cheek to keep from laughing. Jenna knew she was being treated as a joke, but her pride was worth sacrificing if she could get him to agree.

"It's only fair to tell you, there's nobody in this town that's got a better head for figures than me. Why should I waste my time with this contest?"

Jenna was prepared for his question. "If I should lose, I'll bring you a complete meal every day at noon, for one week." She looked to his large stomach. "Stan Tearle can verify that I'm a good cook. But . . ." She met his eyes. "If I should win, you hire me as your bookkeeper for five dollars a week."

Marcus's eyes left her face, and he looked to the interested men around him. He'd be damned! The little lady played them right into her hands. He couldn't back down without looking like he thought she had a chance. Rubbing his stomach, he just hoped she was a good cook.

By nature, he was a good-hearted man, and he looked on the whole episode as an amusing break in an otherwise boring afternoon. Deciding to play along, even though he knew no human being could possibly calculate his books in so short a period of time, Marcus magnanimously offered his own glass-enclosed office for the contest.

Jenna was almost jubilant as she sat down at the expansive wooden desk. She looked out beyond the glass to the men watching her and smiled. Mr. Cheney had already explained to her what was expected, and she casually rearranged his ledgers in front of her.

She sat one of his books open so it would shield her work. Still smiling at the men through the glass, she watched them place bets among themselves as she reached into her skirt pocket. Withdrawing her handkerchief, she could only guess they were wagering on how long it would take her to lose.

Well, she thought, as she placed the folded white hankie in front of the upright book, she had no intention of losing. This was no harebrained scheme. This wasn't pretzels. This one was well thought out.

Faking a sneeze, she quickly brought the handkerchief to her face. Jenna didn't feel the least bit of guilt as she looked at her insurance. Lying innocently on the desk was her Texas Instruments solar-powered calculator.

Chapter Fourteen

Jason watched her walk toward him. He could see by her face that she was happy, tell by the way she moved that she was excited. He'd seen her enter Cheney's lumber mill over an hour ago and used every excuse he could think of to clean the front of the saloon in order to spot her when she reappeared.

Turning back to the bar, he yelled, "Okay for me to take my supper break now?"

Stan looked up from the glasses he was polishing. "Yeah, sure. Go ahead." He watched the boy quickly place his broom behind the counter and untie his long white apron. "You just be back early, you hear?" he added. "Red Mary got word that some of the boys are comin' down from the mountain today instead of tomorrow."

Jason nodded and hurried to the door. He didn't bother to tell Stan that he'd already heard about the loggers. Red Mary, Gert, and the other sorry-looking women who made their living upstairs had beaten him to it. Besides, he didn't want to miss Jenna.

She was almost to the deserted barber shop when he stepped outside. Immediately, she recognized him, and his heart felt strange when she smiled and waved.

"Jace! Guess what?"

Her steps quickened, and he grinned while waiting for her to reach him. "You look happy, Jenna."

She took a deep breath. "I got a job!"

The smile stayed frozen on his lips. "A job?" he asked when he was finally able to move his mouth. "What about your pretzels?"

Jenna quickly shook her head. "Oh, forget them. I found out this morning that it was a waste of time. This is a real job. I'm going to be doing Mr. Cheney's books. Isn't that great?"

He tried to join in her delight. "You must be very good or Chaney wouldn't have hired you. If you're going back to the farm, I'll walk with you. I'm on my supper break."

"Wait until I tell Morgan. I do believe he's going to be thrilled. No more pretzels!" Playfully, she linked her arm through his and, together, they left Verdi behind them.

They had gone no more than a hundred yards when she looked into the young boy's impassive face and asked, "What's wrong, Jace? I thought you'd be happy for me."

Jason's eyes never left the twin paths of dirt that years of wagon wheels had turned into a makeshift road. "I am happy for you." Pursing his lips together, he refused to look at her.

Jenna took her arm away and stopped walking. "What is it then? I can tell you're upset about something."

He didn't want to look at her. He was afraid if he did, she would see the envy in his eyes.

"Tell me what's wrong?" Jenna persisted.

"What you have done today, I have been trying to do for months," he finally admitted. "It isn't your fault, Jenna. I'm sorry I couldn't hide my feelings better."

Immediately, Jenna realized how unthinking she'd been. Jace had told her of his problems in trying to find employment and here she'd been, bragging about something he needed more than her.

"God, I'm sorry, Jace."

"Don't be sorry. Your husband isn't able to support you now. I'm sure he'll be proud." Finally, he looked at her. "And I am happy for you, Jenna."

She smiled, wishing there was something she could say that would make him feel better. "Do you ever have time off?"

It was Jace's turn to smile. "Even Stan Tearle closes on Sunday."

Jenna brightened. "Let's do something on Sunday then. Do you have any plans?"

They were almost to the barn. "I go out into the woods. Since they started cutting down the trees, I'm not always successful in finding game, but I'd be glad to take you with me . . . if that's what you really want."

Jenna tried to bring the smile back to her face. What had she gotten herself into? "You mean, you go hunting every Sunday?"

Jace stopped at the door to the barn. "I try. Would you like to come with me?"

She could see the hope in his eyes and didn't have the heart to say no. "Sure. Why not? See you the day after tomorrow."

The happiness on Jason's face was genuine. "I'll come for you in the morning. And Jenna . . . congratulations on your job."

"Thanks, Jace." Jenna found her lips curling up as she opened the barn door. She couldn't exactly say that luck was her constant companion of late, but, maybe, just maybe, on Sunday, all the furry little

184

animals who lived in the nearby forest would be on holiday.

Jenna flung open the door to the small room and stood smiling at Morgan. She watched as his brows arched questioningly.

"I take it there's a reason for your dramatic entrance?"

She continued to smile at the handsome man lying so casually on the bed. "I got a job! A real job!" She felt as if she had just accomplished the impossible.

"A job? What kind of job?" Morgan straightened his legs and sat up higher against the pillows.

Reaching behind her, Jenna flicked the door shut and walked closer to him. Lifting her chin, she said with pride, "I'm the new bookkeeper at Cheney's lumber mill."

He didn't say anything for a few seconds, just continued to breathe deeply and stare at her.

It wasn't exactly the reaction Jenna had hoped for. "Well?"

Morgan's eyes narrowed. "And just how did this come about? The last thing I knew, you were going to sell your pretzels down at the depot. How did you go from being a pretzel vendor to a bookkeeper in a matter of hours?"

What was wrong with everybody? Why isn't *anyone* happy about her job? Trying to ignore the resentment that she could feel growing inside her, Jenna again attempted to lighten the mood. "I challenged Mr. Cheney to a contest . . . and I won! Pretty good, huh?"

"You what?"

The smile quickly left her face. "I won. What's the matter with you?"

"What kind of contest?" he demanded.

Listening to his angry tone of voice, her mouth

opened in shock. "Why are you so upset? I got a job. You should be happy."

"What kind of contest?"

Jenna walked over to the stove, grabbed the large cast-iron skillet resting on top, and slammed it back down. "What kind do you think?" she threw over her shoulder. "It was a spitting contest. I spit furthest, so I get to be bookkeeper." She spun around and faced him. "Dammit, Morgan, what the hell else could it be, other than an accounting contest!"

Morgan could feel the pressure on his back teeth as he ground them together. So she gets rid of the pretzels and jumps right into something else! Only this time, she doesn't even discuss it. Well, he wasn't about to have it. "You'll quit tomorrow."

Jenna looked at him as if he was unhinged. "You're joking! You can't be serious."

"Oh, I'm serious. You'll go back tomorrow and tell Cheney it was a mistake. You're not working for him."

Jenna could feel her pulse beat faster as her anger built. "Like hell I will! I'm going back tomorrow because I'm going to work for the man. Who are you to tell me whether or not I can work? *Somebody* around here has to bring in some money!"

Morgan glared back at her. "I've already told you, I have money. Only you wouldn't listen. I don't want my wife to work. How do you think I'll feel, knowing those men think you have to support me?"

"Well, I do have to support you, but I don't care. You can't work in your condition. And where is this money you keep talking about? Just where is it, Morgan?"

"I told you. It's in Baltimore. I can wire my bank and have an account set up here."

Jenna picked up an egg and rolled it in her hand. "If this money really exists, why haven't you let me send a telegram to your bank? It could have been here days ago."

Morgan couldn't answer her. What could he say? That he'd waited because he liked having her with him? That he was afraid if she had money, she would leave? That he'd purposely isolated her in this shabby room, wanting to keep her to himself?

Seeing a look of guilt cross his face, Jenna turned back to the stove and said, "Let's just forget it. I'm going to make dinner."

Morgan watched her stiff back as she worked at the stove. Quietly, he simmered.

"This is dinner?" he asked, as he looked at the plate of fried eggs. Cradled beside them were two pretzels.

Jenna impatiently ran a fingernail across her eyebrow. What had started out as a tension headache was turning into monumental pain. "Now what's wrong? You'll have to forgive me, but I've been a little busy today. I didn't think you'd mind the eggs."

Morgan looked up from the plate. He was still angry over her insistence that she take the job. Picking up the pretzels, he handed them to her. "I don't care about the eggs. It's *these* damn things. Here."

Taking them from him, she stared at her hand. "I thought you liked them. I saved a few."

"Well, you saved a few too many. I hate to tell you this, Jenna, but I can't stand to even look at them."

That was it! She'd taken enough abuse from him since she entered the room. "Oh really? Then you should be thrilled to know that I won't be baking them anymore. I won't have time . . . now that I'll be working at the lumber mill."

Morgan slammed the fork back on the plate.

"Dammit, Jenna! I told you. You're not working there. What do I have to do to get through to you?"

Jenna almost laughed. Was he serious? Did he really think she would give up her job, just like that? Once again, she tried to be understanding. It must be very hard for him to stay in this room, bedridden. "Look, Morgan, let's not argue. I have a splitting headache, and I'm hungry. Why don't we talk about this after we've eaten?"

Not waiting for him to agree, she turned around and walked back to the stove. Filling her own plate, she put one of his discarded pretzels on it and sat in the chair by the window. It only took a few mouthfuls for Jenna to realize the small tin knife she was using wouldn't be sharp enough to cut the tension in the room and, uncomfortable, she tried again.

"I met the most extraordinary woman today," she said as if their argument had never taken place.

To his credit, Morgan politely put his fork on his plate and looked up at her. "Oh, really? Does she live in town?"

Seeing that he meant to be agreeable, Jenna smiled. "No. She and her husband were on the train. I guess they were going to Sacramento, or maybe, San Francisco."

"What was so extraordinary about her?"

Jenna held her plate with both hands. Her look was intent as she said, "I know this is going to sound crazy, but I had the strangest feeling that she was like me."

Morgan was confused. "Like you? What do you mean?"

"You know . . . from the future."

He could only stare at her. Oh God, not again! he thought. She was constantly throwing him off balance, asserting her independence, as if she were a

188

man; insisting she was from the future, sounding as if she were an escapee from an asylum. For all he knew, she could be. "You're right," he said calmly, "it does sound crazy."

Jenna wasn't going to let him upset her again. "I know you don't believe me, but this woman called my pretzels, *Philly soft pretzels*! Don't you see, Morgan? That's what they really are! She *knew*! I could see it in her eyes . . ."

"Am I to believe," he said, "that you could tell this woman was from the future because you saw it in her eyes?"

"Yes, dammit!" He was infuriating! "I know it sounds ridiculous—"

"No, you were right the first time," he interrupted. "It sounds crazy. Why do you stubbornly cling to something so ludicrous? Do you find living in 1870 so dreadful that you must make up this fantasy world of the future?"

Jenna stood up. Her hands were shaking as she held the plate out in front of her. "Dreadful? Why, that's too mild a word to describe *your* world. How about repulsive? Offensive? Oppressive? Take your pick. They all apply."

She could feel all the anger returning, only now it had grown in size and nothing would stop her from venting it. Taking her tin plate to the stove, she made a loud clatter as she forcefully threw it into the empty skillet. "I have tried to be patient with you. What more proof do you need? You've heard your own voice on a tape recorder, seen letters that have the date on it, my date . . . 1987! Have you ever seen a flashlight before? You know how I won the contest today? With another nifty invention from the future. A calculator. I was going to show it to you tonight, but why bother? You'll just try and explain it away, just like the others."

Morgan sat up straighter. "So you cheated today!" He actually sounded pleased.

"No, I didn't cheat. I merely used the advantage I had to get the job. You know why Cheney didn't want to hire me? Because I'm a woman! The same reason you don't want me to work! I just bet if I were another man, you'd be grateful as hell that someone in this room was earning money!"

"I knew it! You're a bloody suffragette!"

Jenna didn't know whether to laugh or cry. She decided to laugh. "You're damn right, Morgan. Only I didn't know it until just this minute. You are what was known in the latter twentieth century as a male chauvinist pig!"

Morgan's thumb and index finger followed the line of his thick mustache. When both met at his chin, he quietly asked, "I beg your pardon?"

Jenna smiled confidently into his glaring blue eyes. "I said, had you been the one transported into the twentieth century, you would be a classic male chauvinist pig."

"With your habit of using shocking language, I don't know if I want you to define that term."

She could see he was barely controlling his temper, but she plunged ahead anyway. In truth, there was no stopping her, and she found that since she had released her anger, her headache had lessened considerably. "I'll try to keep it clean enough for your delicate ears, Mr. Trahern. A chauvinist pig happens to be a man whose masculinity is threatened when a woman tries to become independent."

"Are you implying I'm not a man?" He spoke quietly, yet his tone made the sound of his words grate along the nerves at the back of her neck.

"What I'm implying," she ground out between her

teeth as she took his plate away, "is that you're a direct throwback to the cave man. You can't provide for us, yet it offends your ego if I pick up the club, leave the cave and go out into the world."

From behind, she heard his shocked voice. "First, you're saying I'm not a man. And now you tell me I can't provide for you."

"That's not—"

"I'll have you know, madam, that you are the single, most infuriating woman I have ever had the misfortune to meet. You will have your money in three days. I'll open an account in your name as soon as the bank opens tomorrow." His face turned even more red. "That should be in agreement with your suffragette notions."

She watched as he ran his hands through the silky black hair at his head. He was furious, yet like the foolish skater who knows he's on thin ice, Jenna couldn't help sticking her toe out further.

"And where, may I ask, is this money supposed to come from? What are you, Morgan? A drifter? A simple cowboy who happens to have a fat bank account in Baltimore? Or, could you possibly be a spy?"

His head jerked up, and his shocked eyes quickly became slits of suspicion. "What did you say?"

She couldn't back down now, especially since she felt she was coming closer to the truth. "I asked if you're a spy."

His face transformed into an impassive mask. "And what makes you ask that?"

Jenna grabbed hold of the iron rail at the foot of the bed. "You talked when you had the fever. All sorts of interesting things came out. Politicians, President Grant. By the way, who's Billy? A fellow agent? Sounded like the poor guy wasn't very good at the job."

Morgan threw off the covers. "Shut up! My God, you can be a bitch!"

She knew she had gone too far, yet some perverse instinct made her continue. "Look, this all started because I got a job. Why are you getting up?" she asked as she saw him rise from the bed with surprising ease. "Do you have to go outside?"

He ignored her questions. Looking at her, he asked quietly, "Do you intend to go through with this? Even if I forbid it?"

Jenna gave a short, incredulous laugh. "You can't forbid it. You don't have the right to do that."

"I'm your husband." He continued to stare at her, waiting for something she was unable to give.

"That wasn't real. We both know that."

Quietly, very softly, he asked as he pulled on his jeans, "And what would you call the night our marriage was consummated? Was that real?"

He stood, buttoning his pants and staring into her eyes, waiting. They both knew whatever happened in the next few minutes would determine their relationship.

But it was too new, too confusing—and she was too hurt. "I think I'd call that a mistake," Jenna said slowly, hating the quivering of her chin, the hot tears forming at her eyes.

At her words, he winced, but didn't say anything for a few seconds. He didn't even move. Did she only imagine the pain in his eyes? Or was it because her own pain was wrapping itself around her, constricting her ability to take back the angry words?

She became aware that he was moving around the room quite easily. It amazed her to turn her eyes back to him and find him fully dressed, right down to his boots.

Seeing her look of confusion, he said, "If you'd been around, you would have known I've been getting up for days now. Where do you keep the money, Jenna?"

Still shocked by his near recovery, she pointed to her purse. "In . . . in the center pocket. Why?"

He picked up her purse and opened it. "I'm taking five dollars. I'll see you get it back."

"Morgan, what are you doing? Where are you going?"

He placed the money into the top pocket of the plaid shirt that she'd bought him and couldn't wait to see him in. Turning around at the door, he smiled bitterly.

"I'm about to rectify a mistake, *Miss* Weldon. I'm leaving."

Chapter Fifteen

"Stan, how about another?" With only five dollars to his name, Morgan couldn't afford anything better than the house whiskey. He'd have to be careful, not only with the money, but with what he was drinking. This stuff could play hell with the stomach, he remembered, and make your head feel like twenty guys with hammers were having a contest inside it.

Contest! Just the word made him grit his teeth. It brought back mental images of Jenna, flaunting her job, saying things she had no right to say. Thinking about their argument, Morgan looked down the long length of bar.

"What about that drink, Stan?"

"Comin' right up." Stan Tearle placed the bottle in front of the tall man and poured a little more than normal, but not too much for a first time customer. Stan needed to cultivate all the business that he could, and he was eager to please. What surprised him was this customer. He wasn't expecting Jenna Trahern's husband quite so soon.

"How about one of your wife's pretzels to go with

it?"

Morgan glared at the man. "No thanks."

Stan had seen all kinds pass through his bar in the last few years. He prided himself in accurately judging a man within minutes. Stan's opinion was that Morgan Trahern could very easily become a dangerous man. And Stan was nobody's fool.

"Guess you could have 'em anytime you want, huh?"

Morgan lifted the small glass and, throwing back his head, downed the drink in one swift gulp. The corner of his lip unconsciously lifted in a sneer. "Not anymore, my friend."

Stan was surprised. Caution told him to back off, but curiosity pushed him further. "You sayin' the wife isn't going to be making 'em anymore?"

Morgan took the bottle from Stan and poured his own drink. "The *wife* seems to be through with pretzels . . . among other things."

Stan knew enough not to inquire what that meant. "Too bad," he said, wiping the bar in front of Trahern. Sometimes, a man just needed a place to get away and blow off whatever was eating him up inside. Stan tried to make sure the Four Mile Saloon was such a place and, leaving the bottle, he also knew when to turn back to his other customers.

Morgan watched the barkeeper walk away. What the hell was he supposed to say? That Jenna wouldn't be making her damn pretzels anymore because she boldly challenged the owner of the lumber mill to a contest . . . and won? That she didn't think of herself as his wife? That she didn't want anything more to do with him? That she considered the night they had made love as a *mistake*? It was the last which grated along his spine, just like the incessant buzzing of

195

Verdi's sawmills. He could forgive her strange behavior, her crazy notions, maybe even her remarks about Billy. What made him furious was that she'd said the two of them were a mistake.

God! A mistake! He'd spent frustrating days and nights thinking, reliving each moment. He'd lain in that lumpy bed and carefully planned how he would seduce her. He'd even let her take precedence over his assignment. Damn! Never before had he let a woman come before his job. Tomorrow, first thing, he'd wire Frank Adams, just to let him know he was still alive.

Morgan poured himself another drink. He must have been a little crazy, he reflected, allowing Jenna to take over his every thought like that. Bringing the drink to his lips, he closed his eyes. That had to be it. The fever had made him temporarily insane. What else could explain the unnatural craving he had for the woman?

Swallowing the drink, he vaguely noticed that it no longer burned as it went down his throat. With a drawn-out sigh, he replaced the small glass on the bar and, looking beyond it, saw his reflection. It was the first time he'd seen himself in over a week, and he was shocked at his appearance. His hair was too long, his mustache was in need of attention, yet it was his eyes that bothered him the most. They didn't belong to a respected Baltimore importer. They were too hard, too angry—and too familiar.

It was as if he were the one taken back in time, along with Jenna. Only his journey into the past was shorter. The man looking back at him was someone he had thought he'd left behind with the war. Morgan had hoped never to see him resurface. He, too, wanted to go back to his own time, his own world, the one he had worked so hard to build. He'd been so close, so damn close, when Jenna had walked into his life and turned it upside down. Now, he didn't know what he wanted, except he knew with a certainty that, in spite of everything she'd said and done, he still wanted her.

Jenna brought the already damp pillow closer to her chest. The shock she had felt when Morgan walked out on her had lasted but a few minutes. It was as if her brain had ceased to function during that time. She'd stared at the closed door and refused to allow the truth to sink in. Then, little by little, she began to accept it. He was gone. Gone!

The tears she'd been holding back, since her argument with Morgan, were slowly released, and it was then that she walked back to the bed and climbed into his place.

Bending her head, she could still smell his scent on the pillow, and Jenna's chest felt caved in as a fresh flood of tears joined the others on the wet cotton case. How *could* he? How could he just leave her like that? After all they'd been through together? Did she mean so little to him that he could walk away with so little thought?

Her eyes looked about the small room. Its shabbiness closed in on her and she quickly shut it out. Behind her closed lids, she could again see him as he left her. He seemed like a different man, cold, cruel. She knew she had insulted him, but she didn't think she'd penetrated that hard shield and actually hurt him—not like he had done. If only she could call back the angry words, tell him the night they had made love was the most beautiful moment in her life, but it was too late and her pride was too strong.

It wasn't gratitude she wanted from him; it was

something more, something she couldn't put into words. Never, never, had she wanted another human being as much as she wanted Morgan, and she was frightened. Her *old* life was orderly. She depended on no one but herself. Discounting college, and a few silly involvements where she thought she'd been in love, she had never been emotionally dependent on anyone. She didn't want it.

Relationships like her parents' were rare, and she had been willing to wait for that special someone to come into her life, or do without.

Thinking about her parents brought more tears. Her mother. Claire. Dear God! What was she going through now? Were people searching for her? Jenna knew her mother wasn't strong anymore, not since her father had died. Please God, she prayed, watch over her. She pictured her mother's soft face and longed to feel the security of her arms. It wasn't fair! What had she done to deserve this exile?

By the time Jenna thought of all those she had left behind, she was sobbing. Her tears were those of anger, self-pity, and abandonment. To whom could she scream at this injustice? Who would listen?

"Who the hell would even *believe* it?" she cried in frustration.

"Little lady, you got one head for figures! I'll give you that." Marcus Cheney shook his head in amazement as he went over the books Jenna had been working on. "I never seen anyone work this fast."

He put the large green ledgers back on his desk and looked up at her. "I never thought I'd have hired a woman. You're very good, Mrs. Trahern."

She almost winced when she heard him address her.

"Thank you. Why don't you just call me Jenna?"

Marcus smiled. He liked her, even if she did beat him in front of his men. "Jenna, then. Shall I just pay you for today, and then we can start with a full week on Monday?"

Grateful that he had suggested it when the thought was uppermost on her mind, Jenna returned his smile. "That would be fine, Mr. Cheney."

When she was out on the street, Jenna put her palms into the pockets of her brown skirt. Her one hand touched her trusty calculator while the fingers of her other hand played with the one dollar coin. Her pay. She was working for a dollar a day! Turning the corner of Mill Road, she stepped up onto the wooden sidewalk that lined the stores on Center Street.

She lifted her chin and took a deep breath. She was done being sorry for herself. She'd needed last night, and it was probably healthy for her to have cried out all her frustrations, but it wasn't her style. It always made her feel better to accept the inevitable and work from there to change things.

Looking into the small window display of Dodd's Apothecary, Jenna heard a familiar voice behind her.

"How're you doing, Jenna?"

Her head snapped up, and she saw Morgan's reflection in the glass. Willing her heart to slow down, she gradually turned around to face him. "A lot better than you are, I think. What happened to you?"

Morgan ran a hand over the short stubble of beard on his chin. "I . . . ah, I left my bag last night. Razor and things. Okay if I walk back with you and get it?"

She wanted to slap him. How could he undo all her hard work? He looked like he was in pain, but it was probably just a hangover.

She ignored his question. "How's your shoulder?

You ought to see Dr. Marshall and have him remove the stitches."

"I'll see him tomorrow. You just get out of work?" It was a stupid thing for him to ask, since he'd been watching Cheney's for the last half hour, waiting for her to come out.

Jenna nodded. Why did it hurt so much, just looking at him? She wanted to tell him to straighten out, but she knew she didn't have the right, not anymore. "Where are you staying?" It killed her to ask.

Morgan looked uncomfortable; she could read him that well. "I took a room at the Verdi Inn. Guess I'll be staying there for a few days."

Again Jenna nodded, each word laying heavy on her heart. Why did she allow him to have this affect on her? God knows what the people of the town were thinking. She'd permitted them to assume that the two of them were married, and now her husband was living elsewhere.

The silence was painful for both of them, and it was Morgan who broke it. "You never answered. Can I get my bag?"

She wouldn't let him see what he was doing to her. She'd fought hard last night to regain her pride, and he wasn't about to rip it away again.

"Of course, you can get your bag." She hoped she sounded nonchalant.

"Can I walk you home?"

Jenna doubted that she would survive the short walk with Morgan. She knew if she spent any more time in his company, she would start to say things she would regret later. Things like apologies, self-recriminations and, God forbid, pleadings. No. Better for her to stay away from him than risk humiliation.

She tilted her head toward the store behind her. "I was going to go in here and look around."

Morgan quickly inspected the store window, then looked back at her. "That's all right. I'll wait."

Jenna took a deep breath. "I might be awhile. Why don't you just go on yourself. The room is open."

She could see the hard look return to his face. Touching the brim of his hat, he said, "Take care of yourself, Jenna," and turned away.

She stared at his back for only a few seconds. She wouldn't watch him walk away from her a second time. Closing her eyes tightly for a brief moment, Jenna tried to block out the pain—and the crazy impulse to run after him.

"You must be quiet, Jenna, or we will lose him."

Turning her back, she hugged her arms. "Please, Jason," she whispered over her shoulder. "Let him go."

"Shh!"

Dear God! Why had she ever agreed to this? It was barbaric, standing in the forest, waiting to kill an animal. The only thing she had thought of this morning was getting away. Away from Morgan, the town, and the small room that was starting to resemble a prison. Jason had surprised her by bringing two horses to the barn when he picked her up. He said the animals belonged to his family, though Jenna had never seen them before on the farm. Rather than question him further, she'd overcome any doubts she had and hurried back into the room to change her clothes. When she'd returned, she had on the shrunken gabardine that now resembled short pants, and she'd stuffed the bottoms into her high boots.

Sitting on the black and white spotted horse, Jenna had felt the worries, cares, frustrations of the last two weeks melt away with the cool morning breeze. It was her first moment of pure fun since she'd met Morgan, and she reveled in the freedom and escape. It hadn't lasted long enough, though. Reluctantly, she had followed Jason to the edge of the forest and dismounted. He'd told her that they would be going the rest of the way on foot.

Now, as she stood back to back with him, she shuddered, thinking about the beautiful antelope they had stalked for over half an hour. Again, she wondered why she'd ever gone along with this.

"Jenna, move back. I need room."

Without speaking, she carefully walked away from him. She couldn't watch what she knew was about to happen. When it did, it was almost soundless, except for the vibration of the string as it was let go and the quick rustling of bushes as the antelope bounded away. Reaction was fast, and Jenna turned around to see the handsome animal moving deeper into the woods with a long arrow piercing its graceful neck.

"Oh God!" Jenna moaned and turned her eyes away. Shock mixed with revulsion, and she brought her hand up to her mouth. She was afraid she might be sick and drew in great amounts of air through her nostrils.

"Jenna, I'm sorry. I shouldn't have brought you with me."

She looked at Jace and tried to keep accusation from her eyes as he continued to speak.

"Wait here. I'll be back in a few minutes."

Jenna tried to push the vision of the wounded animal from her mind as she paced back and forth in a small clearing, but the picture resisted banishment and she knew it would haunt her. How she hated being caught in time. How she longed to return to civilization.

She pivoted at the sound of Jason's return. There was no antelope, though she knew it would be too heavy for him to carry himself, and she watched as he held his right hand out in front of him and searched the ground. Several times he looked to the sky and, in spite of her sick stomach, Jenna couldn't help but be intrigued.

"What are you doing?" she asked as she came closer.

Jason continued to inspect the ground until, at last, he seemed satisfied with a small, flat rock. He tilted it, stuffing brush under one corner, until it lay just right. Jenna thought he looked like a young scientist, preoccupied with an exacting experiment and, now curious, she asked again, "What are you doing?"

He lifted his dark head and looked at her. "Hunting."

Jenna's eyes went to his hand and she shuddered. Cradled within his palm was blood. Animal blood. She watched in both fascination and revulsion as Jason spit into it and mixed it with his finger. Carefully, he turned his hand sideways and scraped the mixture onto the rock.

Knowing the Indians were very mystical, she asked, "Is this some sort of ritual?"

Standing, Jason wiped his hand on the leg of his pants. "Ritual?"

Jenna looked again to the blood and saliva, starting to congeal in the bright morning sun. "You know, some sort of offering. You and the antelope, together."

Jace laughed and sat down beside the rock. "That's

203

pretty good, Jenna, but no. It isn't a religious ritual."
He grinned up at her. "Why don't you sit down and
I'll explain it."

She wasn't sure she liked the idea of sitting beside
whatever it was that he was doing, but her legs still
felt shaky and, since it looked like Jace was settled in
for some time, she lowered herself to the ground.

"Well, what is it then?"

Jace turned his head and looked at her lovely face.
Even though he knew she was still upset with him, he
couldn't help but take joy in the fact that she was here
and he had proved himself in front of her. His eyes slid
to the rock. "When that is dried up from the sun, the
antelope will be dead."

Jenna's mouth opened in disbelief. "You're joking.
You believe that?"

I don't just believe it. I know it."

Jenna couldn't help but look at the flat stone.
"How? I mean, what if there was no sun?"

"Then it would take longer, but the blood would
still dry when the antelope was dead." He looked at
the furrows on her forehead and the way she held her
mouth. "Would you rather I made up a story for you?
Shall I tell you that the good Wolf-god, who always
had the welfare of the Washoe close to his heart, asked
that we make this sacrifice to him? Or perhaps, you
would prefer to hear about the bad, jealous Coyote-
god, who demands tribute or threatens to eat us? Or
shall I just tell you the truth? My grandfather taught
me to hunt, and this was part of it. Why track an
animal through the woods, when mixing your saliva
with his blood and waiting for it to evaporate will tell
you when to follow the signs of blood and lead you to
him?"

Jenna played with the blades of grass in front of

her. "I sounded pretty silly, didn't I? I guess I'm like so many other white people and expect everything an Indian does to have some hidden mystical meaning. I'm sorry."

"Don't be sorry, Jenna. At least, you come right out with what you're thinking and ask questions."

He appeared to be finally at ease. Jenna could tell that he was comfortable, almost happy in the woods. "Jace, why don't you and your mother live with her people? I would think you both would be happier."

He sat up straighter. "My mother believes that I must make my way in the white man's world. She made a promise to my father that I would be brought up white. He insisted that we only speak your language in the house, but he allowed me to spend time with my grandfather. He, along with the Elders, taught me the way of the Washoe." He checked the rock, then sat back down. "I will obey my mother and endure the white man until she gives up and returns to her people. I will not allow both of us to forever be outcasts. We don't belong in your world."

With his last words, Jenna's shoulders sagged. She looked down to her hands. "You're not the only outcast, Jason," she whispered. "I, too, don't belong in this world."

He looked at her, and Jenna could feel a wave of compassion coming from the young boy. "Why do you say that? I have known for some time that you are special, Jenna, yet I don't see how you can say that you don't belong to this world. You are what makes this world bearable for me right now."

What she had only guessed before was confirmed. Jason was infatuated with her. Not wanting to hurt him, she said, "Jace, you have your whole life ahead of you. I left my life behind."

"Behind?"

She took a deep breath and looked into his black eyes. "I'm from another time, Jason. I don't know how it happened, but I belong in the future . . ."

He didn't interrupt, just sat and quietly listened as she told her story. She told him everything, except the night she and Morgan made love, and finished with telling him of the argument that had led to Morgan's departure. It felt good telling someone. Hearing it all out loud put it in better perspective, and she realized now that she had been too harsh with Morgan, too rash in calling the night she had spent with him a mistake. Her only mistake was in not realizing that what she felt for Morgan was more than sexual attraction. It was much more than that.

"I believe you, Jenna."

Her head popped up and she stared at him. "You do?"

Jason grinned. "Before, you spoke about Indian rituals. Well, it's true. There are a lot of spiritual beliefs. Someday I will take you to a special rock, right here in Verdi, that is filled with unexplainable symbols. We believe the ancients carved them into caves, canyon walls, rocks. Many have contemplated their meaning, but I think their secrets are still held by Father Sky and Mother Earth. Sometimes, when I'm out here, I can almost hear the gods speak to me with the voice of the wind. Yet I know that only when my spirit is free of loneliness will I be able to understand what they are saying. Their secrets are great, Jenna. You may never understand them, or why they have brought you to this time."

Jenna felt like crying. He believed her! She wanted to thank him for his absolute acceptance, but before she could gulp down her unshed tears, Jace stood up.

Touching her shoulder, he said, "Look, Jenna. I think the Sun-god has given us a sign."

She brought her head up and gazed at the rock. There was only a dark brown stain. As she listened to the sound of Jason reentering the woods, she felt overcome with the magnitude of nature, those things explainable and those which are still a mystery.

Sitting in a small clearing in the woods, Jenna Weldon pondered her own insignificance and, in that place which now seemed almost holy, she paid homage to Father Sky, Mother Earth, and the Sun-god: Jason's gods who were all different personalities of her own.

Chapter Sixteen

As Morgan walked the cobblestone streets of Sacramento, his thoughts turned to Jenna. How she would love the culture of this city, he thought. She didn't belong in Verdi. She belonged somewhere where she could be appreciated, yet it annoyed him to be thinking of her at all, when he was still smarting from her rejection.

He'd spent four days in Verdi, watching her, waiting for her to come to her senses, but she'd avoided him like the plague. He'd had enough of it. He'd found himself walking around like a lovesick kid, just hoping to catch a glimpse of her until he had been disgusted by his own actions. It was then that he had gone to the bank and established an account in her name and left. It was overdue, anyway.

The telegram that he'd sent to Frank Adams proved to be just in time. Frank hadn't ordered his contact to leave the city, and Morgan hurried past the late afternoon crowd, on his way to meet him. He'd already made up his mind to finish this investigation and get back to Baltimore. He had a normal life waiting for him there, with normal people. No scheming businessmen, no corrupt big-time politicians, no crazy, beautiful women who claimed to be from the future. Just normal people.

Yet, he knew from the past few days that his life had unexplainably changed, and Baltimore would probably seem dull without Jenna. He didn't know how he was going to go on with his life when she occupied so many of his waking thoughts. And she wasn't satisfied with disrupting him during the day. For the last two nights, she'd crept up on him and haunted his dreams. Last night, he had awakened in a sweat. Somehow, she had entered the nightmares of his past, and now it was he and Billy and Jenna who were caught behind enemy lines. She had taken Billy's place in his arms. It was her life's blood that ran over his hands and, even now, his stomach tightened as he felt the terror, grief, and frustration once again. It was the thought of losing her to death that had made him scream at her—telling her she had no right to leave him, not when he'd just found her, not when he loved her.

Loved her? Holding his small valise closer to his body, Morgan tried to banish the disturbing thought from his mind as he entered the Santayana Hotel. This was too important. It was the final leg of his investigation, and thoughts of Jenna would just have to wait.

As he brought his hand up to knock on the wooden door with the number four hanging from a long nail, Morgan's body automatically tensed. Within moments, the door opened a crack, and a pair of brown eyes stared back at him.

"Yes?" The voice was cautious, yet gruff.

"I was told you have the last bottle of Gibbons Red Eye. I'll give you five dollars for it."

"You made a mistake, gringo."

Damn! Morgan knew Frank had said this hotel,

and he was sure the room number was correct. Not wanting a confrontation, Morgan followed his first instincts and touched the felt brim of his hat in the form of an apology. "My mistake, senor," he said, before turning away and walking down the hallway.

From behind him, he heard a vaguely familiar voice. "Hey, hombre . . . I only got tequila. From what I remember in Natchez, you don't handle that any better. I can still see you puking your guts—"

Morgan swung around and a wide smile replaced the scowl. "Mano! Why, you sorry-looking son of a bitch! I don't believe it!"

Emmanuel Estevez threw back his head and laughed as Morgan quickly retraced his steps. Mano opened the door to his room wider, and the two of them walked in. Quickly, Morgan flung his bag on the single bed and wrapped the smaller man in his arms. "Goddamn! How many years, Mano? How many?"

Mano slapped Morgan's shoulders a few times before stepping back. Looking into his friend's eyes, he said quietly and sincerely, "Too many, amigo. Too damn many."

Pleasure at seeing his old friend was mixed with shock and, watching Mano pour them both drinks, he asked, "What're you doing here? Last I had heard, you married and settled down in Texas."

Mano handed him a glass filled with tequila. Although Morgan hadn't touched it since Natchez, he accepted the drink and touched Mano's in a silent toast before bringing it to his lips.

"Last I heard was you were some important businessman. Why are *you* here, Morgan?"

He looked into the handsome, Latin face of his friend. "Frank got to you, too, huh?"

Mano shook his head. *"Mierda!* If what he said is true . . . What the hell did we fight so damn hard for?

210

The lousy politicians won't be satisfied until they break this country one way or another."

Morgan cautiously sipped his drink as he looked to the suitcase on the bed. "It's true, Mano. There's enough evidence over there to hang half of Congress."

"Jesus!"

"How're you supposed to get it back to Frank? Grant's going to be up to his whiskers in scandal unless he's warned and warned fast."

Mano put his drink on a table and walked over to the bed. He opened the case and immediately emptied the clothes onto the mattress. When his fingers slid the latch and revealed the hidden bottom, he lifted his head and smiled. "You ever worry, Morgan, why it all comes back so easily?"

"Manolito, I've been going nothing but worrying this entire trip. I'm too old for this game."

Flipping through the papers, Mano whistled. "You've got some pretty important names here. If you think you're too old, guess who I'm to deliver these to?"

Morgan shook his head.

"Hogan."

Now Morgan's head jerked back in surprise. "Why the hell would Frank have him in on this?"

Mano shrugged. "Guess he wanted the old team together again. We did some good work, the three of us."

Morgan looked away and ran his thumb over one side of his mustache. "Yeah. But I'd always thought Hogan was out of the picture. Truthfully, I'd hoped he was dead."

Mano studied the face of his friend. He'd known that Morgan always blamed Hogan for leaving him and Billy behind enemy lines, but he'd hoped he would have left it in the past. "Mike Hogan must have the angels on his side, Morgan. Heard he's turned mean as hell. I'll be glad when I see the last of him in San Francisco. Listen," he said, as he picked up the bag from the bed and joined his tall, pensive friend, "I'm to put this in a box at Wells Fargo until I leave. Come with me, and then we can go somewhere and catch up on old times. I have a feeling you and I will be doing some heavy drinking tonight, and, gringo, we both know you can't handle what's in your hand now."

Morgan looked down at the tequila and then at his friend, a man who had proven his friendship many times in the past. Smiling, he said, "If I remember correctly, amigo, I wasn't alone that night in Natchez. I had a friend who was so drunk, first he embarrassed himself with the ladies and then joined me in the street. Mano, you and I were holding up the side of that cathouse like it was glued to our backs."

They laughed together briefly before Mano challenged him. "Come, old friend. Let's see if you've improved over the years."

Morgan watched him open the door and, smiling, he put down his drink and left the small room, eager for the coming night.

"Morgan, before we get too drunk to remember, Frank asked me to talk to you." Mano put both his elbows on the table and leaned closer.

Morgan tensed. It was a scene that had been played out many times in his past. More than once, Frank had used Mano to convince him to take on another job. But that had been during a war and the convincing hadn't been that difficult. Now, things were different. Looking around the dimly lit bar, Morgan took a deep breath. "Forget it, Mano. For me, this

212

job is finished. I'm going home."

Mano's mouth slowly broke into a wide grin. "Ah, amigo. I think I know you too well. You wouldn't want to leave a job without wrapping it up."

Morgan sipped his drink and put the glass back onto the table. He looked at his friend and wondered why the hell he had returned to this work. Emmanuel Estevez had always been an enigma, of sorts. He had first met Mano when he was no more than twenty-two. Morgan knew he'd been sent East to study. His father, a wealthy Spanish rancher, had decided his son would learn about America by living with its greatest minds. Senor Estevez hadn't counted on his son's dropping out of school and joining the Union army, though. But Morgan knew Mano had done it for more than adventure. The two of them had spent countless hours together and, in the early period of that relationship, Mano had revealed his fierce possessiveness of his new country. His father had fled to the United States from political corruption and intrigue, and Morgan remembered his friend telling him that his family's hopes, as well as finances, were tied to it. Compared to Spain, Mano had described America as a child, an innocent child, that could be influenced to achieve greatness or, under the wrong guidance, fall prey to the greed and power of a corrupt few. And then, there was his Latin sense of honor. America was his home now.

Mano lifted his chin. "You are deep in thought, yet you haven't even heard me out. Aren't you even curious to know what I've been doing on this end?"

Morgan crossed his arms over the edge of the table and leaned into the space that separated them. "You've been conducting your own investigation? Why the hell does Frank keep everybody in the dark?"

Mano smiled. "Didn't he always? You know the rules. If one of us gets in trouble, the others are safe . . . and the information gets back to Washington. Did you expect he would have changed?"

Morgan took a thin cigar from his breast pocket and lit it. Blowing out a long trail of smoke, he shook his head. "Tell me what you've got."

For the next thirty minutes, Morgan listened to his friend's revelations. It seemed the Central Pacific was into as much as the U.P. The Central Pacific had its own version of the Credit Moblier. It was called the Credit and Finance Corporation, but it was held even more closely than the Credit Moblier. The big four of California—Stanford, Huntington, Crocker, and Hopkins—kept this golden goose all to themselves. He found his temper rising when he thought of what a handful of greedy men were doing to this country. Americans were still glowing with pride over the completion of their transcontinental railroad, and it was a real positive step toward healing after the years of war.

"Nobody knows exactly how much they got away with. Estimates are in the hundreds of millions. Much of it was given away to congressmen, neatly tucked away in the pockets of the U.P. and C.P." Mano ran a hand through his hair in frustration. "From what I gathered, and from the little I read of your information, these two holding companies, along with Congress, have stolen this railroad right out from under the American people. I want to see those bastards shamed publicly."

Morgan ordered another drink. "The game doesn't change, Mano. Just the players."

The smaller man nodded. "But here we are again, Morgan. Trying to stop them."

Morgan quickly shook his head. "Not me. I told

you. I'm out of it."

Mano ignored his statement. "I told Frank, and now I'll tell you. There's some whispers right now about the large amounts of payroll that leave this city for the silver mines in Nevada. You and I both know the kind of people this job puts you in contact with. Talk is that pretty soon that shipment won't reach Carson City. I've heard some say it's an inside job. Frank wants to know if it's planned by an independent, or if the railroad, itself, is in on it. He thought you'd be better than me because you're a new face."

Morgan was angry. "Where the hell does he get the right to play with our lives like this? We're not in the army anymore. If he still wants to keep his fingers in the game, why not recruit someone new? Damn, Mano, it's been five years! I've seen enough from Bull Run in '61 to Wilderness in '64. Enough to last me a lifetime. I don't want it anymore."

"And you think I do, *mi compadre*?" He didn't expect an answer. Instead, he asked another question. "Do you find it easy to tell the ones that saw action during the war? I do. It's the eyes, Morgan. They look back at you with the eyes of old men. Just like yours a minute ago."

Blue eyes shot forth a glare that was easily deflected by a pair of warm brown ones. "How long have you had the nightmares?"

Morgan stared at him. Despite the steady consumption of liquor, his throat felt dry. Seeing Mano after all these years had thrown him, and his emotions were too close to the surface. In a cracked voice, he said, "Three months. Ever since I started out from Baltimore."

"Then you're lucky. My ghosts have been visiting for the last two years."

Morgan's face showed his surprise. "You too?"

215

Mano smiled back at him before ordering two bottles: whiskey for Morgan and tequila for himself. Watching the pretty, dark-haired barmaid place the bottles on the table and walk away after giving him an inviting look, he asked, "Remember in the hotel room you asked why I was back into it? Well, my wife died giving me a son. This country will be Ramon's one day, if the greedy bastards don't have their way. And I also do it for my ghosts, my fallen warriors. I must find a way of putting them to rest."

Neither man said a word. When looking into the other's eyes became too painful, Morgan cleared his throat and said quietly, "So tell me, amigo, what have you heard about this payroll shipment? But tell me fast, before I change my mind."

Five years slipped away, and the two friends, two ex-spies, two hardened soldiers, sat across from one another like it was yesterday.

Three hours later, Morgan watched the woman as she came across his hotel room. She'd said her name was Maxine and that she was French. Morgan didn't care what she claimed to be, though her accent sound more like it came from the mountains of Arkansas than the Pyrenees. He was so drunk he didn't even want her to talk. All he needed was her body. He needed her to wipe Jenna from his mind.

Maxine equaled Jenna in beauty, only exactly the opposite. Where Jenna was tall and graceful, Maxine was short, with softly rounded curves. Jenna's shoulder-length blond hair was replaced with dark brown curls that reached the waist, and Jenna's eyes—those lovely blue eyes that reached down inside him and brought up feelings of protection, adoration, and passion—those, too, were changed to light-brown ones that, surprisingly, he now discovered couldn't even stir up his lust.

He must be exceedingly drunk if he didn't want the lovely Maxine. Thinking about that witch in Verdi had robbed him of his manhood. Pleading exhaustion and overindulgence, he paid her and had enough wits about him to send Maxine down the hall to Mano. Knowing his friend's appetite from the past, he knew Mano would welcome the extra partner and appreciate her far more than he ever could tonight.

When he was alone once more, Morgan hid his money under the mattress and put his gun under the pillow. He didn't even bother to undress as he threw himself across the bed. Behind his closed lids, he saw Jenna, giving more of herself than any woman before her ever had. Or maybe, it was the first time he'd allowed a woman to enter his private void, that part of him he had thought was lost; the part he now feared that only Jenna could fill.

Chapter Seventeen

Jenna was furious. On her way home from work, she'd been stopped by Bill Drayton, president of Verdi's only bank, asking her to come in and sit down at his desk. There, in the quiet of the small establishment, he explained that Morgan had opened an account in her name, and he needed her signature on some documents. She hadn't said a word as she watched him slide the papers across the desk, and her mind was in a state of confusion as she tried to read them.

Quickly, she scanned the documents until her eyes reached the bottom where a space was provided for her name. Only, under that space it was another that was neatly printed: Jenna *Trahern!*

"Has Mr. Trahern also opened an account for himself?" she asked in a tight voice.

Bill Drayton straightened in his chair and smiled. "Why, yes. He transferred a sizable amount from his bank in Baltimore." Looking somewhat more serious, he added, "Though, I'm sorry to say that before he left town, he transferred most to a bank in Sacramento. Have you any idea of when he'll be back?"

Jenna felt as though she'd been punched in the

stomach. *Left town!* Dear God, he was *gone?* And he never even thought to say good-bye!

"Mrs. Trahern?"

Jenna frantically searched for composure. She found her breathing was heavy as she stuttered, "Ah . . . no. He's . . . he's away on business. I'm . . . ah, I'm not sure when he'll be back."

The bank president looked as uncomfortable as Jenna. "Well then, if you'll just fix your signature to those papers, I'll see that the account is opened to you."

Jenna stared at the papers, at the man, then again at the papers. "I . . . can't! Not now. I'm sorry."

She stood up and Dayton rose with her. "Mrs. Trahern! You must sign, otherwise you won't be able to withdraw."

Jenna was desperate to get away. Shaking her head, she literally ran out of the bank and down the street. Within less than two minutes she was on the path that led to the Eberly farm. She didn't slow down, just kept right on running, her mind devoid of anything except reaching the privacy of her room. She couldn't even acknowledge Willow's called greeting across the yard as she struggled with the burning in her throat and in her lungs. Mostly, it was the tremendous shattering of her heart that rendered her speechless.

As soon as Jenna shut the wooden door behind her, she leaned up against it for support. Closing her eyes tightly, she gasped for air.

How *could* he? Pay her off as if she were some cheap whore he'd had for the night! No, she angrily corrected herself. Not cheap. Not if she'd read the figure written on the document correctly.

Opening her eyes, she rushed to the pitcher of water and poured herself a glassful. Gulping it down without taking a breath, Jenna collapsed onto the bed.

Five hundred dollars for sleeping with him! Or, maybe, he'd thrown in something extra for saving his miserable life; or for cooking for him, cleaning up after him, washing his lousy clothes; Worrying, night and day, about his health, whether he was happy or not. He didn't even have the decency to fire her in person. Oh, no. Like some disobedient servant, she was given her severance pay and her walking papers. And he let a stranger do it!

The water must have replaced the moisture in her body for she could feel a steady stream of tears sliding down her cheeks. Why hadn't he just slapped her in the face before he left? What he'd done was much more cruel—to silently slip out of her life. But, he couldn't even do that cleanly. He left behind reminders. His damn money!

Five hundred dollars! That son of a bitch had watched her work her fingers to the bone and all the time, he'd had money! She thought herself three times a fool for questioning her feelings for him. In the last week, since he'd left her alone, she'd actually considered going to him and apologizing for their fight. Apologizing! And he wasn't even in town!

Well, she wouldn't touch his conscience money. It could rot in that bank for all she cared. No. Better yet, she'd wait awhile, and let him think she was using it, then, have Drayton transfer the whole amount back to him in Baltimore. Let him wonder how she was surviving without his payoff.

Feeling somewhat better, Jenna wiped her face on her arm and sat up. Looking about the room, she realized that she was truly all alone. While she had thought Morgan was in town, she hadn't been completely on her own. No matter what he'd done, no matter how she'd hurt him, they shared a strong bond. No two people could go through what they had without giving it a second thought. But then, Jenna always judged other people's feeling as if they were own.

She wasn't going to be stuck here forever. Someday, somehow, she knew she would be taken forward to her own time. The man, the right man, was in the next century, and it was almost comforting to know that as of right now, why, he hadn't even been born.

Perhaps she just needed Morgan as a diversion, to take her mind off the incredible, insane situation she found herself in. Even mentally, it sounded hollow and untrue. Plunged once more into depression, Jenna left the bed and found her purse. Coming back, she dumped the contents on the mattress and, searching through the mess, she found what she was looking for.

Almost reverently, she held her last cigarette in her hand. She'd lost track of how many days she'd gone without one. She'd been keeping this for an emergency, a time of real need. Picking up her lighter, Jenna knew this was it. It was a time of endings. Finally, she will have stopped smoking, and, now, Morgan was out of her life. Maybe someday the pain of his departure will be as easily forgotten as her dependence on cigarettes. She didn't think so.

Inhaling deeply, Jenna was shocked at the immediate dizziness that accompanied smoking. Slightly nauseated, she blinked a few times before trying again. This was her last cigarette for God knows how long! It should be better than this! Disgusted by the very taste of it, she was staring at the crumpled cigarette when she heard the frantic calling of her name.

"Jenna! Jenna!"

Quickly, she wiped her face and ran her fingers through her hair as she rose from the bed.

221

"Jenna!"

First, she cleared her throat, before shouting through the door, "I'm coming. I'll be right there."

Plastering a smile on her lips, Jenna took a deep breath and pulled open the door.

Jace stood with his hands on either side of the rough molding, an excited look on his face. "Guess who just pulled into town?" he asked secretively.

Her heart lurched, her stomach tightened, and she found she could barely get out the words. "I don't know. Who?" Please God, she prayed, let it be him.

Walking past her into the room, Jason abruptly turned around. "The Randolph Ames Theatrical Troupe! Can you believe it? Here, in Verdi!"

Her shoulders sagged as she stared at him. "Who?" she asked in disbelief—and disappointment.

"The Randolph Ames Theatrical Troupe. They're a bunch of actors, and they're putting up posters all over town. Surprised you didn't see any of them when you were walking home. It says they're doing something called *Macbeth*. You ever heard of it?"

Jenna shook her head, still not believing what she was hearing. *"Macbeth?* Here in Verdi?"

"They're putting up a big tent just outside of town. Daegal and even Cheney, are shutting down the mills tomorrow night so everyone can come. This is the biggest thing that's ever come to Verdi, since the railroad. I can't wait. I've never been to a play. Have you?"

Thinking of some wonderful nights at the theater in Philadelphia and New York, Jenna nodded. "As a matter of fact, the first play I ever saw was outside. I guess I was only twelve or thirteen, but I remember not caring that the mosquitoes were biting me, or that it was terribly humid. I was too wrapped up in what was taking place on the stage."

"What did you see? *Macbeth?*"

Jenna laughed. "No. It was called *Inherit The Wind*." She watched as Jace sat down in the chair and, realizing that he expected her to explain, she ambled to the bed and lowered herself onto its edge. Taking a deep breath, she said, "It was about a courtroom trial. I remember the man who played the teacher was very good."

Jace leaned forward. "What did he do? Why was he on trial? Did he kill someone?"

"No. He taught Darwin's theory." Knowing Jason had no idea what she was talking about, Jenna carefully said, "He believed that Man is descended from the apes." Seeing his look of confusion, she attempted to clarify her statement. "Animals."

Jace's bottom jaw dropped. "The white man believes that? I did not think he was that smart. Our gods are animals. Would you not want to be as powerful as the gods?"

Jenna shook her head. "The trial I'm talking about hasn't even occurred yet in this time. You can feel superior, Jace. Over a hundred years from now, the white man is still arguing about the origin of Man."

Jason nodded, happy that his Indian ancestors beat out the white man at something. "And this *Macbeth?* Is it also about animals and gods?"

Jenna couldn't help but giggle. "No. It's a tragedy. A sad story about a king and his trusted warriors. One of them, Macbeth, well, he and his wife want the king's throne . . . his power and his lands in Scotland, and they take it."

"How?" Jace interrupted. "Is he not a strong chief?"

"If I tell you, I'll ruin the play. Just be patient and wait to find out for yourself."

Seeing he wouldn't get much more out of her, Jason

leaned closer to Jenna. "Will you come with me? I have yet to tell her, but I'm going to take my mother. She has never seen a play either. She would feel better if you came along."

Jenna smiled into his dark, expressive eyes. "I would be happy to go with you and your mother. Thank you for asking." And thinking about attending a play lifted Jenna's spirits considerably. Morgan was gone, without even saying good-bye, so why should she cloister herself in this tiny room? No, tomorrow night's entertainment was just what she needed.

Heads turned and Jenna, Willow, and Jace were subjected to curious stares as they entered the high canvas tent and took their seats in the back. Jenna could tell Willow was nervous, and she smiled at her reassuringly, before raising her chin and returning a few of the more obvious looks that were directed at the three of them.

"May I say you ladies look lovely? Mind if I join you?"

Jenna looked up and smiled at Dr. Marshall's lined face. "That would be nice." Standing to let him pass in front of her, she whispered, "Why don't you sit beside Willow? That way you can explain Shakespeare, if she has any questions."

Behind his spectacles, Clinton Marshall's eyes sparkled. "How very thoughtful you are, Jenna," he whispered back, a grin appearing on his lips. As he settled himself between her and Willow, Jenna turned her attention to the stage.

The talking stopped, the crowd, almost as one, stretched their necks toward the wooden platform, and an atmosphere of expectancy filled the wide tent.

Almost as if it were payment for their good behavior, the play immediately started, and Jenna grinned with anticipation. Done correctly, *Macbeth* was one of the greatest tragedies, swift and dark, with death and battle and witchcraft bound together in wonderful poetry, spinning one into the story of a man and woman who destroyed themselves. That's the way it should have been. What came across to her was a comedy. It wasn't just the whispers of a member of the audience who swore one of the witches was his mother-in-law he'd left back in Kansas, it was more the actors themselves.

She had to bite the bottom of her lip not to laugh out loud as she listened to Shakespeare with a heavy, southern accent: *"Faiah is fowul, and fowul is faiah. Hovah throu the fowg and filtha aiwr."*

No one but her seemed to think it was outrageous, and Jenna tried to stifle the surging giggles that crept up her throat. She had to close her eyes when the witches hailed Macbeth. Maybe if she didn't see it, it wouldn't seem so bad. But she had forgotten the words of the honorable Banquo who asks if there is any more to the prophecy: "If you can look into the seeds of Time, And say which grain will grow and which will not, Speak then to me . . ."

Jenna wanted to shout her request. Tell me! Look into the seeds of my time, she mentally screamed. Show me how to get back to it! But the moment passed as quickly as the end to the scene, and she chastened herself for falling back into self-pity. Instead, she returned her attention to the stage and decided to enjoy every mispronounced line.

It wasn't more than five minutes before Jenna realized that no amount of concentration was going to help her and her case of silent giggles. Lady Macbeth did her in, long before she got around to good King Duncan. To put it kindly, she was no Dame Judith

Anderson. Looking sideways, Jenna glanced at her companions. All, but her, were held in rapt attention; their eyes riveted to the stage. Jenna felt like she was in church, and the need to let loose with laughter was unbearable. Not wanting to spoil the play for the others, she crossed her arms over her chest to contain the threatening chuckles while silently making her way to the opened flap of canvas.

Once outside, she let her peals of laughter be carried away with the heavy wind. It felt good to laugh again, and she was just sorry that it was at someone else's expense.

"I think Shakespeare would agree with you."

Jenna spun around at the sound of his voice.

"Morgan!"

She could barely believe her eyes. Through the blown-up dust, she watched him walk closer to her.

"How are you, Jenna?"

He had no right to look so handsome, so casually male. His hat was low on his forehead, braced against the wind, yet she could see his blue eyes clearly as they swept up her skirt and blouse and finally settled on her face.

"What are you doing here? I thought you'd left."

He smiled. "I was away on business. And now I'm back."

She could feel her heart opening to him, her body invisibly being drawn toward his, and she had to grind her heels into the ground to stop herself from closing the space between them. "Well, maybe you'd better go back to wherever you came from, Mr. Trahern. And you can take your money with you!"

She was proud of herself. It took every ounce of willpower to tell him to leave. "If you'll excuse me, I should be getting back inside." Jenna walked past him and was congratulating herself on her control when his hand shot out and stopped her.

Looking at her arm, she heard him say, "We're back to *Mr.* Trahern, I see. Should I be calling you Mrs. Trahern, then?"

Jenna almost growled. "Go away, Morgan."

"Ahh, now that's much better," he whispered, as he quickly gathered her into his arms. "I missed you, too, Jenna."

"Ha! What you missed is someone to take care of your clothes, cut your hair, and give you a proper shave." Looking at the heavy growth of whiskers on his face, she asked sarcastically, "When *is* the last time you shaved?"

Morgan chuckled, relishing her provocative squirming within his arms. "About a week ago. I was waiting for you to do it."

Hating the betrayal of her senses as they again responded to his hard body, she forced herself to say, "Well, if that's what you've been waiting for, be prepared to be tripping over it. I'm through being your barber." Pushing at his chest, she demanded, "Let me go. I have to go back."

Morgan merely tightened his hold, bringing her closer. "Do you like Shakespeare that much? You're really going to sit through that?"

Jenna stopped struggling. She wouldn't look into his eyes, afraid that he would see the desire in hers. Studying his throat, she said, "Yes. Anything would be better than being here with you."

Morgan refused to be angered, and Jenna felt relieved when he removed one of his arms, but her release was short lived as she watched him lift her chin up to his face.

"Look at me, Jenna. Are you afraid?"

Defiantly, she raised her eyes to his hoping they showed disgust. "Now, why would I be afraid of you,

Morgan?"

"Because of this . . ." And without any further warning, he quickly brought his mouth down on her opened, shocked one.

She didn't fight him; she didn't have the strength or the willpower. Honesty was stronger than deception, and Jenna willingly gave herself over to the sweet, yet powerful kiss that seemed to go on forever.

It was Morgan who broke the spell. Pulling back from her, he whispered against her lips, "Let's go home, Jenna."

She tried to fight his mastery over her. Burying her face at the base of his throat, she managed to get out, "You don't live there anymore, remember? And anyway, I have to go back inside."

"You want Shakespeare?" he asked, a note of disbelief in his voice.

Not trusting herself to speak, Jenna merely nodded. What did she care about Shakespeare? It was Morgan that she needed to get away from. A few more minutes and she would be lost, her resolve swept away with the wind, like the tendrils of hair floating about her face.

When he started, she could feel the timbre of his voice as it came up from his chest. If she weren't so shocked, she would have laughed.

Fondling, she saith, since I have hemm'd thee
    here
Within the circuit of this ivory pale,
I'll be a park, and thou shalt be my deer;
Feed where thou wilt, on mountain or in dale:
Graze on my lips; and if those hills be dry,
Stray lower, where the pleasant fountains lie

Her breasts began to ache for his touch. She could

228

visualize his hungry mouth upon them. So moved by his recitation, Jenna slowly lifted her head and whisperingly finished the passage:

> Within this limit is relief enough,
> Sweet bottom-grass, and high delightful plain,
> Round rising hillocks, brakes obscure and
>   rough,
> To shelter thee from tempest and from rain:
> Then be my deer, since I am such a park;
> No dog shall rouse thee; though a thousand
>   bark.

Overwhelmed by the erotic imagery of their words, Morgan could only stare into her vulnerable blue-gray eyes.

"Did you think you were the only one who had ever read *Venus and Adonis*?" she asked in a small voice. "That happened to be one of the most memorized and quoted passages of my freshman year at college."

He leaned into her and kissed the tip of her nose. "You continually amaze me. Let me take you home, Jenna. It's your turn to be amazed."

Chapter Eighteen

She couldn't help but laugh. "So now, on top of every other conceited thing you've said and done, you're amazing, too?"

Morgan lifted his head and smirked down into her eyes. "I'll leave that opinion up to you," he quipped. "C'mon, Jenna, let's not stand here in the middle of a field and let the wind blow at us, when we could be very comfortable in our room."

She pulled out of his arms. "Our room? Since when did it regain that title? If I remember correctly, it was you who left it, so that makes it *my* room."

Morgan took a deep breath and eyed her with speculation and guarded impatience. "All right. May I take you back to *your* room?"

The old annoyances started to resurface. "Why should you? I think you made it very clear, when you slipped out of town, that communicating with me wasn't very high on your list of priorities."

Morgan bit his upper lip in frustration, while taking a deep breath. "I want to communicate with you *now*. God, I'd hoped you would have cooled off by now. Listen, I can't stand here and argue. I'd rather if the good citizens of Verdi didn't know I'd returned just yet."

Jenna stopped thinking of a quick answer. "Why? Why are you hiding?" she demanded.

Seeing he had her interest, Morgan began to walk away. Not noticing that he was walking in the direction of the Eberlys' farm, Jenna followed. "Why don't you want anyone to know that you're back? What are you up to, Morgan?"

Shrugging off her questions, Morgan entered the woods, and Jenna had an eerie feeling of deja vu. This had all happened before. He leading; her following. "Are you going to tell me or not?" she persisted.

"I will tell you," he threw over this shoulder, "as soon as we get out of this wind." Without another word, Morgan quickened his steps, and Jenna had no choice but to try and keep up. Lifting her skirts over a fallen branch, she looked up to his strong back. She had no doubts as to what Morgan wanted from her once they reached the seclusion of *her* room. The trouble was she wanted it, too. Jenna knew she would have to be very careful or she'd wind up tomorrow morning worse off than before.

As they entered the barn, Jenna stopped him with her voice before he could open the door to her small bedroom. "I don't think we have to go in there. You can tell me here what you've been up to."

As if he didn't hear her, Morgan reached for the latch on the door and walked right in. She stood, fuming at his presumptuous actions for at least a full minute before gathering up her anger and marching in behind him.

"Look, I think you assume too . . ." Her words trailed off as she looked at the array of clothing on her bed. "What have you done?" she asked, with a trace of humor in her voice.

"What I have done, madam, is purchase you something suitable to wear. God, but I'm sick of that skirt."

Jenna touched the drab brown material at her waist and again looked to the bed. Piled on top were silky undergarments, nightgowns, blouses delicately embroidered with fine intricate lace, and skirts—skirts of black, gray, forest green, and beige. But it was the dress that beckoned Jenna. Coming closer, she touched its square neckline. Creamy off-white material was adorned by countless tiny seed pearls arranged in the shapes of delicate flowers and leaves. The full skirt smoothly ended in graceful scallops, and Jenna had a hard time picturing herself wearing the dainty creation after a lifetime of tailored clothes.

"Well?"

Jenna looked up at the man standing patiently by the bed. "I don't know what else to say, except, thank you . . . and you shouldn't have."

Morgan threw his hat on the nearby table. "That's not what I meant. If you think I carted this all the way from Sacramento just for your gratitude, you're wrong. I intend to see you dressed properly. Go ahead, pick something out."

Jenna's eyes returned to the beautiful clothes. She knew she shouldn't accept them, but she was honest enough to admit that she, too, was sick to death of the brown skirt. Raising her fingers to the plain, white cotton of her blouse, she decided it wouldn't hurt to just try something on.

"You choose, Morgan," she whispered, not yet ready to accept the tender feelings that were starting to emerge within her.

"You'll let me choose?" he asked in astonishment.

"Of course. After all, you bought them." Jenna

immediately regretted her words as she recognized the devilish glint in his eyes, and she knew she was in trouble when she saw his hand quickly reach toward the nightgowns.

"This," he proclaimed, as he brought out from under the others a pale-blue flimsy gown with a matching satin wrapper. "I want to see you in this."

"Morgan," she said his name reproachfully. "I meant the other clothes, and you know it."

Offering what was in his hand, he came closer to her. "Now, Jenna. You did say I could choose; this is what I've chosen. Don't disappoint me. I've imagined you in this at least twenty times since I purchased it. Please?"

They looked at each other. His eyes were imploring; hers showed doubt and traces of fear.

What did it matter? Jenna thought. He might be gone tomorrow, or he might stay. She had no idea what his plans were. But it didn't matter. Her body was telling her to stop thinking and start feeling. And God knows, he had awakened something deep within her that couldn't be forgotten. She needed him.

Without saying a word, she took the clothes from his hand and walked into the barn. Her heart was hammering a fast beat, and she tried to block out the whispers of her conscience as she started to undress. She knew it was foolish to do as he asked. She knew what was going to happen. Was it so wrong to want it as much as Morgan? Was she more than a fool for wiping him out of her life and so easily painting him right back in? Did she have no pride? No self-respect?

She shook her head, willing the words to go away, and as soon as she felt the sensuous silk and satin next to her skin, she knew there was no turning back. In her heart, she admitted that she could no more walk away right now than return to the future. A course was already set; fate had brought her to this moment, and Jenna slowly unpinned her hair while stepping forward to meet it.

It took him a moment before he found his voice. Morgan felt the immediate stirrings of arousal and, staring at the doorway, he could only breathe, "My God!"

Jenna was embarrassed yet thrilled at the transformation she saw reflected in his face. She knew the gown clung to her, outlining and revealing even through the satin of her opened robe.

Wetting her lower lip, she watched with a nervousness belonging to a much younger woman as Morgan came closer. He looked into her eyes and smiled.

"I have missed you, Jenna. Let me show you how much."

She couldn't answer him, didn't trust her voice, as a trembling took over her body. By mutual consent, they leaned into each other and, lifting her head, her lips fused with Morgan's. It was soul stirring, breathtaking, as his tongue seared her with its heat, teasing and nipping the inside of her lower lip. Along with her breath, he took all her willpower to resist. She gave of herself freely, letting his lips roam over her. Whatever he kissed, his mustache would dry, and the tingling sensations left her legs weak as he gave her eyes, her ears, her cheeks, and mouth his full attention.

When he found her ear, his tongue laved it, his teeth caressed it, and his hot breath inflamed it. Jolted by the provocative course of his mouth, Jenna didn't think she could bear another frantic assault. "Please, Morgan," she begged. "Please, no more."

He leaned back from her and looked into her face.

"No more? Jenna, this is just the beginning. I've waited weeks for this night," he whispered. "I don't think I can wait any longer."

Without another word, he took her hand, kissing her fingertips before leading her to the cleared bed. Slowly, he removed his clothes, and Jenna found she couldn't tear her eyes away from his arms, his chest, his legs, his manhood—each part of his anatomy that she already knew so well. But it was different this time. This time he wasn't prone on the bed, injured. This time he was standing before her with pride—and passion.

Boldly, she stepped forward and gently kissed the jagged scar at his shoulder. Morgan, moved by her action, buried his face in her hair and he was engulfed in its softness. "Please, Jenna," he whispered. "Let me do it my way. I've dreamed about this night . . . about you . . ."

In silent acquiescence, she brought her head up and offered her waiting lips. Morgan kissed her with a wild hunger, setting her pulse racing, as his fingers moved through the dark blond strands of her hair, down the plane of her neck, and clutched at her shoulders.

Jenna yielded, welcoming his touch, needing him as desperately as he needed her. Eager hands found the hard muscles of his back, the lean contours of his hips, and the firmness of his buttocks. She reveled in the sharp gasp of arousal that escaped his lips as her fingers traveled ever closer to encircle him. Moving quickly, Morgan swept her up in his arms and gently laid her down on the bed. Kneeling over her, his eyes locked with Jenna's. "Night and day I've pictured you like this. You haunt me, *desperada*," he whispered in a husky voice.

Her hands moved to the satin robe. Swiftly, with Morgan's help, she stripped the delicate material from her body. With nothing to separate them, Jenna lifted her arms, and Morgan covered her warm flesh with his own. With an agonizing slowness, he worshipped her from head to foot, and then back again. His course was set, his lips unhurried, as he intimately explored her body. Jenna thought she would go mad from the scratchiness of his beard, the dampness of his mouth, and the soft caress of his mustache as each passed over her sensitive skin in gradual succession.

"Please, Morgan . . . please." She didn't even recognize the begging voice as her own, as she implored him to end her astonishing torture and, weaving her fingers through his raven-black hair, she brought his head up to hers.

"I don't want to stop."

Throaty, deep, his voice filled her mind, making her frantic for complete surrender. "I don't want you to stop," she murmured against his mouth, tasting herself on his lips. And with yielding, welcoming thighs, she cried out to him, showing him how much she wanted him to continue.

Morgan needed no further urging; his own body was screaming for release. Gently, almost reverently, he entered her, and curbing his own raging passions was the hardest thing he ever had to do. But this was the night of his fantasies, a night he had patiently waited and planned for, and he wouldn't hurry its conclusion—for the reality of Jenna was so much better than his frustrated dreams.

Surrounded in her warmth, Morgan moved slowly at first, committing to memory her fragile beauty, her exquisite body, the way she exposed the graceful column of her throat as she dug her head into the mattress and arched her hips to meet his. Never did he want to forget this moment. But it was fleeting; their pace increasing, the wild hunger beginning to devour them.

"My God . . . Morgan!" His name tore out of her mouth as he almost withdrew from her, then delved deeply to claim her as his own.

It was building, coming at first as gentle caressing waves, and quickly elevating to a surging wall of desire. But Jenna steadfastly held back the tide. She would not enter this sea of passion alone. Morgan had brought her to its edge, and she waited for him to join her. Moments later, her control was rewarded, as palm to palm, mouth to mouth, she brought him with her. Together they reached high and dove under the waves, crashing, thrashing, then hurtled to the surface—emerging as one.

It was then, as they drifted, gently floating back to the shore of reality, that Jenna Weldon gave up fighting and became Jenna Trahern.

Lying quietly next to him, she lightly ran her nail over the edge of Morgan's black mustache. She couldn't speak; she was afraid of breaking the spell they had so delicately woven together. She watched as his breathing gradually slowed, felt his heartbeat under her arm as it returned to near normal. He needed a shave, she again observed, though she had to admit the dark growth on his face gave him a rakish, almost dangerous look.

Feeling her eyes on him, Morgan turned his head and looked down at her. He brought his hand up and brushed the hair back from her forehead. "It's going to be hard leaving you, Jenna. You will wait for me, won't you?"

A cold chill washed over her, and Jenna couldn't help the shudder from shaking her body. "You're *leaving? Again?*"

Chapter Nineteen

Reaching for her arms, Morgan tried to bring her back to his side. Appalled by the very thought of his leaving, so soon after making love, Jenna slid away from his grasp and quickly wrapped the satin robe around her.

"Listen to me, Jenna. I was going to tell you about it, but we seemed to have gotten carried away. I'm only here—"

"Carried away? Is that what you call it?" she interrupted, now embarrassed by his nudity. She turned her eyes away and presented him with her back. Spying the beautiful clothes piled high on the table, she asked in a broken voice, "And what are they, Morgan? Additional payment for falling into bed with you again?"

Jenna heard a movement behind her, and she tightened her arms about her chest. Very quickly, she felt his hands on her shoulders, and when he turned her around, she noticed that he had slipped into his jeans.

"If you think that, you not only insult me, but also yourself." Looking deep into her eyes, he pleaded, "Don't ruin what just happened."

Afraid she was only guessing at the emotion she saw in his dark-blue eyes, she pulled back from him and demanded, "Then, just what would you call it? What is all this . . . the money, the clothes, the quick tumble in the bed? Isn't this your way of saying good-bye . . . again?"

He actually looked hurt. "That was no quick tumble, and you know it. I have to finish some work. It's business, Jenna. That's all."

"What business? What are you doing, Morgan?"

Now he looked uncomfortable. "When I met you, outside of Reno, you knew I was on my way to Sacramento on business. I told you how important it was that I get there. Last week, I found out that it's going to take longer than I expected to wrap it up."

Jenna brought her chin up higher. "You still didn't say what kind of business you're engaged in. What are you hiding?"

He gave a quick laugh before bending to pick up his shirt from the floor. "Hiding? Don't be silly. The work I'm doing is confidential, that's all. If I were free to tell you, I would."

"You're some sort of spy, aren't you?"

"You have an overactive imagination," he said without looking at her.

Jenna watched him concentrate on the tiny buttons of his shirt. It was obvious she had touched on something he'd rather she hadn't. Instinct told her she was right, and it gave her the confidence to come closer to him. "Overactive imagination? No, I don't think so, Morgan. I think you're a spy for President Grant."

As soon as the word tumbled out of her mouth, she saw the change in him. What had passed for feigned amusement turned into anger as his face transformed into a hard mask of suspicion. "A spy? Where would

240

you get such an idea?"

Jenna didn't like the look in his eyes, but decided that she was already walking on thin ice and she might as well leap right in. "You told me."

She couldn't believe how swiftly he reached for her. Holding her tightly by the arms, he demanded, "When? Tell me, Jenna. When did I ever say such a thing?"

She was shocked by his reaction and a little frightened. "You . . . you mumbled something when you were feverish. Something about Grant, about politicians ruining everything, and warning the president. You wanted to keep him out of something. Morgan, you're hurting me," she said, scrutinizing his fierce eyes.

She would never know whether the look of disgust was directed at her or himself as he quickly let her go. She watched as he turned around and started pulling on his boots. "Well? Am I right? Is that why you're sneaking around town? Dammit, Morgan, answer me!" she yelled to his back.

She could almost see the anger build in his shoulders as he stood and stamped his foot into his boot. Spinning around he demanded, "What the hell do you want from me? What I'm doing is none of your business, so stay out of it!"

"Stay out of it? These people think I'm married to you. If you're doing something illegal, I'm going to be dragged right down with you. I think that gives me some right to know what you're involved in."

Morgan didn't look at her as he tightened his belt. "Forget it, Jenna. The less you know, the better."

"Ha!" She gave a short sarcastic laugh. "So now you just disappear out of my life? What do I do? Wait to read your obituary in a three-month-old newspaper?"

He straightened his collar, pushed back his hair and looked at her. "I'm coming back, Jenna. What do you want from me? You say you don't to be married, yet you act like a nagging wife. If I could tell you any more about what I'm doing . . . I would. You're just going to have to trust me."

Jenna wrapped the robe around her even tighter, almost as if it could protect her from the hurt she knew was coming. He was going away, and she didn't know when, or even if, he would ever come back. She wanted to plead with him not to leave her again, for she knew in her heart, somehow, he was her link to the future. Instead, because she had never pleaded, or even needed a man before, Jenna let the hurt envelop her, and she turned cold.

"I have never nagged anyone in my life, and I won't start now. You're free to skulk about the country as much as you want, only don't think you can sneak back into my bed."

It infuriated her that Morgan took her words so humorously. Smiling with confidence, he came closer, and she took a step backward.

"I had the distinct impression you welcomed me, Jenna. Since you didn't take our first marriage seriously, would it make you feel better to have a second one?"

Jenna stopped backpedaling. The audacity of the man! She glared into his laughing eyes and stood her ground. "Don't flatter yourself. Why would I want to be *married* to you? Believe me, Morgan, I can't think of a worse fate."

"Then you'd agree to be my mistress?" he asked, surprised.

The words tumbled out before she could stop them. "Even that would be better than being your wife. I can't imagine you and I spending the rest of our lives together. Of course, the way you're going, I'm sure I would be a widow before too long."

"You don't want to be married?" he asked, shocked that he had actually offered and she had refused.

Looking at the expression on his face gave Jenna satisfaction and the confidence to walk around him. Reaching the stove, she struck a match and waited for the coffeepot to heat up. "You see, Morgan," she said, keeping busy at the stove, "where I come from, the twentieth century, women don't necessarily have to be married to enjoy sex. The freedom you men have enjoyed and abused for centuries has now been given to the women. Hopefully, we'll be more responsible than you've been. It's *our* choice when and with whom we go to bed."

"We have that now, Jenna," he said in a tight voice. "Only there's an exchange of money beforehand. Would you prefer cold cash next time?"

Her hands had a life of their own, and one of them instinctively hurled the empty tin cup at his head. "You bastard!" she screamed. "Get out of here! There won't be a next time!"

Easily deflecting the cup, Morgan came forward and picked up his hat. "I wouldn't wager money on that. I'll be back."

"Why? There's nothing here for you." She would not cry. She wouldn't let him see how his words cut into her very soul.

He stopped at the doorway and turned back to her. "Why?" he asked, with that infuriating grin back on his face. "Because there're two things you and I do well together: argue and make love. It'll be up to you, Jenna, which of them we engage in when I return."

* * *

She spent the next week in a near daze. At work, she couldn't concentrate, going over columns of figures two and three times to make sure she hadn't made a mistake. When she returned home, Willow and Jace would invariably ask her to share their supper, and she was tired of making excuses to be alone. The worst thing that could have happened, did. She, who had always prided herself on her independence, found herself staying awake at night, waiting for Morgan to return. It took three sleepless nights with the chair wedged in front of the door to admit she now wanted him to show up. Four days ago, she had taken the chair down.

The simple act of removing the chair was a monumental step in admitting that she was taking down all her emotional barriers as well. During those sleepless nights, listening for the sound of his return, she confessed that the attraction she felt toward Morgan was more than sexual. She wanted all of him, his humor, his strength and, most of all—his trust. She was afraid to label what she felt as love. The emotion was too foreign.

"Where are you?" she whispered in a tired voice, as she pulled back the blanket. Preparing to spend another restless night, Jenna climbed into bed and brought the cover up to her chin. She was too exhausted to play the same game of waiting. If he was coming back, he would have shown up by now. She was even too tired to cry.

Closing her eyes, she tried to block out Morgan's handsome face, his tall, strong body, his magical hands, but he continued to intrude into her thoughts. What if he were killed? she thought in panic. What if he were caught spying, and now he was dead? She shook her head to brush away the horrible thoughts. No. She couldn't believe that. The very thought of never seeing Morgan again was unacceptable.

Instead of dwelling on Morgan, Jenna decided to concentrate on anything else. Perhaps then, sleep would come. She thought about the second play the troupe of actors had put on. This time she'd stayed for the entire performance. It was a strange adaptation of *Richard III*, and she'd found that she had enjoyed every minute of it. In the darkened room, Jenna pictured the stage and started giggling again. Some playful, literate lumberjack must have smuggled a jackass into the tent and hidden it behind the scenery. When the poor young man who played Richard sank to his knees exclaiming, "My kingdom for a horse!" someone must have kicked the animal so that it responded with a loud braying and ran across the stage and right through the crowd. After the initial shock, even the actors found it funny, and soon the play continued as if nothing had occurred. When it was over there was a small farewell party for the traveling actors, and the entire town took part.

It was there that Jenna again met Swede, the tall blond giant of a man who had brought Morgan out of the woods. He kept introducing her to his friends as Mrs. Trahern, and the strain of smiling was almost unbearable. Then he'd asked to walk her home, since he was leaving for the logging camp the next day and her husband was absent. Jenna had started to say no and looked around for Jason. Spying him with a young, dark-haired teenager, whom she assumed to be working with the acting troupe, Jenna decided to let him stay with the girl and had accepted Swede's offer.

All the way back to the Eberlys' farm, he'd treated her with the utmost respect. He'd "ma'amed" her at least fifty times before Jenna realized he was nervous at being with what he considered a rare find: a good woman.

245

Now, lying in the dark, Jenna didn't feel like she deserved the title. The thoughts that ran through her head and the desire that coursed through her body were anything but good. She had a wanton craving for a man who was wrong for her. He was involved in something shady; he used her when it was convenient for him; he evaded the truth. Yet, he also made her come alive as no other had before, and she threw the cover from her now hot body as she again whispered in anguish, "Where *are* you, Morgan Trahern?"

At that moment, Morgan Trahern was sitting in a darkened corner of a bar in Sacramento, waiting to see who would join the three shady-looking fellows he had trailed for two days. Mano had put him on their track, and the three had led him on a merry chase, all over eastern California, only to wind up right where it all began.

Now, leaning back against the wall of the saloon, Morgan brought the darkened ale to his lips and thought of all the time wasted, when he could have returned to Jenna. Just her name brought a smile to his face, and he wiped away the frothy foam from his mustache as he pictured her in her anger. Damn! She sure could get her feathers riled, and she had the uncanny knack of saying just the wrong thing to him. Comparing herself to a whore! When she started that crazy talk of being from the future and choosing her own lovers, he'd come close to slapping her in the mouth. She'd just insulted herself, and *he'd* wanted to defend her. Now, he knew it was all talk, another way to get to him. She respected herself too much to try anything like that. And if she didn't, well, he'd rather not entertain swinging from a rope—because he'd kill the first son of a bitch who tried to take his place in her bed.

He admitted he missed her. Hell, he could feel himself growing excited just thinking about her. It was a week, seven days, since he'd held her in his arms, and he couldn't wait to see who the bastards were waiting for, because as soon as the ringleader showed up, he was heading back to Verdi, back to Jenna.

He already regretted that it would only be another short trip. The Virginia City payroll was scheduled to go out this week, and it was up to him to stop what he was now sure was its planned robbery. From the past few days he knew the three sorry-looking men across the room were too stupid, too unorganized to plan something of this size. Someone else, someone with brains and inside information, was behind it all. Once they were caught in the act, Mano and the local authorities would take over, and he and Jenna would be on their way back to Baltimore.

Oh, he knew she'd fight him, but he didn't care if he had to gag her and tie her up, he wasn't about to leave her behind. She'd gotten under his skin, made herself a very important part of his life, and if he had to take her to the best doctors in the country, he was going to make her stop her talk of being from the future and be content with staying here, in the present, with him.

Bringing the mug back up to his mouth, Morgan's arm stopped in midair. His eyebrows came together, and he held his breath as Harry Bullmason walked into the bar. He watched as the heavyset man looked about the square room before spying Morgan's three suspects and making his way over to them.

"I'll be damned!" Morgan barely breathed aloud. Harry Bullmason! He would never have given the bastard credit for such intricate thought. He smiled evilly, thinking how much he was going to enjoy giving

247

Harry his due. He had his own score to settle with the crooked train conductor. His smile widened when he thought of how Jenna would enjoy the irony of it. Here he was about to pay back Harry Bullmason in spades, and he knew just how to do it. He couldn't wait to approach him. But that would have to wait until tomorrow. What remained of tonight belonged to his *desperada*.

Never had her dreams been so vivid. Never before could she actually feel Morgan's touch, smell his masculine scent, hear his heavy breathing. Moaning softly, she let her dream image of Morgan cup her breast while feathering the side of her face with gentle kisses.

"You had better be moaning for me, Sleeping Beauty," he whispered into her ear, lightly biting her lobe.

Following the shivers of delight, as his breath traveled straight from the small channel of her ear to settle in her belly, Jenna opened her sleepy eyes and was able to make out Morgan's face before her.

Immediately, she was awake. "You've come back?"

Kissing the tip of her nose, he asked gently, "Did you ever doubt I would?"

Not giving her a chance to answer, Morgan captured her mouth in a hungry, wild kiss, and Jenna never thought of struggling, as her arms quickly reached up and took hold of his back. Pressing him tightly against her, she breathed the lie into his mouth, "Never. Just don't expect me to wash your damn clothes . . ."

Morgan chuckled, right before his tongue silenced any further words.

Watching him bring the cover back up onto the bed, Jenna admired his strong body, the way his muscles glistened in the early morning light. She loved him. It was that simple—and that complicated.

She felt frightened, holding the knowledge of her love deep within her. It was insane. How could she love a man who didn't even exist in her own time? What if she were to somehow get back to the future? How could she go on, knowing she'd left Morgan in the past? And what about Morgan? He had never once said that he loved her. He had never even said that he *liked* her. He needed her. Tonight proved that.

She felt his breath at her temple. "You're deep in thought," he said quietly.

Jenna turned her head slightly and looked into his eyes. Dear God, but he was handsome! How could she bear to exist without him? He had become a part of her, as real as an arm or a leg, and when he was gone, her worst fears would be realized—she would be emotionally crippled.

"When are you leaving?" she whispered.

Morgan closed his eyes briefly and took a deep breath. "In a few hours. Let's not talk about me leaving, Jenna. Come closer. Let me hold you for a little longer."

She wouldn't nag, not again. She would take whatever he could give and hold the precious memories close in the lonely hours and days to come.

When she woke, he was gone. Tears welled up in her eyes as she felt his side of the bed, now cold. He must have left hours ago, long before she could have stopped him. The hurt she felt that he would leave without saying good-bye was quickly forgotten, as she admitted that it was better this way. This way he didn't see her cry. She didn't want that. Whatever he was up to, he certainly didn't need her tears. He needed her support. If only he could trust her. Oh God, if only he could love her!

Three nights later, Morgan again woke her from a fitful sleep. It was a night she would always remember. She gave of herself without any reservations, and the term making love had a new meaning for her. She wanted Morgan's pleasure more than her own and spent hours memorizing and then devouring each part of his magnificent body. Looking into his eyes at the last moments, just as the waves started to wash over them, she mentally told him everything that was in her heart. Later, as they both lay quietly, she prayed there would be a time when she could voice her love aloud.

This time she didn't fall asleep, but had to bite back asking him to stay as she watched him get dressed.

"Do you know how long you'll be gone?" she asked in a quiet voice.

Morgan looked up from buttoning his pants. Damn! he thought, but she's beautiful. He wanted nothing more than to jump back in bed and make love again. This time long and leisurely. But he was too close now. He had Bullmason just where he wanted and in few more days, he and Jenna would have all the time in the world. Only one thing bothered him, and every time he thought of it, it made him physically ill. What if Jenna got dragged into this somehow? What if they used her against him? It was one of the reasons he'd come back so soon, when he should have been in Sacramento, getting ready.

"I'm sorry. What did you say, Jenna?"

"I asked how long you'll be gone."

"Not more than three days, four at the most," he replied absently, as he buckled his holster and tied the

250

thin rawhide strips around his upper thigh. "Listen, Jenna, I brought you something," he said as he picked up a gun from the table and brought it to her. Sitting on the edge of the bed, he held it out. "Here, I want you to have it."

She stared at the huge pistol, then looked up into his eyes. "Why?" she asked in a shocked voice.

Morgan took her hand and laid the cold metal inside it. "For your protection. Look, you probably won't need it, but I'd feel better knowing it was here."

The gun felt heavy in her hand. And deadly. "But why? Morgan, I don't even know how to use it."

He grinned. "I seem to remember you using it once before. Just do the same thing again." He kissed her briefly and stood up. "I have to go. I'll be back in a few days. Take care of yourself, beautiful."

He walked to the door, and Jenna stopped him with her voice. When he turned back to her, she was kneeling on the bed.

"Morgan, promise me you'll be careful," she demanded. Whatever he was doing was coming to a close. She could sense it, and she knew his life was in danger.

He put his hat on and whispered, "I promise. Don't worry, I'll be back."

They looked at each other for timeless seconds, each wanting to say important words to the other. In the end, neither could speak. Morgan could only nod his silent understanding. Then he was gone.

Chapter Twenty

Stepping back into the cold morning air, Jenna wrapped the woolen shawl tighter around her shoulders. What she wouldn't give for a warm bathroom instead of the primitive building she'd just left. Even though she'd been here for weeks, she still had a passionate yearning for the modern conveniences she'd left behind.

As she made her way across the yard, her eyes were drawn to a young woman coming out of the Eberlys' door. Jenna stopped as she watched the female walk in her direction. The closer she came, the more Jenna realized that she wasn't a woman at all. Not yet. She looked to be about fourteen or fifteen, and her face was distantly familiar.

"You must be Jenna," she said with a shy smile playing at the corners of her lips.

Still surprised by her appearance, Jenna could merely nod as she stared at the pretty girl. Long brown hair hung down her back and nearly reached her bottom. Her clothes were plain, a smaller version of Jenna's old brown skirt and white blouse, yet the shawl protecting her from the morning cold was a complete contrast. Red and green vines intertwined amid a blue background, while from its edge hung long gold fringe.

"My name's Coral. Coral Nevlins."

Jenna tore her eyes away from the gaudy shawl and looked into the open friendliness of her lightly freckled face. Recovering, she extended her hand and smiled into the girl's expectant brown eyes.

"Actually, my real name's Mary, but I changed that last year," she said after shaking Jenna's hand. "Randy, he was my boss, well, he said Mary was too plain for the stage."

That was it! Coral/Mary was the girl she had seen Jason talking to the night of the farewell performance. "I think they're both lovely names," Jenna commented, looking over her head to the Eberlys' house. "Do you know where Jason is?" she asked, curious to know how the girl came to be on the farm.

Coral looked out to the woods. "He rode off early this morning. He said he had something he had to do."

Looking at the distant hills, Jenna realized she had ignored Jace for the past few days. In her despair over Morgan's erratic visits, she had been completely wrapped up in herself. Otherwise, she would have known about Coral much sooner.

"Are you staying here?" Jenna asked, bringing her eyes back to the girl.

Coral looked to the ground and nodded. "Randy promised I would be an actress, but that wasn't what he had in mind. Jace said I could stay here until I figured out where I wanted to go. Isn't he nice?" she asked, bringing up her head and smiling in girlish innocence. "And he's half Indian. I've never known an Indian before."

Not knowing how to answer her, Jenna just smiled.

253

"Well, I'd better get going," Coral said as she moved toward the outhouse. "Willow said she's going to teach me how to make bread."

Jenna continued to watch her walk away, her mind in a state of confusion. When Coral turned back to her and yelled, "Guess you and I'll be seeing a lot of each other. Nice to meet you, Jenna," she could only raise her hand and wave.

Shaking her head as she approached the barn, Jenna made up her mind that as soon as she finished work, she was going to saddle the horse and find Jason. What the heck was he up to now?

It had taken her less than a half hour to find him. Letting the horse have its way, she relied on the animal to find its mate, and it hadn't disappointed her. Quietly, she dismounted and tied the reins to a nearby branch. As she made her way into a small clearing, Jenna's mouth opened in surprise. With his back to her, in the privacy of the forest, Jason Eberly was practicing drawing a gun that hung low on his hip.

"Jace?"

She said his name softly, not wanting to startle him, but she instinctively ducked when he spun around and pointed the pistol at her head.

"How'd you find me?"

Jenna couldn't take her eyes off the gun, and slowly, thankfully, it was lowered and replaced in a leather holster that seemed too large for him.

She swallowed, trying to bring the moisture back into her mouth. "The horse found you; I didn't. What are you doing with that gun?"

Jason's chin lifted defiantly. "It's time I carried

ne. This was my father's."

"You aren't planning on using it, are you?" she asked, coming closer.

Taking the gun back out, he ran his fingers over the barrel. "I may."

Annoyed with his secretive attitude, his almost sullen voice, Jenna grabbed his arm. "I thought you and I were friends. Tell me, Jace, what are you planning?"

He looked into her eyes and Jenna cringed. Gone was the young, sometimes intense boy. A hard young man had taken his place. "I will tell you, Jenna, because I have kept your secrets. And now you will keep mine." He pulled himself up to his full height and stated, "I am going to rob the Virginia City payroll tonight."

"What?"

He ignored her shocked expression and, with his eyes, defied her to ridicule him. "I think you heard me. Tonight I intend to get my revenge."

When he turned away from her and began to once more draw the gun in and out of the holster, Jenna's patience broke. "You've got to be kidding! You can't get away with it. You want revenge against the railroad and the white man, and you're going to get yourself killed instead!"

Without missing a stroke, he flashed the gun with increasing speed and answered, "I have a plan."

"What plan? How can you possibly expect to stop a train and then rob it? You know it's going to be guarded."

She couldn't believe her ears when he laughed. "They'll let me. Jenna, working in that miserable saloon finally paid off. I heard that conductor, the one that threw you off the train, planning it with three

255

others. They were here in Verdi, yesterday, but I guess they took off for their hiding place. I heard it, Jenna," he proclaimed, with an excited look on his face. "I know just how they're going to do it. Nobody pays attention to a *breed* sweeping the floor."

"You're telling me Bullmason is planning on robbing his own train?" she demanded, an incredulous look on her face. "I didn't think he was that stupid."

He put the gun back in his holster and looked at her. "Stupid? It . . . it's brilliant! They plan to stop the train outside of Hunter. They'll wait for it to refuel and uncouple the engine and express car. When the train takes off, they have the money, and the passengers are left behind. Can't you see it? They'll only have to worry about the engineer and whoever's in the express car."

He was serious. Dear God, he was going to rob the train. "Jace, what about Bullmason and the other men? Surely you don't think they're just going to let you waltz in there and take the money right out from under their noses."

Jason ran his hand over the wide grin that covered his lower face. "I'm going to do it five miles before they expect it. I'll use their plan and be long gone before they even know what happened."

Jenna was furious. She couldn't believe he would get away with such a thing. Switching tactics, she said, "And what about your mother? What's going to happen to her when you're arrested?"

"I won't be arrested. Can't you see it's foolproof?"

She'd had enough and grabbed his arm again. "*Nothing* is ever foolproof. Don't you think every crook has thought the same thing?"

Twisting his arm, he walked away from her. "I'm no crook. You know why I'm doing it."

Placing two shaking hands on her hips, she faced him. "Oh, that's right. I forgot. This is a noble cause, isn't it? You finally get revenge on everyone who's made your life miserable. Well, guess what, Jace? If you ever had a chance at being happy, you're about to lose it. Those men aren't going to let you walk away with that money any more than the railroad will. Can you live like that? Hunted? Always looking over your shoulder?"

"You're not going to stop me, Jenna."

His statement was clear and full of conviction.

She was desperate. "I can tell the sheriff. Ask him to lock you away until this thing is over."

He looked deep into her eyes and ignored the silent plea for reasoning. "You won't do that."

Jenna stared at him for a few seconds before she admitted, "You're right, I won't. I can't stop you. Can I, Jace?"

He tried to smile, then shook his head. "No, Jenna. You can't."

She took him into her arms. She didn't care that he was planning something illegal. All she could think about was a young boy, fighting so many unfair odds, trying so desperately to become a man. Nor could she help the tears as they slid down her cheeks. "Oh God, Jace," she whispered against his hair. "What are we going to do?"

Accepting his role of comforter, he patted her back. "We're going to act normal, that's what we're going to do. Tomorrow, it'll be all over."

Jenna sniffled and, smiling, pulled back from him. "When were you going to tell me about Coral?" she asked in an attempt at lightness.

Jace looked embarrassed as his dark eyes slid away from hers. "She was in trouble. I thought I could

257

help."

Jenna grinned. "She's pretty, don't you think?"

Jason shrugged. "I suppose so," he mumbled. Then, quickly, he looked up at her and smiled. "Yeah. She is pretty."

She laughed and wiped at her eyes. Linking her arm through his, she said, "C'mon, Superman, let's go home."

They were almost to the horses before Jace asked, "Who's Superman?"

Jenna stood outside the stable and stared at Willow's small house. If ever she needed Morgan, it was now, she thought, as she shivered in the late night air. How was she going to stop Jace alone? She'd dressed in her shrunken gabardine split skirt, and tucking the hems into her boots had made them look like pants. She had her hair pinned under Morgan's old hat, yet the most outrageous thing of her disguise as a man was the heavy, cold gun that rested inside her belt.

She fidgeted as she pulled at the tight material that she had used to bind her breasts, making her look almost flat chested. Jenna wasn't sure what she was going to do if she couldn't stop her young friend. Morgan would be able to stop him. Even if he had to knock him out. But Jenna didn't think she would be capable of forcibly restraining Jace. She had to appeal to his strong sense of honor.

"I have seen you watching my mother's home. You aren't going to stop me."

Jenna spun around. "Geez! You scared the wits out of me! Why do you have to walk around like a . . . ah . . ."

"Indian?" Jace offered, then smiled. Walking

around her, he looked over Jenna's outfit. "Why are you dressed like that?" he countered.

Pulling up to her full height, she stated, "I'm going with you."

Even in the dark, Jace looked angry. "You're not going anywhere, but back in your room. If anyone asks where I was tonight, you can say I was with you. If you want to help, that's the way to do it. Not like this." His eyes traveled up her body with distaste.

Where was the young boy who had been infatuated with her? She'd thought if she had insisted on going with him, he'd back down. Instead, he was trying to humiliate her into following his orders. "I won't let you do this alone. You'll get killed. I know something about railcars. I can help."

They stood, face to face, each knowing they were powerless to stop the other. Jace looked at her for the longest time before he spoke. "We'll have to take the horses to the spot I've picked to stop the train. I was going to take both horses and ride one back, but since there's going to be two of us, we'd better leave now. We're going to have to walk back to town and board the train."

Silently, Jenna watched him saddle the horses. What the hell had she gotten herself into? Maybe she could still stop him. There had to be time before they boarded the one o'clock train. If not—Dear God, she didn't want to think about the alternative.

Nothing had gone right. Nothing! We'll both get killed, she thought in a panic, as they crossed the railroad tracks and used the cover of darkness to approach the refueled train. The steam that shot out from under its frame hid her and Jace as they climbed

259

up to the express car. Using makeshift tools, they soon were able to work the coupling pin loose.

"Hurry, Jenna. Uncouple the cars, and then let's get out of here!"

"No . . . no . . ." she whispered, as she and Jace fought with the heavy steel. "We'll place it upside down. Then when the train moves out of Verdi, the passenger cars will come with it. If those cars remained here, somebody would come after the train. If we wait, the vibration of the train will make this come loose in about three minutes, and we'll leave the passengers behind, outside of town, but not able to contact anyone right away."

"Great! You think it'll work like that?"

Jenna looked sideways. "I sure as hell hope so."

Minutes later, she and Jace had hidden themselves amid the firewood in the tender. Jenna found herself barely breathing, her mind refusing to register that she was about to commit a crime. When she heard voices, she thought her heart would surely give her away. She was either hyperventilating or she was having a heart attack! Dear God! Here she was about to rob a train and she couldn't breathe! It was the damn kerchief over her face, she thought irritably. That, and the panic she could feel quickly building up.

Jace must have sensed her fear because his hand found hers, and he gave it a tight squeeze. Mindful not to disturb any of the carefully placed wood, Jenna pulled her fingers out of his grasp just as the train started to move.

They could feel it when the passenger cars became detached. Without the extra burden, the steam engine quickly picked up speed, and moments later, Jace popped up from behind the wood and yelled.

"Stop the train!"

It was hard to tell who was more shocked: the engineer, the fireman—or Jenna.

She automatically stood up when Jace yelled. But she just stood, staring at her young friend pointing his pistol at the two frightened men.

"You ready, Jay?" Jace asked, a nervous tone to his voice.

Jenna nodded. She was about to rob a damn train!

She was astonished to see the two railroad men doing exactly as Jace asked. Weren't they going to fight? Argue? Something?

In the end, it was easier than either Jenna or Jace could have imagined. Jace ordered the engineer to stop at the culvert up the track, and they obliged him without a whimper of protest. When the train came to a complete stop, Jace held his pistol on the men, and Jenna jumped down from the cab and ran to the nearby woods. Within minutes, she located the horses and pulled her tape recorder out of her saddle. Bringing the animals back with her to the edge of the trees, she turned the recorder all the way up and hung it from the pommel. Quickly, she tied the horses to sturdy limbs and ran back to the now hissing train engine.

Jace had the men standing in front of the red express and mail car when she returned. Out of breath, she was aware that the kerchief covering her mouth was waving like a flag with each labored gasp of air that entered, then left her lungs. Trying to control her breathing, Jenna stood next to Jace and stared at the two frightened men. She felt sorry for them and wanted to explain that they had no intention of hurting them. The younger one, the fireman, looked about ready to cry.

"Your gun!" Jace hissed across his shoulder.

"Oh, right. Sorry," Jenna mumbled as she brought out the heavy pistol.

Satisfied that he now had help, Jace looked up to the Wells Fargo Express Car and shouted, "Open that door! I have a gun pointed at the engineer and his man! If I have to, I'll use dynamite!"

Jenna couldn't help the surprised look she shot at Jace. He didn't have dynamite! Nor could she suppress the shocked gasp as the wide door slowly slid open. My God! It was so easy!

Just as Jace motioned for the two men to climb inside, from the woods came a loud shout, *"Open that door. There's more guns out here!"*

Everyone, including the weathered engineer and his shaking assistant, looked at each other in surprise. Over the red kerchief, Jace's eyes showed his chagrin while Jenna merely shrugged. She couldn't help it if the timed recording of her voice was slightly off.

Looking out to the woods, Jenna yelled back in her deep disguised voice, "That's okay, Joe. We got it. Just keep the train covered."

Hoping she had made up for the mistake, Jenna pointed her gun toward the open door. She and Jace followed the men inside, and quickly, the railroad employees lined up next to the Wells Fargo messenger. Seeing the fear in all three men's eyes, Jenna felt she had to speak up.

"Nobody's going to get hurt," she said in a deep voice. "Just do as you're told and we'll be out of here."

"Right," Jace added. "Now, open those treasure boxes."

The nervous express agent looked horrified. "But those are holding the payroll for the Yellow Jacket Mine on the Comstock!"

Jace brought the gun up closer to the man's chest. "Glad to know we stopped the right train. Now get those boxes open."

Jenna kept her gun on the other two as the agent bobbed his head and walked over to the heavy-looking boxes. Within seconds, he had the lid open, and Jace quickly emptied a canvas sack of mail and started dumping the money inside it. Jenna's brain kept hammering out an insistent message. This was wrong. She should run away. Get away before someone gets hurt. But she knew if she followed her woman's instinct, Jace would surely be the one who got hurt. He needed her. Perhaps she could talk. . .

Her breath caught in her throat as a huge arm came over her right shoulder and caught her under her left armpit. She never gave her intruder the time to speak as the self-defense training she had forced herself to learn took over. In a lightning flash, Jenna's left elbow connected with the hard flesh between his rib cage. As she felt him bend over, she quickly grabbed hold of his arm and, using leverage, she gained the advantage and flipped him over her shoulder.

She stood over the guard, breathing like a cornered animal. Her reflexes were accurate, and her nerves were pulled as tight as a string. Picking up her gun, she held it in her shaking hand and, furious that this tall man had almost caught her and Jace, she watched his broad back as he attempted to rise.

He stood with his hands on his knees, trying to get his breath, and as he started to straighten, Jenna put the gun against the inside of his right upper thigh.

"You okay?" Jace stood, his gun in one hand, the sack of money in the other.

Jenna didn't take her eyes off the heavy breathing man in front of her. Even though her hand was still

263

shaking, she kept the gun aimed at his manhood.

"Just breathe too heavy, mister," she growled at him, "and I'll send them right back to your grandfather!"

At her words, the man lifted his head, and Jenna thought her heart would drop to her knees as she stared into angry deep-blue eyes. Familiar eyes. *Morgan's!*

Chapter Twenty-one

He knew her! The kerchief hiding her face did nothing to conceal her eyes, and she could do no more than blink rapidly while swallowing several times in an attempt to bring moisture back into her mouth.

"Let's get out of here!" she screamed in a croaked voice, not even bothering to look at Jason.

"I just got started! Give me a few minutes more," Jace called out to her.

Still watching the horrible fury build in Morgan's eyes, Jenna demanded, "Now! Leave it!"

The gun was still nestled where his long legs were joined together, and Jenna quickly removed it. She wasn't foolish enough to take it off him, though. No words could describe the anger, the rage that she felt coming from her lover's body. Frightened, she backed up.

"I'm getting out of here!" she exclaimed to her partner's back. "Leave the damn money!"

Jace spun around. "Are you crazy?"

"I must have been," Jenna almost sobbed, and indicated Morgan with her head.

Never having been able to see the guard's face, Jace turned his head and recognition was instant. "Damn!"

"Put the bag down and let's go," Jenna ordered, assuming the role of leader. "There's going to be people all over this train in a minute."

The canvas bag dropped from Jace's hand with a loud thud. His shoulders drooped with defeat. Jenna kept her gun on Morgan and the railroad men until she heard Jace jump to the ground. Moving backward, she felt with her hand for the open doorway. Touching the splintered wood, she looked at Morgan and shrugged her shoulders. What could she say?

"Sorry about this, gentlemen," she apologized. "It was all a mistake."

She could hear the horses behind her and, turning around, she didn't even hesitate before jumping onto the animal's strong back. She watched as Jace slid the heavy door closed, then quickly, the two of them dug their heels into the horses' soft flanks.

The wind howled through her hair as Jenna's hat blew off. She never noticed. Her brain was a confused center, sending out partial messages, screamed warnings, and frantic instructions. Only instinct kept her on the back of the horse as the two sped out of the Peavine Mountains and across the valley. She felt as if the hounds of hell were at her heels, waiting to devour her. Morgan! She couldn't believe he was on the train! *Morgan!* His name repeated and repeated inside her head. Jenna knew he would come after her, and she didn't intend to be around to face his wrath. Sighting the Eberlys' farm in the distance, she made up her mind to get out of Verdi tonight! Even that wouldn't be soon enough.

The bitch! She'd held his gun—*his gun*, dammit, against his balls and threatened to blow them away! *The bitch!* The brazen *thieving* bitch! Morgan could never remember being so infuriated, and he tried to bring his temper back under control as the engineer turned to him.

"Do you believe that? They didn't even take the money!"

Morgan didn't answer him. He couldn't. His throat welled up with unsaid curses, and the muscles in his neck hurt from swallowing back frustrated shouts of indignation. Not only had she deceived him, but she'd screwed up the entire case against Bullmason! His heart continued to pound against the wall of his chest; the veins in his neck had not even begun to recede, and his hands began to itch. He couldn't wait to place them on Jenna. She wanted to dress up like a man and play men's games? Well, he was going to teach her the consequences of losing.

A menacing smile appeared on Morgan's face, and he turned his attention to the men inside the cab. "Let's back this train up to the passenger cars. We're returning to Verdi!"

Sliding off the winded horse, Jenna looked up at Jace. "You have to get out of here. Go to your grandfather's. I'll make up some story for your mother. Now, go!"

"What are you going to do? You know he'll come back here. You can't stay either."

Jenna took her recorder off the saddle. "I'm not staying. I'm picking up a few things and then I'm going into town. I'll ask Dr. Marshall to take me in until daylight. When the next train pulls out of town, I'm going to be on it."

Jace didn't move. "Where will you go?"

"Wherever the train's going. We don't have time to talk about it," she said, giving her reins to Jace. "Now, get out of here. Go on."

"Won't I ever see you again? I'm ashamed that I got you into this."

"Of course you'll see me again. I'll come back. I promise. If only to see what happens between you and Coral," she teased. Bringing her fingers up to her lips, she blew him a kiss. *"Go!"*

Her eyes filled up as she watched him disappear into the night. Maybe he wouldn't get into any trouble. They didn't actually take any money. All they'd done was stop a Central Pacific railroad train, break into the treasure boxes, scatter the United States mail and assault their guard. The groan that escaped her lips contained all the frustration of the past three hours. There would be time enough later to berate herself. Right now, she had to gather her few things and get out. She wanted to be long gone before Morgan showed up. Jenna knew this was one night Morgan Trahern wouldn't miss.

After writing a short note to Willow, she ripped the cover off the bed and dumped her clothes onto the sheet. Thank God there wasn't much to pack, only the few things Morgan had bought for her. Morgan! Just thinking his name was painful. It was hard to believe that for the first time in her life she loved someone and had to walk away. It wasn't fair. But then what had been fair since she entered that damned smoking car?

Nothing! She answered her own question while bringing up the corners of the sheet and tying them into a knot. She would be sorry to leave here, she thought in surprise, as she reached for her briefcase and purse. Looking back, it hadn't been too bad. In fact when Morgan was here, it was almost—

"Who are you running from, *desperada*?"

The whisper was soft, yet its tone and its unexpectedness had the impact of a full-blown scream. her briefcase fell from numb hands; her legs felt incapable of supporting her, and she sank to the stripped mattress.

Swallowing a few times as she looked at him lounging against the door, she attempted to speak. "I . . . ah . . . why no one," she managed to get out, aware that her voice squeaked when she spoke.

"No one?" Morgan smoothly asked as he came further into the room. "Not the railroad? Not Bullmason? Not even the sheriff?"

"Morgan, let me explain. You see, Jace—"

"Shut up! When I ask for explanations, you can lie to me then. Right now, I want you to get undressed."

Jenna's eyes opened in shock. "You can't mean . . . Now? My God, you can't be serious!"

Morgan's hand moved to his holster. Slowly, he brought out his gun. "I am serious. And I do mean now. *Get undressed!*"

Jenna blinked a few times in disbelief. "I won't," she emphatically stated.

Morgan brought the pistol up and pointed it at her chest. "You will. You like to play with guns, Jenna. The trouble is, so far, you've been pointing them at me. Now it's your turn. What part of *your* body shall I threaten first?"

Her fingers hurried to the buttons on her shirt. Quickly, she removed it and pulled off her boots. Slipping the gabardine down around her ankles, she was bending to pick it up when Morgan stepped forward and placed the cold, hard shaft of the gun inches away from her thigh.

"How did that go again? Oh yes, *'even breathe too hard and I'll send them back to your grandfather'*. What shall we send to *your* grandmother?" he asked in a deceptively innocent voice. Not waiting for an answer, for he knew she was incapable of giving one, he added in a much angrier tone, "I didn't like it. How does it feel, Jenna?"

The tears started forming, and she realized there wasn't any way of stopping them. "I didn't know it was you, Morgan. I swear! I never would have touched you. I was scared. I thought it was Bullmason who grabbed me, or some guard. What were you doing on that train?" she cried out.

He straightened and brought the gun with him. "What do you know about Bullmason?"

Able to breathe easier, Jenna kicked the shrunken skirt away from her bare feet and wiped her eyes with the back of her hand. "Jace overheard him and some other men planning the robbery. He said he was going to pull it off sooner than Bullmason expected it. I tried to talk him out of it, but he wouldn't listen. I was afraid if he went alone, he would get killed. Where were you, Morgan?" she cried. "If you were here, you might have stopped him."

"You will not turn this around and blame me. You and your young friend committed a crime . . . and now you have to pay."

"What do you mean?"

"Get dressed."

Jenna touched the top of her chemise. "But you said—"

"Don't flatter yourself, madam. The very last thing

270

I want to do is take you to bed." Lifting his foot to the bed rail, he crossed his arms over his raised knee and seemed quite relaxed as he continued to hold the gun on her.

"Put on something decent. Something a *woman* would wear. There's a whole trainload of people in town. As a matter of fact, I wouldn't hesitate to say that there's more than a few people anxiously waiting for you. Do hurry, Jenna. They've already been delayed enough as it is."

"You're turning me in?" She couldn't believe it! "Morgan! We didn't take any money! Nobody got hurt!"

His eyes looked deadly. "You're wrong, Jenna. Jace took three hundred dollars. And somebody most definitely got hurt. Me! I believed in you. *Now get dressed!*"

She walked in front of him, her thoughts in a turmoil. What was going to happen to her when Morgan handed her over? She had grown up with movies and television shows about the Old West. They hung people for stealing horses. They hung everybody for everything, didn't they? What the hell would they do to her?

He made her carry her makeshift baggage, and she shifted the heavy tied sheet over her shoulder. "Listen, Morgan—"

"I don't want to listen. Keep walking."

"But what are they going to do to me?"

From behind her, she heard his voice. "You should have thought about that before you robbed the train, *desperada*."

"Stop calling me that! And I didn't rob the damn

train! I only helped stop it."

Morgan snickered. "Before I was only teasing you when I called you that. Now you've earned the name. That's what you are . . . a bandit, an outlaw. A criminal. Three hundred dollars is missing from the payroll, and you were there. Why Bullmason might even recommend that I receive an award when I come back with you."

She stopped walking and dropped her sack to the ground. Turning around, her eyes widened, and she looked at him with a shocked expression. "I've finally figured it out. You're working for the railroad. You must have known Bullmason was up to something and hired on as a guard. You're angry because Jace and I messed up your plans. You wanted to catch him in the act."

Even through the darkness she could tell his eyes were still angry. "I was hired as a guard by Wells Fargo, not the railroad."

"When?"

"What difference does that make?"

Jenna was insistent. "When?"

"Last week," Morgan sighed, eyeing the dark woods that surrounded them.

"How did you get the job, Morgan? Didn't somebody have to recommend you? Somebody trusted by the railroad?"

"Let's go. You're wasting time."

Jenna's mouth dropped open. "That's it! It was Bullmason wasn't it? Bullmason got you that job!"

Morgan impatiently ran his hand over his mustache. "Pick up your clothes."

Jenna wanted to shake him. "Don't you see? Bullmason planned to rob his own train. As the new guard, suspicion would be directed at you, not him.

He was using you, Morgan!"

He almost smiled at her intelligence, but quickly overcame the urge. Instead, he produced his fiercest scowl and hissed, "Pick up your clothes!"

She reached down and hoisted the sack over her shoulder, not caring if she hit him in the process. "Why are you being so dense?" she demanded, as they resumed walking. "You know I'm right. And now you want to hand me over to that man. He hates me!"

Morgan didn't answer her until Verdi was in sight. Walking down the middle of Center Street, with the sheriff's office on one side and the depot on the other, he stopped.

"I never said I was handing you over to Bullmason. I just said people are waiting for you. You have two choices. One, we walk over to the sheriff and tell him the whole story, including the name of your partner, or, you come to Sacramento with me until this mess is straightened out."

Seeing the hopeful look on her face, he hurried to add, "If you choose to come to Sacramento, you'll come as my wife. Not that I want to claim you as one, but Bullmason thinks you are. If you say yes, you'll play the part of obedient spouse. What I say goes. No arguing. Understand?"

Jenna could barely contain her relief. *She wasn't going to hang!* But she knew Morgan wouldn't stand for it if she were to throw her arms around him and kiss his gorgeous face. In the end, she only nodded, and from then on made a point of keeping her eyes downcast. It wasn't going to be easy. She was sure he was going to make her pay for her misadventure. But right now, anything was better than a hangman's noose. Besides, if she played this right, a few days of

273

sickeningly sweet, obedient wife and, Morgan would be ready to tear his hair out.

Thinking of the role she intended to play, Jenna had to bite the inside of her lower lip to keep from smiling. She knew she shouldn't. Not now. It would be so out of character.

Chapter Twenty-two

The depot was crowded with people standing around talking about the daring attempted robbery. As Jenna walked next to Morgan, she couldn't help overhearing snatches of conversation from the curious townspeople and passengers.

"Pretty smart the way they unhooked the cars. My bet is one of them fellas worked for the railroad."

"Way I hear it, they could've got away scot-free. Just left all that money. Pretty stupid, if you ask me."

Morgan took hold of her upper arm. "Let's go. I've already bought you a ticket."

Jenna held her bundle tighter to her chest, but didn't say a word. She could feel the anger build inside her. So. He'd made up his mind about her *before* he'd surprised her at the farm. All of his threats were to teach her a lesson, and he never had any intention of turning her over to Bullmason. How could he scare her like that?

As they boarded the train, Jenna couldn't help but think about his words. She'd really hurt him this time. Something special had been happening between them. If it hadn't been for the robbery, they might have been able to— She shook her head. What good did it do to remember the last few times they had been together? She'd lost his trust, and it was up to her to regain it. If Morgan wanted to make her pay by forcing her to be subservient, then so be it. She could take it—for a little while.

"You'll sit here," Morgan said, indicating an uncomfortable-looking seat.

Jenna didn't argue. She sat down by the window and placed her tied sheet on the floor in front of her. Straightening, she looked up at Morgan, just in time to see him nod to a dark-haired man standing a few feet away. Immediately, the man came forward and took the seat next to her.

Confused, Jenna questioned Morgan with her eyes.

"This is Emmanuel Estevez. He'll stay here until we reach Clark's Station. I have to ride in the express car and deliver the payroll to the Comstock's agent."

He didn't bother to introduce her to her guard, just touched the man on the shoulder and walked out of the train. From the corner of her eye, she looked at her new traveling companion. His dark, Latin features were definitely appealing, and Jenna imagined that if he ever smiled, he could be downright handsome. At the moment, he sat straight up against the back of the seat with his arms crossed over a leather vest. His expression was solemn, and she wondered if he was allowed to speak.

Within ten minutes, the train was moving, and Jenna stared out the window and into the darkness of night. She'd certainly made a mess out of everything, she thought dismally. At least, Jace got away. *With three hundred dollars!* She honestly didn't think he'd taken it on purpose. He must have stuffed it in one of his pockets before he'd emptied the mail sack. She only hoped he was smart enough not to spend it; she didn't doubt that if even one dollar of that money showed up too soon, he'd be caught.

Jenna continued to watch the darkness outside her window. She didn't even know what time it was. It had to be somewhere between three and four in the morning and, just guessing at what was in store for her, she made up her mind to shut out the gossip of the other passengers and get some much needed sleep.

She closed her eyes and tried to concentrate on the sound of the train passing over its tracks. If she could let her mind wander, forcing away everything that had happened this night, she just might be able to doze off.

No sooner did she close her eyes when the man next to her spoke up. "You may not fall asleep."

So he *could* speak! Thinking he meant she might have trouble sleeping with so much noise surrounding her, Jenna smiled and said, "I'm so tired I don't think anything could keep me awake."

She turned her head away and, again closing her eyes, tucked her cheek into the hollow of her shoulder.

"I'm afraid you misunderstood me, senora. You are not allowed to sleep."

Her head jerked up and she stared at his profile. *"What?"*

Very calmly, the man explained, "I was told you must remain awake until Reno. Morgan will take over then. Possibly you might wish to speak with him about his orders."

Jenna took several deep breaths before she trusted her voice. "Yes, I think I'll do just that," she said between clenched teeth. *His orders!* How can you order a person not to sleep? What was he trying to do to her? Closing her eyes tightly, she attempted to control her temper.

"I'm sorry, senora. It would be better if you kept your eyes open. That way I wouldn't have to continually disturb you to see if you're awake."

She blinked several times before her vision finally focused on her clasped hands. Eyeing her white knuckles, she vowed not to cry. She had survived her father's death, the near bankruptcy of his company, being transported back in time, and the disaster of a train robbery. She would survive Morgan Trahern.

The gray dawn did little to revive Jenna's sunken spirits. She'd been awake for almost twenty-four hours, and she didn't know how much more her body could endure. She had said good-bye to her guard, Mr. Estevez, in Reno, and Morgan had taken his place on the returning train to Sacramento. Her body ached, her head throbbed, and her patience was held together by a fine string.

All she wanted to do was sleep and shut out Morgan's annoying, nonstop talking. As soon as he had sat down beside her, it was obvious he'd settled in for a *long* chat. She didn't even know what he was mumbling about now; she stopped actually listening to his tirades about an hour ago. The most she was capable of was an occasional nod. She knew she wasn't fooling him, for every time her upper lids would rest on her lower ones, his elbow would find its way into her arm. Beginning to feel like a bruised jack-in-the-box, Jenna once more straightened as his elbow connected.

"You mustn't fall asleep now, Jenna. We'll be in Sacramento in a few minutes . . . and there's *so* much to see."

Yawning, she couldn't help the quick shiver that followed it. "I don't suppose we could see the inside of a hotel room first," she mumbled, and brought her shawl tighter about her shoulders.

Morgan's mouth made a disapproving noise. "Now, Jenna. You'll have to control yourself. As your husband, it will be up to me to tell you when I want to take you to bed."

She gave him a look of disgust. "You must be joking. I want to go to sleep . . . alone!"

"That will have to wait, my dear. I plan to show you the city first. You aren't thinking about disobeying me, are you?"

Jenna let her breath out in a frustrated rush. Putting up with him was going to be harder than she'd imagined. Gathering her last reserve of willpower, she shook her head.

Morgan smiled. "Good."

By the time they were finally showed to their rooms, all Jenna could remember of Sacramento were some beautiful Victorian houses. Everything else had passed before her in a blur. Not even the jostling of the carriage had helped to wake her up. Looking around at the lovely suite, with its brocaded sofas and chairs, she felt almost drunk with exhaustion. Her sheeted bundle of clothes felt like they weighed a ton as she carried it into the next room.

She had gone no more than two feet before she stopped and stared at a huge, high-postered bed. Jenna almost cried from the beauty of it. Dear God, she never would have thought a piece of furniture could mean so much to a person and, dropping her heavy bundle, she closed the short distance between her and the inviting sight.

It was almost sensuous, the way the mattress caressed her tired body, the way the pillow tenderly enveloped her aching head. Finally, finally she could stretch her tight muscles and wait for the blessed relief of sleep.

"You are the laziest wife a man could ever have.

Now up with you. I've just ordered a bath, and then we're going shopping for clothes."

Oh my God! Please, make him go away, she thought, as she hugged the pillow tighter to her chest. "I don't need clothes," Jenna mumbled against the clean fresh cotton. "I need sleep."

"What you need, my dear," he said in a voice that was much closer, "is a bath. You forget I've sat next to you all night. You smell of horses . . . and fear."

Her eyes opened, and she was so shocked she had to remind herself to breathe. She couldn't believe it! He, who had refused to give her a chance to get cleaned up in Verdi, was telling her she—she smelled! Burying her fists into the pillow, she asked in a quiet, strained voice, "What do you want from me, Morgan?"

"What I want," he said as he took hold of her shoulders and forced her into a sitting position, "is for you to be awake and out of bed when the bath is delivered. Why don't you put your clothes away until then? It shouldn't be too long."

Looking at her, Morgan had to refrain from smiling. She looked just like a disheveled, cranky child. Teaching her a lesson wasn't easy on him either. He was exhausted and more than tempted to join her on the bed. But he was determined to go through with his hasty plans. If it was games Jenna wanted to play, he'd play them. Only this time, he had every intention of winning.

Placing the tied sheet on the bed, he stood and watched as her fingers struggled with the tight knot. When she finally succeeded in opening her makeshift luggage, Morgan sat down in a comfortable chair and observed her neatly arranging her clothes in the huge armoire and tall wardrobe. He could tell she was nearing collapse, and his heart almost softened. Almost, but not quite. Thinking she had been through

280

enough for one twenty-four hour period, Morgan rose and called out over his shoulder, "By the way, the clothes are for me, not you," as he left the bedroom to answer the door.

After the hotel employees left, Jenna looked at the steam rising from the tub. It seemed to call out to her, beckoning her to come and relax in its warmth. Raising her eyes, she glared at Morgan, seated in a chair with a thin cigar in one hand and a drink in the other.

"Well?" he asked. "What are you waiting for?"

Jenna looked at the connecting door to the sitting room, then back at him. "For you to leave."

He smiled contentedly. "I don't think there's any need for a show of modesty. You forget I've seen you nude before. Besides, I'm leaving the life of drifter behind. I find it's time to return to my own identity. And as such, I require a bit more refinement than before." He waved his hands, as if giving permission. "Go ahead. The sight of you undressed will no longer hold the same charms as in the past."

Refinement? He required *refinement?* He was just trying to embarrass her, shame her in front of him. Well, he'd thrown out the challenge, and she might be too tired to be embarrassed, but never too tired for a dare. She demurely lowered her eyes to her chest and brought her hands up to the buttons on her blouse. Slowly, ever so slowly, she let her fingers push each tiny pearl button through its hole. It must have taken her a full minute to unfasten her long-sleeved blouse. She never looked at him while she performed an excruciating, drawn-out striptease. Each garment that she discarded, she would carefully fold and place on the bed, allowing even more time to pass.

When she was down to her underwear, and about to pull the tiny ribbon that held the chemise tightly against her breasts, Morgan abruptly stood and muttered a curse.

"Damn! You're slower than a snail! I'm not about to waste half the day waiting for you to finish your toilette." Slamming his drink onto a nearby table, he jammed the cigar into his mouth and muttered, "I'll choose my own damn clothes!" That was right before he quickly strode out of the room and slammed the door behind him.

Completely nude, Jenna walked over to Morgan's bag. Rummaging through it, she found what she was looking for and leisurely came over to the table where he had left his drink. Picking it up, she sniffed the dark amber liquor and was pleased to identify it as brandy. A good brandy, she thought as she took a small sip while settling herself in the steaming bath.

She put the crystal glass on the small ledge of the tub and brought her lighter up to one of Morgan's thin cigars. After a few tries she had it sufficiently lit, and she slowly leaned against the high back of the portable tub. Reaching for the drink, she took another puff and smiled. Refinement? Damn, there was nothing like a good cigar and brandy after a refined striptease, she thought, finally letting loose her laughter. Score one for her side.

When Morgan returned to their hotel, he could hear her light snoring even before he entered the bedroom. Smiling, he quietly walked over to her and gazed down at the beautiful, exhausted woman. Her blond hair was lying in tantalizing disarray across the pillow, the tips still wet from her bath. Poor Jenna, he thought, as he laid his packages on the nearby chair. His eyes slid to the small table and spied the remainder of one of his cigars and the empty glass that had contained his brandy. He'd have to remember that she liked brandy and cigars. Jenna was like no other woman he had known. She wasn't anything like the wives of his business associates. Definitely not. There was no resemblance to the staid, proper and rather boring women who had made up Baltimore's society. Jenna was unique. And she was his. He didn't care how long it took him to convince her of that. They weren't leaving Sacramento until Jenna admitted that she was his wife and would always remain so.

Removing his clothes, Morgan kept his eyes on her. Secretly, he admitted his admiration. He was certain she was telling the truth about her involvement in the robbery. While in Verdi, he'd noticed her growing friendship with the young boy, Jace, and he was sure it was just as she said: Jason Eberly overheard Bullmason and saw the opportunity to make it rich in a hurry. That she'd risked imprisonment or death for a friend told him a great deal about her. Loyalty. He admired that quality in anyone.

Letting her sleep, he quietly climbed into bed and lay down next to her. Her back was turned toward him, and he spent some time watching it rise and fall with her steady breath. She was like a beautiful wild horse, he thought with a smile, in need of taming. He didn't want to break her, just tame her—a little. Closing his eyes, he slowly let out his breath and relaxed. He would need sleep if he intended to keep one step ahead of Jenna. The little minx didn't fool him one bit, and this afternoon had proved she still had more than enough fight left in her. He refused to think about her provacative removal of clothing. He was too tired and might not be able to control his body. Instead, he chuckled, thinking about the test of wills to come in the next few days. It ought to prove interesting, if not downright enjoyable.

"Wake up, woman! Do you expect to sleep right through dinner? Up with you!"

Jenna's nose wrinkled at the sound of Morgan's voice, and she snuggled deeper into the pillow. "Go away," she whispered irritably.

"Did I hear you right? I wouldn't think of going downstairs to have supper without my wife. Do you intend to refuse your husband?"

Jenna fluttered her eyelids. Her mouth opened in an exaggerated yawn, and her limbs moved in a feline stretch. "You're not my husb—"

"I beg your pardon?" Morgan interrupted her sentence before it was finished.

Jenna was about to repeat her statement when she looked up at him—really looked. Her eyes widened in surprise and reluctant appreciation. Morgan, her old Morgan, had disappeared. In his place was a handsome, polished gentleman wearing a well-fitted, old-fashioned tuxedo. His hair was neatly brushed back, and the only thing remaining of her old lover was the thick, impeccably trimmed mustache.

She forced herself to sit up and again eyed him from head to foot. As she looked back to his face, a smile crept up the corners of her mouth. "Well, well, don't we look . . . dapper."

Morgan brought his cigar up to his mouth and drew on the thin tobacco. Exhaling, he gazed at her through a swirling haze of gray smoke. "If that was supposed to be a compliment, then thank you. However, *we* happen to be quite hungry, so if you wouldn't mind, please get up and get dressed."

"Morgan, I'm so tired."

"Then splash cold water on your face. I've waited long enough. Your clothes are laid out for you."

Turning from her, he walked out of the room, and Jenna rubbed her eyes, trying to wake up. Not yet ready to give up the comfort of the soft bed, she returned to the warmth of her pillow and sighed with contentment.

From beyond the connecting wall, she heard his impatient voice, "I would be very displeased to miss the first seating. Don't make me come back in there."

Groaning, Jenna made a childish face at the flocked wallpaper and dragged her body from the bed. He was going to push this subservient role to the limit, she realized, as her hands cupped the cool water and brought it up to her face. Gasping with shock, she quickly reached for a towel and held it to her. Breathing into the thick cotton, she waited for her breath to warm her skin before throwing it back onto the commode.

Reluctantly, she gave Morgan credit. He was right. She was definitely awake now. In the chair that he had occupied earlier was the beautiful gown he'd brought her in Verdi. Picking it up, she realized he must have had someone press it, for the many wrinkles she had viewed when she hung it up were now removed. Under it were matching underwear, hose, and shoes. The shoes were new, and she lifted one for closer inspection. Creamy white, they matched the dress, and the tiny heels would be perfect as they peeked out from under the delicate scallops of her gown. Nestled inside each shoe was an exquisite comb for her hair. Both were identical and adorned with the same tiny seed pearls that graced her dress.

Touched by his generosity, Jenna looked toward the open door. He must care about her. Why else would he have taken the time to purchase the lovely accessories? Wanting to please him, she quickly replaced the gown and hurriedly removed her robe. She couldn't wait to get dressed.

Twenty minutes later, Jenna stood at the doorway and looked across the room to Morgan. His back was facing her as he gazed out the large, heavily draped window, and she admired the clean cut of his tuxedo as it fit snugly across his shoulders. His right hand was casually inserted inside his pocket, and Jenna had to admit he was extremely handsome. He handled the look of a polished, sophisticated gentleman with indifference. She was intrigued because he looked quite natural and comfortable, just as he had looked when he was the drifter and spy. Either way, he was devastating to her senses, and she found herself equally drawn by this new version of Morgan.

Almost as if he felt her scrutinizing his back, Morgan turned around. His eyes traveled up and down her body in appreciation, until slowly, without realizing it, he let out the breath he'd been unconsciously holding. Good God! He'd known she was lovely, but not like this. She was a vision in soft cream, from the tiny combs that held back her thick blond hair to the dainty slippers upon her feet.

Touching those combs, she shyly smiled at him and said, "Thank you, Morgan. They're lovely. And so are the shoes."

Unnerved by her extraordinary beauty, he felt almost flustered and, grinding out his cigar, muttered, "I expect my wife to be properly dressed. You look very nice."

Was she supposed to thank him for that? Was it even a compliment? Or was it merely a way of telling her she looked adequately proper? Why, she thought as she pulled on long matching gloves, did he have to take the good out of everything? Couldn't he have said she looked pretty? Thinking all he wanted was a proper wife, Jenna made up her mind to be just that.

See if he likes that any better, she mentally challenged, as she walked ahead of him and exited the hotel suite. This should prove to be a very interesting night, and she might even enjoy herself.

Chapter Twenty-three

More than a few paused in their dinner as Morgan and Jenna entered the elegant dining room of the Traymore Hotel. Diners of both sexes found themselves drawn to the handsome couple. Women looked in open admiration at the tall, distinguished man who radiated money, power, and sexuality. Men, on the other hand, quickly picked up Morgan's fierce aura of possessiveness, and were more discreet in glancing at the beautiful creature on his arm.

"Tomorrow, we're buying you a wedding ring," Morgan stated as they sat down. He wanted to mark her as his territory, letting any man know that, if he approached, he would be trespassing.

Placing the damask napkin on her lap, Jenna looked across the sparkling crystal, the delicately painted china and a small bowl of lovely spring flowers. "Whatever you wish, Morgan," she said in a subdued voice. "I realize you want to keep up appearances."

Placing his napkin across his right thigh, Morgan leaned into the table. "Appearances?"

"That is what you said in Verdi, isn't it?" she asked innocently. "Something about not wanting to claim me as your wife, but Bullmason thought we were married and we would keep up the charade until you straightened out the robbery? I hope I didn't misunderstand you," she pleaded, as if the very thought of upsetting him was a punishable offense.

Morgan studied her for a long, silent moment, not quite sure what she was up to. Thinking she meant to make him regret those words, he said in a slightly bored voice, "Rest easy, Jenna. You didn't misunderstand me."

Liar, she thought, and had to bite back saying the word aloud. She would play his game, give him the obedient wife he sought, and turn the tables around. If it took every bit of willpower she possessed, she would make Morgan Trahern beg for the return of the real Jenna Weldon. If she could love him, even as a drifter, then he would have to admit he loved her for herself—not this submissive shadow he was trying to create.

Looking over the top of the menu, she gave him a shy smile. "Why don't you order, Morgan?" she offered, trying to look flustered. "I'm afraid with so many entrees, I just can't choose."

Morgan glanced at the printed paper in front of him. "There's only five. You can't choose among five?"

She gave him a helpless look and lifted her shoulders. When their waiter appeared, Jenna's curiosity was roused by listening to Morgan order in French. She didn't understand a word. It wasn't until her dinner arrived that she knew she hadn't fooled him one bit. It wasn't going to be easy, she told herself for the tenth time, while looking at the pale mass on her plate.

"What is this?" she asked, swallowing down her

distaste.

Morgan looked up from his serving of rare roast beef. *"Ris de Veau a la Creme."* The words slid easily off his tongue.

At her look of non comprehension, he said with a smile, "Since you seemed so helpless, and couldn't choose for yourself, I ordered something I thought was appropriate. Brains, my dear. Creamed brains."

By the time they returned to their room, Morgan and Jenna watched each other with speculation. Neither one trusted the other to behave normally, and the atmosphere inside the sumptuous suite was charged with expectation.

Walking into the bedroom, Jenna took a deep breath as she heard Morgan following. She stepped over to the armoire and opened a drawer. Watching him from the corner of her eye, her fingers felt for a suitable nightgown.

He was standing in front of a low dresser, casually removing his gold cuff links. He did it slowly, as if he had all the time in the world. Next, his tanned fingers moved to the black tie at his neck. Again, he was slow as he unwound it and carefully placed it next to his links. He looked to be deep in thought, unconscious of her, and her hand abandoned its search for a nightgown. Unwillingly, she turned around to watch him.

Jenna felt hypnotized as she stared at him undressing in almost slow motion. He took infinite care in removing his shirt. In fact, he took so long, she wanted to scream at him to hurry so she could view more of his chest. When his strong muscles were revealed, she couldn't help the audible gasp.

He looked at her, a glint of laughter in his eyes. "Aren't you going to get ready for bed?" he asked innocently as his fingers moved to the buttons on his pants.

Jenna drew in a long, rasping breath. "Ah . . . yes, of course. But I think I'll go into the other room to get undressed," she managed to get out as she grabbed her nightgown and quickly fled the bedroom.

Suppressing a chuckle, Morgan called after her, "You may undress anywhere you wish, but you're sleeping in here!"

When she walked back into the bedroom, she did so with a shyness that belonged to a much younger, less experienced woman. He'd played her just right, she thought, and she'd been an eager participant. Okay, she admitted. He got her back for this afternoon. She'd reacted exactly as he did—ran away—but she couldn't afford another slipup. If she let him get away with this, making her into someone she couldn't possibly be, she'd be lost forever. Besides, she wanted an admission from him. She wanted his love. Her only choice was to make him want the old Jenna so much, he'd give up his silly plans and admit he loved her for herself.

Jenna's eyes lifted from the oriental rug, and she looked at Morgan. He was lying in bed, and she saw her side of the cover had been turned down, waiting for her to enter.

Just knowing under those covers that he was nude brought a shiver of apprehension. How was she ever going to pull this off? It didn't help matters when Morgan patted the sheet, almost in an invitation. Slipping beneath the cover, Jenna tried not to think how sexy, how blatantly male Morgan looked. And how confident. It was the last that gave her the courage to withstand whatever he had planned.

Turning down the oil lamp, Morgan said, "I must compliment you on how well you're behaving. It shouldn't take more than a few weeks to get this robbery thing straightened out."

As her head rested against the plump pillow, Jenna's mind screamed. She wouldn't be able to take a few weeks of this! It had only been one day, and already she desired him. How could she possibly last a few weeks?

"Come closer, Jenna."

The whispered words sent a shiver down her spine. It was starting. She prayed for strength as she murmured, "If that's what you wish, Morgan."

She moved a few inches toward the center of the bed.

"Closer."

It took her three times before she was where he wanted her—right in his arms. She tried to control her breathing, as he gently kissed the side of her face. She willed her heart to slow down as his hands moved from her neck to her shoulder. She prayed for the willpower to resist when he lifted her nightgown over her head.

"Jenna . . . you're so soft. I love the feel of your skin."

She wouldn't answer. She didn't trust her voice.

When he cupped her breast and lowered his mouth to hers, she forced herself to think of the new quality control welding system that had just been installed at Weldon Transit. Jenna tried to picture her employees, the flash of the arc as stainless steel material was joined through the welding process.

She knew she had been successful when Morgan raised his head and stared into her eyes. "Why are you fighting me? Don't do this, Jenna. Not now."

She didn't know how to appear impassive when her senses were reeling, but she tried. "I'm not fighting you," she said quietly. "I'm obeying you. That is what you wanted, isn't it?"

He let his breath out in a long, frustrated rush. "Well, now I'm ordering you to enjoy yourself! All right?"

Looking into his beautiful blue eyes, Jenna was caught between heartbreak and hilarity. "You can't order someone to enjoy themselves, Morgan. Either it's there . . . or it isn't."

"And you're trying to tell me it isn't?"

She attempted to conjure up a look of pity. "I'm sorry. As a proper wife, though, I'll allow you to continue, if you feel the need."

His jaw dropped in disbelief. "If I feel the *need*? Dammit, Jenna. I'm not going to let you do this."

Panther quick, Morgan wrapped her in his arms. His mouth became an instrument of torture as it hungrily explored her body. Jenna was driven to the brink, trying to resist his lips, his hands, the hard muscles of his body as it pressed against her betraying flesh. When he swiftly entered her, Jenna thought she would scream out from the frustration. It wasn't working. Weldon Transit had receded from her mind's eye; mental pictures of her mother, even her great-aunt, Madeline, who had always voiced her disapproval, didn't help to stop the flood of delicious sensations from erupting throughout her body. Her arms ached to bring him closer, her legs twitched with the need to wrap them around his strong hips. She was losing the battle and, afraid it would also eventually mean losing him, she forced her mouth to say the words.

"Are you almost through, Morgan?" she asked with a falsely bored voice.

He became deathly still. She could barely feel his chest move as he took in shallow gasps of air. She could, however, feel him still throbbing inside of her. It was cruel, and she knew it. But it was something she felt must be done. Morgan wanted two women in one. A proper, little wife outside of bed and someone entirely different within. It wasn't fair. He had to want *her*.

"Damn you!" His curse resounded throughout the quiet room.

He gave her a look of disgust before moving away from her and returning to his side of the bed. He turned his back and brought the sheet up to his shoulders. She could tell by his breathing that he was furious and suffering from the pain of unfulfillment.

Immediately, Jenna was ashamed. Never in her life had she been a tease. Even though she didn't provoke him, even though he had initiated it, Jenna was shamed by her actions. Reaching out, she touched his shoulder. "Morgan?"

He shook her hand off. "Go to sleep, Jeanna. It's what you do best lately"

She cringed from the anger in his voice and, settling back against her pillow, she stared at his rigid back.

Score two for her side. Brushing away the moisture at her eyes, Jenna admitted this one brought no pleasure. This victory was painfully hollow.

The next morning he acted as though nothing had occurred. Jenna was grateful, yet confused. She wanted him to talk, to admit he was also unhappy with their present situation. If Morgan was acting, he

294

was doing a good job. He took her shopping, brought her beautiful clothes, shoes, and ribbons for her hair. Always, she let him pick out the articles, and it irritated her to find his taste impeccable. It was when he guided her inside a small jewelry store that Jenna finally protested.

I won't have it, Morgan. I don't care what you say."

He cocked one eyebrow and looked into her face. "Can we be having our first show of disobedience?" he asked, a glimmer of hopefulness in his eyes.

How she hated this role, she thought, as she lowered her smoky-blue eyes to the floor. "Please, Morgan," she whispered in a tight voice. "I would prefer not to get a wedding ring right now."

"I thought we discussed this last night."

She clamped her mouth closed to stop the angry words. She didn't want a ring. All it would symbolize is Morgan's dominance over her. If she were to give in now, every time she looked at it she would be reminded of the sham the two of them were living. They *weren't* married. She wanted a real marriage, a real wedding, with Morgan's accepting her and loving her for the woman she was. "We didn't discuss it," she said quietly, trying not to attract the attention of the other shoppers. "You made a statement, and I agreed to keep the peace."

Morgan lowered his head until he was looking directly into her eyes. "You call what we have *peace?*"

She met his gaze. "It's what you wanted. You wouldn't listen to me in Verdi. I tried to explain, but you'd already made up your mind."

He gave her an exasperated look. Taking her upper arm, Morgan steered her out of the store and into the street. "We'll discuss this back at the hotel," he stated as they made their way through an odd assortment of people. Dangerous-looking cowboys mixed with disillusioned miners. Elegantly dressed men and women sidestepped somber-looking Orientals. Neither Jenna nor Morgan paid attention to the strange crowd. Both were too caught up in their own thoughts, as they made their way to the hired carriage that contained their packages and would take them back to the hotel.

As it turned out, they never got the chance to have their discussion. Entering the hotel suite, Morgan placed the wrapped packages on a brocaded sofa just as a knock sounded on their door. Jenna watched him answer it, her curiosity aroused as she noticed him accepting a small white envelope. She tried to act disinterested as she observed him reading the note inside. Whatever it was, it brought a smile to his face.

"Well, well. We've been invited to a small dinner party tonight. Make sure you wear something special."

Jenna briefly closed her eyes, envisioning an entire evening playing out the sweet, obedient wife. She knew it was a night she could do without. "I don't think I'm up to it, Morgan. Would you mind if I didn't go?"

He seemed annoyed and held up the envelope. "Of course I'd mind. This invitation is made out to Mr. and *Mrs*. Trahern. I'd rather not show up alone."

She swallowed several times. "I'm not feeling well," she stated simply. It was the truth. Ever since early in the afternoon, a persistent ache had grabbed hold of her lower abdomen and hadn't let up. Since she was thirteen years old, her body had given out this signal, and she knew what was coming.

"What's wrong? You seemed well enough while we

were shopping."

"It's nothing," she said, placing her shawl over the back of a chair. "Just a little . . . hmm, stomach problem."

"Perhaps it was something you ate. Did anything disagree with you?" he asked, concern in his voice.

What was she supposed to tell him? No, you fool, I'm getting my period. The only thing that disagreed with her was this stupid game the two of them were playing!

"I don't know," she finally said. "I just think I'd be more comfortable staying here. Would you mind?"

Actually, he was hurt that she wouldn't accompany him. He was proud of her and wanted to show her off. Thinking she had refused his company out of spite, he said brusquely, "Suit yourself. Just make sure you don't leave this room."

Walking into the bedroom, he raised his voice. "You'll never know if I've had a guard posted, so I wouldn't try running away."

She could feel the tension in the muscles surrounding her eyes. God, she didn't want to cry. Not now. Wait until he leaves and then give in, she told herself.

But nature has a way of not accommodating itself to one's wishes. As she waited for Morgan to emerge from the bedroom, Jenna pulled a desk chair over to the window and sat watching the early evening population of Sacramento rush off to its entertainments. Even if she managed to escape, she had nowhere to go. And, in truth, did she really want to leave Morgan?

"I'm leaving. I'll give your regrets to our host."

She turned her head and watched him pick up his hat from a table. His tuxedo looked fresh, and she realized that while they were out, it had been pressed.

Why did he have to look so damn handsome?

Knowing there was no comforting answer to her foolish question, Jenna rose and walked across the room. She stood before him, waiting patiently for him to say good-bye.

"I'd like you to lock this door when I leave. I'll pick up another key downstairs at the desk."

She nodded and silently watched him slip his hand into a white glove. Holding the hat under his arm, his fingers pulled the edge of the glove tighter, and the hat fell to the floor.

Without thought, Jenna bent down and picked it up. Just as she straightened, she was overcome by stomach cramps and doubled over. She heard him exclaim, "My God, Jenna! What's the matter with you?"

Startled by his words, she stood up and looked into his shocked face.

"You're sick!" he proclaimed in horror as he continued to stare at her. "What's wrong?"

She cringed. What more could happen? What other humiliation must she endure before she was allowed some peace? It was too much. She didn't even think about her resolve not to cry in front of him as she freely let the tears run down her cheeks. Reaching for the door, she cried, "Just go, Morgan. I'm fine."

He grabbed her arm. "*Fine?* Tell me, what's wrong with you? Shouldn't you see a doctor?"

She didn't know whether to laugh or cry. It felt better to cry.

"Jenna . . ." he urged. "Tell me."

"It's not what you think, Morgan," she whispered, feeling a hot blush creep up her neck. Sniffling, she forced herself to continue. "It's normal. Every woman goes through this once a month."

It took a moment for her explanation to sink in, and she was touched by the quick change on his face as relief made him smile.

Drawing her into his arms, he soothed her whimpers of misery and rubbed her back. "I thought you were hurt. Don't most women prepare for this?" he asked gently.

She broke into fresh tears. It felt so good to be held by him. "I don't know how to prepare!" she cried into his shoulder. "If I were in my own time, it would be different. I just don't know what women do here."

Ignoring her reference to the future, he pulled back from her and held her face between his hands. Rubbing his thumbs across her chin, he smiled and asked in a tender voice, "You don't know what to do?"

Shaking her head, her bottom lip came up as Morgan let one of her tears soak into his gloved thumb. "I have some ideas, but I'm not sure."

His smile spread and he briefly held her to his chest. "I'm ruining your suit," she murmured, bringing her head away from the dark tux.

"No . . . no you're not," he whispered as he left an arm around her shoulders and walked her into the bedroom. When they reached the middle of the room, he pulled away and brushed her hair back from her forehead. "Wait here," he said gently. "I'll ring for a maid."

As she watched him leave the room, she broke into a fresh flood of tears. She cried for herself, she cried for him, and she cried for the growing love within her heart that had to be kept secret.

If she ever doubted that love, and in the last few days she'd had many occasions to do so, there was no denial of it now. Tonight, after insisting that she'd feel better if he attended his dinner, Jenna Weldon stayed in bed and watched Morgan leave for his appointment. He'd seen to it that she was comfortable and secure. How he had presented her problem to the older woman who earned her living as a chamber maid, she'd never know. It was that he did it himself that made her heart expand with an increasing love.

It was over, she resolved, as she brought the soft comforter closer to her chin. She would fight no more. She would be his any way he wanted her.

Chapter Twenty-four

"Really, Morgan, I'm fine."

"You're sure you wouldn't rather rest today?" The question was asked as he watched her hang up his jacket from last night. His eyes caught the way she gently ran her fingers across the padded shoulders, trying to smooth away any wrinkles. "You don't have to do that," he stated, a little uncomfortable by the contented smile on her lips.

Placing his tux in the wardrobe, Jenna gazed at Morgan's finely tailored clothes. "I don't mind taking care of your things," she sighed, touching a pair of fawn-colored trousers.

His eyes widened. "You don't? I thought you hated it."

Jenna turned around and faced him. The smile that played at the corners of her mouth was soft and sweet. "That was before. If it makes you happy, I'd be glad to do it."

Morgan gave her a look of suspicion. What was she up to? Was he to return from some outing and find his clothes in shreds? What plans were running through that beautiful head?

"I've already employed the hotel's valet service.

You don't have to bother with my clothing."

"But I want to, Morgan," she said, coming closer to him. "It isn't any trouble."

He didn't trust her. She was too sweet, too accommodating. "Why don't you oversee the valet? That way you won't be tied up resewing buttons, and such."

Jenna looked into his handsome face. Her fingers itched to make contact with his thick, silky black hair, to touch the softness of his mustache, the gentleness of his lips. Instead, because she knew it was too soon, she settled for patting his shoulder as she walked past him. "Whatever you wish. I just want to please you."

Morgan turned his head and watched her as she approached the window. Pulling aside the drapes, she gazed down in the street, and he again wondered what new game she was playing. *I just want to please you?* That didn't sound like his Jenna at all. And what about the way she'd been looking at him? Ever since he'd awakened to find her blue-gray eyes inches away from his face, he'd been uncomfortable. Over breakfast, he'd found her staring at him. At any given moment, he could glance up and there she would be: a strange, almost adoring look accompanying an unexplainable smile. It was as if overnight she had discovered some wonderful secret, and he hadn't been let in on it.

"How was the dinner party?"

Morgan blinked a few times and turned around in the chair so he could see her better. "The party? It was . . . fine. It's a shame you couldn't come. I think you'd have enjoyed the host."

Jenna left the window and came to sit in the chair next to his. "Really? Why?"

"He's a fascinating man. Not too long ago, he was the proprietor of a dry-goods emporium, and now he's one of the wealthiest men in the state."

The description piqued Jenna's interest. "How did he make his money?"

"The railroad."

"Oh." Morgan's brief explanation squashed any further inquiry. The very last thing she wished to discuss was the railroad, or anything pertaining to it. She was too afraid that one thing would lead to another and they would be back to arguing about the robbery. No. Better to change the subject than bring up her past mistakes.

"Morgan. It's a beautiful day outside. Why don't we pack a lunch and have that picnic you were talking about earlier?"

He looked into her hopeful face. "I said sometime this week. It doesn't have to be today. I think you should take it easy for . . . well, for a few days. Besides, I have to go over to the Wells Fargo office. I'll probably be there most of the afternoon."

She tried not to show the disappointment that she felt inside. "Oh."

Morgan stood and reached for her hand. Rising, she gazed up into his eyes and smiled. It hurt her to know that he was eager to leave.

"When I come back we'll have a nice dinner," he said while patting her hand. Even when he let it go and she stood with both hands clasped in front of her, she continued to smile.

Nodding, she murmured, "That'll be nice, Morgan. I'll see you then."

He grinned politely. "Try to rest."

When the door shut behind him, Jenna slumped into one of the sofas in the sitting room. What was she supposed to do with herself for an entire day? She was alone, penniless and bored. Being in love, and acknowledging it, wasn't easy either. Morgan was too polite, too careful about his manner. That wasn't the man she fell in love with. She wanted her Morgan back. The old Morgan who knew how to make her laugh, who teased her and then drove her to the edge of sanity as he created magic within her body.

Where had he gone? In playing her silly games, had she destroyed him? Or was he just waiting to see if she was really accepting the role as his wife?

Pouring herself another cup of coffee from the urn Morgan had ordered delivered with their breakfast, Jenna decided to wait a while longer. After all, she did love him. Maybe she could grow to enjoy this role. Maybe.

Even as a child, Jenna was never able to handle idleness with a great deal of patience. By the time Morgan returned to the room, she was fully dressed for dinner and pacing the floor like a caged animal.

"You're back!"

She announced his entrance as if it was the most important event of the day. In truth, it was. Walking over to Morgan, she helped him off with his coat and, like a lonely puppy, followed him into the bedroom. "What did you do today?" she asked, impatient to hear any interesting news. "Who did you see? What are the people at Wells Fargo like?"

He stopped short and Jenna walked into his back. Turning around, he looked into her startled face. "You haven't even given me a chance to say hello. Or to ask what you did today. Did you rest?"

Jenna loved the way his smile extended to his eyes, creating tiny lines that radiated outward. She nodded, returning his smile. "That's *all* I did. Hurry, Morgan. Get changed so we can go down to dinner."

He took his coat from her arms. "I thought I might have dinner sent up tonight," he stated, turning his back to her and biting the side of his cheek to keep his chuckle under control.

"No! You can't!"

He didn't trust himself to look into her face. "I can't?" he asked, forcing his voice to sound stern.

"Well . . . I mean, don't you want to relax and have a nice dinner? The dining room was so lovely the other night." He *couldn't* keep her cooped up in this room. She would go mad if she didn't escape. Just for a few hours.

"I think dinner here would prove very relaxing," he said while hanging up his gray coat. "However, if you would prefer to go downstairs, then give me a few minutes to clean up and I'll join you in the other room."

She could've kissed him. Instead, she smiled into his serious face and left the room. Almost skipping to the sofa, Jenna sat on its edge and impatiently tapped her foot. Freedom. It tasted as good as the expertly prepared cuisine that awaited her in the dining room. No, she mentally corrected the comparison. It was better.

This time Jenna ordered for herself. Her appetite was ravenous, and she had to stop herself from inhaling each course as it was presented to her.

"I'm glad to see that you're enjoying the food," Morgan remarked, raising one eyebrow as she attacked her entree.

Swallowing the delicately seasoned beef, Jenna looked up from her plate. "It's delicious. *Everything's* delicious." Her eyes left his and gazed about the elegantly appointed dining room. "Isn't it beautiful? And look at the clothes the women are wearing!"

Her roving inspection took in the surrounding tables. Women, some clothed in demure pastels, others in stark, vivid colors, were seated across from their handsomely dressed dinner companions. The men were as beautifully attired as the women. No matter what color jackets they wore, most sported contrasting vests and elaborate ties that ended in large bows under their chins.

Her eyes swung back to Morgan. She wouldn't trade him for a single one of them. She preferred Morgan's quiet elegance. He was dressed completely in charcoal gray, except for the ruffled white shirt and satin tie.

Feeling her vision on him, he lifted his eyes from his poached salmon and returned her stare. He noted that, again, she had that puzzling look on her face: that serene little smile at her lips, that dreamy glaze to her eyes. "What's wrong with you, Jenna?" he couldn't help but ask.

She shook herself and smiled. "I suppose I missed you this afternoon."

Pleased as he was to have that admission from her, Morgan wished she wouldn't continued to stare at him. It was unnerving. He couldn't help but think she was planning something outrageous while lulling him into a false sense of security with her sweetness. And, if he were honest with himself, he had to admit that the thought of Jenna as a sweet, adoring wife was infinitely boring.

Knowing that before he had forced her into playing this role, he had never once been bored, and he realized that his plan had backfired. The woman seated across from him was a copy of his friends' wives, those women he had observed and promised never to marry. The lady across the table wasn't his Jenna. He had made her into someone she was never meant to be. He wanted to replace the strange, adoring look in her eyes with the fire, the anticipation, the excitement that had so often shown there before.

Smiling, he turned his attention back to his dinner. He would get his Jenna back. All he had to do was wait for the right opportunity.

An hour later, Jenna felt the waistband of her dress cut into her as she rose from the table. She had eaten far too much. She'd had the ridiculous urge to consume every tasty morsel that was offered to her. It had to be the afternoon's boredom that had given her the need to ingest all the sights, smells, and tastes that the brief hours of freedom afforded. Wondering how such excellent food could cause such a terrible feeling in her stomach, Jenna left the dining room on Morgan's arm.

"Mr. Trahern! Well, isn't this a nice surprise."

Jenna and Morgan turned as one at the loud voice. If Morgan was surprised by the greeting, he didn't show it. Jenna, on the other hand, couldn't stop the astonished stare, nor the dropping of her lower jaw as she watched a huge man break away from a small group of people and make his way over to them.

The man was huge, but not in height. Dressed like an overblown peacock, he extended his hand and Morgan shook it.

"It's good to see you again, sir. May I present my wife?"

Bringing her forward, Morgan said, "Jenna . . . Mr. Charles Crocker."

Smiling, she extended her hand. If she was taken aback by his size, she was astounded when Mr. Crocker brought her hand up to his lips and planted a wet kiss on her fingers.

Looking into her eyes, he said, "I'm certainly sorry you couldn't make our little party last night. A lovely lady such as you should never be alone." Keeping his eyes on her, he added, "And, Morgan, I told you it's Charlie. All my friends call me that."

Jenna pulled her fingers back and looked into Morgan's grinning face. He was staring across the room. Following his line of vision, she saw a small, attractive woman return his smile.

"We were about to have brandies before we called it a night. What do you say, you join us?" Mr. Crocker offered. "Give me a chance to get to know your wife, and maybe we could continue that talk we started last night."

Morgan turned his attention back to the man in front of him. "Why don't you and your friends come up to our suite? I'd like to repay your generous hospitality." Looking at Jenna, he asked, "You don't mind, do you?"

What could she say? Both men were expectantly waiting for an answer. "Of course not. If you'll excuse me, I'll make arrangements with the hotel for our guests."

She could feel Morgan's eyes on her back as she walked away from him. Why couldn't she have listened to him when he said he wanted to have dinner in their room? she anguished, as she made her way to the front desk. The cost of a few hours of freedom was dear. Now she had to suffer through a party. But then, if she had stayed upstairs, she would have missed the intimate look that passed between Morgan and the beautiful dark-haired woman. Who was she? Who *was* she?

Ten minutes later, Jenna had her answer. Mr. Charles Crocker introduced Mrs. William Maxwell.

Jenna offered her hand, and Mrs. Maxwell seemed amused as she placed hers inside it. "How do you do,

308

Mrs. Maxwell," she said, trying to appear friendly.

"Please, call me Charlotte," she answered in a cultured voice. "I hope you're feeling better tonight."

Jenna straightened her shoulders. "Yes, I am. Thank you for asking." She smiled at the woman and took in her appearance. Charlotte Maxwell was lovely. Her thick brown hair was braided into a coronet where tiny jeweled hairpins rested. Her complexion was flawless; only the slightest application of rouge was evident. Large, expressive brown eyes seemed to be as busy taking stock as Jenna's blue ones. Jenna viewed the woman's exquisite satin gown. Its deep wine color and plunging neckline contrasted sharply with creamy, pale skin. She forced her gaze to return to Charlotte's.

Seeing a similar appraisal written on the other's face, Jenna tried to ease the tension between them. "Would you care for something to drink? I've also ordered coffee and tea."

Charlotte startled her by throwing back her head and laughing. Looking into Jenna's surprised face, she remarked, "Coffee and tea is for the morning, my dear. You wouldn't happen to have a good whiskey handy, would you?"

Taken aback by the woman's request, Jenna swallowed down her surprise and nodded. "Why, yes . . . I'm sure we do. If you'll excuse me?"

Charlotte barely inclined her head as Jenna left her and walked over to the silver tray with several bottles of liquor resting on it. Spotting Morgan, she changed direction and approached him.

Touching his sleeve, she apologized for interrupting his conversation with several men and asked, "Do you think you could pour Mrs. Maxwell's drink? She'd like a whiskey."

It didn't help her insecurity to watch Morgan raise

his head and search the room for the woman. Finding her examining a huge ring that adorned her gloved finger, Morgan smiled. "Certainly, Jenna. Why don't you see what the other ladies are having?"

Feeling as if she'd been dismissed, Jenna mingled with the four other women. All were attired as extravagantly as Charlotte Maxwell, yet they seemed pleased and almost relieved that coffee and tea and a large assortment of tiny cakes were offered. The four were married to the men surrounding Morgan, and Jenna deduced that Mrs. Maxwell must be escorted by the loud Mr. Crocker.

She stood watching Morgan talking and laughing. It pleased her to see the respect the other men had for him and to observe him as he handled himself so well.

"He's quite a man. I understand congratulations are in order on your recent marriage."

Jenna half turned at the sound of Charlotte's voice behind her. The woman's dark eyes were fixed on Morgan's form. An unknown protective, perhaps even jealous response rose up inside her. "Thank you," she murmured as she let her eyes follow Charlotte's. "Is Mr. Maxwell here in Sacramento with you?" Please don't let her be a widow, Jenna prayed.

"There is no Mr. Maxwell," she said easily. "There never was."

Jenna turned back to her. "Then why would you call yourself Mrs. Maxwell? Why not just use your real name?"

Charlotte smiled. "Maxwell is my real name. A few years ago, I attached the Mrs. I suppose I did it for respectability."

The look Jenna gave her was confused. "Respectability? Surely it's not unrespectible to be unmarried."

Charlotte sipped her drink. Holding the glass in both hands, she continued to look at Morgan. "I made my fortune in the building of the railroad and in the mining camps. Women were in great demand . . . and I supplied them."

Jenna's mouth opened in astonishment. "You were a . . ."

"Madam," Charlotte finished. She finally tore her eyes away from Morgan and looked at Jenna. Regarding her with amusement, she continued. "Charlie and I met years ago. He's the only one here who knows the truth. And now you do."

Jenna wished she had a drink in her hand, something to steady her nerves. "Why? Why are you telling me this?" she asked, already afraid of the answer.

Charlotte brought her glass up to her mouth and neatly sipped from it. Looking back to Morgan, she said quietly, "I thought you should know. I have very few scruples, Mrs. Trahern. And the fact that Morgan's a married man only makes him that much more interesting."

Jenna couldn't believe her implications. "Are you saying that . . ."

"What I'm saying is that you're married to a very attractive man," Charlotte stated, stopping any further words that Jenna could have said. She placed her drink on a nearby table and smoothed the skirt of her gown. "Thank you for your hospitality, Mrs. Trahern, but I'm afraid the hour is late, and you look as if we've stayed too long. I hope the next time we meet, you'll be fully recovered."

She glided away toward the men, and Jenna could only blink as she watched her stand between two of them. What had just happened? Was she correct in assuming that Charlotte Maxwell had just given her fair warning? Was it possible that she felt the need to inform a man's wife before she engaged in an affair with him? Or, am I being paranoid? Jenna thought.

311

Because we're not really married, and Morgan hasn't looked at me like he's looking at Charlotte since before the train robbery.

Throwing back her shoulders, she lifted her chin. She was losing him by being his perfect wife. It wasn't her, and if he weren't so damn stubborn, he'd admit his strategy was a miserable failure. Well, she was done with his stupid experiment. It wasn't worth losing the man she loved. Grinning, she crossed the room to join him. Feeling almost light-headed, she linked her arm through Morgan's strong one and smiled at Mrs. Charlotte Maxwell. Just let her try, she thought with confidence.

Jenna Weldon was back—to stay.

Chapter Twenty-five

This time she was waiting in bed for Morgan. Dressed in the pale-blue nightgown he had brought to her in Verdi, Jenna watched him undress. She felt better, knowing she was through playing games and, raising her hands, pulled her dark-blond hair up over her head, then let it quickly fall as she stretched the muscles in her arms and back.

"What did you think of our little gathering?" he asked, unbuttoning his shirt and revealing the dark curling hair at his chest.

Jenna's fingers clutched at the sheet and brought it up closer to her breasts. How she ached to touch him, to let her hands roam the strong muscles, the small mat of crisp curls that covered his upper body and trailed— She shook herself. She must remain controlled for a while longer. If her body cooperated, she would be back to normal in two days. In the meantime, she would prepare Morgan for the return of the woman he'd first met and desired.

"I thought everyone was . . . interesting." She stressed the last word. "Especially, Mr. Crocker."

"He's quite a character, isn't he?" Morgan said while shedding his trousers.

Jenna averted her eyes and spent a few seconds smoothing the sheet after she finally let it go. "Yes. I would say so. And his companion, Mrs. Maxwell. She certainly is unusual."

Glad that he'd left his underwear in place, she watched his face as he came to his side of the bed. "Ah . . . Charlotte." He smiled before adjusting the lamp and bringing the room into darkness. "Yes. I would say she is definitely unusual."

Jenna's eyebrows came together in annoyance. Ah . . . Charlotte? What the hell did he mean by that!

"Good night, Jenna."

It was the most polite dismissal that she had ever received. The sharp pain she felt in her heart worked its way up her throat, and she had to force the whispered words through it. "Good night, Morgan," she murmured, before rolling over to her side. Staring into the darkness, she tried not to think of the man behind her or the possibility that she might have played the game too long. Could Morgan be *that* interested in Charlotte Maxwell? Closing her eyes tightly, she prayed she wasn't too late.

"How do you . . . ah, feel?"

"I'm perfectly fine, Morgan. What's in your hand?"

He waved the small invitation. "A return engagement. This time I hope you'll accompany me. You made quite an impression on our host, and I know two of your gowns were delivered yesterday. You have no excuse, Jenna."

"But I *want* to go, Morgan," she said, looking at him through the mirror as she brushed her hair. Seeing the pleased expression on his face as he reread

314

the note made her want to scream. If she'd had to crash Mr. Crocker's party, she had no intention of letting Morgan go alone. "I think I'll wear the black. What do you think?"

"Hmm?" He was still absorbed in the handwritten invitation, almost daydreaming. "Oh . . . the black. Fine. I'm sure you'll look stunning."

Placing the brush on the dresser she turned around and gave him a look of impatience. "Thank you for that vote of confidence," she said with a hint of sarcasm in her voice. "And where do you have to run off to today?"

He looked up from the stationary, as if just noticing her. "There're still a few minor details to straighten out with the Wells Fargo people." Picking up his jacket, he placed the invitation in its pocket.

Jenna bit the inside of her cheek in frustration. "Those Wells Fargo people certainly don't move too quickly, do they? Especially since this *robbery* never really took place. You would think a big company like that would have better things to do than detain you, for days, while you fill out reports."

His eyes showed his surprise, and the way his thumb smoothed the one side of his mustache in the familiar gesture showed his unease. Jenna took it all in, and, for the first time, she wondered if he had lied to her. All those afternoons, all those hours. If he weren't tied up with business, what had he been doing? Picturing him with a small, dark-haired woman made her stomach lurch upward toward her chest.

"But it was a robbery, Jenna," he said softly, putting his arms into the jacket. "I told you Jace stole three hundred dollars."

"Then are they looking for him? What exactly are

315

they doing, Morgan? You've never told me a single thing." Annoyed that he had withheld information about the investigation from her, Jenna snapped, "And why don't you just pay the three hundred dollars back to them and be done with the whole thing? I've seen you spend more than that when you took me shopping!"

He came to stand in front of her. Looking beyond her shoulder, he straightened his tie in the mirror. "But I *have* paid it back, Jenna."

"You have? Why didn't you say so?"

"I just did." Satisfied with his tie, his eyes held a glint of laughter as he turned them on her. "The money was withdrawn from your bank account in Verdi days ago."

He placed his index finger under her chin and closed her open mouth for her. "I should be back by half past six. Since you once voiced a desire to take care of my clothing, please see that my dark-blue velvet jacket and gray trousers are pressed." He quickly kissed the tip of her nose. "That's a good girl," Morgan said almost happily before he turned and disappeared from the room.

Jenna heard the door open and then close, yet her legs felt rooted to the thick, patterned carpet. She forced her feet to move and slowly made her way to a chair. Collapsing into its soft cushion, Jenna stared about the room. She couldn't believe the gall of the man! He transferred money from a bank account that he had established for her. Granted, she never intended to use it, except to do exactly as he had already done. But, he didn't even think to inform her! And what about his ordering her to see to his evening wear? Sure, she admitted, she'd once made some ridiculous statement about wanting to take care of his

316

clothes, but he had no right to order her about, as if she were his paid servant.

Jenna turned her head and looked out from the bedroom door and into the adjoining room. Spotting the door, she made a childish face. *That's a good girl!* Just thinking it made the hair at the back of her neck stand on end. Wait until tonight. She'd make him eat those words!

Her gown was midnight black, as dark as the night they ventured into, and Morgan couldn't keep his eyes off her. Neither, it seemed, could any other man, as he returned the stares of several. Lifting Jenna into the hired carriage, he settled himself next to her and, again, looked at her. She was lovely. Her light hair was lifted up and off her face, held back by the tiny combs he had bought her. It fell in soft curls to her shoulders, just brushing the bare, satiny skin. When he'd ordered the gown, he didn't realize it would be so revealing, and he swallowed down his rising desire as he viewed the soft swells of her breasts. She was without any adornment, save the combs, and Morgan regretted leaving the jewelers when they had first reached Sacramento. She was his wife, and he wanted her to outshine every other woman there tonight.

Looking out the window, he seemed absorbed in the activity on the street, until he spotted the store he had seen in his travels throughout the city. Rapping on the inside wall of the carriage, Morgan told the driver to stop.

"What are you doing?" Jenna asked, a look of confusion on her face.

Morgan smiled into her eyes. "Wait here," he gently ordered. Without waiting for her to speak, he quickly left the carriage.

Jenna peeked through a window and watched Morgan pounding on the door of a shop. Looking closer, she could see it was the jewelers where he had wanted to buy her a wedding ring. She saw a light emerge from the back of the store and heard Morgan's mumbled speech as he talked through the closed door.

When he was admitted into the store, her curiosity was heightened. What was he doing? She could only see two heads bent over in concentration, looking at something. Sitting back against the leather seat, Jenna nervously bit her bottom lip. He was buying a wedding ring. That had to be it. He didn't want her showing up at his friend's party without one. Well, I won't wear it, she vowed. He's paid the money back to the railroad. He has no hold over me, nor can he continue to threaten me with revealing my part in the robbery. Or Jace's. They were both in the clear. Wells Fargo probably dropped the whole thing. Unconsciously preparing for the battle, she crossed her arms over her chest as she waited for Morgan to return. She would *not* accept a wedding ring from him—not yet.

Within ten minutes, he was seated next to her and holding out a wide black box. "Open it," he said with a hint of anticipation in his voice.

Jenna felt the carriage begin to move as she reached out a hesitant hand. It's too big to be a ring, she thought as she lifted off the top of the box.

Viewing its contents, her breath caught in the back of her throat. Lying on black velvet was the most exquisite necklace. Three strands of small pearls were held together by a large, yet fragile-looking pink and white cameo. Her finger shook as she touched the tiny interlacing gold threads that weaved around it, forming a delicate filigree. "It's beautiful, Morgan," she

318

breathed, still in awe.

"Try it on. Let's see it out of the box."

She looked up at him. "But . . ."

"I won't hear any objections, Jenna. It would please me to have you wear it tonight." He reached over and took the necklace. Holding it up in front of her, he said, "Turn around and lift your hair. I don't want to catch it on the clasp."

Touched by his generosity, she did as he asked. When his hands crossed over her shoulders, she could smell the faint masculine scent of his cologne, and it was an act of self-control not to tilt her head and rest her cheek against one of them.

The necklace was heavy, yet warm. Turning back around, she lifted her eyes to his. If it was approval she was looking for, she found it. His lips lifted in a satisfied smile; his eyes held a look of pride and seduction. "You look beautiful, Jenna."

The sincerity of his words, the huskiness of his voice reached deep within her and warmly wrapped around her heart. Dear God, how she loved him! When was he going to admit he felt the same about her? How long must she be silent when she wanted to shout the words to him? Instead, she pushed the declaration down and whispered a soft "thank you." Her heart battled with her mind, one telling her to wait, to be patient while the other demanded immediate release, immediate satisfaction.

Looking at Morgan's handsome profile, Jenna knew her heart was winning out. It had to be soon.

The large Victorian home sparkled with light and was the perfect setting for the small gathering of people inside it. Twenty-four men and women mingled under the huge crystal chandelier. Each had a plate of food and a compliment for their host as they passed the man.

"Lobster, Charlie? I'm impressed."

"Not just lobster, Morgan. *Maine* lobster." Charlie Crocker popped a large piece of white meat into his mouth.

Seeing his host's obvious pleasure, Morgan smiled and listened as he continued. "Had 'em brought out here in barrels full of sea water. It's all part of what I've been telling you. The East would give plenty for all the fresh fruit and vegetables that we can provide. I got a dream. Going to bring 'em strawberries right in the middle of winter. Pack 'em in ice from Alaska, and they'll do fine. Can you picture that?" His silver fork pierced another piece of lobster. "You're an importer. Can't you see the fortune to be made by the railroad?"

Morgan looked about the heavily decorated room. "Looks like you already did that, Charlie. What's left for a small fish like myself?"

Charlie laughed, somehow managing not to choke on his food. "I like you, boy. Heard about you when I was back East. You've got a reputation for being honest. And you're some sort of war hero, aren't you? That still holds some weight."

Morgan's posture stiffened. "It's gratifying to know my business reputation has traveled as far west as California," he stated, already weary of the conversation. "Excuse me. I want to make sure my wife tastes this lobster."

Jenna sat on the edge of a Louis XV chair, clutching the long stem of her champagne glass. *He was Charlie Crocker!* The Charlie Crocker, of the big four: Stanford, Huntington, Hopkins, and Crocker—

Charlie Crocker. Her brain refused to digest such startling information. She was sitting in the home of the legendary Charlie Crocker, a man so instrumental in building the transcontinental railroad. Since her father had made his living building cars for the railroad, Jenna had devoured any history on the subject. Her interest had started as a child, when her father had taken her into Weldon's manufacturing plant and showed her around. From that time on, she was hooked.

"Are you enjoying yourself, Jenna? You look lost in thought."

Blinking a few times, she focused her eyes on Morgan's tall form. "What . . . I'm sorry?"

He smiled, reaching for her hand and bringing her to her feet. "I asked if you're enjoying yourself."

"Do you know who he *is*?"

Morgan looked about the room. "Who?"

"Our host! Morgan, he's Charlie Crocker. *The* Charlie Crocker!" Only now was it really sinking in. She hadn't just traveled back in time. She'd stepped back into history.

"Yes?" He waited for her to continue.

Frustrated, she placed her glass on a table and grabbed his arm. "Charlie Crocker . . . the big four Crocker? Don't you see, Morgan?"

He gazed intently into her eyes. "He's Charlie Crocker. What is it you want me to see?"

Jenna stared back at him, unsure if she should continue. And what could she say? That she'd read about him when she was a teenager? That he was a chapter in history, come alive? He wouldn't believe her, any more than he'd believed what she'd told him about the tape recorder, the flashlight, the calculator. If he doubted tangible evidence, then just her words would sound ridiculous.

Forcing a smile to appear on her lips, she said, "Never mind. I . . . I don't know why I was rambling like that. I must be nervous." She tried to hide the frustration of not being able to share her excitement.

He took her hand and let it rest on his forearm. Drawing her with him, he led her from the room while whispering, "I know what you need. Food. You must be hungry. Wait until you taste the lobster Charlie brought in from Maine. Melts in your mouth."

Morgan never had a fondness for musicals of any kind. And a local matron, trying out her vocal cords for what seemed like the first time, held even less interest for him. Since he was standing behind Jenna's chair, and that was placed toward the back of the room, Morgan did the sensible thing and quietly left. Hoping no one had noticed his hasty departure, he made his way back to the dining room and slipped out the partially opened french doors.

Inhaling the fragrant, night air, Morgan reached inside his jacket and withdrew a cigar. God, early summer was beautiful out here in California, he thought, as he brought more fresh air into his lungs. Feeling in his pocket for a match, he smiled, picturing Jenna tonight. Now, *she* was beautiful.

He was about to strike the match when his eyes caught a movement by the Chinese lanterns Crocker had set up around his garden. He didn't move, didn't even breathe, and his heart started racing.

No! It couldn't be! He drew in a long, rasping breath and the match dropped from his lifeless fingers. His training overcame his immobility, and quickly, he pressed his body against the wall of the house. His eyes never left the two men deep in discussion as he inched his way along the back of Crocker's home. When he reached the edge of the garden, Morgan entered the bushes and painstakingly tried to close the distance between him and the men.

Within seconds, he knew he need not come any closer. The light was faint, but it was enough to confirm his worst suspicions. Unconsciously, his fists curled into tight balls of rage. The corner of his upper lip lifted in an animal-like sneer. His ears could only pick up snatches of garbled, hurried conversation, but his eyes could definitely identify the speakers. The short one was Bennett, one of Crocker's many flunkies; the other, the taller of the two, was much more familiar. He was the unwelcome visitor to Morgan's recent nightmares, the deserving recipient of his hatred: Michael C. Hogan.

What the hell was he doing here in Sacracmento? Why wasn't he on his way to Washington with the information he and Mano had unearthed? And more importantly, why was he sneaking around in the bushes with one of Crocker's men? Staring at the man's sinister profile, Morgan had the strangest feeling in his stomach. Looks like Frank Adams finally made a mistake, he thought with disgust, as he turned back to the house. It wasn't over.

Jenna didn't mind leaving the party early. In fact, she thought, as she removed the lovely cameo, she was pleased to be back at the hotel. Tonight had shown her that she must find a way of making Morgan believe her. She would try talking to him this time unemotionally and logically. He had to start believing that she was from the future. It would answer so many of his questions.

Placing the delicate cameo on the dresser, Jenna turned around to speak. Her eyes widened in surprise and shock.

"What are you doing? Why are you dressed like that?" she demanded, staring at the worn denim jeans and old plaid shirt.

"I'm going out, Jenna," he stated, tightening the belt around his waist.

She lifted the hem of her gown and walked across the room. "What do mean *out*? It's after midnight. Why are you wearing those clothes again?"

He seemed in a hurry as he searched the wardrobe for his old boots. "Just out. Don't wait up for me."

Without thinking, she brought her hands up to her hips in an angry posture. "I wanted to speak with you tonight."

He shoved his foot into one boot and picked up the other. "It'll have to wait. I'm sorry."

Immediately, her senses came alive. Those same instinctual warnings she had when she'd thought Morgan was in trouble came rushing back. He stood up, and she hurried after him as he left the bedroom. "Morgan, tell me. What's going on? Are you in trouble?"

Putting on the suede hat she had used in the robbery, he stopped at the door and turned around. "I don't have the time to explain. Not now. I'm sorry Jenna. Lock the door after me."

She didn't know how long she stared at the wooden door or how many minutes passed by before she realized that the hotel suite was as quiet as a tomb. She commanded her legs to move and carry her back into the bedroom. Picking up Morgan's discarded jacket, she held it to her cheek and inhaled the lingering spicy scent of him. He'd said he had left his days of a drifter behind: that he was through with that way of life. Hanging up his jacket, her fingers caressed the material. Why was he sneaking off into the night *again*? Walking back to the bed, Jenna reached for his shirt and clutched it to her breasts. The heavy sick feeling in her stomach told her it wasn't over. She and Morgan had only been granted a lull, and they had wasted it by playing games with each other. Instinct told her there was a far more dangerous game waiting to be played out to the end.

Chapter Twenty-six

Morgan started at the bars, the very same bars he had frequented when trailing Bullmason's accomplices. If Hogan was still in Sacramento, Morgan hoped he could pick up his trail there. Hell, he thought, as he entered the third, it was the logical place to begin. Unless Hogan had reformed, which he doubted, he was still a heavy drinker.

It hadn't always been that way, he remembered as his eyes scanned the dimly lit room. When he'd first met Mike Hogan, he seemed just like the farm boy from Ohio that he was. But war had a way of forcing one to grow up too fast. They'd split up for a time, each on difficult assignments, and when Morgan had seen him again, he was different. He knew his work, never tried to get out of a dangerous job, but handled it differently—like he almost enjoyed it. That was when Morgan noticed the ever present bottle. It was almost as if Mike couldn't get through the day without it. Morgan understood that. Hell, there were times he'd drowned the horror in whiskey and never wanted to sober up. But it wasn't like that for Hogan. He got mean.

Not seeing the familiar face, Morgan exited the bar

and walked up the street to the next one. God, he wished Mano hadn't left the city and returned to his father's ranch. He'd feel better if his old friend handled this one. Morgan admitted he was afraid. Not of Hogan but himself. He had Jenna now, and he wanted to believe that she meant more to him than settling an old debt.

He wanted to believe that, he thought, pushing open the swinging door to a saloon, but the churning in his stomach told him differently. Maybe Mano was right. Maybe it was time to give the fallen warriors their rest. God, he thought as he again failed to recognize any of the men in the bar, he wanted Billy to rest. Perhaps then, he would be free to go on with his own life.

Five hours later, while the rest of the world slept, Morgan sat in a chair and watched Jenna. Through dawn's gray haze, he could see the outline of her delicate profile. Quietly removing his boots, he couldn't help but smile as he listened to her light snoring. She still refused to admit to that unladylike affliction. Unbuttoning his shirt, he let it hang at his sides and settled back against the soft cushion of the chair. Maybe he should try to use her echo machine and capture the steady sound, he thought, amused by imagining her reaction.

He needed her, he admitted, the smile leaving his mouth. And it was never more obvious than tonight. The confusion, the rage, the disappointment he had felt by seeing Hogan and then being unable to find him would have been unbearable, if he'd returned to an empty room. Without any overt actions, any annoying feminine wiles, Jenna had worked her way into his heart and took possession of it. The admission startled him.

327

He had always thought of himself as being independent, never needing a woman on a steady basis. Looking back, he could see he was never really satisfied with such casual relationships. And since tonight seemed the time for revelations, he could further admit that all those years he had been afraid, terrified to care so much about another human being. The war had taught him that lesson. Not wanting to work his way through the hurt of again losing someone close, he'd closed his heart.

Looking back at Jenna, he felt a burning in his eyes, a tightness in his throat. Letting the moisture build up and overflow his lids, Morgan allowed the tears to slide down his rigid cheeks. He couldn't lose her!

He never felt as alive as when he was with her, nor as tender as when they made love. She was his mystery woman, and now he wanted to know everything about her.

Inhaling, he brushed at his cheeks with the back of his hand and rose. As he walked over to the bed, he knew the time had come for the truth. He didn't care what it was, he just had to hear it. *Where did she really come from? Who was this incredible woman?*

Gently, he sat on the edge of the mattress and reached over to pull a few tangled strands of hair away from her face. "Wake up, *desperada*," he whispered.

The grin returned to his mouth as she abruptly stopped snoring and wrinkled her nose. "Jenna?" He quietly called her name.

Eyes still closed, she inhaled deeply and turned away from him. "Not again, Morgan," she begged in a hoarse voice. "Go away. Please . . . let me sleep."

Not more than three seconds passed before she quickly turned back to him, a look of astonishment on her face. "Morgan!" Wide awake, she exclaimed her relief. "Thank God you're back!" Then just as quickly, she admonished him. "Dammit, Morgan, where were you?"

"We have to talk, Jenna."

She blinked a few times. "Now?" she asked, looking out at the breaking dawn. "I wanted to talk to you last night. Remember? Where did you go?"

"I'll explain that later," he said. "Right now I'd like to hear what you know about the railroad, and Charlie Crocker, in particular."

"What?" She couldn't help but rub her eyelids. Holding the sides of her face, she stared at him. "You woke me up, before daylight, to discuss the railroad?"

Morgan grinned at her childlike pout. "It's almost daylight. And I haven't even been asleep. Maybe I should order coffee?"

Groaning, Jenna sank back into the warmth of the covers. Her voice was muffled when she spoke. "Forget the coffee, Morgan, and go to sleep. This is crazy."

She felt the bed move as he lifted his weight from it, and she sighed in relief. Thank God. He was leaving her alone. Closing her eyes, she promised to give him her rapt attention when he approached her at a more civilized hour. What did he think she could tell him about the railroad?

Although she didn't immediately fall back to sleep, Jenna was sure no more than five minutes could have lapsed before he returned. She had no need to turn around to know he didn't have any intention of letting her sleep. Even before she heard the rattling of china, her nostrils were filled with the distinct aroma of freshly brewed coffee.

Resigned, Jenna tried to be patient as she sat up in bed and plumped the pillows behind her. "I see you're determined to have this conversation," she stated while watching him pour the coffee. She noticed that he fixed it exactly the way she liked: cream and one teaspoon of sugar. She also noticed the grin had returned to his face.

As he handed her the cup, she looked closely into his eyes. They were bloodshot; the tiny lines surrounding them seemed a bit deeper, and the healthy tan coloring of his face appeared to have faded. "Why are you doing this?" she asked. Waiting until he sipped his coffee, she continued, "My God, Morgan, you look terrible. Even if you have something against *me* sleeping you should try it."

He held the cup and saucer in his hands as he resumed his position on the edge of the bed. "Thanks for the compliment, my dear. And may I say how marvelous you look in the morning?"

Jenna lifted her chin. "If it was actually morning, I would accept your sarcasm. Since this is practically the bewitching hour, then I think I'm entitled to look slightly witchy." Narrowing her eyes, she said in a threatening voice, "And I dare you to make any remarks about my personality . . ."

He couldn't resist. "Truthfully, I was going to mention that your delightful snoring would have kept me awake anyway . . ."

"I've told you. I do not snore."

He wanted to tell her that she looked nothing like a witch, and it was all he could do to keep his hands off her. Clearing his throat, he tried to steer the conversation back to where they had left off before the coffee. "You were going to tell me about your involvement with the railroad and whatever knowledge you have about Charlie Crocker."

Jenna blew on the steaming brew. "I was? I seem to remember you demanding I tell you. What is all this with the railroad? And Crocker's your friend. Don't

330

you know him?"

"Jenna, just tell me what *you* know. All right?"

She heard the patience in his voice and decided that the sooner she told him, the quicker she could return to sleep. Anyway, she could also use this conversation to serve her purposes, if she told the truth.

Taking a large steadying sip of the strong stimulant, Jenna placed her cup on the night table. She returned to her pillows and stretched her arms toward the ceiling. Lowering them slowly, she crossed them behind her head. "I read about both in school. I told you my father owned a company that manufactures railcars. It was only natural that I developed a curiosity in the railroad."

Only showing a slight interest, Morgan asked, "And why have I never heard of this company? Weldon Transit, you said?"

Jenna smiled, anticipating his reaction. "Because, dear Morgan, in *my* time, you don't even exist."

He expelled his breath in a rush of frustration. "Not again, Jenna," he implored. "For once, why don't you stick to the truth?"

She refused to be angered. This conversation afforded the best opportunity for him to accept where she really came from. It didn't take much of an effort for her to produce a smile as she lowered her arms. "But I'm not lying, Morgan. And somewhere in your subconscious, I think you know it. Now, what kind of details would you like me to give you? Shall I tell you that railcars in my day measure eighty-five feet, each one, and the best are made of stainless steel? Would it impress you to know my company has made coaches that, even with a weight of over one hundred and fifty thousand pounds, the cars are capable of reaching a speed of one hundred and sixty miles an hour?"

Ignoring his look of bewilderment, Jenna refused to

331

give mercy. "Or, perhaps, you'd be more interested in our new ultra high-speed transport system, in which vehicles are magnetically levitated, guided and propelled along an elevated guideway at speeds over two hundred and fifty miles an hour?" She raised her eyebrows. "Now that's the one that excites me. How about you?"

She knew he wasn't capable of answering, so she continued. "You know, Morgan, I just gave you part of the speech that I was supposed to deliver in 1987, in this very city." Reaching for her cooled coffee, she shrugged. "Too bad. Judging from your reaction, I would have had them in the palm of my hand."

When she replaced the cup, Morgan's hand shot out and captured her arm. "Stop it, Jenna. I've never heard anyone with your . . . your imagination. I promise I'll try to get you help. You don't have to continue this—"

She pulled her arm away and glared at him. "What do you want me to tell you about *your* time?" she interrupted. "How about this transcontinental railroad that you're so interested in? Shall I tell you that it was built on corruption?"

Seeing the look of surprise on his face, she said, "I see that got your attention."

"What do you know about it?" he asked quietly.

"Just that it was one of the biggest scandals this country has ever known. And they thought Watergate was bad!"

He looked puzzled. "What's Watergate? I've never heard of it."

Jenna shook her head. "That's my generation's political scandal. Forget it. What you're itching to know about is the Credit Moblier, isn't it?"

His jaw dropped. "You know about that? How?"

"I told you, Morgan, from textbooks on American

History. It was covered quite thoroughly. And, of course, my natural interest, because of my father, remember?"

He leaned forward. "Tell me," he demanded in a low, rasping voice.

And so she did.

Chapter Twenty-seven

Her eyes felt strained from following him as he furiously paced the bedroom.

"So who was involved? Tell me!"

She tried to repress the giggle that was slowly building in her throat. "You expect me to remember something like that? Please, Morgan. It's been years ago."

He stopped pacing and grabbed hold of the carved wooden bedpost. His eyes held an intense look. "It's important, Jenna. Try. Names, places, anything."

She sighed. "Okay. I'll try." Biting her bottom lip, she attempted to visualize the textbook pages. "I think it was Durant who found an old charter in the Pennsylvania archives and called it the Credit Moblier. He used it as a construction company for the railroad. If his own engineer gave him an estimate of, say, three million, Durant gave the Credit Moblier a construction contract for five. But he held the company only to the original three million dollar specifications." She shook her head. "It was something like that. It's hard for me to remember."

He didn't take his eyes off her, and she could see he

was swallowing several times, as if having difficulty attempting to speak. When he did, his voice was hoarse. "What else? What other names do you remember?"

"Morgan, I don't know. Why is this so important to you? Is this what—"

"*Jenna! Try!*"

It was like being on the witness stand with a hostile interrogator. She took another sip of her coffee and resumed her position on the bed. "Let me see," she sighed, trying to remember. "The big powers, besides Durant, were Oak Ames and his brother. And I can't remember his name, so don't shout at me."

"It's all right. I do. His name's Oliver."

Now it was Jenna's turn to be surprised. "You know him?"

"I know of him. Continue."

"Well, a New York newspaper prints letters from Ames, stating that he had distributed shares of Credit Moblier stock to the vice president and members of congress in an effort to influence them."

Morgan leaned even closer to her. "Who were they, Jenna? That's what I have to know."

Her eyes widened. "My God, Morgan. How can you expect me to remember *that*?"

His hands filtered through his hair in frustration. "Wait. What if I tell you the names I know, and then one might stand out as missing? How about that?"

Jenna's shoulders lifted in a helpless shrug. "Whatever you want. I just don't see how you can expect me to pull these names out of thin air."

He ignored her statement and intently stared into her eyes. "I've got William Allison of Iowa, James Brooks of New York, John Logan of Illinois, Schuyler Colfax—"

"And don't forget the one with the funny name—

What was it? Oh yes, Blaine from Maine. I don't remember his first."

Morgan's eyes showed his astonishment. "It's James," he said quietly. "Who else?"

Jenna smiled. "You missed the most important one. James Garfield. Don't you think that says something significant about the American public, if they knew all this and later elected that man for president?"

Morgan looked almost ill, and he sat down heavily on the bed. "How could you have all this information?"

"I told you. I read it. When are you going to believe me, Morgan? Do you want to hear about your friend, Charlie Crocker?"

He didn't answer her, but just continued to stare at her, as if she weren't real. Uncomfortable, Jenna cleared her throat and began to speak. "On this side of the country, Crocker resigned from the Central Pacific board and set up his own construction company. It was another facade and the big four siphoned off huge profits from government subsidies. Crocker and his friends got off much easier than their East Coast counterparts. I think it was Huntington who reported that their books had been destroyed when the construction company disbanded. Anyway, they're all written down in history as stock manipulators and robber barons."

"You read this." It was more of a statement rather than a question. When she nodded, he asked in a whisper, "When did it all come out? Did you read that?"

Jenna didn't like the look on his face. It wasn't what she had expected. "Sure," she said hesitantly. "It was 1873."

"*No!*" He jumped up from the bed and hurried to

the window.

She watched him, outlined against the now bright daylight. Suddenly, he turned around and glared at her.

"I didn't waste four months of my life to have this buried for three more years!"

Slowly, Jenna left the bed. Pulling her robe around her shoulders, she walked over to him. It wasn't easy, but she tried to ignore his intense, angry look. "That's what you've been doing, Morgan?" she asked gently. "Investigating the railroad?"

He didn't answer.

"Then you might want to talk to somebody named McComb. He's the one who breaks the story."

Suddenly, his arms reached up and grabbed her shoulders. She had never seen such a look of intense inner pain, anger, and confusion mixed together at once. Shaking her, he demanded, "Just how the hell do you *know* all this! *Dammit, Jenna, tell me the truth!*"

"I did! I . . . I told you." She was breathless when he released her. He stood, looking over her head, and stared at the wall. Her nerves were strained, her hands were shaking, but she commanded them upward. Placing one hand on either side of his face, Jenna forced him to look at her.

The anger she saw brought tears to her eyes. "Morgan . . ." She whispered his name. "What I've said may have sounded ludicrous to you, but you know me, Morgan. You know me as no other man ever has. And you know I'm not insane. Listen to me now. Believe it this time, for there's no other answer, but the truth. Something, I don't know what, happened on that train. When I stumbled and fell . . . I fell into your world. I'm from the future, Morgan." She forced a sad smile. "Why, I haven't even been

337

born yet in your time." Quickly the smile disappeared, and her fingers tightened at his head. "And you . . ." The tears flowed freely until she was almost sobbing. "And you, my . . . my husband, in my time you're . . ." She couldn't continue, couldn't say the word.

He did. *"Dead."*

Bringing her hands down from his face, he backed away from her. "That's what you were going to say, isn't it?" he demanded. *"What are you*? What the hell *are* you?"

She could feel herself shrinking away from the look of horror on his face. Bringing her fist up to her mouth, she tried to stop the choking sobs. He hated her. She should never have pushed the truth on him. How could she have expected him to accept it? Wanting nothing more than to flee from his terrible stare, Jenna ran past him.

Forgetting she was clad only in her nightgown, she hurried to the door. She had to get away from that look. "Open, dammit," she cried as she struggled with the lock. "Damn . . . damn . . ." In her fury she pounded on the immobile wood.

He came up behind her, leaning into her body and covering her flailing hands with his own. She could feel his labored breath by her ear. It was too much, and her forehead rested against the wood in defeat. "I . . . I'm not a freak," she cried. "Do you think I *wanted* to leave my life behind?"

Quickly, he turned her around and held her to his chest in a tight, possessive grip. "Do you think I *care*? Dammit! It doesn't matter where you came from, or even who you are! I won't *let* you go back!" He buried his face in her hair, and she heard his soft, muffled cry. "I love you . . . I love you . . . Don't leave me . . . Please . . . I love you, Jenna . . ."

He felt her immediate surrender. She was so still, for a moment, he thought she might not have understood. Then, slowly, almost hesitantly, her hands worked their way into his hair.

Lifting his head, she searched his eyes. "You . . . you love . . . me?" Her voice sounded tiny, afraid.

Morgan stared down at her perfect face. Soft blue-gray surrounded huge black pupils, and in a shattering fraction of time, he saw himself reflected in her eyes. He was surrounded by her, by the soft color of the woman. The woman who offered him love, caring, understanding—And just as quickly, something hard and hurting deep inside of him dissolved.

"I've been afraid, Jenna," he whispered.

She sniffled and tried to smile. "I know."

"I thought if I let you come too close, I'd lose you."

"I know."

Almost frantic, his hands entered her hair and held her head tightly. Staring into her eyes, he prayed he wasn't misreading what he saw reflected there. "You love me!" he stated in a hoarse, rasping voice.

Jenna brought his lips down to hers. "I know . . ." She breathed the words into his mouth just before it took possession of her own.

It was a communion, a tender giving and taking, binding two lovers in a life-sustaining bond. Jenna and Morgan sealed their spoken love, yet very quickly, tenderness gave way to desperation, and kissing wasn't enough.

She slipped her hands under the back of his opened shirt, pressing him into her as her fingers reached his collar. Taking hold of it, she pulled it down and away from him. His arms easily withdrew from the material.

Letting the shirt fall from her hands, Jenna's splayed fingers roamed over his naked chest. "I love

339

you, Morgan Trahern," she whispered as she let her fingertips trail through the soft curling hair. Hearing his quick intake of breath, she frantically unbuckled his belt and disposed of the buttons on his jeans. His hands joined hers and, within seconds, Jenna pressed his naked body against her.

She raised her face to his, and his mouth crushed her own. Their hands moved over the other in a feverish, possessive sweep, wanting to touch, to explore, to memorize. Morgan felt her body begin to sag as her legs went weak, and he slowly lowered them to the ground. He sat on the polished wooden floor, his thighs against the back of his legs, the woman he adored straddling him.

He left her nightgown in place, letting it fall around them. Using one hand to support her back, he used the other to pull the light-blue silk away from her breasts. The fragile material strained under their weight, yet lifted them up in an extravagant offering.

Wanting him as much as he wanted her, Jenna lowered herself, unable to stop the gasp of pleasure when she felt his warmth enter her body. He brought his head forward and captured first one already erect nipple and then the other, but she forced the pleasure to end as she pulled his head back from her.

"Morgan . . ." She kissed his eyelids. "I want you to know why I love you . . ." His heavy lashes lifted, and she was engulfed in a dark warm blue. "I love your strength," she whispered in a husky, emotion-filled voice. "I love your compassion, your sense of honor . . . your laughter. And right now, I love the way you make me feel wanted, needed."

Words no longer could convey what was in Jenna's and Morgan's hearts. Concentrating on each other, they communicated silently, sharing a sense of wonder, elation, joy, and passion. Emotions passed from one to the other and then back again, filling them both with an overpowering sensuality. They went beyond physical need and awareness, and entered the other's soul. Timeless seconds passed as they mutually surrendered all barriers, a total giving and receiving. And when their breathing quickened, they released the tender hold and withdrew, taking with them a piece of the other's identity to meld with their own. Slowly moving in the ancient ritual of love, they both knew, with conviction, neither would ever again be alone.

"I suppose I should do something romantic and carry you into the bedroom."

Jenna smiled and looked down into his tired eyes.

"Frankly, I don't think I have the energy," he admitted while running a hand through his hair.

"You forget," she said, a look of laughter in her eyes, "you're speaking to a twentieth century woman." Standing up, she adjusted the nightgown over her body and held out her hand. "Here, I'll help you."

He never hesitated. The moment his larger hand grabbed hold of hers, she brought him up. Once he was standing, she took his arm and brought it around her shoulders. As she led him into the bedroom, she could feel his weight, and Jenna relished the fact that he wasn't too proud to let her help.

Standing at the bed, he brought his other arm around her, and she lifted her face. "Nothing like that has ever happened to me, Jenna," he said with a sense of wonder. "I don't know whether I feel ten years younger in body, or ten years older in wisdom. I just know I love you."

She smiled tenderly. "I love you, too, Morgan, but I think you should get some rest. You've been up over twenty-four hours."

"You'll come with me?"

She nodded. "Hmm. Just try and keep me out of your bed," she lightly challenged.

Ten minutes later, she watched him drift off. She couldn't stop watching him, couldn't tear her eyes away from his handsome face. She was torn between shedding tears of tenderness, when he'd quickly open his eyes to make sure she was still there, and whoops of silent elation. *He loved her!* After everything, Morgan Trahern loved her!

Discarded dishes lay haphazardly on a silver tray at the bottom of the bed. Clothes were strewn over the soft hues of the oriental rug, and the heavy haze of cigar smoke rose and hung about the huge copper tub. Inside it, Morgan and Jenna relaxed at opposite ends, each with a large snifter of brandy and a thin cheroot.

"Explain it again," he demanded, with the insistence of a child.

Jenna blew at the curling tendrils of hair that brushed her damp forehead. "I'm not a mechanical engineer." She sipped the smooth liquor. "Ask me about trains. That I can tell you about."

His toe dipped under the steaming water and tickled her inner thigh. "I want to hear about the coaches that fly through the air . . . and that thing, what did you call it? Tubevision?"

"Stop it!" she giggled. "All right! Only it's television. You got part of it right."

"Television." He said the word slowly, testing it on his tongue. "This seems the most disturbing. You say it comes into your home? People fight wars, ride horses . . . right in your sitting room?"

Jenna laughed, enjoying his confusion. "And if you have the right equipment . . ." Her voice lowered to a conspiratorial whisper. "They even . . . make love!"

He sat up straighter, a look of indignation marring his face. "Stop teasing, Jenna! I don't believe that!"

It was impossible to control her laughter. "I'm not teasing! Though, on conventional television you don't see that much."

"*You watched*?"

She lifted her chin and gave him a look of perfect innocence. "I admit I've never seen an X-rated movie, but you get a pretty good idea from the—"

"Jenna Trahern! You should be ashamed! Do you realize what you've been describing?"

She relaxed and took another puff from the thin cigar. "I like that," she said, ignoring his outburst. "That sounds nice . . . Jenna Trahern. When are you going to buy me my wedding ring?"

He, too, relaxed and brought the snifter to his lips. "When we get married . . . again. I don't think either one of us is too comfortable with the Reverend Hobart's improvised ceremony."

Jenna slowly ran her foot along the long length of his leg. "I never thought I'd say this, but I'm glad he was on that train. If he'd never insisted that we be thrown off, if he'd never gotten the inspiration to marry us, who knows? You might never have given me a second thought."

He placed his drink on the floor and his cigar in a crystal ashtray alongside it. Putting his hands behind her knees, he quickly pulled her to him. She slid along the bottom of the tub, splashing water over its sides, until she came to rest directly in front of him. He leaned forward and wrapped her legs around his waist. "Given you a second thought? Woman, you have, and always had, my complete attention. Tell me, *desperada*, more about this television. Do they show people doing this?" And he kissed her shoulder.

"More," she said, throwing back her head in laugh-

343

ter.

"This?" he asked, burying his head at her wet breasts.

"Don't ask, Morgan," she breathed, inhaling and feeling her body begin to melt. "I . . . I think this is the part where they just play music and let your imagination take over."

Morgan lifted his head and smiled into her flushed face. "Then this is one time I'll be grateful for your vivid imagination. Let me know, beautiful, when you begin to hear the music . . ."

Chapter Twenty-eight

"How could this have happened, Jenna? How could you have traveled into the past?"

She looked up into his eyes and sighed. "I don't know, Morgan. I've tried to figure it out, but there's no answer. It just happened."

Morgan sat on a blanket with Jenna's head cradled in his lap. Leaning back against the trunk of a tree, he lifted his head and stared beyond the leaves and into the sky. "For so long, I resisted. I can't anymore." He looked down at her. Kissing the tip of her nose, he said, "You've told me about the money cards—"

"Credit cards," she interrupted.

"Credit cards." He said the words like a child learning a new language. "You've explained television, telephones, comp . . ."

"Computers," she helped out when she heard the uncertainty in his voice. "Though I really didn't explain them. I don't know how."

He smiled while playing with a soft blond curl. "Nor could you explain the airplane or the auto. You are certain such things really exist in the future?"

Jenna laughed. "Yes, Morgan. I have flown in airplanes many times, and I own my own automobile.

345

We call them cars."

He looked out to the deserted valley that they had chosen as the site for their long postponed picnic. "Cars. Try to explain them again. I think I would like to drive such a vehicle."

Jenna smiled as she watched him daydream. "I'm not quite sure how to explain it clearly. Gasoline is refined from oil, from under the ground. When it's put into a car, it travels to the engine, and a small explosion takes place with something called spark plugs." She kissed his stomach. "Let's not talk about cars. Let's talk about us. It's so much more interesting. Don't you think?"

He brought his knees up, and she rested her back against them. Staring into her eyes, he whispered, "Let's go home."

Jenna's lips curved upward. "We don't have to go back to the hotel, you know. I don't think there's another person around for five miles. It's just you, me, and—"

"Not the hotel. I mean *home*. Baltimore."

Seeing her shocked expression, he hurried to explain. "Neither one of us is from the West. There's nothing for you in Philadelphia, and I have a home and business in Baltimore. Come home with me, Jenna."

Sitting up straight, she looked out to the swaying reeds of grass. "My mother, my home, my father's company . . ."

"Jenna. I'm sorry." He touched her shoulder with compassion. "I shouldn't have put it like that."

She took a deep, steadying breath and shook her head. "No. You're right. There is nothing for me there now. I have to face it. Nothing . . . exists yet."

Hearing the torment in her voice, he gathered her into his arms. He held her close, wishing he could erase the pain, take away the grief that racked her body. "Shh . . ." He whispered into her hair, gently rocking her as she continued to sob against his chest. "It's all right, Jenna. You have good reason to cry. But it's for yourself, not for them," he said gently. "Don't you see? If they haven't even been born, they have their whole life ahead of them."

She brought her head up. "Then what about me? Don't I exist? *What about me, Morgan?*"

He gazed into her eyes, swollen with tears. "You exist for *me*. And we're going to go home and begin *our* life. But first . . ." He gently placed his hands on either side of her face. "I have something to ask you."

She sniffled and raised her eyebrows in a silent question.

He looked at her mouth, at her hair, and finally, her eyes.

"Will you marry me, Jenna? I never did ask you properly. Will you consent to be my wife?"

She stared at him, wanting to commit to memory this precious moment. He'd asked her! He had finally asked! Nodding, she broke into fresh tears and wrapped her arms around his neck. "I love you, Morgan. I love you so much."

Kissing her shoulder, he murmured, "I know . . . I know . . ."

The next few days were taken up with plans for their wedding and departure from Sacramento. Jenna bought the sexiest lingerie she could find, but resisted Morgan's pleas for a wedding gown. She wanted to wear the cream silk he had brought to her in Verdi. It didn't matter that it wasn't new. What did matter was that Morgan had picked it out, and it meant something special to her.

347

He had arranged with a minister to marry them, and it was this news that prompted Jenna to ask questions. Folding clothes into a new leather trunk, she turned around and faced him.

"You know, Morgan, I've told you about my life in detail, yet you haven't filled me in about yourself. For instance, I would have thought with a name like Trahern, you would have wanted a priest to officiate at our wedding. I don't know your religion, what your family is like, or if you even have any in Baltimore."

Morgan handed her another of his jackets. As he watched her fold the two shoulders together, he said, "A priest would have taken too long, wanted too much information. Does it bother you not to have one?"

She smiled and shook her head. "No, not at all. I just want to be married . . . legally. But what about your family? What will they think when you return with a wife? Should I be worried?"

He came up behind her and enclosed her in his arms. Feeling her lean against him, he bent his head and kissed the skin right below her ear. "They will probably think I'm the luckiest man alive. And my mother will be thrilled to finally have her wish of seeing me settled."

Jenna gave a short laugh. "That doesn't sound too exciting, does it? Settled. That was one of the last things my mother and I talked about. I guess it doesn't matter whether you're male or female. I imagine all parents want the same. But you have no brothers, sisters? Someone who could have taken the pressure off you? I know I had wished for a sister."

His grip tightened, and Jenna stared into the half full trunk as she listened to his words.

"I had a brother. He was younger than me."

"What happened? she whispered.

She could feel him inhale deeply. "He died. In the

348

war."

Turning around, Jenna looked up to his face. She could easily read the pain in his eyes. "I'm sorry, Morgan."

He shook his head. "Too many people lost brothers, and husbands . . . and sons."

His arms fell to his sides, and he walked away from her. Touching her ribbons lying on the dresser, he seemed lost in thought. Suddenly, as if making up his mind, he turned to her and asked, "Tell me more about this McComb? The one you say breaks the story to the newspapers."

Jenna blinked a few times in confusion. "McComb? What does he have to do with—"

He impatiently dropped the ribbons and walked back to her. "Listen to me. I've tried to put this investigation out of my mind in the last few days. I wanted to. But I can't, Jenna. Something's gone completely wrong. All the work Mano and I have done is in jeopardy." He sat on the bed and brought his hand up to his forehead. Rubbing it, he said, "There's a man, Mike Hogan. All three of us were partners in the war. Frank Adams, my superior, sent me on this assignment, just as he recruited Mano and Hogan. Mano gave the information to Hogan, and he was to see that it got back to Frank."

He looked up and stared into her eyes. "When we were at Crocker's party, I saw Hogan in the garden. I think he's going to sell it to the highest bidder."

Jenna was amazed. When she could find her voice, she asked, "Why do you want to know about McComb? You think he's going to buy the information?"

Morgan shook his head. "Not if this story doesn't come out for three years. I didn't have any positive proof, but I thought McComb was heavily involved.

That's why I didn't figure he'd be the one who exposed it."

Jenna sat down next to him, deep in thought. "I think you're right, Morgan," she said slowly. "I may be mistaken, but I sort of remember that McComb and Oak Ames have an argument over the ownership of some shares of stock. McComb loses and is so vindictive that he hands over to the newspaper letters from Oak Ames, which names almost everyone involved."

Morgan's face showed his astonishment. "He incriminates himself?"

Jenna raised her shoulders. "I know. It seems crazy, but that's what he did."

She watched him stare at the patterns on the oriental rug. When he stood up, so did she.

He faced her and was silent for a few, uncomfortable seconds. "Jenna, I can't let him get away with it."

Her eyes widened. "Who? McComb? I've already told you . . . that's how it happened. It's written down in history books. You can't change it!"

The hard, cold anger returned to his eyes, and Jenna's stomach tightened.

"I can try! It's Hogan. He's the key."

"Morgan, what does it matter to you?" she demanded, frightened by what had unexpectedly come out of their discussion. "It's all going to be exposed. They'll all be caught. Please . . . stay out of it! What about us? What about going back to Baltimore? *Please*, Morgan!"

She recognized the closed expression on his face before he spoke. "I have to stop him. We'll postpone the wedding. We can always—"

"No!" She was desperate and grabbed hold of his arm, as if it might keep him with her. "Morgan, listen to me. How many chances does a person get at happiness? How many? I'm terrified that this might be our last. Don't throw this one away. Please!"

Her pleading cracked the hard outer shell he had placed around him. Gathering her into his arms, he kissed the top of her head. "Don't be foolish. You were never superstitious before. We'll have our chance. I promise you."

Listening to his heart, she quietly asked, "You won't leave this alone? Not for me?"

She heard his breath leave his lungs in a quick rush. "I can't, Jenna. It isn't only this assignment. I've just realized something. I can't go on with the future until I've taken care of the past. Trust me? Please?"

In the end she knew she had no other choice. If he didn't go through with this, he would always blame her for stopping him, for not letting him settle his old life. Yet, as she watched him leave, she knew she would've accepted that, rather than risk losing him.

Shutting the door behind him, Jenna leaned against it and closed her eyes. Dear God, she prayed, don't be impatient with us. Give us one more chance.

Two days later, Jenna thought she would go mad if he didn't return. She'd done exactly as he'd said. She hadn't left the hotel, just stayed in her room and waited. She'd even taken her meals in the hotel suite, afraid she might miss him. But nothing. And the enforced waiting was driving her crazy.

In the beginning, she'd pushed all thoughts out of her mind and concentrated on planning their new life together. She had envisioned Morgan's home in Baltimore, his parents, what his business might be like, and how she might help him. But it hadn't lasted long. In the back of her mind lurked nightmarish thoughts that something was going to happen to

351

Morgan.

Now, she was convinced of it. Morgan would never leave her for two days without trying to communicate. *Something* must have happened. Who could help her? She hadn't the slightest idea of where to start looking for such a person.

Pacing the floor of the sitting room, Jenna almost didn't hear the slight knock. She stopped, standing completely still, and waited. There! Again she heard it, this time a little louder. Picking up the hem of her skirt, she ran to the door.

"Senora Trahern?"

Jenna looked down into the frightened face of a young, dark-haired boy. Ignoring his mispronunciation of the last name, she quickly nodded. "Yes?"

He shifted uncomfortably and wiped his small hands on his white shirt. "I was to tell you to go out through the service entrance and he would meet you."

"Who?" she asked urgently. "Tell me who."

The child nervously looked down the hall. "The big man with dark hair. He paid me to come here."

Morgan! For some reason he didn't want anyone to know he was back. Who cared why—he was back! Closing the door behind her, she said, "Show me where he is. Quickly!"

The child's almost black eyes widened. He didn't move, but just pointed toward the end of the hall.

"Down there?" she asked. "The service stairs are back there?"

He nodded once, then quickly turned around and ran in the opposite direction. Jenna watched him for a few seconds before she turned back and walked toward the end of the hall. Opening the last door on the right, she found the stairs and hurried down them. When they ended, she heard noises coming from her left and listened to the sounds of dishes and muffled talking. Knowing that would lead her to the kitchen, she opened the door directly in front of her.

She was behind the hotel. Looking around in the dark, she whispered his name. "Morgan! Are you out here?"

Not hearing anything, she looked over to the piled boxes and garbage. "Morgan . . . where are you?"

Bringing her arms up, she hugged herself. Not from the cold, for it was a warm summer night, but from an instinctive sense of foreboding. Why didn't he answer?

She was beginning to be frightened and decided to call out one more time before she went back inside. "Morg—"

She never finished his name as a dark, suffocating cloth was swiftly placed over her head. Panicked, she clawed at the heavy sack, but her arms were caught by someone and held in a viselike grip. Her cries were muted by the material, and she lost her equilibrium several times as she tried to get away from her assailant. When she felt him dragging her across the ground, she realized that her only hope was to scream.

Taking a deep breath, she let out a yell and almost immediately, her hands were loose. Instantly she raised them to the sack that covered her, but before she could remove it, a sharp, piercing pain exploded on the left side of her face, and all she could think of was that she was going to die as the darkness behind her eyelids flashed silver. And then it, and everything, went black—and silent.

All he could think about was getting out of his filthy clothes and taking a bath. Then, he wanted to hold Jenna in his arms until he fell asleep. God, he missed her. Maybe she was right about his not being able to change history. Maybe he should just let it be. But he was so close. He could almost sense Hogan's anger, even though he hadn't caught sight of him yet. Crocker's man was too nervous after he'd talked with him. He'd been easy to follow, and Morgan had known he would lead him right to Hogan. But he'd underestimated his old partner. The run-down hotel room was deserted. Instinct told him Hogan knew he was after him.

That was when he made up his mind to return to the hotel. It wasn't worth it. Morgan didn't want to take any more chances with Jenna. She was what was important. He would telegraph Frank in Washington and let him handle it, and he didn't care that he was breaking silence. This time it was really over. He had Jenna now.

354

Chapter Twenty-nine

"Jenna? Where are you? *Jenna!*"

Morgan left the deserted bedroom and walked back into the sitting room. Looking around, he noticed a cup and saucer on the small writing desk. As he came closer, he saw that it was three quarters full. What was she doing? Why did she leave? It wasn't like her. He'd told Jenna not to go out, to stay put until he came back.

Touching the tea with his finger, Morgan noted its coolness. She'd left some time ago. He looked around the empty hotel suite. She'd probably gone shopping. That's it, he thought, as he walked back into the bedroom. She must have thought of something else she needed and couldn't wait any longer. Removing his shirt as he waited for the bath he had ordered when he'd entered the hotel, Morgan remembered Jenna's desire to buy gifts for the Eberlys. He just wished she could have waited.

Refreshed after his quick bath, Morgan toweled his hair dry and wandered into the sitting room. Several times, he looked out the window and down into the street, hoping to catch a glimpse of Jenna. He'd been back over an hour, and she had yet to return. Turning back to the room, he left the towel across his shoulders and untied the belt of his robe. He looked over the elegant furnishings as he walked back into the bedroom to finish dressing, and out of the corner of his eye, he caught sight of a small white paper in front of the door.

Knowing it wasn't unusual for the hotel to slip messages under the door if they couldn't get an answer, Morgan walked over to the paper, believing it had come while he'd been in the bath. Almost carelessly, he picked it up, and it was only a vague curiosity that made him open the note before he placed it on a nearby table.

His stood still, staring at the scrawled words. He could feel his heartbeat increase, the tightening of his stomach muscles, and hear his own labored breathing. His hands shook as he brought it closer to his eyes and read the single sentence over again.

If you ever want to see her again, stay out of it.

For a brief moment, he felt immobilized, incapable of taking action. Then, slowly, a terrible anger grabbed hold of him, and his body continued to shake as he ran into the bedroom—only this time from fury. Even though there was no signature, Morgan knew the man's identity.

The son of a bitch couldn't face him, like a man. Throwing aside the carefully folded clothes in the trunk, Morgan brought out his familiar old garb. It was fitting that he dress the part. For if Hogan harmed one hair on Jenna's head, he'd kill the bastard quicker than the blink of an eye. Casting off his robe and picking up the faded denims, he let out an animallike growl. He wanted Hogan permanently out of his life. It was time.

The El Boleto de Ida Hotel was appropriately named. It was a one way ticket to nowhere. In its three years of operation, more robberies, drunken brawls, and murders had taken place there than at any other establishment in the city; and nobody, including its owners, could put a figure on how many incidents went unreported. It was a place that didn't ask questions, and its reputation grew among the unsavory crowd that frequented it.

Above the cantina, on the second floor, were rooms that could be rented by the hour, day, or, on rare occasions, by the week. In number eight, a small cubicle of space, a man sat in the dark, waiting. Through a great deal of threatening, he knew the room was paid for until the end of the week, and he'd spent almost six hours inside it—in the same place, in the same uncomfortable chair—just waiting for its occupant to return.

Morgan didn't notice the growth of whiskers on his face; his ears had shut out the loud noises from the first floor. Even his nose no longer wrinkled in distaste from the foul air that permeated the place. In one hand was a bottle of whiskey, almost gone; in the other, his pistol. What kept him awake and alert was the sound of people walking in the hallway. Each time, he held his breath, wanting so much for the footsteps to stop, to pause in front of the tobacco-stained door. But each time, they kept going right on past. He hadn't seen daylight since he'd left the hotel to take up his vigil in Hogan's room, and his eyes watered from fatigue and frustration.

Jenna! Her name swirled around inside his tormented brain. What had he done to her? How could he have placed her in this danger? He had to believe she was all right. If he thought differently, he would go mad. He kept hearing her voice telling him there was nothing he could do. The vision of her begging him to leave it alone, not to jeopardize their last chance for happiness nagged at him, berated him, and continued to torture his mind. He had placed revenge above her, made it more important, and now he might lose the most valuable thing in his life.

It was impossible to sit in Hogan's room, to know the man had slept in the narrow, unmade bed, had sat in the same chair, without remembering the man himself. The last six hours had been a mental journey into the past.

He and Mike Hogan had been good, better than good. They each knew the other's mind and reacted accordingly. They worked so smoothly together that when Mano had joined them, both were afraid that the new man would disrupt their efficiency. But Mano's easy disposition and quick mind soon blended with theirs, and the three of them became a formidable team. No one was sure, probably not even Frank, how many times they'd crossed over the enemy's lines and brought back the necessary information about troop movements.

Each man had a specialty. Wearing a Confederate officer's uniform became almost second nature. Countless times he'd mingled with Lee's upper echelon. Hogan normally posed as his corporal, developing such a strong southern drawl that even the infantry southerners had a tough time understanding him. Between the two of them, they usually managed to figure out what was going to take place. Even if the officers changed their minds, the infantry gossip filled

358

them in on supplies and troop strength. On occasion, Mano, drawing on his coloring and breeding, became a wonderfully effeminate Creole, too cowardly to actually fight for the southern cause, but more than willing to contribute financially. So grateful were the Confederate's officers that they thrilled him with daring stories of how the money would be spent. Most of the time the information wasn't accurate, but he was a genius at infiltrating the more powerful civilians beyond the Mason-Dixon Line.

He and Hogan had thought Mano's specialty to be the most dangerous, especially when he would return and rant about barely escaping with his manhood intact after fighting off an amorous southern gentleman.

It hadn't all been bad, Morgan thought. In war, a man develops friendships that can never be replaced. It would be hard to explain to someone who hadn't experienced it. You could never really explain it to a woman. How could you say you'd loved another man? How could you tell of that bond when you're crouched back to back in the woods, or in a deserted barn, with the enemy all around you, and you know with a certainty that the man behind you will never leave you to face death alone? That at that time, your lives, your heartbeats, are so entwined, you'd die for each other? It can't be explained or understood. Not unless you've been through it.

They'd all been so close, so protective of each other. But that was before Hogan took to drink and became careless—and before Billy.

Bringing the bottle up to his mouth, Morgan took another long swallow. His tongue felt numb and, using the back of his hand, he wiped the whiskey from his lips as he continued to stare into the darkness.

Billy.

Just saying the name in his head was painful. He'd seen so many men die, so many—just boys, deprived of the full life that they deserved. But Billy was different. He wasn't supposed to be there in Vicksburg. He was supposed to be safe in Washington. Frank had promised him that. But he wanted to be a damned hero—like his older brother.

Morgan broke his silence and whispered a fierce obscenity. Hero. *Hero*! He hated the word! He'd only done what he was told, and anything else was done to save his own life, or his men's. Hell, three quarters of the time, he was scared to death!

Billy shouldn't have been there. When his younger brother had enlisted, Morgan had made sure he was safely tucked away at the War Department in Washington. But he should have remembered how headstrong his seventeen-year-old brother was. Seventeen! So damned young! When he showed up, outside Vicksburg, Morgan had been furious. He'd cursed Frank, Frank's superior whom Billy had gotten to, anybody connected with the lousy war. It was Hogan who had talked to him, tried to calm him down, telling him the kid deserved a chance to find out what the war was really like. Let him find out for himself what it's like on the line, Mike had said. Who the hell wouldn't go back to Washington? Mike'd promised to watch out for him.

The nightmares of his dreams silently played out in the darkness surrounding him. Billy, fresh, eager to be a real soldier, had started calling him major. Never Morgan, just major. At the time he'd thought it was because he didn't want special treatment. Hell, nobody got special treatment. Not then.

Word had gotten to them that Mano was being held

360

for questioning by the Rebs inside Vicksburg. He and Hogan were to pose as attachés for Lee, with forged orders to bring the Creole with them for further questioning. It should have been quick, in and out. Yet when they'd been ready to leave, Morgan had found Hogan drunk, too drunk to convincingly pull off his role. Deciding to chance going in alone, he'd left Billy with Hogan and the horses, just outside of town.

Clenching his back teeth together, as he let the memories freely come, Morgan tried to picture the confusion that had taken place next. It was as if they were waiting for him. Gunshots rang out all around him, and when he looked back, the sight of Billy running to him, and Hogan taking all the horses as he fled into the woods, burned into his brain. When he reached his brother, lying in the grass, the dim moonlight couldn't hide that Billy'd been shot in the chest. There was an ugly dark stain rapidly spreading across the front of his shirt. Dragging him into the woods, he'd held the young boy in his arms and—

Morgan couldn't relive watching his brother die twice, and he closed his eyes tightly, shutting out the horrible image. Perspiration broke out all over his body as he tried to forget the sound of Billy's labored voice: "Tell 'em . . . tell 'em I . . . I was a hero. You . . . you'll do that, Major? Jesus, Morgan, it hurts! Morgan? *Morgan . . .*"

His eyes snapped open and he shot out of the chair, throwing the bottle onto the filthy mattress. He had to get out of here, he thought in desperation, as he put the gun back into his holster and flung open the door. Hogan knew him too well. He wasn't coming back. Morgan realized he had no choice but to wait for Hogan to contact him. But he'd be damned if he would add Jenna to his nightmares. This time Mike Hogan would answer for his actions!

Sutter's Fort was the beginnings of Sacramento. When John Sutter, a German, settled along the American River in 1839, he envisioned a place where all he'd seen, in his worldwide travels, could be incorporated. It was a model for pioneer settlements. A huge center building sat atop a knoll, housing a carpenter shop, brandy distilleries, a blacksmith shop, saddle shop, and kitchens. A little over twenty-five years later, nothing remained of the walled fort, except the deserted, deteriorating, two-storied adobe center building. Everything had been picked over by scavengers, people trying to make a city out of rubble.

In its dark, musty basement, Jenna sat on the dirt floor and watched the tall man tap more wine from the old barrel.

"Some kind of luck, huh?" he asked, not really expecting an answer. "They took every other damned thing and missed this beauty."

Mike Hogan brought the tin cup up to his mouth and took a long swig. Using the cuff of his black silk shirt, he wiped the droplets of red from his lips. He stared at the silent woman and walked closer. "You're not much of a talker, are you?"

Again, Jenna tried the rope that bound her wrists together in front of her. It only made her inhale with pain as the fibers cut into her raw skin. Glaring at the tall, dark-haired man, she muttered, "What do you expect me to say?"

"Tell me about Morgan."

Her lips clamped together in anger. Ever since she'd awakened in this place, he'd harassed her with questions about Morgan. She hadn't answered one. Instead, she'd watched his every movement. She supposed, at one time, he might have been handsome. His auburn hair was thick; his height over six feet. Yet in the hours since her abduction, she had watched him deteriorate. She knew it wasn't just the faint light coming from the single lamp that made his complexion sallow; nor was it whatever caused the whites of his brown eyes to look yellow. The man was an alcoholic. She'd seen him clutch at his stomach in pain, until he stopped it with alcohol. And when that ran out, he'd opened the hidden barrel of wine.

"What're you waiting for? You think he's going to find you here?" He gave a derisive laugh. "You're married to him. Don't you know Morgan hates being the hero?"

He crouched down in front of her and touched her swollen cheek. "You shouldn't have screamed," he slurred, a look of regret in his eyes.

Jenna jerked her head away from his finger, disgust written on her face. "He'll come," she stated with conviction.

"You think you know him better'n me? I know that man's mind, inside and out. We were as close as brothers." He threw back his head and laughed. "That's funny, you know?"

Tracing the line of her shoulder with his finger, he whispered, "You're right. He's not goin' to let you go. I wouldn't. What do you think he's going to do, pretty woman, when he gets here?"

Jenna pressed her back against the adobe wall in an effort to get away from him. Her lips trembled from fear, but she forced them to move as she said the words. "I think he's going to kill you."

Hogan slowly smiled as he came closer. "I'm countin' on that, lady . . ."

He hadn't washed, except to throw cold water on his face, but he had sobered up. Morgan had forced the breakfast down his throat along with nearly the entire contents of a pot of coffee. He couldn't say he felt better, just stronger to face whatever was coming. It was the waiting that got to him, the feeling of being helpless, nothing more than a pawn in Hogan's greedy game. But he'd stayed in the room, not wanting to miss the message when it came. He was sure Hogan would contact him, once he'd traded the information. Sitting in a chair that faced the door, he waited.

Two hours later, the knock was loud and firm, and Morgan jumped for his gun. Bringing it with him, he slowly walked to the door and stood behind it, the barrel of the pistol pointed at the brass knob. Swiftly, he reached out and opened it, ready to kill whoever was on the opposite side.

"Dear God! Put that thing away!"

Charlotte Maxwell's face went completely white, but she recovered enough to enter the sitting room. Collapsing into a chair, she looked up. "You could have killed me!"

Morgan impatiently shut the door and gazed in her direction. "What the hell do you want, Charlotte? I don't have time for your theatrics."

Ignoring his words, she lifted the white netted veil on her hat and stared at him. "You look terrible, Morgan. No one would ever take you for a successful business man. You look more like a gunslinger than an importer."

Morgan laid the pistol on a table and sat down. "And I suppose you know a lot about gunslingers?

What do you want, Charlotte?"

Turning her head, she looked around the room. "Where's your lovely wife? I thought I might pay you both a call."

Morgan stared at the purse in her lap. "She's not here. Why don't you come back some other time?"

Charlotte cocked her head to one side and smiled sweetly. "But will she be back then? I'm afraid you're not being very hospitable, Morgan. Especially when I've come here to offer my help."

He leaned forward in the chair. "Your help? What are you talking about?"

She rose and slowly walked over to him. Standing in front of his knees, she reached out and placed a small hand on his shoulder. "Poor, Morgan. You really love her, don't you?"

His jaw became rigid. "I asked what you're talking about."

She withdrew her hand and studied the large diamond on her finger. "I think I'd like a drink first."

He impatiently indicated with his head several bottles on a narrow table.

Turning around, Charlotte glided over to it and poured herself a glass of straight whiskey. Over her shoulder, she said, "Here I thought all you Easterners had manners." Delicately sipping the amber liquor, she turned back to him.

He glanced over her expensively tailored gown and matching jacket. Letting his eyes travel up to her face, he noted her coloring had returned and that her eyes held a look of anticipation. "Just what is it you know, Charlotte?" he asked slowly.

She returned to her chair and held her drink in both hands. "I know where he's holding Jenna."

"*What?*" Morgan came to his feet.

Seeing that his hands were clenched into fists, Charlotte's voice was deceptively calm. "If you're thinking of harming me, I doubt whether you'll ever see her again. I'm your only hope, Morgan. So sit down and listen."

"Where is she?" he demanded, feeling his anger build once more.

She remained undaunted. "You're wasting time. If you want your wife back, stop being angry with me and listen." She waited until he gained control and reseated himself before she continued. "First of all, I had nothing to do with Jenna's kidnapping. All I want are the papers Hogan is selling."

Morgan's jaw dropped. "You? Why? Who do you work for?"

Charlotte laughed. "We're not all spies, you know. I'm not involved in any of your intrigues. I want them because they could hurt a friend of mine."

"Crocker?"

She nodded. "My reasons are none of your business. Let's just say I owe him a favor. He doesn't know about this, and I don't want him to. Bennett came to me with Hogan's offer. He used to work for me before Charlie hired him." She smiled. "Sometimes it's very advantageous that his first allegiance is to his former employer."

"Where does Hogan have Jenna?"

She finished her drink and looked across at him. "Let's get one thing perfectly straight, all right? I don't give a damn about Hogan. All I want are those papers. If he should have ah . . . an unfortunate accident, well then, I would be able to keep my fifteen thousand dollars and you would have your wife. Everybody would be happy, with the exception of Mike Hogan. It doesn't matter to me whether he's dead or alive, as long as I get that information."

"You're a cold bitch, Charlotte. What's Crocker got on you that you'd have a man killed?"

She raised her chin, giving back as hard a look as she was receiving. "I'm protecting him, not myself. Forget my personal life, Trahern. Will you, or will you not, trade your wife for those damn papers?"

Standing up, he tried to control his temper as he picked up the gun. Walking over to the desk, he placed the Colt .45 in his holster and turned around.

Automatically, his fingers buckled the worn leather into place, and he glared at the smiling woman across the room. "Where is she?" he demanded in a hoarse whisper that sounded too old and too tired for a man his age.

Chapter Thirty

He stood in the shadows, watching the deserted fort. Resisting the urge to charge right in, Morgan tried to calm down and think logically. Hogan had to have Jenna in the basement. Nothing remained of the building, except its shell. Even the staircase to the second floor was gone. He had to give Mike credit. It was the perfect place to hide someone. Old Sutter's Fort stood right in the middle of Sacramento. It must have been for sentimental reasons that it was still standing, for California's state capital grew and prospered all around it.

Keeping to the shadows, he entered the adobe building and listened. Several times he heard the rustling of rodents or the larger scavengers—stray cats. Taking out his pistol, he tried to see any light coming from the several rooms that lined one wall. Starting at the first, he kept his body flush with the adobe wall and brought out Jenna's small flashlight. His heart started pounding as he inched his way toward the room, his gun ready in his right hand, the thumb of his left hand poised over the small button on the flashlight. Taking a deep breath, he spun on his heels and faced the dark entryway, instantly shining the light into the room.

Large furry creatures scurried amid the litter, but there were no human occupants. Releasing his breath at the same time as he lifted his thumb, he allowed the room to return to darkness. Morgan repeated the same procedure three more times as he checked each small cubicle.

Nothing.

With only two more rooms to go, Morgan's nerves were stretched tight as he realized he was playing a deadly game of cat and mouse. And, as each space had failed to produce Jenna, he had the queer feeling that he was the mouse.

Standing outside the entryway to the fourth room, Morgan pushed the strange thoughts out of his mind. Leaning the back of his head against the wall, he deeply inhaled through his nose in an attempt to control the building frustration. Every nerve ending came alive with the expectation of immediate danger. Once again bringing his hands up to his chest, he quickly flipped his body around and stood poised at the threshold to the room, gun and flashlight now thrust out toward the unknown.

Within half a second, his brain registered the form huddled in the corner; yet before he could turn the light on it, the small room was quickly illuminated by a large oil lamp.

"Welcome, old friend. We've been waiting for you."

His eyes flicked over Hogan before they returned to Jenna. Staring into her frightened eyes, he tried to gain control over his anger as he took in the gun pointed at her neck and the dark bruise at her cheekbone.

"What have you done to her?" he growled, his need to run to Jenna curbed by Hogan's pistol pointing at her neck.

"Throw your gun back outside the room and come on in. We have a lot to talk about."

Without hesitation, Morgan flipped the gun backward and came closer. Hogan backed away from Jenna, and Morgan rushed to her side. Crouching on the floor, he gathered her into his arms and whispered, "It's all right, Jenna. It's all right now."

She lifted her head and he winced at her appearance. She was filthy. Her right cheekbone was purple red and swollen. Her lips looked dry and cracked, and they quivered as tears rushed over the dirt on her face.

"Morgan. Thank God you're here!" she murmured in between sobs.

Now standing across the room, with his gun pointed on the couple, Hogan stated, "She's not hurt."

"What the hell do you call this, then?" Morgan ground out through clenched teeth as he lightly touched Jenna's cheek."

"She's not hurt," Hogan repeated.

Morgan gave him a look of disgust. "I'm untying her hands," he shot back, and reached for the rope at Jenna's wrists.

As the painful tingling started, returning the circulation to her hands, Jenna hissed and briefly closed her eyes.

"Shh . . ." Morgan soothed, while taking her hands and placing them in his. Lightly rubbing them, he whispered, "I know it hurts, but it'll be over in a few minutes. Are you all right? He didn't . . ." When Jenna shook her head, he kissed her fingers and gently placed them in her lap.

Standing up, he turned around and faced Hogan. Morgan eyed his old partner as if he were a stranger. The past years had taken their toll. Mike looked like hell. It didn't take more than a few seconds to note the dissipation that ravaged his once handsome face.

Morgan lifted his chin. "You shouldn't have taken her. This is between you and me."

Hogan snorted and grabbed his stomach with his left hand. "You had no business sticking your nose around where it didn't belong," he gasped. "I've got fifteen thousand dollars coming to me for this. When the hell did the government ever pay us money like that?"

On closer inspection Mike looked sick, and although the gun in his hand wavered slightly, Morgan knew he wouldn't risk jumping him. Not yet.

"What have you done with the papers?"

Hogan straightened and patted his chest. "Right here. Got a little business to take care of tonight."

"Gonna just take the money and run. That's the way you figured it, Mike?"

"Something like that."

They stood across the small room, staring at each other. After so many years, neither one had ever imagined this scene would actually take place.

Jerking his head in the direction of the wine barrel, Hogan said, "How about a drink? We used to be able to put many a bottle to rest, as I remember."

Morgan walked over to the barrel. Picking up the battered tin cup, he opened the tap and filled it. As he handed it to Hogan, he looked him straight in the eye and said, "Those days are over. Looks to me like you shouldn't be drinking anymore, Mike."

Hogan grabbed the wine, spilling some onto the ground. "What's wrong, *Major*? You gonna get self-righteous on me, or something?"

"Or something. What the hell are you doing, Mike? Why aren't you and those papers on the way to Washington?"

Licking his lips to savor the taste of the wine,

Hogan brought his head up in a proud stance. "I already told you. I'm getting fifteen thousand dollars. What were you going to get from Frank this time? Hell, you'd be lucky to get a thank you. This stuff you and Mano dug up is worth more than that."

"Then give it to me and let us leave. You won't be doing any selling tonight. Charlotte Maxwell's the one who told me where to find you. You're not getting her fifteen thousand."

"That double-crossing bitch!" He sat down on an overturned wooden box and finished his wine. Glancing up at Morgan, he held out the empty cup. "How about some more, friend? There was a time—"

Grabbing the cup away from him, Morgan snapped back, "Forget there ever was such a time! It doesn't exist anymore. You and me, we don't exist anymore . . . not like before. We were soldiers. And now we're not. It's that simple."

"*Simple?* It's been that easy for you, Morgan? I don't think so. I *know* you've got your ghosts." He looked toward Morgan's boots. "I know I got mine," he said quietly.

Looking back up, his eyes pleaded for understanding. "I was drunk, Morgan. When I heard the shots . . . " He shook his head. "I don't know. Something made me run. I forgot about Billy, everything, just . . . "

He got no further in his explanation. In a lightning flash, Morgan's fist connected with his jaw and slammed him against the wall behind him. He heard the woman scream, yet it took a moment for the pain to register, and only slightly longer to realize that he'd lost control of the gun.

Hogan felt like he was in a foggy daze. His whole head throbbed, and he casually wiped at the blood coming from his mouth as he tried not to listen to

Morgan's shouts.

"Don't you *ever* talk about my brother again, you hear me? *Not ever!*"

Hogan glanced up to see Morgan picking up his gun. The woman ran to his side, and he watched Morgan wrap an arm around her while continuing to keep the pistol pointed in his direction. "I think it's time we did some talking, my friend," he said with a false calmness.

Morgan watched him spit out blood, yet kept the gun on him as he straightened. "The only talking we need to do is good-bye . . . after you hand over the papers."

"Look, Morgan, I'll make a deal with you—"

"No deals. You forget who's got the gun now. *I'll* give the orders."

"Just like the old days, Major?" Hogan cut in. "We were a pretty good team, you and me. Even Mano was okay. Why not one more time? Who's it gonna hurt?"

Morgan shook his head. "Just give me the papers."

Hogan brushed his hair back from his face, and the look he gave Morgan was one of agony. "Still so damned self-righteous, aren't you!" he shouted. "What about me? What about the rest of the world, who just wants a little bit for themselves? This is my chance, Morgan. Let me have it."

Morgan leaned slightly against Jenna. "You're chance is gone, Mike. You lost it a long time ago. I'm going to ask one last time: Give me the papers."

Hogan seemed to crumble before them. His hands shook as he reached inside his shirt. "Listen, Morgan, I have another deal. You want these." He held up the small sheaf of paper. "And I want something from you." Just then, he grabbed at his stomach as a spasm doubled him over. When he again straightened, his face was perspiring, and his eyes reflected his pain.

"I'm dyin', Morgan," he whispered. "Heard too many doctors in too many towns tell me the same thing. My liver's shot to hell. I've only got a couple of months, if I'm lucky." He took several deep breaths, before continuing. "You got this thing about honor . . . okay, I expected that. That's why I took your wife. What I want from you is a release." He looked straight into Morgan's eyes. "Don't make me die slow. It'd be different if I'd had the fifteen thousand, but not now. I don't want to die like this. Do it quick, Morgan. I choose you."

Morgan let loose a string of curses while Jenna buried her head against his chest. Still holding the gun on Hogan, he gently pushed her away and slowly said, "Go get him a drink, Jenna."

She stared at him. "Morgan! Please, don't do this! Think about—"

"Get him the wine!" he interrupted, never taking his eyes off Hogan.

Slowly, she moved away, looking at Morgan as if he had turned into a stranger. His mouth was set in a grim line; his eyes were hard glints of blue steel as they locked with Hogan's.

"Just do it, Jenna!"

So shocked by the sound of Morgan's voice, she half ran to the barrel. Neither Morgan nor Hogan had taken their eyes off each other. She struggled with the tap, spilling the wine, and watched as it soaked into the dirt floor. Finally, she filled the cup and held it in her shaking hands.

"Give it to him."

"Morgan . . ."

He ignored the pleading sound of her voice. "Give it to him."

She looked at Hogan, and then back at Morgan. Both men were determined.

"Take him the wine, Jenna."

Slowly, she walked over to Hogan and handed him the tin cup. His hand, too, was shaking.

From behind her, she heard Morgan's voice. "Give her the papers, Mike. You get what you want . . . I get what I want."

Handing her the folded, wrinkled papers, Hogan looked into Jenna's eyes and smiled. "You got one hell of a lady, Morgan. Be sure you treat her good."

Jenna read the pain, the resignation, and the fear in his eyes, and despite everything, she returned his sad smile.

"I don't need you to tell me about her. I'll make up to her for what you did."

Hogan shrugged as he continued to stare at Jenna. "I never did mean to hurt you. I'd like you to believe that."

Jenna bit her bottom lip as she turned to Morgan. "I won't let you do this. You're both crazy!"

"Stay out of it, Jenna. And get away from him."

She didn't move. "What's wrong with you, Morgan? We're talking about death here! That's final. Whatever you think Hogan has done, it can't deserve this!"

It was Hogan who spoke. "Oh, you're wrong there, Jenna. In your husband's mind I deserve to die. In my mind . . . I want to."

She jerked her head back and stared at him. *"Why?"*

He brought the wine up to his lips, closed his eyes, and drank. Opening them, he took a deep breath and smiled again. "It's all pointless anymore. I'm gonna die anyway. Might as well be Morgan who does it. He's probably the last man on this earth that I still respect."

Looking over her shoulder, his eyes locked with

Morgan's. "I can't live with them anymore. If I'm not going to have the money to drink them away, then let me join them."

"Who?" Jenna whispered, thinking his mind was snapping.

His eyes slid back to hers. "Ned Froman, Tom Baxter, Max Simpson, Billy Trahern . . . too many to name. I can't fall asleep unless I'm drunk. Even then, they don't always leave me alone. I've had enough."

Again, he looked at Morgan. "How about you?" he asked. "Do righteous, honorable men like you, Morgan, don't they ever think back and wonder what it would be like if they'd stayed home, stayed on their small farms, tended their own business, and never went to war? Or are honorable men free from ghosts and nightmares?"

Jenna looked at Morgan, waiting with Hogan for him to answer. She saw a slight narrowing of his eyes, a tightness that seemed like a crack in his rigid attitude.

Never taking his eyes away from Hogan's, he said, "Bring the papers to me, Jenna."

She walked over and handed them to him. "I hope they're worth it, Morgan. This isn't the way to stop the nightmares . . . for either of you. Please don't do this."

He took them out of her hand and slipped the papers down the front of his shirt. "Go wait by the door."

She felt desperate. "Please . . ."

His eyes flicked over her and he smiled. "Trust me. Go over by the door."

Jenna backed away from them until she felt the wall against her back. Her mind refused to believe that Morgan was going to do this.

"You know, Mike, I used to lie awake at night

thinking of ways to kill you. I hated you more than any man should. I hated you for Billy, for me." He shook his head. "Now that I can kill you . . . I can't. It was a war. A damn, lousy war. Billy was in the wrong place at the wrong time. And you were drunk at the wrong time. I think it's finally time to stop all the hatred. Maybe that's what all our ghosts want, Mike. If they all really died for peace . . . then let's give it to them. I'm through with it. I have a whole new life waiting for me, and there's no room for all the old hatreds."

He put Hogan's gun into his own holster and walked toward Jenna. As he put an arm around her shoulders, he felt her body go weak with relief. Turning back toward the pathetic man still leaning against the wall, he said, "Good-bye, Mike."

Picking up his own gun by the doorway, he heard Hogan's yell. "*No!* You got the papers, Morgan. Don't leave me like this!"

"C'mon, Jenna," Morgan urged her into the large center room of the fort.

They had gone no more than four feet when they heard the woman's voice. "I'll take those papers now. If you don't mind."

Morgan and Jenna turned as one. Charlotte Maxwell came out of the shadows and stood bathed in the light coming from the room. In her hand was a small, but deadly looking gun. And it was pointed at them.

"What is she doing here?" Jenna asked Morgan.

"I'm here," Charlotte quickly answered, "because your husband made a deal with me. Your life for the information he's carrying. I'm here to collect, Morgan."

Morgan looked at her outstretched hand, then up into her face. Gone was the stylish outfit of this afternoon. Instead, she had on a black skirt and blouse, and black gloves. The only thing not hidden by the darkness was her face and the expectancy in her eyes.

"I hate to disappoint you, Charlotte, but I'm keeping the papers. I'm taking them to Washington myself."

Her mouth opened in astonishment. "We made a deal. You got your wife, now I want those papers. Hand them over."

"I lied," Morgan calmly admitted.

She blinked a few times in disbelief, then stuck out the gun further. "What do you think this is? It may be small, but it'll kill you just the same." Pointing it at Jenna, she asked quietly, "Shall we try it out on your wife first?"

Morgan quickly put Jenna behind him and faced the woman. "Charlotte, put that thing away before someone does get hurt. It's over. The papers are coming with me. Go home."

He turned around and, keeping Jenna in front of him, slowly pushed her toward the door leading to the outside. His heart started beating a fast staccato against his chest wall. Perspiration broke out over his body and ran down the middle of his back, while the hairs at the back of his neck stood straight up, anticipating a bullet. He didn't think she would do it. She might be greedy, tough, and a manipulator, but he didn't think she was a murderer. He sure as hell hoped not!

Whether it was instinct or his senses, which were heightened by the danger he had placed himself and Jenna in, but Morgan's ears picked up the very faint, very deadly click of the hammer being pulled back. Reacting out of habit, he pushed Jenna down and fell with her, just as he heard the loud, angry shout.

"Noooo . . ."

Morgan quickly rolled to his side as he brought out his pistol. From the light streaming out of the small room, he could see Hogan and Charlotte in a struggle over the gun. He felt frozen as he watched the scene unfold. To him, it was almost as if they were in slow motion. His eyes squinted as he tried to see who had control of the small gun. He couldn't tell—it was buried between them. Shaking his head to clear it, Morgan started crawling to his feet to help out, when the sudden explosion resounded over and over in the deserted fort.

Now it was Morgan who yelled, his lips pulled back in a grimace of pain as he watched Hogan slowly slip to the ground. *"Mike!"*

Charlotte backed away as Morgan ran to Hogan's side. Kneeling down next to the bleeding man, he cradled his shoulders against his chest. "Why? Why the hell did you do that?" he demanded while pushing auburn hair back from the sweating brow.

Mike Hogan looked up into Morgan's face and tried to smile. "I . . . I think I owed you that one, Major."

Morgan cursed, then looked up at Charlotte. Ignoring her horrified expression, he shouted, "Don't just stand there, you bitch, get a doctor!"

Mike reached up and grabbed Morgan's shirt. "Don't . . . don't!"

Morgan looked back down at him.

His breathing was coming in short little gasps, the intense pain of the fatal stomach wound evident on his face. "It . . . it's better . . . like this. We were . . . good, though. Right? *Right?*"

Morgan looked down into his glazed eyes and nodded. "We were . . . we were good, Mike," he whispered in a choked voice and held him closer as a long, shuddering rush of air left the man's body.

379

He didn't know how long he held the still shoulders, how long his face was buried in the familiar auburn hair. He felt Jenna kneeling beside him and, reaching inside his shirt, he removed the damn papers. Giving them to Jenna, he heard her shove them at Charlotte.

"Here! You killed a man for them, now take them!"

"He jumped me! I didn't want to kill anybody!" Taking them, she started to back away. "He wanted to die! You heard him. He was dying anyway! He was nothing but a sick drunkard!"

He didn't raise his head until he heard the woman's shrill voice. Slowly, Morgan looked up at her, and his face was contorted with grief as he spoke.

"How the hell would you know? He was more than that. Once he was so much more . . ." He took several deep breaths before his eyes returned to the man in his arms.

In an almost inaudible voice, he whispered, "He was my best friend."

Chapter Thirty-one

"From Dust Thou Art—And To Dust Thou Shalt Return . . ."

Through a dark-netted veil, Jenna briefly glanced at the young minister as he read from the Bible before turning her face up to Morgan's. His features were set in a rigid mask as he stared at the mound of dirt that covered Mike Hogan's grave.

Morgan had insisted that his old partner receive a decent burial, and they stood together on a slight hill outside the city saying their good-byes. Besides the two men who had dug the grave, they were his only mourners.

Continuing to scrutinize Morgan's face, Jenna thought back over the last thirty-six hours and sighed. Tomorrow, they would leave Sacramento. It seemed they had no choice.

She had insisted on going with Morgan to report the shooting, wanting to verify what had actually happened. Of course, Charlotte Maxwell was nowhere to be found, and it was only her and Morgan's word. The sheriff and his deputy had escorted them back to Sutter's Fort and had forced them to reenact the entire incident. Going through it the second time had seemed almost as bad as the first, and Jenna's heart went out to Morgan when the sheriff gave him a lecture on honor and decency and how Morgan's *kind* wasn't needed in a respectable town like Sacramento. How, despite his money and eastern reputation, trouble seemed to follow him. She'd started to protest, but Morgan had held her back.

And now they were to leave tomorrow, by request. Pursing her lips at the unfairness of the sheriff's order, Jenna forced her attention back to the minister in time to hear him say, "We ask God to accept the soul of Michael Hogan, and to ease your hearts. For in Revelations it is written, 'He will wipe away all tears from their eyes. There will be no more death, no more grief or crying or pain. The old things have disappeared.' "

How à propos, Jenna thought and, slipping an arm through Morgan's, she smiled up at him. Her heart expanded with love as she watched his lips slowly curve into an answering smile. He understood. The old things have disappeared for Mike. It was what he wanted. It's what he finally got.

No one spoke much on the short ride back to town, and when the carriage stopped in front of the small church, she and Morgan stepped out with the minister.

Joseph Brady was young, but seemed dedicated to his calling. Gently shaking Morgan's hand, he said, "I'm so very sorry, Mr. Trahern. This must be especially hard for you, since today was to have been your wedding."

Morgan stared at the man for a few seconds before turning back to Jenna. There was a new, almost pleading look in his eyes as he spoke. "Jenna. Remember what you said about our last chance for happiness. I thought you were superstitious. Now maybe I am. Let's get married right away. Let's not wait any longer."

She wasn't prepared for such a request. "Now?" she asked, looking down at her heavy clothing. "But I'm dressed in black!"

Morgan looked at the somber gown, then back to the minister, as if asking for help.

The young sandy-haired man smiled at the couple. "Miss Weldon, it's what you feel inside that's important, not what shows outside. Do you want to marry Mr. Trahern?"

"Yes!" The answer was immediate.

The Reverend Brady waved his hand toward the front doors of his church. "Then I think we should go inside and make it legal. Just let me get my wife to serve as your witness."

Standing inside the small church, Jenna nervously looked toward the altar. "I don't believe we're doing this! What about our plans? This isn't exactly how normal people get married!"

Morgan gathered her into his arms and whispered, "Admit it, Jenna. Nothing that has taken place between us has been normal so far. Why should this be any different?"

When she looked up into his eyes, they were soft with love. "Besides, I don't want to leave the city without being married to you. Today was a day for endings, Jenna. But it can also be a day for beginnings. Our beginning."

She would have kissed him if the door hadn't opened at that very moment. The reverend introduced his wife, and Mary Brady smiled warmly, trying very hard not to stare at the bride's strange choice of wedding colors.

Morgan and Jenna stood before God, the reverend,

and Mrs. Brady, and pledged their love. For the second time they were married without flowers, white satin, or a wedding ring; only this time it wasn't in the middle of nowhere, and they weren't standing before a fanatic. This time it was their choice—because of a love so deep, so timeless, that their spoken commitments to each other became solemn vows.

When it was over, and they were pronounced husband and wife, both were so shocked that they had to be reminded to kiss. Lifting back the black-netted veil of her hat, Morgan lowered his face to hers. The brief brushing of lips was more affectionate than passionate and, looking up into Morgan's face and seeing the satisfied expression, Jenna couldn't help wondering if marriage, a real marriage, was going to change the way they felt toward each other.

Within minutes, the small wedding party was again outside. Standing in the hot sun, Jenna glanced up at the man who was now truly her husband. He looked confident and in complete command as he politely engaged in conversation. When Mrs. Brady asked them if they could stay for dinner, Jenna was relieved when Morgan graciously declined, stating that they had a good deal of packing to do before tomorrow.

Once more in the carriage, Mr. and Mrs. Trahern waved good-bye to the minister and his wife and made their way back to their hotel. It was only a short distance away, yet the ride was uncomfortably strange. Neither one spoke, and Jenna was starting to have a terrible feeling in the pit of her stomach that they had just done something extremely foolish.

Perhaps, they should have waited to be married, she thought as Morgan handed over the reins to the livery man and steered her in the direction of the hotel. She just wished he would *say* something, anything to make her feel that they hadn't made a mistake. But he was silent.

Turning the key, he opened the door to their suite. Jenna was about to walk past him when his arm came out and stopped her. Before she could question him, he reached down and picked her up in his arms.

"Everything up till now might not have been normal for us," he said huskily, "but not anymore." Holding her close to his chest, he carried her over the threshold to their rooms.

Jenna couldn't help the nervous giggle as she let go of his neck with one hand and closed the door after them. He set her down before a window in the sitting room and ordered her not to move until he returned. As she watched him walk into their bedroom, she felt her body go weak with relief. It was going to be all right.

Within half a minute, he was back. Standing before her, Morgan smiled as he removed her hat and placed it on a nearby chair. "I love your hair," he said as he took out the pins and ran his fingers through it until the soft blond curls fell down her back.

Reaching for the buttons on her gown, he quickly undid each one and helped her out of it. Gathering the heavy material, he added it to the hat. When he turned back to her, his smile was devastating as he leisurely eyed her from head to foot.

Clad only in her frilly white camisole and slip, she started to protest. "Morgan, what are you . . ."

"Shh." He brought his finger up to her lips and gently clasped her left hand. Reaching into his pocket, he took out a ring and slipped it on her third finger. Watching his movements, she let out a gasp.

"Now it's legal."

She looked up at him, noticed the single dimple had reappeared on his cheek, and smiled with pleasure as she looked back at her hand. "It's beautiful, Morgan," she sighed as she admired the delicate filigreed gold band. "I have a wedding ring for you, too," she stated and started to turn away.

Morgan grabbed her hand and brought her back. "Hold back the curtain, love," he asked.

"I can't. I'm not dressed."

"Stand behind it then. Just hold it back for a minute."

Jenna's eyes nararowed as she tried to figure out what he was planning. Doing as he'd asked, she stood behind it and pulled the heavy material to one side. Immediately, fresh air entered the room from the opened window.

She watched as he picked up her clothes and came closer.

"Morgan. What are you doing? Morgan? *Morgan!*"

Jenna couldn't believe it as she watched her hat sail through the window, quickly followed by her gown. So astonished was she by his actions that she forgot herself and leaned closer to the opening to see where they had fallen. Before anyone could see her, Morgan grabbed her hand and twirled her back toward him.

Picking her up once more, he kissed her shocked lips and stated, "I never want to see you in black again! Never!"

With one arm around his shoulders, she tweaked the side of his mustache. "Did you have to throw them out the window? What are the people in the street going to think?"

Walking into the bedroom, he pulled his head back from her assault. "I warn you, woman, it would be foolish on your part to injure me on our wedding day. And what do we care what the rest of the world thinks? They're throwing us out tomorrow." Reaching the bed, he winked. "But we've still got today."

Very gently, he placed her on the plump satin comforter and stood back. He reached over to the night table and brought out the roses that had been placed there that morning by the hotel. Pulling at the velvety red petals of one flower, he slowly scattered them across the pillow. As he sat down on the mattress, Morgan smiled at her quizzical look before handing her the small bouquet.

"I appreciate what you did today," he said softly. "I know every woman wants her wedding day to be special, and I want you to have everything you ever desired. What we said in the church was to make it legal. What I'm saying now is to make it real."

Taking her hand, he brought it up to his lips and kissed her fingertips. "You're in white. You have a ring. And you have your flowers." Looking into her eyes, his voice cracked as he whispered, "I'll love you, Jenna Weldon Trahern, for as long as I live. If I've ever done anything right in my life, then you're my gift . . . my payment from the gods. I promise to cherish you, to take care of you, to build a life with you. All I ask is that you love me in return."

Jenna's lids closed briefly as she tried to control the tears. It was impossible. Opening her eyes and her arms, she whispered, "Come here."

When she held him next to her, she felt overcome with love and found it difficult to speak. But like Morgan, there were words she felt compelled to say aloud. "You've become my life, Morgan. A part of me will always wonder how I came to be in the past . . . what has happened to my mother, my father's company . . . so many things. But a stronger part belongs to you and never wants to leave. I love you, Morgan Trahern, and promise to cherish you, take care of you, and build a life with you."

He lifted his head and stared into blue-gray eyes

that were glazed with tears of happiness. Holding her face, he ran his thumbs across her cheekbones and wiped away the salty liquid.

"Let's start now," he whispered with a sexy smile playing at his lips. "We've never discussed this, but I'd like a large family. Maybe six or seven."

Jenna's mouth opened in astonishment. Obviously, the man had never heard of planned parenthood or overpopulation. Knowing now was not the time to inform him of such developments, Jenna answered his smile with one of her own. "That's a tall order, Mr. Trahern." She couldn't stop the giggle as she removed his tie and stated with false security, "I think we'd better start immediately."

Unbuttoning his shirt, Jenna continued to smile at him. Maybe it would be nice to have a baby, especially if he looked like his father, she thought, as Morgan's experienced hands once again started to work their special magic.

Jenna could have stayed there forever. There was something about the moments after making love that were beyond natural. There wasn't a tense muscle in her body. Every organ seemed to be renewed. Her breathing was better, her senses more heightened, even more so than when they had been making love. It was as near perfection as the human body was capable of being, she thought, as she continued to hold Morgan close.

When she felt him move, she was reluctant to let go, wanting to keep him within her for as long as possible.

"No." The word came out as a plea.

Leaning on his elbows, Morgan brought his head up and looked into her eyes. "I'll be right back," he whispered and kissed the tip of her nose.

She couldn't stop the moan as she felt him leave her, and her body automatically curled up with an overwhelming sense of loss. Turning to her side, Jenna took a deep breath and watched him as he took a towel and soaked it in a bowl of water.

Her eyes never left his magnificent body as he wrung out the cloth. She had just loved every inch of him, every corded muscle, every jagged scar, and she licked her lips, tasting him all over again.

"Is it different, Morgan?" she asked a little hesitantly.

Bringing the damp towel with him, he sat next to her. "Different? What do you mean?"

Jenna found it hard to speak, as Morgan lightly, ever so lightly, brought the cool cloth across her face, her breasts, and her stomach.

Wanting to know his answer, she attempted again. "You know—now that we're officially married. Is it different?"

She closed her eyes as the towel dipped further, grazing the insides of her thighs. God, he was driving her crazy. She couldn't think straight!

"Do you believe it's different, *desperada*?"

For a man of such strength, he was so gentle, she mused, as the course cloth was brought down each leg and around each foot. Opening her eyes, she watched him gaze at her body as his hand continued its maddening course.

She knew she was expected to say something, but it had become increasingly difficult to string two thoughts together as her heart began to beat faster and primitive instinct took over. "If it means now I get service like this . . . then . . . then yes, it is different . . . better," she gasped haltingly. "Only don't . . . don't call me *desperada*. Not now."

She heard Morgan's chuckle. "But now is the

perfect time. Now it has a new meaning. You came into my life, Mrs. Trahern, and stole my heart. Completely and forever. Nothing, not even time, will allow it to be released.'

And finally, mercifully, he allowed the towel to meet the soft delta of her femininity. Gasping at the contact, Jenna opened her eyes just as Morgan lowered his head to seal the pact.

Chapter Thirty-two

Jenna sat back against the plush seat and looked out the curtained window of the train. Within moments, they would leave Sacramento. She could already see and hear the steam rising from under the elegant car. How different it was this time, she thought, just as Morgan took his seat opposite her.

"Well, we're all set," he announced cheerfully. "Are you happy to be going back?"

Jenna smiled as she watched him settle himself. She would never tire of looking at the man. "I'll be happy to see Willow. I just hope Jace is there."

"Is that what brought on those serious thoughts a moment ago? While you were staring out the window?"

Jenna smoothed the linen of her traveling suit over her knees. Looking up from the deep green material, she smiled at her husband. "Actually, I was thinking how different this trip is going to be from the last time I traveled on a train." She raised her eyebrows. "Or the time before that."

As the train pulled out of Sacramento, Morgan chuckled. "Your last trip was to teach you a lesson."

Jenna didn't even look out at the disappearing

station. Although many wonderful memories were created in the city, she knew she would always associate Sacramento with Mike Hogan. Keeping her attention on the handsome man across from her, she returned his laugh. "But to keep me awake! Morgan, you were cruel!"

He pulled at the white cuff of his shirt that peeked out from under his dark-gray jacket sleeve. "Mano said he had a hell of a time keeping you awake. If it makes you feel any better, he thought I was cruel, too."

Seeing the single dimple appear on his cheek, she nodded her head. "I knew there was a reason why I liked that man." Unconsciously, she leaned closer to him and whispered, "Does he know *everything*, Morgan?"

"Depends on what you mean by everything?"

She leaned back. "You know . . . us. I mean . . . does he know the two of us were . . ."

This time Morgan leaned closer to her. "Lovers?" he asked in a quiet, teasing voice.

Jenna took a deep breath, trying to ignore Morgan's baiting tone. "Well . . . yes. I'd hate to think Mano left Sacramento with the idea we were casually involved."

Morgan couldn't help the hearty laugh that attracted smiles from the other passengers. "Jenna." He said her name in a whisper. "Nothing, absolutely nothing, between us has been casual since the day we met." Sitting back in his chair, he added, "Which brings us to the first train trip we took together. Although, actually we couldn't have traveled more than a mile together by rail. The rest of that trip took place on foot."

Seeing his smile gave her the courage to ask, "What did you think, Morgan, when you first saw me? I

392

must have looked strange, the way I was dressed and everything."

He looked above her head and smoothed the sides of his mustache down with his fingers, as if lost in thought. "You, my dear, were the most astonishing woman I had ever seen. When I first saw you, I thought, My goodness, she's tall. Then I saw you were wearing high-heeled boots. When you sat down next to me and asked me for a light and I lowered that paper and looked into your eyes—I think that's when I was lost."

Jenna felt embarrassed and wished she had never asked. It sounded as if she wanted complements. "Don't be silly. You couldn't stand me. You thought I was insane." She shook her head and looked out the window. "All that talk about hundred-year-old newspapers . . ." Then she giggled as she remembered. "Those men . . . remember? I had accused them of being actors! I told them they would never work for the railroad again! What a spectacle I made of myself."

He nodded and laughed as the scene rose in his mind. "Don't forget, you said I was one, too. In fact, for some time, you had insisted I was an out of work actor."

Jenna smiled. "Ah, but you looked like one. Rugged cowboy, the quiet, silent type." She sighed in remembrance. "You, Morgan Trahern, were devastating."

He looked deeply into her eyes and stated, "Then I must remember to wear those old clothes more often."

He was looking at her with the same intense longing that always preceded making love, and her thighs started to feel heavy in response. Squirming in the chair, she said, "Just make sure you never put them on and go out on business again. You promised me that's over."

He held her gloved hand between his tanned fingers. "Believe me, it's over. Your husband, Mrs. Trahern, is an importer. A very fortunate man who's taking his bride home to Baltimore."

Unconsciously, she pulled back her hand and nervously straightened the already straight hat perched on her head. It was a large creation of deep-green silk, complemented with white curling feathers in back. Jenna had thought she looked ridiculous, but Morgan had insisted she was dressed in the height of fashion. Bringing her hands together in her lap, she gave him a worried look. "What if they don't like me?"

He shook his head in confusion. "Who?"

"Your parents!" she exclaimed in an exasperated and nervous voice. "You know they're going to be suspicious. *I'd* be suspicious if I were in their place."

She looked back out the window, not wanting Morgan to see her face. They were entering the Sierras, and she swallowed a few times as the altitude blocked her ears. Soon, they would be back in Verdi. Where it had all started.

His voice was soft and soothing. "They're going to love you, Jenna. Stop worrying. My parents will have the time of their lives throwing parties for us, introducing you to their friends. Trust me. They're going to be thrilled with you. Only don't start talking about working in the business with me right away. That, I think, is something we'll slowly ease into."

Seeing the familiar Juniper pines, Jenna smiled and turned her attention back to her husband. "So. You've finally decided I can join you in your work."

"Did I have a choice?"

She looked into her eyes. They were happy, just like the smile on his lips. "Honestly?"

He nodded.

She shook her head, causing the blond curls to brush her shoulders. "If I couldn't join your business, I'd probably have started one of my own."

His eyes opened wider. "You'd compete against me? Your own husband?"

She was unaware the smile she'd cast in his direction was so openly seductive. "You'll never know, will you? This way our marriage will never be dull. And you, my handsome husband, will never be complacent. I don't want to be taken for granted or sit home while you have all the fun."

A sigh escaped Morgan's lips that was filled with patience. "Jenna, marriage to you couldn't possibly be dull. Dangerous, maybe. But never dull."

"What do you mean, dan—"

"Well, well. Now isn't this a surprise?"

Jenna and Morgan both looked up into Harry Bullmason's beefy red face. "Come up some in the world, didn't you, missy?"

Morgan gave Jenna a look that told her he would handle the annoying conductor. "You're addressing my wife, Bullmason. If you should ever attempt to speak with her again, though I'd strongly advise you not to, make sure it's done with respect. "Now, what is you want? Our tickets?"

Both Morgan and Jenna could see Harry was having a difficult time keeping his temper under control. Straightening his conductor's hat, Bullmason retorted, "Let's just hope this time they're in order."

Reaching inside his jacket, Morgan brought out their tickets and handed them over with a smile. "I'm sure you'll find everything satisfactory."

They watched as Bullmason inspected their tickets and finally punched out the proper places.

"I see you're headed back East, after a stopover in Verdi. Kinda got attached to the place, did ya?"

Morgan took back the tickets and replaced them inside his jacket. "Not that it's any of your business, but my wife and I are visiting friends before we go home. How about you, Harry? Have any friends left since the last time I saw you? Looks to me as if you didn't get that office promotion you were looking forward to."

Jenna thought Morgan was foolish to taunt Bullmason and remind him of the attempted robbery.

She knew she was right when he gave them both a frustrated, angry look and said, "I'm not forgetting you were on that train, Trahern. Funny how that missing money was returned and the whole thing dropped, don't you think?"

Morgan look very convincing as he answered in a perplexed voice. "That is a puzzle, isn't it? I suppose we should both be grateful. After all, I was the guard . . . and it was your train. Seems to me we should be happy whoever took it, returned it."

Knowing the mining payroll could have very easily been his, Bullmason's eyes glittered with his hatred. "Yeah, they returned it. And now you two show up lookin' like a couple of fancy Easterners. Makes a man think."

Jenna looked at Morgan and resisted making a remark about Bullmason's lack of ability in that area. Instead, she watched Morgan silently acknowledge Bullmason's quick tip of his cap.

Neither spoke as the conductor moved on. When he was no longer in their car, Jenna was fast to scold Morgan. "Why did you say that? What are you trying to do? Have him get suspicious all over again?"

Morgan seemed unmoved by her words. "Come now, Jenna. Do you really think Harry ever gave up being suspicious? If we sat here, meek as kittens, he'd have thought we were hiding something. I don't like that man, and I have plenty of reasons to be suspicious of *him*."

"Just the same, I think you should be careful. I won't feel completely safe until we reach Baltimore and are through with trains. Promise me you won't antagonize Bullmason. We still have to see him again in three days, when we go on to Reno. That is the end of his line, isn't it?"

Morgan nodded. Trying to take her mind off the conductor, he said, "Tell me again what you got for Willow and Jace."

Heading the rented wagon up the narrow path that led to the Eberlys' farm, Morgan glanced over as Jenna removed her large hat.

"It's a bit much. I told you so. Didn't you see the way people were staring when we got off the train?"

Morgan grinned. "Nonsense. How did you expect them to look? The last time they saw us, we were both dirt poor. You would have stared, too."

Jenna threw the hat into the flatbed of the wagon behind them where their trunks were. "I suppose so," she admitted. "It's just that I don't want Willow and Jace to think we're flaunting wealth."

Clearing the woods, they could both see the small farm. Slowly, Morgan stopped the wagon. "You know, it's crazy, but I think I'm going to miss this miserable place."

Jenna smiled as she looked at the rundown barn where it had all started. "I know," she breathed dreamily, and let out a small yell when she saw Willow emerge from the wooden building.

Without thinking, she quickly jumped down from the wagon and hiked up the full skirt of her suit as she broke into a run. *"Willow!"*

Smiling, Morgan made a noise with his mouth and kept the horse to a slow trot as he followed his wife.

Willow dropped the basket to the ground as she stared at the tall, beautiful woman running in her direction. Her eyes were tired from packing up the farm, and she imagined they were playing tricks on her as she thought she recognized the figure.

As the woman came closer, Willow brought her hand up to her chest and said the name out loud. *"Jenna?"*

They met in a tangle of arms and cries of delight. Pulling back from the tall woman, Willow seemed embarrassed by her actions. "It is so good to see you again, Jenna." Turning toward Morgan, who had just stepped down from the wagon, she smiled in his direction. "Both of you. It is good to see both of you once more."

Morgan took off his hat in a gesture of respect. "It's good to see you, too, Willow. We couldn't go home without stopping for a visit."

"I'm glad you came," she said, smiling at them both.

"Is Jace around?" Jenna asked, looking toward the house. "Or is he working?"

The happiness left Willow's face. "No. My son no longer works for Mr. Teale at his saloon." When she again looked at them, both Jenna and Morgan could see she was trying to hide something. "You will be staying here again?" she asked.

"Only if it isn't any trouble," Morgan said. "Our train for back East leaves in three days."

Willow smiled. "Then it is good I haven't cleaned out your old room yet. Let me get you bedding."

"I'll help, Willow," Jenna offered as she followed the small Indian woman, eager to know what had brought about such a look of disappointment.

She waited politely in the front room of Willow's home. Something strange is going on, Jenna thought with a worried look on her face as she took in the bare floors, the stacked wooden boxes, the near empty kitchen area. Where were the colorful Indian rugs, the many pots and pans that once hung from the wall? Why did it look as if Willow was in the process of moving?

"I will help you carry these back."

Jenna turned around at the quiet statement. Looking into Willow's beautiful dark eyes, she couldn't help but ask, "What's happening here? Where's Jace?"

Willow Eberly placed the blankets and clean linen into Jenna's arms. Turning away, she rooted through a few boxes before she found a cast-iron pan and two heavy pots. "I will bring over some food later," she said, a hint of weariness in her voice.

Jenna wouldn't budge. "Willow?"

The two women stood staring at each other for a few painful seconds. Finally, the smaller one spoke. "Since you left, Jason spends most of his time in the mountains with his grandfather, my father. Last week even Coral left the farm, and since then, my son has not returned. His life has never been easy, and I think you know, Jenna, how hard it has been for him since his father died. He refuses to fit in here and has told me he will not live with the white man."

"You're going to join him? You're going back to your people?"

Willow smiled sadly and shook her head. "Now it is I who no longer fits in there." She looked around at the near empty room. "I will keep this place for my son. That is a promise I made to his father. Maybe someday Jason will claim it. I hope so." She looked at Jenna. "I am moving to Dr. Marshall's home. I will be his housekeeper."

Jenna's mouth opened in surprise. "His housekeeper? But I thought . . ."

Willow smiled kindly. "Verdi is Clinton Marshall's home. He is a very good doctor and cares for the people who live here. They respect him now. If he were to marry an Indian, he would lose their respect."

Anger quickly rose up in Jenna. "You mean he won't marry you because you're an Indian?"

Again, Willow smiled. "You misunderstand, my young friend. I won't marry *him* because I'm an Indian. I care for Clinton Marshall too much to bring him shame."

Jenna moved closer to the woman. "Willow, if he asked you to marry him, it must mean he doesn't care. Why deny yourself the happiness of being his wife? What do you care what these people think? You're twice as good as any of them!"

Willow startled her by issuing forth a small, completely feminine laugh. "You are a very good friend, Jenna Weldon," she declared. "Look at us, arguing with pots and pans and sheets in our hands, while Morgan patiently waits." The laughter showed in her eyes as she added, "Jenna, I am embarrassed to tell you that Clinton and I are married in every way that is important. I tell you this to make you feel better. It doesn't matter to me that we have not stood before one of your priests. We know what we are doing."

Jenna shifted the linen in her arms and returned Willow's smile. "Then I'm happy for you both. When are you leaving the farm?"

Walking toward the door, she said, "In four more days, I will join Clinton in his home. I was hoping Jason would return before then. As you can imagine, he is not happy about this change."

Following Willow out the door, Jenna said to her, "I

hope he comes back. I really wanted to see him again. Maybe I could visit him at your father's camp."

"You are a good friend, Jenna Weldon," she repeated. "To both Jason and me."

They were almost to the barn when Jenna stopped her. Although they had never talked about it, Jace's mother was too intelligent not to have realized what was going on while she and Morgan were living here. Stretching out her hand, she showed Willow her wedding ring. "It's Jenna Trahern, now," she said shyly. "We finally made it legal in Sacramento."

Willow stopped and admired her ring. Smiling, she looked up at Jenna. "In your heart, you were his wife long before this. I remember him looking at you. Your Morgan claimed you before Sacramento. It is a beautiful ring to show others. I think you and Morgan have what is important inside."

If her arms weren't filled, she would have hugged the smaller woman. "I have missed you, Willow. Come, let me show you what I found in Sacramento."

Within less than a hour, Willow and Jenna had swept out the room off the barn, put fresh linens on the narrow bed, and started a small fire, while Morgan had gone into town to pick up the ingredients for their dinner. The sudden decision was made to invite Willow and Clinton Marshall to share their supper, and Jenna and Willow had struggled to bring the larger table into the room.

Jenna regretted that she couldn't make it more special for the couple, but Willow had brightened her spirits when she returned from her house with a small bouquet of wildflowers. Placing them in a tall drinking glass, Jenna stood back from the table and surveyed it.

"Not too bad. What do you think, Willow?"

Jenna turned around and looked at her. She was

staring at the table with a wistful expression. "It is very lovely, Jenna. I don't know if Clinton will be able to come. He is a very busy man."

Jenna smiled. "I gave Morgan strict orders to bring him back. See what marriage has done to me? I've turned into a very bossy woman. Maybe you're smarter not to marry. This way—"

She never finished her sentence as the door burst open and Morgan entered the room, his arms filled with packages. "Guess who I brought?" he asked with a wide smile.

Clinton Marshall followed him, carrying as many packages as Morgan. "Couldn't rightly pass up such a friendly invitation now, could I?" First he smiled at Willow, then Jenna. "Mrs. Trahern, you get lovelier every time I see you. Thank you for asking me to join you."

Jenna looked at the middle-aged man, his spectacles low on his noise, his ruddy complexion a sharp contrast to his graying hair. Even though Jenna considered Willow to be a beautiful woman, all she had to do was catch the adoration that passed from the doctor to the small Indian woman to know Willow was right. She would be happy with Clinton Marshall, and she would find that happiness any way she could.

"We're pleased you could come, Doctor. We just arrived this afternoon, and Willow told us your good news."

She didn't mean it as a test, but couldn't help the small flicker of satisfaction as Clinton Marshall looked at Willow and smiled.

"Good," he stated emphatically. "I'm glad there won't be any pretending tonight. I don't suppose you managed to talk any sense into this woman?" he asked while walking closer to Willow.

Watching her take the packages out of the doctor's arms, Jenna gave a small laugh and said, "Clinton, I think you know by now that Willow has a mind of her own. Now what's in those packages? I don't know about the rest of you, but I'm starving."

"Hold on there," Morgan said as he took the paper-wrapped bundles away from Willow. "Clinton and I had a talk and decided that since the two of you had to do some pretty fast work fixing this place up, the two of us would make dinner."

Jenna stared at her husband. "You're joking! *You're* going to make dinner?"

Morgan looked insulted by her tone. "Not alone. Clinton will help. I can cook, you know."

"I can't wait," Jenna proclaimed with a grin.

Returning her smile, Morgan said, "Well, you're going to have to. Why don't you show Willow her present in the meantime?"

Willow looked embarrassed as Jenna handed her the package. Unwrapping the paper, she whispered, "You shouldn't have brought me anything. I have nothing to give you."

It was Morgan who spoke. Putting an arm over Jenna's shoulder, he said sincerely, "Were it not for you, Willow, I don't think I would be standing here today. Neither Jenna, nor I, can ever repay your kindness to us."

Jenna nodded as she watched Willow take the large leather book into her hands. Opening it, she flipped through its pages before looking up. "I don't know what to say. Clinton has many valuable books such as this in his home."

Jenna smiled. "You have a natural instinct for medicine. I thought you might enjoy reading about it." She laughed. "Of course, at the time, I didn't know you'd have free access to an entire medical library."

Willow held the book as if it were priceless. "Thank you, Morgan. Thank you, Jenna. I will treasure this always."

Morgan gave Jenna a squeeze. "All right ladies, we will leave you to entertain yourselves while Clinton and I create a culinary delight. Prepare for a masterpiece!"

Jenna's eyes rolled toward the ceiling. "Just make it edible, okay, Morgan?"

Chapter Thirty-three

Jenna took the plate from Morgan and wiped it with the long length of cotton. "I think it went well, don't you?"

Looking up from the small tub of water, Morgan smiled in her direction. "I think Clinton and Willow were very pleased." He leaned closer and kissed her cheek. "Stop worrying. I really believe they're going to be happy." Dunking his hands once more, he washed the last tin plate. "You can't organize everyone's life to fit your idea of happiness," he gently warned. "It's their decision, Jenna. Not yours."

She held her hands out, waiting for the plate. "I'm not worried about Willow and Clinton," Jenna said with a smile. "I have a feeling Clinton Marshall isn't a man who likes to hide his feelings. I'll bet a year from now, Willow is his legal wife—town be damned."

"So what's wrong?" he asked, coming closer to dry his hands on the bottom of her towel.

She looked up at him. "You know me that well?"

"Better than any other, I hope. What are you worried about?"

"Jace."

Morgan nodded. "You want to see him, don't you?

You want to go up to that Indian camp of his grandfather's."

Finished drying the dishes they had used for dinner, she folded the towel and turned to him. "How can I leave without seeing him?" she asked, a pleading look on her face. "He's lost now, Morgan. I know it. His mother's going on with her life and he doesn't have the slightest idea how to even begin his. I have to talk to him. I have to try."

A smile played at the corner of his mouth. "Were you always like this? Did you always involve yourself in everyone's problems?"

Jenna shrugged. "My mother accused me of spending too much time with my causes. But Jace isn't a cause. He's just a boy trying so hard to be a man. I don't know if talking to him will do any good. I just know I have to see him before we leave."

Morgan walked over to her and wrapped her in his arms. Kissing the side of her neck, he whispered in her ear, "If we're going up into the mountains tomorrow, then I think we'd better get some sleep."

Jenna's head snapped up. "You'll go with me?" she asked, an excited look on her face.

Morgan smiled. "You're not going anywhere without me, Mrs. Trahern. C'mon, let's go to bed." Taking her hand, he led her to the small night table and extinguished the oil lamp. Bathed in moonlight, he leisurely undressed her, removing each garment with exquisite slowness.

"My God, I love you, Jenna," he whispered running his palms up her arms, over her shoulders, and finally weaving his fingers through her hair. Very gently, he brought her face closer to his. "This room is so special for us. Yet here it was always over so quickly. Each time, I hated to leave and go back to Sacramento. Tonight I'll make it up to you. Tonight will last forever."

Jenna gasped, her body already aroused by his touch, her mind now inflamed by his words. She moved closer, allowing her breasts to barely touch his chest. "Are you seducing me, Morgan?" she asked quietly, her eyes never leaving his, yet letting her hands unbutton his clothing.

He smiled widely as his fingers joined hers. "That I am, madam."

Jenna's lips curved seductively as she returned his smile. "Then don't stop," she softly commanded in a breathless voice, just before his mouth took possession of her own.

They both wanted it to be slow, to savor what had been denied to them the last time they had shared this bed, yet, like most good intentions, it was difficult to follow through. For Morgan and Jenna, it was impossible. The overpowering magnetism that had always held them quickly resurfaced, pulling them together. The brush of lips became demanding; the gentle caress, a possessive stroke. Nature had entered that small room and taken command. For the two lovers, entwined in a feverish giving and taking, to have held back would have been as futile as trying to capture the wind. Instead, they gave in to their love and were swept away with time.

"I don't remember it being this small," Morgan whispered into her hair.

Lazily stretching in the early morning light, Jenna giggled and snuggled closer to his chest. "It was always narrow. We just didn't notice it before." Lifting her head, she looked into his peaceful face. "Do you think that says something about us? Now that we're married, has some of the wonder left?"

Looking down at her he tried to hide a smile. "You can say that? After what just transpired in this bed?"

She giggled again.

"I don't think the wonder has left, just because half of my rear end is suspended in air. And freezing, I might add. Move over."

Doing as he'd asked, Jenna laughed and wrapped her arms around Morgan. "Here," she offered. "I'll give you my body heat. That ought to warm you up a bit."

Morgan growled as her soft body fit closely next to his. "Keep it up, madam, and the only Indians you'll be seeing are in picture books."

Sighing loudly, Jenna laid her head on his warm chest. "I suppose we have to get up, don't we?" She could feel Morgan's chin move above her head as he nodded, yet his arms continued to hold her.

"I prepared dinner last night. I even washed the dishes. It's your turn to cook, woman."

She gave a short sarcastic laugh. "*You* prepared dinner? Let's get this straight, for the record. That ham was already cooked by the Verdi Inn, along with the vegetables. You *served* dinner, Morgan, not cooked it."

She could feel his chest move as he silently chuckled. "You have to admit it was delicious. I should be complimented on using my head. We would never have had enough time to cook a proper meal. And I did make the coffee."

Nodding, Jenna dragged herself away from his warmth. "I think I can do that much. How does coffee and left-over biscuits sound?"

Morgan frowned. "it sounds like I'll be hungry an hour from now."

Grinning, Jenna leaned down and kissed the side of his mustache. "Then I guess I'll just have to fix you

408

eggs. I noticed you remembered to buy them. And since you've very unselfishly given over today to take me to Gray Wolf's camp, I might be persuaded to fry a little of that ham from last night."

Morgan ran his hand up her arm until it curled around her neck. Bringing her back to him, he whispered into her mouth, "And how might you be persuaded, Mrs. Trahern?"

"You're doing a splendid job, Mr. Trahern. Absolutely splendid."

Following Willow's directions, Morgan was able to locate the Indian camp within less than an hour. Seeing it in the distance, in a small clearing, he turned to Jenna and said, "Let's walk the horses in. I want to appear as peaceful as possible."

Nodding, Jenna dismounted and waited for Morgan to lead the way. Walking through the sagebrush thickets, she noticed both she and Morgan were quickly covered with a yellow powder. The pollen coming from the bush's yellow blossoms clung to their clothes as they made their way closer to the camp. Absently brushing the powder away from her skirt, Jenna took in the scene before her. She could see several women and children walking about the crude shelters. They weren't anything like she'd expected. Here were no colorful teepees she had imagined from movies and books. These looked to be fashioned from brush, piling the scrubby growth against a few upright poles to provide a partial covering. To one side was a larger structure, looking more permanent. It appeared that a number of poles had been erected in a circle and connected at the top, then covered with layers of brush, weeds, and mud to form a cone-shaped shelter.

As they walked through the center of the camp, Jenna could feel dozens of eyes watching her and Morgan. All activity had stopped as the Indians stared at the strangers.

"We'll go to the wickiup," Morgan whispered out of the corner of his mouth, as he led the way. "Gray Wolf's gotta be in there."

Passing the cruder shelters, Jenna kept a tight smile on her face as she looked at the Indians they passed. The women continued to roll or chew what looked to be bark, with partially finished baskets lying on the ground near them. Although their mouths or hands were busy, their eyes never left the two white strangers in their midst. The men stood quietly, distrust clearly showing in their eyes.

As they reached the wickiup, Morgan stopped by the small opening and waited.

"Should you call out to Jace?"

"Shh!" Keeping his eyes on the hide flap that served as a door, Morgan whispered, "We wait until Gray Wolf comes out."

Their wait couldn't have been more than a minute, yet to Jenna it seemed so much longer. She could feel the eyes of the camp on her back as they came closer to encircle her and Morgan. The whole camp waited.

Finally, the hide was pushed outward against the reeds, and an older man appeared in the opening. Gray-haired, he couldn't have been more than five and a half feet, yet when he pulled himself up to his full height, he appeared so much taller. Dark, dark eyes ignored her and stared into Morgan's face. Neither man said a word as they silently took measure of each other.

"We have come with greetings from your daughter, Willow," Morgan said slowly.

Not getting a response, he tried again. "We wish to

speak with her son, your grandson, Jason."

"I don't think he understands you, Morgan," Jenna whispered in a frightened voice.

The dark eyes widened slightly. Suddenly, the creases of age increased as Gray Wolf's face broke out into a smile.

"You may tell your woman I understand, Morgan Trahern."

Both Morgan and Jenna looked at each other in surprise, then back at Gray Wolf.

"My grandson, who you call Jason, has told me of you. He said you might try and come after him." Looking at the packed horses and Jenna, he added, "I do not think you have come after him. I believe you were sent by Willow."

With his hand, he indicated that they should take the packages off the horses. Quickly, Jenna and Morgan untied their gifts.

First Morgan handed Gray Wolf the bolt of heavy blue cotton Willow had picked out, but Morgan had bought at Verdi's dry-goods store. "This is a gift from your daughter, Gray Wolf."

Silently, a woman appeared at his side and took the cotton from Morgan. Both he and Jenna watched as she unfolded it for the camp to see. They heard murmurings of approval from behind them, and it gave Jenna the courage to speak.

"Is Jason here?" she asked hesitantly.

Gray Wolf looked directly at her for the first time. Without saying a word, he turned around and walked back into the wickiup.

Jenna looked at Morgan and watched as he shrugged his shoulders. The small woman came back and indicated with her hand that she and Morgan were to follow. Taking their packages with them, they entered the large round structure.

It was dark and warm, the only light coming through a hole in the top. Sitting in the center of a soft beam of sunlight was Gray Wolf. They sat opposite him, a small depression in the ground separating them. Jenna realized from the charred debris that it must be where they cooked during colder months.

Placing their packages on the ground beside them, Morgan and Jenna waited for the old, silent man to speak first.

"I will call you Star Dancer," he said in a whisperingly soft voice as he stared at Jenna. "My grandson has told me how far you have traveled to be his friend."

Seeing her surprise, he added, "The Old Ones tell tales of the ancients. You will talk to me, and I will tell tales of the future."

"I have no powers to tell the future," Jenna whispered back.

"You have been sent here for a reason. Have you not tried to find it?"

"She is only a woman," Morgan stated firmly. "She was sent here to find me. She is my wife."

Gray Wolf nodded. "Then you cannot tell me if the Washo regain their hunting grounds," he said in a sad voice.

"I'm sorry . . ." Again, Jenna whispered. She could not tell this man that his people would lose more than just their hunting grounds.

"You speak English very well, Gray Wolf," Morgan interrupted, sensing Jenna's unease.

The old man accepted the compliment with a nod. "Many years ago, a white man named John Blocker lived with the Washo. He was hunting for the yellow dust—what you call gold. He was found near death, and the people took him in. What I did not learn from John Blocker, my daughter, and then my grandson

412

taught me."

Jason's grandfather stopped speaking, and Morgan said quietly, "We have brought you gifts, Gray Wolf," and handed several wool blankets to him.

Gray Wolf reached across the small fire pit and accepted the offering. "Our women and children will remember your kindness during the winter months."

Jenna next handed her package. Watching Gray Wolf unwrap the paper, she held her breath as he took out her gift.

Gray Wolf held the brocaded vest up to the light to get a better look. Seeing the sun catch the silver threads that were woven through the red gaudy garment, she felt Morgan's eyes on her, but refused to acknowledge them. This particular vest had been the object of a prolonged discussion only days ago, when they were packing to leave Sacramento. Always so meticulous in his taste, Morgan held an unnatural fondness for this newly purchased garment. Jenna had tried to explain it wasn't his style, that he didn't own another like it in his wardrobe, and that she thought he was holding on to his alter ego, the drifter and spy. Morgan had laughed and told her she was nagging.

Now, as she watched Gray Wolf's pleasure as he tried on the vest, she knew she had been right. She just wasn't sure if Morgan would agree. Not able to stand his glare any longer, Jenna slowly turned her head. Eyes wide, Morgan jerked his head toward the vest in a silent question, and she had to bite the side of her cheek to keep from giggling at his expression.

"Jenna!"

Her eyes were drawn to the entrance of the wickiup. "Jace!" She said his name in an excited rush as she scrambled to her feet. Quickly, she crossed the distance between them and threw her arms around him.

"Oh, It's so good to see you," she said in a happy voice. Pulling back from him, she searched his face. "How are you?"

Looking over her shoulder to Morgan, he whispered, "I'm fine. Are you all right?"

Following his line of vision, she, too, looked to her husband. "Everything's wonderful. Really. Don't be worried. We've come to see you before we return to Morgan's home."

Taking his hand, she led him over to where she and Morgan were sitting. Jace sat down next to her, and Jenna gave Morgan a meaningful look. Happily, she watched as Morgan reached across her to extend his hand.

"Glad to see you again, Jason," he said as Jace took his hand and shook it. "We were just talking with your grandfather."

Jace looked toward Gray Wolf and noticed the bright vest. "Star Dancer has given me this special gift, my grandson. She is as good and beautiful as you told me."

Jace smiled at the older man's obvious pride. Turning to Jenna, he said, "Grandfather loves stories, and you have just given him another. Generations of Washo will hear how Star Dancer came from the future and honored Gray Wolf with this gift."

Embarrassed, Jenna said, "But it's only a vest." She could hear Morgan clearing his throat at her words and, trying to steer the conversation away from the controversial piece of clothing, she added, "Your mother sends her love, Jace."

She watched the expression on the young boy's face turn into a scowl. "My mother has made her choices. She has decided to live with the white doctor."

Jenna wanted to reach out and hug him again, but she knew to do so would humiliate him in front of his grandfather. Instead, she said softly, "She still loves you. That doesn't change the way she feels about you."

Seeing the look of anger on the young one's face, Gray Wolf interrupted the exchange. "Was your hunt successful, my grandson?" he asked.

Reluctantly, Jace tore his eyes away from Jenna's. "Yes, grandfather. The antelope was too swift for my arrows, but two rabbits will feed our family today."

Gray Wolf nodded. "It is good. Today we will make a feast to honor Star Dancer and Morgan Trahern."

Jenna was about to tell Gray Wolf that they couldn't remain that long when Jace spoke up. Looking at Jenna, he said meaningfully, "You will honor us by remaining."

She looked at Morgan, saw him nod, and turned back to Gray Wolf. "Thank you for inviting us. We will stay and eat with you," she said in a solemn voice.

Seeing the smile light Gray Wolf's dark eyes, she knew she had made the right decision. Together, all three listened as Gray Wolf gave instructions in a soft guttural voice to the Indian women outside the wick-iup.

When he came back, he settled himself before them and offered a basket filled with brown nuts. Gingerly, Jenna took one and popped it inside her mouth. Chewing the tasty nut, she looked at Jace.

Identifying it, he said, "Piñon nut, from the pine tree. It is almost the season for gathering them. They are stored in special pits for winter use."

Morgan swallowed and asked, "That isn't the same tree the loggers are cutting, is it?"

Gray Wolf answered. "We have asked them to stop taking away the trees." He continued to explain that resin from the piñon provided waterproofing and cement for pottery and baskets, which his tribe made, and it was also used to mend their jewelry. But the most important reason, he said, was that his people gathered pine nuts each year as one of their staple foods.

Jena could almost feel Gray Wolf's sorrow and Jace's anger. Seeing that he had upset his guest, Gray Wolf cleared his throat as he again offered the basket, and said, "While we wait for the women to finish their task, I will tell you how the dwarf piñon came to be."

Settling himself, he brushed the front of his new vest and smiled. "Our ancestors tell us exactly why this tree is dwarfed and exactly how it happened."

In a low, hypnotic voice, he began. "It happened very long ago, at the time when two animals were worshipped by the Washoes: The wolf and the coyote. The wolf was good and the coyote was evil. The good Wolf-god tried to keep this valley for the tribe. He created a river and taught the Indian to bathe in it, cleansing away all sin and disease. The happy people came to share the magic of the region. Feasts were held and everyone gathered piñon nuts, for the trees were plentiful. And afterward, they would have a great celebration of singing and dancing."

Jena looked at Morgan and saw his interest was more than polite. Glancing to her other side, she noticed Jace's face was pleased as he listened to his grandfather and, smiling, she turned her attention back to Gray Wolf.

His voice became harder as he continued: "Soon the bad, jealous Coyote-god came and tried to influence these happy people to leave the Wolf-god and follow his wicked ways. He told them if they continued to bathe in the pure water their hands would become like his. 'And when this happens,' he said, 'you will no longer be able to make fire. You will grow weak and die.'

416

"The Indians were frightened, too frightened to disobey. Soon after, a terrible drought struck the valley. The river dried up, but worst of all, the pine forests were destroyed by fire. These trees were the life of the Washo. It was gone.

"Then the barren, foodless land drove the antelope, rabbit, and other animals elsewhere. There was no hunting. Nor was there fur from which to make warm clothing. Babies cried from the cold and hunger. Sickness fell upon the Washo. Many died and the tribe became small. Others made war and took all their ponies. The Washoes grieved bitterly and knew they had made a mistake by listening to the evil Coyote-god."

Gray Wolf paused in his story and again passed around the piñon nuts. Taking one, Jenna looked at Morgan, and he smiled in return. Both of them were eager for the story to continue.

Satisfied that he had his audience's rapt attention, the old man smiled before again speaking.

"Finally, the Washo sent for their friend, the good Wolf-god. When he saw what had happened, he felt great pity. First, he made a number of arrowheads and scattered them widely over the land so the people could hunt for food in faraway places. When the Coyote-god heard of this, he poisoned the arrowheads so any Washo who picked one up died.

"Again, the Wolf-god tried to help his friends. This time he scattered pine nuts over the ground, and these immediately sprang up into forests. But the Washoes were so weak from hunger that they could not reach the nuts on the trees. Then, once more, he came to their rescue. He struck off the tops of the piñons, turning them into dwarfed trees. Now the people could reach up and gather the nuts and cones.

"This made Coyote-god angry. He met Wolf-god

and argued, trying to make him stop shrinking the nut pines. Wolf-god would not listen. He continued to shrink thousands of trees for his friends. The starving Washoes gathered the crop and were saved. For these pines are food not only for the people, but for birds and animals as well."

He sat back in a relaxed posture, indicating that his story was at its end. All three of his listeners unconsciously breathed in appreciation as they, too, relaxed.

"It is a very good story, Gray Wolf," Morgan complimented. "The Washo is fortunate to be a good friend of the Wolf-god."

As Jenna agreed, Jace spoke up. "Now it is not the Coyote-god who threatens the people. It is the white man and his railroad. They take our land so we must travel further to hunt. They rob us of our trees, so our women must work harder to gather nuts. And all because of the railroad." Looking back at Gray Wolf, he said in a hard voice, "Perhaps, Grandfather, it is time to call on the Wolf-god again."

Gray Wolf looked troubled but said nothing as the women silently came into the wickiup and placed bowls of food in front of him. As he nodded to them, they kept their eyes down and quietly left. "Come," he said, in an effort to change the mood. "Share our humble food."

Jenna looked with interest inside the large bowls as Gray Wolf passed one to each of them. There was only a spoon, the bowl of which was fashioned from a nut. She knew it would be rude to bring the food up to her nose, but there was a strange smell coming from it.

"It's the *cui-ui*," Jace said, reading her mind while pointing to a dark mass off to one side of the heavy pottery. "It's a big, clumsy fish. We only see it during spring and early summer. It's considered special."

Jenna nodded. Sensing all eyes on her, she spooned

some onto her crude utensil and brought it to her mouth. Seeing Morgan was doing the same thing, she waited until he tasted the fish she couldn't even pronounce. Morgan chewed a few times and smiled as he swallowed. Looking at his host, he said, "Delicious!"

Feeling braver, Jenna followed suit. Immediately, her stomach rebelled at the oily fishy taste. Her mind fought with her digestive system, and she closed her eyes as she forced the fish down her throat. Taking a deep breath, she opened her lids and smiled at Gray Wolf. *"Delicious!"* she said, a little too brightly, not daring to look at Morgan.

The older man looked pleased, and he nodded abruptly as he started on his own food. She watched Gray Wolf eat with relish and worried that she would insult him by her refusal to finish.

Looking at Jace, who also seemed to be enjoying his meal, she pointed to the two other different foods in the bowl. "And what are these, Jace?"

Swallowing, Jason used his spoon to point them out. "This is the rabbit I brought in today, and this . . ." He touched a flat, small round food. "This is a cake."

Immediately, Jenna knew she couldn't eat the rabbit. The memory of Morgan's rabbit was still very fresh in her mind. But the flat little cakes looked harmless. Picking one up, she bit into it and found it almost tasteless. Wanting to compliment Gray Wolf, she swallowed and said the only truthful thing she could. "It's crunchy." Nodding, she repeated her statement just before taking another bite. "It's very crunchy."

Gray Wolf smiled and spoke to Jace in Washo. Seeing Jenna looking at him, Jason turned to her and explained, "My grandfather wanted to know what 'crunchy' was. I translated."

Gray Wolf wiped his mouth on his sleeve. "It is the . . ." Looking to his grandson, he asked, "How do you say it in the white man's tongue?"

Jace smiled, refusing to meet Jenna's eyes. "Grasshoppers."

She heard Morgan chuckle beside her and turned to glare at him while a shiver of revulsion ran through her. His eyes didn't hold a shred of sympathy as he spooned rabbit into his mouth.

"Try the cakes, Morgan," she whispered harshly. "You'll love them."

Chewing vigorously, Morgan grinned, his smile causing the single dimple to appear. Swallowing, he nodded. "I intend to, Jenna," he said, unable to keep the laughter out of his voice. "Rarely do we get the opportunity to taste such delicacies." Picking up a flat cake, he raised it in a salute to Gray Wolf before jamming it in his mouth.

Jenna watched Morgan and Jace walk off together. She went over in her mind the disturbing conversation she'd had with the young boy earlier. Jason didn't want to return to the farm. He wanted to remain here, with his grandfather. Jenna could have accepted that. She, too, thought Jace would be happier with the Washo. He just refused to see his mother. He'd said that Willow had made her choice, and she'd chosen a white man over her son and her father's people. When she'd asked what he'd done with the three hundred dollars taken from the train, he pointed to the sturdy clothing the Indians wore, the heavy pots cooking over outside fires, and the small herd of ponies off to one side of the camp. She couldn't fault him on his choices.

It was then that Morgan came up to them and asked Jace to walk with him. Seeing them standing in the distance, she could only hope Morgan was more successful with their young friend.

"She wants to see you, Jace. Why don't you come back with us?"

Morgan watched the boy's jaw harden with determination. "If she wanted to see me, she could have come with you today. I will not go to that doctor's house."

Morgan tried again. "You would deny your mother happiness?"

Defensively, Jace shot back. "She has denied me happiness! First, she leaves her people to marry a white man. Then, when he dies, I am left to bear the shame of working for the white man—all because of a promise she made to him! I will stay *here*, Morgan. At least *I* know where I belong."

Breaking off a small twig from a tree, Morgan studied its leaves. "She's keeping the farm for you. You might change your mind someday."

"Never! I want nothing more to do with the white man!"

Morgan looked into his face. "Not all whites have treated you badly. What about Jenna? Haven't you wondered why no one came after you for stealing that money?"

Jace looked to the ground, unable to meet Morgan's eyes.

Quietly, Morgan gave him his answer. "Jenna paid that back. It was her money that replaced what you stole."

Jace's head jerked up. "Jenna?" he asked, a stricken look on his face.

Morgan nodded. "She cares that much about you. I'm not telling you this to make you feel guilty. It's

421

over. No one's looking for you. I just wanted you to know how Jenna feels." Putting his hand on Jason's shoulder, he said, "We're leaving the day after tomorrow. You might never see her again. She, too, has to make a new life. It would mean a lot to her if you would come down to say good-bye . . . and to speak with your mother."

Jace looked across the camp to the beautiful yellow-haired woman. He knew she could never accept the Indian life, and he was glad Morgan would take care of her. Still, in his young heart, he knew another female would never take her place. Star Dancer. How he loved her and wanted to make her proud.

Looking back to Morgan, he nodded. "I will come to say good-bye to you and Jenna. I cannot promise about my mother."

Pleased, Morgan smiled.

Without saying another word, both of them silently turned and walked back to the camp. Jace's eyes were serious, and he couldn't tear them away from Jenna as plans started forming in his head.

Chapter Thirty-four

While Morgan washed up after their trip to Gray Wolf's camp, Jenna stood at the window and towel dried her own damp hair. Looking out into the dark night, she was depressed for some strange reason. It's being back here, she thought, where it all began. The day after tomorrow she would leave Nevada, leave Willow and Jace; leave everything that had become familiar since her own incredible journey.

Turning away from the window, she sat on the bed and looked around the small room. Here they had brought Morgan when he was wounded. In this tiny room, she had nursed him, argued with him and loved him. He was everything to her now. Here, she had no past—no friends, no family.

Standing up, she opened their leather trunk and searched through its contents. Bringing out her purse, she opened it and withdrew her wallet before dropping the purse back. Once more back on the bed, she unfolded the thin rectangular billfold and fingered past the useless credit cards until she reached the pictures. Taking them out, Jenna inhaled deeply as she looked into her mother's smiling eyes. She'd been afraid to do this before, afraid that if she dwelt on those she had left behind, it would be an admittance that she would never return.

Today, after talking to Jace of Willow's love for him, her own mother's image had been strong in her mind. Dear, dear Claire. Jenna's lips curled in a sad smile as she continued to stare at the picture. How she missed her. How she wished her mother could meet Morgan—know that finally her daughter had met the right man and was settling down—just as her mother had always wished.

"Jenna?"

Towel thrown over his shoulders, Morgan stood just inside the door leading into their room. "What's wrong? You looked so sad a moment ago."

Jenna's eyes closed briefly before she smiled. "Come here, Morgan," she softly instructed. "I want you to see something."

He sat on the edge of the bed and looked at her.

Tears formed in her eyes as she held out the picture. "I want you to meet my mother," she said, trying so hard to hold back the sobs of homesickness.

Taking the photograph from her hand, Morgan stared down at the attractive older woman. He could see Jenna in her delicate structure and coloring.

"That's my mom," she whispered, her throat raw from the unshed tears. "Her name's Claire."

"She's lovely, Jenna," Morgan commented while looking up to his wife. Seeing how close she was to crying, he threw the towel to the bottom of the bed and pulled her into his arms.

Feeling her shoulders shake, he held her tighter, knowing there was very little he could say to comfort her.

"I miss her so much," Jenna sobbed against his chest. "She isn't a strong woman, Morgan. I don't know how she'll get through my disappearance."

Rubbing her back, Morgan shook his head at his inability to provide a comforting answer. In all honesty, he felt selfish. He couldn't wish Jenna to be with her mother, for to do that would mean losing her himself. And he would fight anyone or anything that tried to separate them. Wanting to say something, he whispered above her still damp hair, "Do you have any others? A picture of your father?"

She pulled back from him and wiped her eyes on the sleeve of her robe. Nodding, she rummaged through the wallet and brought out another small picture. Looking down, Morgan smiled. Even though they were different sexes, the resemblance between Jenna and her father was strong. It was in the eyes, the proud tilt of the chin, the softness of the smile.

"You are your father's daughter," he stated quietly and looked up. "What was his name again?"

"Keene. Keene Weldon." Jenna said the name as if it were last spoken long ago.

Putting the wallet on the small wooden table by the bed, Morgan lay down and took Jenna into his arms. Still holding the photographs, he brought them up in front of both of them. Tonight Jenna needed only comfort and a release from her past. Realizing that, he said, "Tell me about your parents. I want to know everything about you."

"You have decided to do this, my grandson?" Gray Wolf asked in Washo. "I will tell you: The journey is not an easy one."

Jason looked up at his grandfather and nodded. Ever since Morgan had told him of Jenna's sacrifice, he knew he must do something to repay her. The time was short before her departure, and he only knew of this way to come up with some plan in such a short time. Straightening his bare shoulders, he said in a strong voice, "I am ready."

Nodding, Gray Wolf pulled back the hide covering the entrance to his wickiup and motioned for his young grandson to walk in first. Inside the structure they were greeted by Yellow Hawk, the road man, who would act as master of ceremony.

"Everything is in readiness, Two Faces. Before the light again rises, you will have your dream and your new name."

Jason inclined his head and came closer, already smelling the strong incense of fire and cedar.

Reaching out, Yellow Hawk placed the necklace of beans around Jason's neck and brought him closer to the crescent-shaped altar. Motioning with his hands, he instructed Jason and Gray Wolf to sit down with him before the fire.

Although frightened, Jace kept his breathing normal, not wanting his grandfather and Yellow Hawk to sense his fear. A pipe was placed in his hands and he brought it to his lips, inhaling the strong tobacco. He could feel it enter his lungs and fought the cough that crept up his throat. He would go through with this, no matter what. It was time he became a man.

When all three had smoked, the pipe was put aside, and Yellow Hawk picked up a fan of eagle feathers. Chanting, asking the Goddess of Night to lead Two Faces on his journey, the road man used his fan to draw the smoke over Jace's body. After this was repeated several times, Yellow Hawk held out his hand with the offering.

Breathing deeply, Jace stared at the sacred button. He tried not to think of the incredible stories he had heard of its use. Taking a last calming breath, he reached out and picked up the peyote. His hand shook, his jaw clenched with determination as he brought it to his lips. Closing his eyes, he pictured Jenna in his mind as he opened his mouth and chewed it.

Listening to Yellow Hawk's continued chanting, Jace's first reaction was a clenching and gripping of his stomach muscles. He started to sweat profusely; his muscles started to shake, and unconsciously, he began to sway from side to side. Closing his eyes against the pain in his stomach, he fought the strong, threatening waves of nausea. Concentrating ever harder, Jace struggled to picture his dream: that which would send him on his quest and tell him how to repay Jenna.

Nothing; only flashes of multicolored lights behind his lids. Frustrated, he opened his eyes and looked about the wickiup.

She stood before him, like the goddess she was, and Jace gasped at her beauty.

The Goddess of Night approached rapidly, opening her billowy robe of darkness around him. He felt lifted into her softness, and from far away he heard Yellow Eagle's admonishment: "Do not rise, Two Faces. Stay. Go with your dream only in your mind."

Giving himself over to her, Jace moaned as her dark robe spread from horizon to horizon. He watched as the Sun-god saluted her with his final rays, then descended to his home to rest until dawn. The stars became white crystals against the blackness of the sky as his beautiful goddess reigned supreme. He listened to her sweet voice as she called for her lamp, and the moon rose to her bidding.

"Go now," she whispered softly as she opened her robe and released him.

Jace cried out for her to return, but she left him there in the night. He looked around him, feeling alone and frightened. He wanted the goddess to come back. He wanted to speak to her, to feel the security of her robes. But he was alone.

The voices of the wind gathered strength, and he heard people speaking. Spinning around, he saw the train conductor, Bullmason, fighting with someone. Looking closer, he saw the body of a woman, saw her yellow hair. Screaming her name, Jace ran toward Jenna. Bullmason laughed as Jace fell to the ground beside her. The tears ran down his cheeks as he picked up her still body and buried his face in her hair.

"Jenna! Please, don't be dead. Come back to me! Please!"

Feeling someone touch his hair, Jace looked up, but Bullmason was gone. Feeling the soft touch again, he lowered his head and watched in wonder as Jenna opened her eyes and smiled at him. Pulling his head toward hers, she kissed his lips lightly, and Jace almost cried from the sweetness of her mouth.

Somehow, she faded from his arms, and he slowly turned his head to see her standing next to him. Holding out her hand, she pulled him to his feet. "Come," she said, smiling at him. "Star Dancer will go with you on your journey . . ."

He returned her smile and held fast to her strong hand. Neither spoke as they walked into the night. Clouds drifted across the shrouded heaven as the two wandered. The summer moons passed and winter came upon them. Cold, they clung to each other for warmth. Unexpectedly, a great wind rose up, and the clouds quickly moved backward, bringing them back to summer. He held Jenna to his chest as an unexpected roar surrounded them. Suddenly, the earth shook violently as the wind continued to howl around them.

It came upon them quickly, a great iron monster. Without tracks, the train devoured everything in its path. Gone were the piñon trees. The animals crying out to Mother Earth as they disappeared into its huge dark mouth. The whistle of the train sounded so loud, both he and Jenna held their hands over their ears to stop the pain. When the monster train approached the gentle Washo, Jace screamed his rage until his throat was raw.

Magically, Jenna handed him his father's gun. Aiming it at the massive engine, Jace fired again and again. After what seemed a long time, they watched as it stopped and collapsed before them. Taking his hand, Jenna started running toward it. Together, they climbed into the express car, and Jace marveled at the wealth inside. Money was everywhere. Their feet walked over it. Scooping a pile into his hands, Jace was about to hand it to Jenna when he was swiftly pulled back.

He blinked a few times, trying to clear his head. His grandfather and Yellow Hawk were looking at him, asking him questions. He felt fear because he couldn't hear them. Opening his mouth, he tried to form the words to tell them of his dream, but his voice sounded strange to his ears.

For the next twelve hours, Jace periodically reentered his dream world. Gray Wolf and Yellow Hawk stayed with him, watching over and making sure he did no harm to himself. No one entered, except the women to bring water, for the men's thirst was great. During the night, Jace told his grandfather and the road man of his many dreams and his new name was decided.

"When the Sun-god returns, we will tell the people of your new name. You will be called Iron Warrior," Yellow Hawk proclaimed.

"Iron Warrior . . ." Gray Wolf said the name slowly. He nodded. "I like it," he said after some thought. Looking at his grandson, he smiled. "I am proud of you, Iron Warrior. Tonight you have become a man."

Jace's heart swelled. His own pride was near bursting. "Thank you, Grandfather," he murmured, his smile matching Gray Wolf's. Suddenly a great weariness overtook him, and he lay down on a blanket beside the fire. Looking into its small flames, he smiled again. He had passed the test. He was now a man. And most important, he had been given his dream—and the means to repay Star Dancer. He closed his eyes, a contented smile staying on his lips.

Chapter Thirty-five

Morgan and Jenna stood opposite each other, amused smiles on their faces. It was early morning, and both had decided to help Willow finish packing up the farm. Jenna was standing at the side of the bed, having just picked up her wallet from the small table. Morgan stood at the bottom of the bed, his hands casually inside the pockets of his jeans.

"What're you thinking?" he asked, a smile playing at the corner of his mouth.

Coming to stand in front of him, she laughed. "You know exactly what I'm thinking. Just because I said you look devastating in those jeans, you're going to flaunt yourself, aren't you?"

Morgan threw back his head and chuckled. "What did you expect me to wear when I'm moving furniture? And what about you? We're right back to the beginning, aren't we?"

Looking down at her green split skirt and the once white blouse that showed signs of wear, she nodded her head. "I guess we are," she agreed. "I may be wearing the same clothes as when we met, but yours are different."

Bringing her into his arms, he kissed the top of her

431

head. "What do you mean . . . different?"

Snuggling against his chest, she inhaled his clean scent and turned her head toward the window. Her voice was heavy with nostalgia when she spoke. "I bought these for you." Looking out the window, she held him tighter. "Look! Clinton and Willow have already started packing the wagon. I guess we should join them."

Morgan pressed her closer to his body. "We'll go out in a minute. Right now, you feel too good to let go."

"We promised today—"

"We'll give them today," he interrupted. "Just promise me the night."

"All my nights," she whispered, smiling with contentment. "But look, Morgan. Clinton has that heavy box and he—Oh God!"

Jenna's body jerked, and the wallet fell from her hands as she pulled away from her husband. Following her look of horror, Morgan saw that Clinton had fallen down the porch steps, the box and its contents scattered. Instantly, Jenna raced out of their room to help. Before he followed her, Morgan quickly picked up her wallet and stuffed it into his pocket as he hurried out of the barn.

Running across the yard, they reached Clinton and Willow just as the doctor was attempting to stand.

"Clinton, why didn't you wait for us?" Jenna cried. "We told you we would help."

Not waiting for an answer, Morgan approached the injured man. "Here, lean on me and I'll get you to the wagon."

Smiling sheepishly, Clinton Marshall tried to hide the pain with sarcasm. "Guess I'm too old to be of any use, huh? Maybe you should think twice about coming with me, Willow."

The small woman automatically placed Clinton's other arm around her shoulders as Jenna cleared the steps. "You are too old to be foolish. You should not have tried to pick up something that two men would have trouble carrying." Looking up to his face as the three made it down the wooden stairs, she added wisely, "You have nothing to prove to me."

As Morgan helped seat him into the buckboard, Clinton said, "Look, I'm the doctor here, and I say it's nothing more than a sprained ankle. I'll wrap it and—"

Willow spoke up with authority. "We will take you home and you will put that foot up to take the pressure off it. It is what you would say to one of your patients."

As Morgan took the reins, Willow climbed up to join the men. Looking back at Jenna, Clinton said with a wry grin, "Thank you, Jenna, for giving Willow that medical book." He shook his head. "And I thought she was competition before!"

Jenna grinned. "Just do as she says, Clinton. You know she's right." Looking at Morgan and Willow, she added, "Take your time. I'll start stacking things out here."

Willow smiled her thanks, concern for the injured man showing in her eyes, while Morgan blew her a kiss. As she watched them ride away, Jenna imagined the life between the stubborn Clinton and the equally stubborn Willow. Chuckling, she silently wished them the best and waved as Clinton yelled back to her, "Supper at my house tonight!"

Jenna was slowly maneuvering the same steps where Clinton had fallen, so she was twice as careful and didn't look up right away when she heard the sound of a horse approaching. It wasn't until her feet were firmly planted on the dirt that she lifted her head.

"Jace!"

Lowering the box to the ground, she greeted him with a wide smile when he brought his horse up before her. As he easily slid down from its back, she noticed that Jace was again dressed as a white man. Gone were the buckskin pants and vest.

"Jenna. I don't have time . . . Is my mother here?" His eyes darted about the farm, looking for Willow.

She smiled again, trying hard not to notice his impatience. "No. She just left with Morgan. Clinton fell and injured—"

"Good, I'm glad she isn't here," he interrupted. "Has she packed all my things yet?"

Annoyed, because of his attitude, she replied shortly, "I really don't know. She hasn't had too much help, you know?"

Jace finally looked at her and smiled. "Don't be angry. Everything's going to work out." Without waiting for her reply, he looked into the box she had brought out of the house. Not finding what he was looking for, he hurried up the stairs and entered his old home.

Jenna stared after him for a few moments, confused by his attitude. Unconsciously, she raised her hands to her hips and followed him. When she entered the main room, she stopped short as she observed Jace throwing articles of clothing out of a box.

"What are you *doing*?" she demanded, angry that he was creating more work.

Finding what he was looking for, he straightened and brought up a dark kerchief and hat. Putting them on, he looked back at her and grinned. "I have a plan, Jenna."

Inhaling deeply as a wave of recognition struck her, she whispered in a shocked voice, "Jace, you can't mean . . . You're not going to do it again!"

Without answering her, he strode out of the house and down the steps. Running behind him, she prevented him from mounting his horse by pulling on his arm. "Dammit, Jace! Answer me!"

When he turned to her, Jenna was taken aback by the look of authority on his face. "My new name is Iron Warrior. Do not try and stop me, Star Dancer. I did it once, I can do it again."

Her fingers released him. She felt as if she had been slapped. "Don't you . . . don't you think every thief thinks they can get away with it again? Jace, it's over! No one's looking for you anymore—"

"I am not a thief," he interrupted. "And my new name is Iron Warrior. I received it last night in a dream, along with this plan." Looking deeply into her eyes, he said slowly, "The Goddess of Night came to me and showed me the way. You were there, too."

She was confused and shook her head. "What are you saying? You dreamed that you would rob the train again? That's crazy! Listen to me. It was only a dream! Wait for Morgan to come back, he'll . . ."

He mounted the horse. Looking down at her, his face was sad. "I thought *you* would understand. But I cannot stay here and explain it. It wasn't just a dream, Jenna. It was instructions from the gods."

"Please . . ." She grabbed hold of his leg, desperate to keep him with her. "Don't do this, Jace! You'll get caught. I know it. We were just lucky."

He pulled his leg back and rode a few feet away. Seeing the anxiety and sorrow on her face, he smiled and said slowly, quietly, "I have always loved you, Star Dancer. From the very moment I first saw you. Do not cry. I will see you before you leave tomorrow, and pay you back your money. I promise."

Digging his heels into the soft sides of his horse, he

435 ·

headed away from the farm and toward the railroad tracks, never hearing Jenna yelling after him, "*What money*? What the *hell* are you talking about?!"

She stood, watching him disappear into the woods. Apprehension took over her body, and she held her arms to stop the shaking. What should she do? She tried to think clearly, but it was impossible. Morgan! Dear God, why wasn't he here? *Someone* had to stop Jace.

She thought of going to town to get help, but realized it would only create an uproar. She couldn't do that, not to Jason. He'd said he'd loved her, had to pay her back. Back for what? Knowing she could never catch him on foot, Jenna ran to her room to write Morgan a note. She was out of breath by the time she returned to Willow's house. Placing the paper under a rock, she left her hurried explanations on the porch and pushed her lungs further as she sped to the corral.

Slipping a bridle over the horse she had used yesterday, she didn't even bother with a saddle as she brought the animal over to the fence and climbed on top. Without looking back, Jenna kicked the horse into action and followed her young friend. Wrapping the reins around her hands, she tightly grasped the mane and lowered her body to reduce the wind resistance. If he was going to pull it off like the last time, she knew just where to find him and, shaking off a horrible premonition of disaster, she cursed. Damn it, if she had to, she'd use every self-defense trick she'd been taught to stop him. Spurring the animal on, Jenna prayed she wouldn't be too late.

She pulled the horse up short as she stared at the scene before her. Down the hill, the engine and express car were stopped, great billows of steam coming up from under its frame. Realizing Jace must have uncoupled the cars before he came to the farm, Jenna took a deep breath filled with determination and kicked the animal's sides to make the descent.

She dismounted in front of the huge engine and walked across the heavy lengths of track that Jace must have pried up. As she made her way past the engine and firebox, Jenna could hear Jace's voice as she approached the red express car.

"You heard me . . . fill those bags!"

Her heart hammered away inside her chest, her throat felt incapable of speech, but she knew she had to overcome her fear if she were to stop him. Taking a deep, steadying breath, she forced her feet to move until she was standing at the opened door. Jace's back was toward her, his gun pointed on the engineer, his assistant, and the Wells Fargo man. Afraid to startle him, she eased her weight up until she could crawl into the car. Keeping her eyes on Jace, she slowly straightened.

"Jace . . ." She whispered his name. "It's me, Jenna . . ."

Spinning around, Jace turned startled eyes to her above the bright red kerchief covering his face. "What are you *doing* here!" he demanded in an angry voice while turning halfway back to the railroad men. Keeping his gun on them, he looked at her from the corner of his eye. "Why did you come?"

Coming toward him, she stopped a few feet from his side. "Please don't do this. Tell them it was all a mistake, and let's get out of here. Please!"

He moved the gun in the direction of the Wells Fargo man. "Hurry up!" he commanded.

Up until then, the three men were staring at her as if she weren't real. At Jace's order, the engineer and his man held their hands up higher, and the express agent quickly returned to filling the burlap sack. Looking back at her young friend, Jenna tried again. "Jace, I'm not going to let you do this. We'll work something out. I don't know why you think you have to repay—"

"Better listen to her, *breed*."

Turning with Jace at the sound of the voice, Jenna couldn't stop an astonished gasp as Harry Bullmason appeared from behind several stacked boxes.

Holding a pistol on both of them, Bullmason came out of his hiding place and grinned. "Well, missy, we meet again. I sorta had this half-breed figured out. You—you're the surprise."

Jenna stared at the long barrel of the gun and closed her eyes briefly while she willed her heart to slow down. Opening them, she met Harry's hard gaze. "Look, this is all a mistake," she said in a nervous voice. "He's just a young boy. He didn't mean it."

"I am a man, Jenna. Do not make excuses for me." Now Jace had his gun pointed at Bullmason.

Again, the conductor grinned. "You just made an even bigger mistake, boy. I don't know whether I should take you in, hang you, or shoot you right here."

Jenna wrung her hands together, desperate to make them listen. "Please. Bullmason. He's young. He's watched the railroad take away his people's land. He didn't take anything yet. Can't we just put everything back?" Seeing the determined look in Bullmason's eyes, she cried, "Haven't you ever done something foolish? Something you regretted later?"

From her side, she heard Jace's angry voice. "The only thing he regrets is that the last time we beat him out of robbing his own train." Pulling down the kerchief, now that there was no need for a disguise, he

438

asked, "Isn't that right, Bullmason? I heard you and those other men planning it. It's just eating at you that we pulled it off before you."

Jenna groaned as she watched Bullmason look at the three railroad men behind them. Forcing his eyes back to her and Jace, the conductor's features were red with fury. "Shut up, you lying red bastard! I ought to hang you right now and do the sheriff a favor. Now, hand that gun over."

Willow was the first to discover Jenna's note. Picking it up, her eyes scanned the hurried message. When she looked up, Morgan was coming up the stairs. Without a word, she handed it over, though her eyes told him volumes.

Morgan read it, then read it again. Raising his head, he looked at Willow and muttered a single, explosive curse. "Stay here!" he ordered as he leapt off the steps and ran to the barn.

Watching him ride away, Willow knelt and picked up the crumpled piece of paper. Holding it to her chest, she prayed to all the gods: hers, and the one she had been taught to love through her husband. She stayed there, in her yard, lifting her head to the mid-morning sun, not able to shake away a premonition that this was a day of disaster.

Morgan was no more than thirty feet away when he heard the shot coming from the train. Frantic, he pulled the horse up fast and almost fell from its back. Taking out the pistol from his belt, he held it upright as he cautiously approached the express car. *Jenna!* He was terrified of what he would find when he looked inside! Quickly, relief washed over him as he heard her screams. *"My God! What have you done! Oh, my God . . ."*

There was a faint rumble as the ground shook, and Morgan grabbed hold of the door as he hoisted himself up into the car. Standing behind Bullmason, he looked around him to the scene on the floor.

Jenna was kneeling next to Jace, cradling his head in her arms. "Wake up! Please? Jace, please . . ." Sobbing, she shook the boy's body. *"Jace!"*

"You saw him," Bullmason said, breathing heavily. "He was goin' to shoot me. Crazy breed . . ."

Still holding Jace, she turned her grief-stricken face up to Bullmason's. "You bastard! You *killed* him! He's dead! Do you hear me? *Dead!*"

Somehow, through the insanity taking place in that small car, Jenna spotted Morgan, and her face crumpled as she whispered, "He's dead, Morgan. He was . . . he was just a boy. He killed him. He . . . he just shot him." Hysterical, she could barely breathe as the sobs wracked her body and the steady flow of tears clouded her vision.

When the next tremor occurred, it was so strong Jace slipped out of Jenna's arms, and everyone inside the car stared at each other, trying to figure out what it was. A distant roar could be heard, and it continued as the shaking and rattling slowly stopped. Bullmason was the first to recover.

"Throw the gun down, Trahern!" he ordered, keeping both Jenna and Morgan in view. "You!" he yelled to Jenna. "Get away from that Indian's gun."

Not caring what happened to herself, Jenna continued to reach across Jace's body for his gun. Picking it up, she pointed it at Bullmason and pulled back the hammer. "I'm going to make sure you pay for what you did," she proclaimed in a shaky voice. Sniffling, she brought her other hand up to steady her aim.

"Tell her, Trahern. Drop your gun and tell her to do the same. I'll shoot her. I swear to God!" he yelled over the increasing noise and the returned rumbling of the ground.

The shaking was so violent, now, Jenna had to concentrate on keeping the gun on Bullmason. She knew Morgan was off to her side, but she couldn't see him. Nor could she see the frightened railroad men who had fallen to the floor during the last tremor and remained there.

"I hate you!" she screamed over the deafening noise. "I'm not going to let you go back and lie to everyone about this!" Taking a deep breath, she tightened her index finger on the trigger.

Watching in amazement, Jenna's mouth dropped open as the sound of the gun exploded within the car. Unbelievably Harry Bullmason was lifted up in the air and slammed back against the stacked boxes. She shook her head. It had been so easy. She hadn't even felt the gun go off.

"You always were a bad shot, *desperada*," Morgan yelled from behind her. Shocked, she turned her head and saw him still holding the smoking gun while trying to keep his balance. What was wrong with him? Dear God, why was he fading away like that?

She had no time to wonder as, swiftly, the roar increased again. It felt so close that everything inside the car was moving. Boxes shifted and fell down around them; mail was flying through the sudden wind that had entered the express car and wrapped itself around all within. Struggling against the force of the wind and the roaring in her ears, Jenna tried to stand up. Boxes and debris separated Morgan and Jenna, and she screamed as she identified the noise.

"It's a train, Morgan! Another train!" And it's coming too fast, she thought in a panic as she tried to maneuver her way closer to her husband.

Her eyes locked with his as he attempted to reach her. "Hurry, Jenna! We've got to get out of here!"

"Morgan!" Again, he faded, then quickly came back. Were her eyes playing tricks on her? What the hell was happening? Desperate to touch him, she pulled herself up again and crawled in his direction as he once more fell to the ground. It was almost impossible to move, to hear beyond the gigantic roar of the oncoming train. Please God, she prayed, help me! In a terrifying flash of recognition, she knew what was taking place. It was a modern engine! And it was all around her. She'd heard that same sound too many times to forget. The train that was almost upon them was *modern*!

Seeing the desperation in Morgan's face as he pushed boxes away and crawled closer to her only made her move with determination. She knew she had to reach him! When he faded again, he was less than a foot away. "Morgan!" His name tore out of her. Terrified, refusing to accept what was happening, Jenna made a frenzied grab for him. His face was frozen in fear as he reached for her, but she seemed to pass through him as she fell.

He was already gone.

Chapter Thirty-six

The breath was knocked out of him as he was slammed against a heavy partition. Several painful seconds passed as he waited for his diaphragm to relax and his lungs to function. Gradually, he was able to take short breaths, though his body continued to be held by a powerful unseen force against the wall.

"You okay, man?"

Opening his eyes, Morgan looked into the face of a young man about twenty years old.

"Scared the hell out of me, fallin' like that. You sure you're okay?"

Morgan continued to stare at him, unable to speak. He felt immobilized by the pressure against him.

Pushing back his light-brown hair, the young man extended his hand. "Here, let me help you get up."

Morgan took his hand and noticed that he, too, was having trouble keeping his balance. When he was finally upright, the two men let go of hands and looked at each other.

"Where am I?" Morgan whispered.

As the younger man turned his head to look out a door window, so did Morgan. Keeping a firm grip on a handle just inside the door, Morgan watched the blur of scenery as they sped by.

"I'd say we're just outside Reno. Why don't you go back and sit down? You don't look too good."

Morgan sharply turned his head and looked beyond the vestibule where they were standing. It was a car of some kind. People were seated two and three across, separated by a narrow aisle. He felt chills go up his back and run down his arms. His stomach tightened, and his breathing came in quick gasps. By the car's starkness, it wasn't a palace car. By its inhabitants, it wasn't a passenger car; at least, it wasn't anything like he'd ever seen before!

Turning back to the man standing next to him, he asked in a low, frightened voice, "What year is it?"

The young man's eyes narrowed. "What'd you say?"

Morgan couldn't speak. His vocal cords were rendered useless by fear. He could only shake his head.

"Look, you better sit down, mister. You want me to find the conductor?"

Again shaking his head, he backed away from him and almost fell into a seat in the first row. He could see the man looking at him, and he turned his head toward the shiny steel framed window. *Jenna!* My God, where are you? Perspiration broke out all over him as he felt the incredible speed of the train. His body was rigid with fear, and he held onto the cushioned seat beneath him. *Where am I?* A hundred questions ran through his mind. Only two demanded an immediate answer: What happened on that train? And where was his wife?

He watched the strangely dressed people get up and walk off the train. Joining the women in their short dresses that showed their legs, or pants that hid them completely, he fell in behind a man dressed in a cream-colored suit. Frightened, he forced his legs to move and keep up with the line of people. Once off the train, he stopped and looked back. Through the crowd of busy travelers, he saw it.

It was huge. Smooth and shiny, like fine silver, the sleek train patiently waited on its track. There was no steam coming from under its frame. There was no engine, at all. Morgan could not detect anything that might indicate where it got its tremendous power. He watched as people hurried past him to take the seats in its many cars. A uniformed conductor stood at its side, checking his watch before stepping onto the train. Without any warning, the doors closed automatically and within seconds, he could hear the engine increase. As it moved slowly down the track, Morgan could feel the hair rise at the back of his neck. There could be no denying it now.

This was no world that he knew. It was Jenna's— and knowing that, a great wave of fear, followed by grief, swept over him. He had returned instead of her. His Jenna, his wife, she was back there. He had lost her.

"Don't look so sad, cowboy."

Morgan glanced over toward the soft female voice. His mouth dropped open as he viewed what he *thought* was a female. Young, very young, she stood next to him and smiled. He couldn't help the astonished look as he stared at her from head to foot and then back again. Short, high-heeled boots that ended at her ankles were followed by a long expanse of purple legs. Looking past the stockings, he saw she wore the smallest skirt he had ever seen. It ended at her thighs! Above that was an open white leather jacket showing a brief strapless garment meant to cover her breasts. But what had truly shocked him was her hair. Short, even for a man, it was palomino blond with the front the same color as her purple

445

stockings. And it was sticking straight up in points.

"A real eye-catcher, huh?"

Morgan could only swallow.

She smiled again. Looking behind the theatrical makeup on her face, he could see she was pretty, and her smile was openly friendly.

"Some people don't understand new wave. I can see you have a real appreciation," she said while putting the strap of her white purse over her shoulder. "Listen, I just came in on the last train. Can you tell me how to get to Harrah's?"

Still unable to speak, Morgan merely shook his head.

She picked up her large suitcase and laughed. "You, too? I kinda thought, 'cause of the way you're dressed and all, that you were from Reno. Look, why don't we share the ride into town? That is where you're going, isn't it?"

Knowing he had to say something, Morgan nodded and mumbled, "Yes . . . into town."

She walked a few feet away, then turned back when she realized he wasn't following. "You coming, or what?"

As if waking from a nightmare, Morgan shuddered and forced his body into mobility. "Yes," he said with determination, "I'm coming."

He could feel her watching him as he stared around the train station. Never had he seen so many people, moving so fast. So many strange sights! Once they were outside, she turned to him and said, "Where are you from?" She then put her fingers into her mouth and emitted a shrill whistle. Within seconds, one of the strange fast-moving vehicles pulled up to them and stopped so quickly that Morgan jumped back toward the building.

"Hey, what's wrong?" the girl asked while a man

opened a door and walked around the thing to take her suitcase. Morgan watched in fascination as he opened the back of it and deposited the suitcase in a hidden compartment.

Slamming it shut, the man looked at the girl and asked, "Where to?"

The strangely dressed girl walked over to him and said, "What's the matter? You act like you've never seen a cab before. Are you coming or not?"

Morgan looked at the cab and realized it must be what Jenna had described as a car, an automobile. Nodding, he followed the girl inside. Again, he listened to another powerful engine as the driver started the cab. He could feel his excitement grow as the vehicle slowly started to move away from the station. When they joined other similar automobiles on a many-laned road, Morgan couldn't help turning to his companion and smiling.

She returned his smile and said, "You never did say where you were from."

Lost in the exhilaration of the moment, he answered her while looking back out the window, "Maryland. Baltimore, Maryland."

"No kidding! I would've sworn you were from out here. I mean, you really look like a cowboy." When he continued to look out the window, she added, "I'm from San Francisco. I'm going to try and get a job singing in the lounge in one of the casinos here. After I get a little experience, then I'm going down to Vegas. The money's supposed to be better there."

Not knowing if he'd heard her, she tapped his arm and held out her hand. "Name's Liza Moran. That's Liza with a Z, you know, like Liza Minnelli?"

Morgan turned away from the incredible scene whizzing by outside the window and faced her. Taking her hand, he shook it. "I'm Morgan Trahern. How do

447

you do?"

Liza giggled. "I'm doing pretty good, thank you. You're real formal, aren't you? Sure are strange, Morgan Trahern."

Smiling, he looked back out the window as they crossed a four-laned bridge. Strange? If only Liza Moran knew how true that was, he thought.

When the cab stopped, Liza announced, "Well, here we are! The Biggest Little City in the World . . . Reno. I'm getting out here. Harrah's. You going on?"

Shaking his head, he watched Liza open her purse and say, "It's five-eighty. If we split it, it comes to three-fifty a piece, including tip."

Reaching into his pocket, Morgan felt Jenna's wallet. Bringing it out, he opened it up to the driver. The man turned around and stared at the many credit cards. "You got to be kidding me!" he announced with a disgusted look on his face. "Look, man, I don't take credit cards! This here's a gambling town. Nobody's gonna take a credit card without IDs as long as your arm." He looked toward Liza and shook his head at her appearance. "You got the money, *lady*?"

The girl looked up and gave the driver an equally belittling stare. "Yeah, I got money. What do you think I'm getting out?" She handed him two bills and said, "Keep the change," as she opened the cab door and got out.

Even before Morgan followed her, he heard the man curse as he got out of the car to get Liza's suitcase, then add in an angry voice, "Twenty cents! Why do I always get the weirdos!"

As Morgan stood upright on the street, Liza slammed the door shut and whispered to Morgan as the cab sped away, "The creep didn't deserve any more. A tip is supposed to be for good service. Did you see the way he looked at us?"

Morgan couldn't answer her. His eyes were glued to the front of the casino. He had never seen so many lights before—and in the daytime! They winked at him, blinked names at him, and pointed with arrows toward the buildings. He was astonished by the colors. This wide-open gambling town was not the Reno, Nevada he had visited less than a month ago!

"You going in? Or are you gonna stand here gawking at the place? Geez, what's wrong with you? You act like you've never seen a hotel before, either."

Liza's words reminded him of Jenna. All those times she'd asked what was wrong with him—why he had no knowledge of her incredible inventions. How very different and difficult his world must have seemed. Again, Morgan was speechless, but his curiosity made him move toward the casino's opening. As soon as he and Liza walked across a grating, a gush of cold air ran over their bodies. Surprised, Morgan stopped and turned back to look at the floor. Hesitantly, he walked back to the grating and reveled as the cool air rushed up from the ground and brought chills to his arms. It was as if there was an invisible wall of cold air.

"Now you're going to tell me you've never felt air-conditioning? Where've you been living, Morgan?"

He looked up at Liza and smiled. "You'd never believe me." Shaking his head, he left the air-conditioning and joined her as they walked through the casino. Row after row of brightly lit slot machines captured his attention. Hundreds of people, mostly women, stood before each, depositing silver coins and pulling down arms. He watched in fascination as the machine would spin three rows of fruit and buzz loudly if all three would match. He was amazed as the machine spit out coin after coin and continued to watch as the lucky winners scooped up their money

449

and deposited it into tall cups, ready to try it again.

"If you're looking to make any money, you're not going to do it here," Liza whispered as she stood next to him. "Not unless you watch for one that's not paying off. When the player gets fed up and walks away, that's when you should try it. Those slots are primed to pay off after a certain time." She nudged his arm to get his attention. "If you want to try slots, go to the half dollar or dollar ones over there."

Morgan looked past the slot machines and noticed a large wheel with money attached. On a table in front of it were matching bills. He walked over to it and studied the money. After a few moments, he knew he didn't have any usable money. Even Jenna's credit cards were useless without proper identification. Looking up from the table, he met Liza's curious gaze. "I have no money," he said quietly.

Her eyes widened. "No money?" Waiting until he shook his head, Liza's mouth pursed in annoyance. "Morgan, what the hell are you doing? Coming here, to a casino, without any money?"

This time she shook her head and pinched the material of his shirt as she dragged him toward a wall. Looking up at him, her eyes narrowed as she dropped her suitcase to the carpeted floor. "What about those credit cards?" she whispered.

"They're not mine," he admitted.

"Geez!" She looked around them to see if anyone had heard. "Why didn't you just announce it to one of the security guards!"

Morgan smiled. "I didn't steal them. They belong to . . . to someone I know."

Looking back at him, her expression showed she didn't believe him. "Yeah, sure. Somebody you know. Forget them or you'll be picked up and thrown in jail. I don't even want to know where you got them." She looked at the pockets of his jeans. "Don't you have any money . . . no bills, no change?"

Shrugging, Morgan reached into his pockets while Liza looked about the casino and muttered, "Why do I always get involved with losers?"

Too confused to comment on her remark about losers, Morgan held out his hand and showed her the only money he had. Looking into his palm, Liza picked up one small silver coin and brought it closer to her eyes.

"You really are broke," she mumbled. "You can't have more than a dollar fifty to your name. What kind of man comes to Reno with nothing but a couple of dimes in his . . ." Her neck stretched closer to the coin. "Hey! You know how old this is?" she asked as she turned it over. "Look! It isn't even a dime. It says: half dime. Where you get this?"

Morgan glanced into her hand and shrugged. "I don't know. Probably Sacramento."

"It looks pretty new." Suddenly, her head snapped up, and Liza's expression was filled with excitement. "Did you see that sign when we came in? The one about some kind of rare coin show?"

Morgan shook his head. "I didn't—"

Picking up her suitcase, Liza gave Morgan back the coin and grabbed his arm. "C'mon. Let's find out where it is."

He followed her back to the entrance of the casino, unintentionally bumping into several people as he stared at his incredible surroundings.

"There!" Liza stopped and read the small white letters on a black board. "It's at the Convention Center. It says International Nu . . . Numismatic." She finally pronounced the word. "Authentication Bureau. Dealers Welcome."

Morgan looked over the sign. "I don't know about

this," he said, the coin burning into his palm. "What if they ask where I got it?"

Impatiently, Liza turned back to look at him. "Is it yours?" she asked abruptly.

When he nodded, she continued. "Then that's what you say. Tell them it's been in your family for years. Stretch the truth, if you have to. Look, Morgan, I'm here to audition as a lounge singer. I don't have any promises of a job, so I can't help you out. You've got to help yourself." Seeing the uncertainty on his face, she persisted. "You've got no *money*! No one's going to let you stand around and sightsee. Either you play one of the games or you leave. And since you can't play, sooner or later you're going to be asked to leave."

Morgan looked into her determined face. It was strange that since his initial shock at her appearance, he hadn't given her odd attire much thought, though he remembered several people staring at Liza's hair. She was trying to be helpful. In fact, without her, he would probably still be at the train station, immobilized by his fear. Deciding he had to begin to trust someone, needed someone to guide him through this strange world that he found himself in, Morgan nodded and said in a firm voice, "Show me where this Convention Center is."

Liza smiled and picked up her suitcase. "Follow me," she said and started to turn away when Morgan reached out and took the heavy suitcase from her hand.

She looked up into his eyes and smiled again while pulling the front of her white jacket together. "Maybe you're not a loser, Morgan Trahern. Let's go and find out."

She led him back into the casino, past an entertainment stage. A band played, and a pretty female sang into a thin pole about a boy she knew and dreamed of. In a loud, plaintive voice, she asked, "How will I know, if he really loves me? How will I know?" Morgan was fascinated, wondering how the woman made her voice so loud, and he would have asked Liza except, when he looked at her, she was giving the stage a nervous glance. Remembering her remark about being a singer and auditioning for a job, he thought it would be better not to ask any questions about the other woman's astonishing ability.

It appeared there were three separate buildings to this Harrah's, and as they went across an alley to the hotel side, Morgan was incapable of asking questions. There were so many racing through his head! Trying to take in everything around him, he found himself again frightened when he looked at Liza gliding upward on movable stairs. He stood, staring at the queer apparatus, as stair after stair appeared from out of the ground.

His eyes sought out Liza, and she impatiently motioned for him to follow her onto the thing. He took a deep breath and placed his hands on the black rails on either side. Immediately, his hands were pulled along with the moving, thick revolving belt. He pulled them back, frightened by its movement, and stumbled onto the large steps. One of them seemed to catch his feet and whisk him upward, leaving the ground behind him. The wonder of it! He regained his balance and looked back as others casually stepped on. Turning his head, he saw Liza waiting for him at the top. Anxious to see what awaited him on the next floor of the hotel, Morgan smiled with excitement.

His smile was short lived, yet stayed frozen in place as he noticed that the steps became shorter and shorter—until they disappeared altogether back into the ground. The tight knot of fear returned to his stomach, and his palms began to perspire. How was he to get off the thing?

As he went higher and higher, his anxiety grew as he realized time was running out. Making up his mind, Morgan looked at Liza and motioned with his hands for her to move. "Get out of the way," he yelled, and tried to gauge just how much time he had before his feet disappeared with the steps. Gathering up his courage, Morgan leaped over the dangerous point and landed on his knees three feet away from the thing.

"What . . . are . . . you . . . doing!" Hands on her hips, Liza looked down at him with a strained, annoyed expression on her face. "And where the hell is my suitcase?"

Breathing heavily, Morgan straightened and looked back as the other stair passengers merely stepped over onto the beige carpeting. "It's back down there. That . . . that *thing*," he said, pointing to the escalator, "attacked me!"

Liza slowly let her breath out and briefly closed her eyes. "What's wrong with you?" Not waiting for an answer, she pointed to the floor in front of him. "Don't move," she ordered. "Wait right here until I get back."

As she walked away, Morgan could hear her muttering to herself, "What the hell am I doing, getting involved with a nut case? I must be as crazy as him!"

He did move. He came closer to the moving stairs and studied it, watching as Liza glided down a matching one, picked up her suitcase, and stepped onto the one he had traveled. Their eyes locked, and he watched as her expression changed from annoyance to confusion, and finally, to amusement. Easily stepping over the disappearing steps, she tried to hide the laugh that threatened to escape her lips. Standing in front of him, she giggled. "Do you know how funny you looked? It's an escalator, Morgan. An escalator! You've never seen one?"

Envisioning himself leaping into the air, he couldn't help the short chuckle. "Liza, I don't know how to explain it to you. All this—"

She interrupted him. "I don't know if I'm ready to hear about it. Maybe I'm afraid of what you'll say. Like, you're not from a mental institution, are you?"

Morgan smiled. "No. I'm not from a mental institution, though you might think I belong in one if I told you where I do come from."

Confused, she shook her head. "Don't tell me . . . not yet. First, let's see about that half dime in your pocket. C'mon."

Again, she led the way. This time they walked through a glass-enclosed skyway, and Liza had to periodically pull on his arm as he stopped in amazement. Laughingly, she reassured him that it would not collapse and hurl them to the ground. Once more, they confronted an escalator, and now Morgan approached it bravely, cautiously, but no longer afraid it would chop off his feet.

Soon, they were standing at the Convention Center. Another small sign announced the group of coin collectors who sponsored the display and welcomed members of the Authentication Bureau.

"Well, this is it," Liza said with finality.

Morgan turned to face her. "Aren't you coming in with me?"

She smiled and shook her head. "I don't think I'd be the best person to walk in there with, you know?" She looked down to her purple stockings.

Morgan glanced at them and then up to her face. "Come with me," he asked. "I don't know what to say to them."

"You'll do okay." She pushed his arm. "Go on. If it makes you feel any better, I'll wait here until you come out. All right?"

Morgan looked into her eyes and nodded. "You have been a good friend, Liza Moran. Thank you."

She winked at him and gave him another gentle push. "Go on. Remember, if that coin's worth something, don't be real quick about letting it go. Look around a bit, and then talk to someone who looks like they're in charge."

"I will," he promised.

She indicated the Convention Hall with her head. "Good luck."

Liza Moran watched the handsome cowboy enter the large room and shrugged. It wasn't the first time she'd gotten mixed up with a strange man. Reaching into her white-leather shoulder bag, she took out a cigarette and lit it. Inhaling the tobacco, she picked up her suitcase and walked to a comfortable-looking chair against the wall. Dropping her belongings on the carpet, she sat down and took another long drag, ignoring the looks of some older women as they passed in front of her.

What the hell was she doing here anyway? She should be downstairs looking up the guy who was either going to hire her or send her back to San Francisco. She'd already made up her mind that this was it. If she walked away from this audition empty handed, then she was going back to work as a legal secretary. Unconsciously, her mouth screwed up in distaste when she thought about her job. It was okay, as far as jobs go, but nothing exciting ever occurred— unless you could call typing up bankruptcy proceedings exciting. She didn't. The only excitement took place on the weekends when she sang in Marty's Bar. Then she wasn't Elizabeth Moran, proper middle child of Agnes and Peter. Then she was special. God, how could she explain it to them? How could she explain it to anyone? It wasn't conceit nor disillusionment—at least she hoped not. Ever since she'd been little, she just knew she was special in some way. She didn't find out how until a few years ago. She could sing. It was that simple. She didn't have a great, powerful voice, just clear. Pure, Marty had said.

Thinking about singing, she crushed out the cigarette. So much depended on what happened today. It could either be the beginning or the end to her dreams. She looked down at her boots and shook her head. Maybe she shouldn't have dressed like this. What was fun in San Francisco didn't look like it would go over here in Reno. What if the talent coordinator thought she was strange, a weirdo, as the cab driver put it? God, what being a middle child and looking for attention could do to you!

She mentally shook herself. She had to stop the creeping insecurities from taking hold. It was too late now to do much about her appearance. She couldn't exactly walk into a ladies' room and wash her hair. And if nothing else, she *would* get attention. She just hoped they'd listen to her voice, too.

From her vantage point across the double doors, she could see several men surrounding the cowboy, excited looks on their faces. Very quickly, almost like a wave, they propelled him off to one side, and he was out of view. Shifting in her chair, Liza hoped it was a good sign and that they weren't taking him off to jail. What a strange man! The guy was good looking enough to be in the movies, yet he seemed backward. She couldn't understand his ignorance, his childish wonder. And she couldn't understand why she kept helping him, especially since she noticed the gold wedding band on his finger. The last thing she needed was to get involved with a married man.

"Excuse me, are you Liza Moran?"

Looking up, she saw a heavyset middle-aged man who adjusted his glasses as he waited for her answer. Unsure of what he wanted, she answered a little hesitantly. "Yes."

The man smiled. "Mr. Trahern asked if you'd join him inside."

"Inside?"

Nodding, the man picked up her suitcase and waited for her to rise. "Yes. I suppose you can imagine our excitement when Mr. Trahern shows up out of nowhere and produces such a rare find. I believe the others are planning an impromptu auction. Mr. Trahern asked that you be present."

Liza couldn't help the small laugh. Her audition could wait.

They were gathered in the banquet manager's office, hotly discussing the auction when Liza entered. Morgan turned around and caught her look of amazement. Leaving the others, he slowly walked up to her.

"What's going on? Is there really going to be an auction?"

Nodding, Morgan smiled and looked back toward the group of men. "I think that's what they're arguing about."

Leaning closer to him, Liza whispered, "Do you still have it? You didn't give it over to them, did you?"

Morgan turned back to her. "Only for a short while so they could authenticate it. But it's not just the one. I looked over their display and found I had another that might interest them."

"No kidding! Hey, that's great. How much do you

think you'll get?" She watched him shrug just as the argument stopped and the men faced them. One— tall, thin, and dressed like an ad in *Gentleman's Quarterly*, took a step in their direction. His impatient eyes dismissed Liza.

"Mr. Trahern, after much discussion, some of our members feel it would be inappropriate for us to conduct an auction on such short notice. There are some who think a find such as this should be offered to more than a select few here today. With your permission, the auction will be held in two days, in order for some of us to reach interested clients and act on their behalf." Adjusting the cuff on his impeccably tailored light-gray suit, he added, "And, of course, that would give the bureau the necessary time to draw up its papers."

Liza's family wasn't monied, but in her job, she'd been around enough wealthy people to no longer be impressed. Sensing Morgan's unease, she spoke up. "Excuse me, gentlemen. I'm afraid that puts Mr. Trahern in an awkward position. You see, he wasn't planning to stay in Reno that long." Seeing the looks of almost horror on the faces of the men across from her, she felt her advantage and pressed on. "Perhaps, the hotel could issue him a credit line. Comp him for a room, meals, and so forth. Could you give us a low estimate on how much the coins might be worth?"

The men starting talking all at once. She looked at Morgan and returned his pleased smile. They both heard the man in the blue suit ask the banquet manager if such an arrangement would be possible and listened to the confused man's answer.

"I don't know! This entire floor is banquet facilities. We have nothing to do with those things. I'll have to call Bob Stratton to come up here."

Above the excited talk, Liza raised her voice once

more. "Gentlemen! Have you decided on an estimate?"

The room became hushed, and the now nervous spokesman conferred with the others. In less than a minute, he turned around and faced a very quiet and anxious Morgan. "A low estimate?" he asked.

Both Liza and Morgan nodded and waited.

The man cleared his throat. "For both coins, a low estimate would be somewhere in the neighborhood of three hundred thousand dollars."

Almost as one, Morgan and Liza inhaled with shock. Immediately, the banquet manager was on the phone and quicker than anyone thought possible, Bob Stratton was in the office, making arrangements. The coins would be kept in the casino's safe, and the hotel would handle the auction for one percent of the proceeds. And, best of all, Morgan had a credit line of one hundred thousand dollars, until the coins were actually sold.

As Bob Stratton turned a flushed face toward them, asking if he could reserve a room, Liza had recovered enough to link her arm through Morgan's and announce in a happy voice, "I believe Mr. Trahern would be more comfortable in a suite."

Everyone, including Harrah's casino manager, laughed. No, she thought as she quickly joined in, Morgan Trahern was definitely not a loser.

Chapter Thirty-seven

The walls were covered in rich fabrics and paintings. Handmade duplicates of rare antique furniture were tastefully used throughout the suite—in shades of pink, mauve, and a cream so soft it looked like fine silk. A shell-pink, veined, marble floor gave way to thick, plush, rose-colored carpets. It was elegance—the surroundings of a high roller—where in a land without royalty, one can live like a king, dine like a duke and drink like a lord.

Liza dropped her purse onto a subtly flowered sofa and slowly whistled. "This place is bigger than my parents' whole house!" she said in a low voice meant only for Morgan.

Smiling, Bob Stratton looked at the silent man who viewed the room with less excitement. "I hope you'll be comfortable, Mr. Trahern. If there's anything you wish, just use the phone. I'll have your VIP card sent up this afternoon." Turning as a tuxedoed waiter came out of an adjoining room, he added, "And if there's anything special you'd like to eat, Thomas will have our chef prepare it for you. Just let us know."

Overwhelmed by his surroundings, by the entire episode, Morgan nodded. "Thank you, Mr. Stratton."

Harrah's host came closer. Extending his hand, he smiled and said, "Call me Bob. Remember . . . anything, at all."

"I think Morgan could use some new clothes. As I said: He wasn't prepared to stay in Reno."

Both men looked at Liza. Bob Stratton inclined his head. "That can be arranged. What size are you, Morgan?"

"Size?" With his eyes, Morgan questioned Liza.

"He's a forty-two long," she said, quick to pick up his confusion.

Bob walked toward the double doors. "No problem. Do you want to go downstairs, or would you like them sent up?"

"Sent up," Morgan said quietly. "If it isn't any trouble."

"No trouble. Someone will be up within the hour." Just before he closed the door behind him, he looked at Morgan and Liza and again smiled warmly. "Enjoy your stay at Harrah's."

As Morgan stared at the closed door, Liza said in an awed voice, "They make it hard not to enjoy it. God, look at this place!"

Seeing the sad look return to his eyes as Morgan glanced about the suite, she came closer to him. "Hey, what's wrong? Was I too pushy? I was only guessing at your size."

Morgan shook his head. "If it weren't for you, I'd be back at the train station."

She laughed. "I was thinking the same thing, only the other way around." Spying the patient waiter standing to one side, she asked, "Are you hungry, Morgan?"

He shook his head as he walked about the large room, taking in totally unfamiliar objects scattered

462

about. From behind him, he heard Liza telling the waiter that they would order later. Quietly, the man left.

"Are you okay?"

Turning around, he nodded and had to smile as he watched her fall back into one of the plump chairs and put her high-heel boots onto a low, square marble table.

"Well, well, Morgan Trahern. How does it feel to be rich?"

He issued a small laugh. "I'm not exactly rich yet. I'll have to wait until the auction."

"*This* is not rich?" she asked, waving her hand about the sumptuous room.

He sat opposite her on the sofa. In a serious voice, he said, "Liza, you've done so much for me already. Can I ask for another favor?"

She leaned forward. "Sure. What do you want?"

"Will you stay with me?"

She didn't say anything, just looked into his eyes. Finally, after several tense moments, she spoke. "What about that wedding ring on your hand? Look, Morgan I don't know what you think I am, but—"

"No. That's not what I meant," he quickly interrupted. "I . . . I just . . . I need someone I can trust. Someone who can show me around, tell me how things work."

"Tell you how things work? What things?"

He inhaled deeply several times. "I can't explain it to you. All of this." He looked about the room. "It's completely unfamiliar to me. I need someone to explain it, without asking questions I can't answer. I trust you."

Her eyebrows came together, and she scratched her pointed dyed hair. "I don't know what to make of you. You show up with a wallet full of credit cards that aren't yours, a pocket full of coins that could be worth a fortune, and now you want *me* to answer questions. Answer me this, Morgan. That is a wedding ring, isn't it?"

He looked down at his left hand. Nodding, he said, "It is."

"Then, where's your wife? Why don't you call her? Let her answer your questions."

His face was transformed by a look of intense inner pain. "I can't," he whispered.

Liza brought her legs down from the coffee table. "God, I'm sorry. Are you . . . are you a widower?"

His head snapped up. "No! My wife is alive. She's . . ." What could he say? He refused to believe Jenna no longer existed! "She's gone . . . lost."

Feeling she had treaded on something extremely personal, Liza tried to change the subject. "Well, look, sure I'll stay for a couple of days. But first, I've got to see about that job." Standing up, she said, "I don't know where they put my suitcase. I'm late already. What do you think, Morgan? Do you think Reno is ready for purple hair?"

Looking up, his lips curved upward. "You are different, Liza."

Laughing, she walked around the chair and crossed the carpet. Disappearing into a room, she called out, "Yeah, but I kind of have a feeling I'm *too* different."

Smiling in the direction of her voice, he jumped up when he heard her startled shout. "Hey! Will you look at this!"

He passed two huge bedrooms before he saw her standing at the doorway to another room. Coming up behind her, he saw it was a bath of some sort. A room as large as his mother's sitting room was devoted entirely to bathing.

Liza felt him standing behind her and moved into

the bathroom. Turning her face around to his, she widened her eyes and laughed. "Have you ever seen anything like it before? Four people could fit in that tub."

Like two children, they slowly walked about the room exploring its many delights. A huge black-marble bathtub was raised on a carpeted platform, with a ledge that held towels, soaps, oils, telephone, and a large crystal bowl containing every fruit imaginable.

"Talk about pampered!" Liza turned on the water in the tub and looked up at Morgan. "Look, I can't pass this up. I'm going to call downstairs and see if I can postpone my interview. Would you mind if I used this first?"

"No. Go ahead," he muttered, unable to take his eyes off the heavy flow of water that was forced out of a thick gold pump of some kind. Sitting on the platform, he vaguely heard Liza speak and looked up to see her talking into the small machine beyond the fruit. He could hear her answering someone, as if carrying on a conversation, and shook his head. Marveling at the invention, he reached out with his hand and felt the water. It was hot! Where could it come from? Even though this room's windows were of stained glass, he knew they were high above the ground. How did they make the water flow up instead of down?

"Well, I've got two hours to make myself beautiful," Liza announced across the tub.

Looking up at her, Morgan asked, "How do they get the water up here? It's already hot."

"What do you mean, how? Plumbing."

"But how do they do it?"

"It's a tub, Morgan. You know—hot and cold-running water?"

Seeing the confusion on his face, she swallowed the sarcastic remark on the tip of her tongue. Instead, she smiled. "No questions, right? Geez, it's like leading someone through the twenty-first century."

When Morgan nodded, she shook her head. "I don't even want to know what that nod meant . . . not now. Okay, let's see . . . I guess it has something to do with water pressure. Anything else in here has you confused?"

Looking around the huge room, Morgan stood up and walked to a low apparatus off to one side, surrounded by large, feathery plants. "What's that?" he asked.

Coming up beside him, Liza looked at it and then looked at him. "It's a toilet, Morgan. A toilet," she repeated for emphasis. "You're not going to ask me to explain what it's used for, are you?"

He didn't answer her, but just stared at it. Impatient, embarrassed, but mostly confused, she brought the lid up and said, "You sit on it, all right? And then, *voila*!" She pushed on a small lever, and again Morgan watched water disappear and come back.

"It's amazing!"

"Yeah, right . . . amazing." Wanting to get him away from the toilet, she said, "Look, since you seem fascinated with water, watch this." Walking back to the tub, she switched a button, and the accumulated water began to swish and twirl inside the black marble. "A Jacuzzi. Great, huh?"

"Why does it do that?" he asked, putting his hand into the water and feeling the bubbly currents run over his fingers.

Handing him a towel, Liza said, "It's to relax you. Wait till you try it."

Drying his hand, he walked over to the door to leave her in privacy, but from behind, he heard her exclaim,

"I don't believe it! Will you look at this?"

Turning around he saw her at a long dressing table. Coming back into the room, he watched as she examined the contents of a padded bag. "Look. Shampoo, toothpaste, brushes, deodorant, and even a hair dryer! God, they think of everything."

"I know the others. What are deodorant and hair dryer?"

She exhaled heavily, and her voice was filled with a strained patience when she spoke. "You don't know anything, do you?"

"I told you I know what shampoo and brushes are, and I assume toothpaste is to clean your teeth. I have never heard of deodorant or hair dryer. Does it dry your hair?"

He watched as she picked up a small object with a long round tube at the end. As she lifted the other end of its long cord, he carefully took notice of the way she inserted the two small prongs into a device in the wall. "Deodorant, Morgan, is put on your armpits, and I'm being graphic because I'm afraid if I don't explain it perfectly and say it goes under your arms, you'll apply it from your elbow to your waist."

Seeing how he was trying to stop smiling, she continued. "And if you think about it, it's all self-explanatory. Deodorant. Hair dryer . . ." Picking it up, she flipped a switch and pointed it at his hair.

Immediately, Morgan stepped back as hot air robbed him of his breath. Liza turned it off and chuckled as he pushed back his hair and glared at her. "Sorry. I thought a demonstration might be helpful," she apologized.

"I think I will leave you to your bath," he stated, frustrated at his own ignorance.

Putting the hair dryer back on the long marble counter, she felt ashamed for making fun of him.

"Look, why don't you relax. You've had a strange morning. Watch some television."

Quickly, his face was transformed. Here was something he'd heard about. "Yes. Television. Where is it?"

He followed her back into the spacious sitting room and sat in a chair opposite a piece of furniture whose center was gray glass.

"Now watch what I'm doing," she said, holding a small rectangular device out in front of him. "See where it says On/Off? Push it."

Doing as she'd asked, he depressed the tiny button and jumped when the gray glass immediately started talking to him. Accompanying its voice was a picture of a man asking him, "Do you want to spin, or can you solve the puzzle?"

Startled, Morgan whispered, "No," and listened to Liza's giggle.

"He's not asking you," she gently advised. "Look, he's asking that woman."

Morgan watched as a red-haired woman said, "I'm going to spin," and reached down and gave a large wheel a push.

"It's a game," Liza said. "Wheel of Fortune. Maybe you'd like to see what else is on. Push this button."

Following her directions, he watched in astonishment as the picture quickly changed. He saw brief glimpses of people shooting at each other, and with the push of a button, he could see a man and woman embracing. He saw automobiles engaged in a race, and with the slight depression of his finger, he could make them disappear and be replaced by two men fighting."

"Here! Why don't you keep this on? It's a sports cable channel. You like boxing?"

Nodding, Morgan's eyes were glued to the screen as two men fought with each other in front of him. He held on to the arms of the chair as the picture got bigger and felt as if he were standing right in the ring with them, as if he could but reach out and touch their faces. When a bell rang, the picture quickly changed by itself and was replaced by an older woman with a strangely accented voice. She talked to him about making love and asked if he used condoms. Eyebrows together and his mouth almost hidden beneath his mustache, he looked up at Liza.

"What is she talking about? This time it seems as if she's speaking to me."

"It's a commercial!" Liza squealed over gasps of laughter. Holding her sides as she went over to a long desk, she brought back a piece of paper, a pen that used no visible ink, and a heavy book.

"Thanks to Doctor Ruth," she giggled, "you're going to start your own education right now. This is a pen," she said, handing over each article in succession. "This is a piece of paper. And *this* is a dictionary. Make a list of words you don't understand and look them up." Leaving them in Morgan's lap, she laughed again and walked back toward the bathroom. "Too bad I have to get going," she threw over her shoulder. "Sounds like it's going to be more fun up here."

Using the thick dictionary, he looked up the word and scowled. "A sheath for the—" Slamming the book shut, he picked up the changing device and immediately switched channels. He'd be damned if he'd let a woman old enough to be his grandmother tell him about such things!

He lost track of time as he scribbled words onto the paper. Long ago, he had given up trying to find their meaning—for no sooner had he picked up the dictionary when another confusing phrase would be uttered. Instead, he just listened and wrote, bewitched by the wonderful invention, until a quiet knocking on the door forced him to abandon the addictive entertainment.

He admitted three men, two of whom were pushing a long clothes rack. He acknowledged the single man's handshake and listened as he was told what store the three of them were from. Just as he was slipping his arms into a dark-blue jacket, Liza turned the corner of the room and came into view.

All four men stopped and watched as she crossed the distance and stood in front of them. Pleased by their expression of admiration, she lifted her head and reached out to touch a pair of Lizard cowboy boots. "Mr. Trahern is more conservative. I think these . . ." And she raised a pair of plain brown-leather boots shining with a high gloss. "Yes?" she asked, looking for Morgan's approval.

Unable to comprehend the startling change in her appearance, he merely nodded. Gone were the purple stockings, the matching hair, the strange clothing. Instead of an outlandish young girl, Liza had turned into a pretty, understated woman. Her hair was still blond, but now it was swept back off her face in soft waves. Her makeup was lighter, and she was dressed in black slacks, a white sweater, and low-heeled slippers. A strand of small pearls lay gracefully over her chest, almost the same color as her hair.

"You look . . . lovely," Morgan quietly observed aloud.

Liza smiled. "Thanks," she said self-consciously and turned her attention back to the rack of clothes. "I wish I could stay and help you, but I've already postponed the audition once." Looking at the still staring men, she said with authority, "He's going to

470

need everything, from underwear on out, but I want an itemized list. And remember—conservative."

Nodding, the men began to assemble clothes as Morgan took off the jacket and walked her to the door. Opening it for her, he said, "Thanks, Liza. Good lu—"

She brought her finger up to his lips, stopping him from finishing his wish. "Never say that to a performer. You're supposed to say: 'Break a leg.'"

Shaking his head, Morgan laughed. "Break a leg?" he asked, unable to understand why he was to wish her harm.

Liza squeezed his arm and giggled. "Thank you, Morgan," she whispered a little nervously, and quickly shut the door behind her.

He stood at the window looking down, so far down, at the street below. Life seemed to be moving in slow motion, he thought, and he leaned his forehead against the cool glass as he watched the moving miniatures. The automobiles, some now with lights like two vigilant eyes, glided across the wide black road and over a bridge. At dusk, the entire town seemed prepared for a party, with all its glittering lights proclaiming in a yellow and blue arch to be the biggest little city in the world.

Morgan wasn't in the mood. He could still hear the television's voice behind him, yet, for the moment, it had lost its fascination. He had seen two people kissing—and the woman had been blond. *Jenna!* Even thinking her name was painful.

Suddenly, he was tired, exhausted, and he pushed himself away from the glass pane. Picking up the television's device, he turned it off. In tense silence, he walked through the rooms until he found the one with his new clothes. Without giving them a second glance, he also ignored the room's lavish decor and fell onto the largest bed he had ever seen. Closing his eyes, he pictured his wife. Oh, Jenna, where are you? How could I have been sent to this time when I'm so unprepared? His arms ached for her, and he brought them around his chest while fighting for control. Come to me, Jenna, he silently pleaded. Come to me—if only in my dreams.

"Ladies and gentlemen, the 1870-S half dime, the coin called the numismatic find of the century when it was first discovered in 1978, will be joined by another. Until the coin appeared in 1978, no 1870-S half dime was known to exist." The spokesman for the coin exposition nodded to a security guard, and the man brought out a small glass case. Walking up and down the front aisles of the room, he offered a glimpse to the well-heeled collectors straining their necks to see.

"Some of the mystery surrounding the dime arises directly from the San Francisco Mint itself. We are all aware of the, shall we say, confusion in its management. No coinage records were kept of some issues. The 1870-S silver dollar, for instance, is not mentioned, yet at least a dozen exist. Today, in addition to the half dime, another 1870-S silver dollar will also be auctioned."

Catching the eye of the guard, he again nodded, and the uniformed man brought the coins to the front of the room. Waiting until he had his audience's attention, he looked around the small, yet elegant gathering. "These extremely rare coins were brought to us two days ago for authentication by a party that wishes to remain anonymous." Looking out to his rapt audience, he said happily, "Shall we begin the auction with the silver dollar? Am I bid one hundred thousand dollars?"

Morgan sat in the back of the room. To an observer, he looked like a wealthy businessman. A three-piece, charcoal-gray suit fit him like it was cut on his body and was handsomely offset by a impeccable white shirt and red tie. His legs were crossed, and he leaned back into the soft-cushioned chair, a thin cigar in hand. He looked almost uninterested in the proceedings, and in truth, he was.

It was all part of the strange lethargy that had taken hold of him in the last two days. What did it matter how much money he derived from the sale of the coins? What did any of it matter without Jenna? The only reason he was here was because of Liza. She had nagged at him to get out of the suite until he couldn't stand the sound of her voice. He almost smiled when he thought that. Her voice. She had her job. Lead singer, she said, in the cabaret, and he had promised to go and hear her tonight. She'd also surprised him by telling him she had found a place to stay—with one of the other female singers. Her things were already moved out of the suite. He really was alone now, but he had a great deal to thank her for. She'd given him a good beginning. The only problem was he didn't know where it would all end.

Hearing the sudden cheering, he realized he had missed the final bid and didn't know what the silver dollar had gone for. It really didn't matter. He was afraid nothing mattered anymore.

Forty-five minutes later, he left the auction a wealthy man, far richer than when he had walked into this hotel. Five hundred and twenty-five thousand dollars richer. Half a million dollars for two coins in his pocket that wouldn't have bought him a room for the night in his own time. And he hadn't even shown them the others. Wandering around the hotel, he looked into the expensive shop windows, yet felt no urge to buy anything. He left the hotel part and entered the casino. Even the excitement there couldn't dispel his pensive mood. For two days he'd spent his time discovering new inventions or watching television. He couldn't say this future held any hope for mankind. On the screen he had seen pictures of wars, accidents, fires, and death. No—everything was the same, only now the horror visited you every day through the television.

Apparently the hotel had its own channel to instruct its guests on gambling, and Morgan had watched with little interest. He should have paid better attention.

Standing at a craps table, he listened to the cheers and moans, and within forty-five minutes lost four thousand dollars. It didn't faze him, and it should have. Next he sat down at a blackjack table, and immediately, a pretty young woman in a black velvet and rhinestone dress, ending at her hips, asked him if he'd like a drink. When she delivered his whiskey, he tipped her with a fifty dollar chip, knowing it was outrageous—yet he didn't care. It was almost as if he felt he had no right to the money. Even for a novice, he played poorly—taking a hit on fourteen, when the dealer showed a six—splitting eights when the quick-handed female had a five. This time when he lost seven hundred, he stood up and backed away from the table.

It was then that he saw her. Just her back. His legs moved as fast as the beat of his heart while he quickly maneuvered his way through the crowd.

"Jenna!"

Why didn't she stop? Frantic, he called her name once more as he broke into a faster stride. Reaching out with his hand, he grabbed her arm and turned her around.

An annoyed stranger looked first into his face then at her arm. He felt the breath had been knocked out of him, and he could do no more than loosen his grip, freeing the blond woman. Apologies were never made as he turned away and tried to bring moisture back into his mouth. He was losing his mind! Needing to get away from the noise in the casino, Morgan made his way to the cabaret—anxious now for another drink.

He sat at the bar, nursing his second whiskey, minding his own business, and only turned around when he heard Liza's soft voice behind him.

"You shouldn't have, you know that, don't you?"

Taking in her outfit, he smiled. "It is the one you were talking about, isn't it?"

Looking down at the slinky black dress with its sequined white jacket, ending at her thighs in graceful points, she sighed and smiled. "How did you know my size?"

Sipping on his whiskey, Morgan again looked at the shimmering outfit. "I had one of the women deliver flowers and size you up. You look wonderful, Liza."

She sat on the chair next to him. "I should have known they were from you! Who else would send them? Who else do I even know here? Thanks, Morgan. For everything."

He looked into her eyes, saw the happiness, and wished he could share it. "I have a feeling all that's going to change. Soon, you won't be able to keep your suitors straight."

"Suitors? You sure talk funny, Morgan."

"Yeah, I suppose I do."

Sensing his depression, she linked her arm through his and whispered in an excited voice, "How long are you going to keep me in suspense? The only reason I stayed away from the auction was because you wanted to remain anonymous, and I would have given you away by shrieking, or something. What did they go for?"

"Five hundred and twenty-five thousand."

"What?" Immediately, she pulled her arm away and stared at him.

He didn't repeat the figure, knowing she had heard him correctly the first time. "It's hard to believe, isn't it?"

Not answering, Liza reached out and took his drink. Taking a large gulp, she gasped as she replaced it in front of him. "My God! What are you going to do?"

"Do?"

"Sure. You can't just sit around a hotel room and watch television. Get out there," she said, jerking her head toward the door, "and see the world. It isn't so bad, Morgan," she whispered softly.

He didn't say anything, just continued to stare at his near empty glass.

"It's your wife, isn't it?"

Still, he couldn't form any words. How could he tell her? How could he explain?

Sitting back on the chair next to him, she leaned her arms on the bar and looked at him as soft music began to play behind them. "I never asked any questions, did I?"

He shook his head.

"Can I ask them now?"

He didn't look at her, just nodded—both to her and the bartender who immediately took away his glass and replaced it with a filled one. "I don't know if I can answer them, Liza."

She examined the polished bar in front of her,

476

running her finger across the grain of wood. "Then tell me this. Will I ever see you again? Do you love her that much?"

For a fraction of time, his composure broke. His shoulders sagged, and his face held a look of grief. In a cracked voice, he murmured, "I love her so much that . . . don't you see, it's all pointless without her?"

She put an arm around him and rested her cheek on his shoulder. For just a moment, he took comfort in her friendship and leaned his head against her hair. Then, knowing the break between them had to come sometime, and secretly dreading it, he straightened and said in a falsely strong voice, "When do I get to hear you sing? They're not going to start without you, are they?"

She took her cue and raised her head to look at the band behind them. "I'd better get up there. God, I'm scared to death! All the songs we rehearsed are standards, nothing fast until the end of the set. But what if I forget the lines? What if I fall? What if—"

"Stop it. You worked hard and you look beautiful. Everyone will love you."

She looked deep into his eyes. "Will you stay until I'm done?"

He smiled, brushed her hair back from the top of her ears, and shook his head. "I think the mood I'm in, I'd be better off alone. But I wouldn't miss hearing you sing."

Her eyes were large as she searched his. "Will I ever see you again?"

"I don't know," he admitted. "I honestly don't know." Seeing her quivering chin, he stilled it with his finger. "Break a leg, Liza," he softly whispered.

With a small cry, she buried her face in his neck and wrapped her arms around his shoulders. Kissing the skin under his jaw, she mumbled, "Good luck,

Morgan. I swear . . . I'll never forget you!''

She tore herself away from him and almost ran to the stage. His eyes followed her movements as she conferred with the other members of the band, and he felt proud as he watched her get control of herself and move into the halo of light in the center of the wooden platform.

Bringing his drink up to his lips, he heard her voice as she spoke into what he now knew was called a microphone.

"Welcome back. My name's Liza Moran, and I'd like to dedicate our first song to a special friend.'' She signaled the others, and soon the band started playing a pleasant, drawn-out refrain.

Morgan was shaken when he heard her sing. It was so different from her speaking voice. Strong, clear, and sweet, she asked the audience in a plaintive voice, "Where is the love? . . .''

It had taken every bit of willpower to sit in that bar and listen to Liza sing to him. He had waited until she'd finished two songs before he slipped away. Back in the suite, he loosened his tie and removed his suit jacket. Dropping it onto a chair, he crossed the room and stood at the window. He looked down at the tiny lights crisscrossing over the city and felt his throat tighten. God, he couldn't go on like this—always searching, always yearning. She was back there, back in his past, and the future held nothing for him. What had happened to her? Did she take the blame for the second robbery? For Bullmason's death? Was she in a jail right now, waiting for— Even tightening his face couldn't stop the tears from sliding down his cheeks. Would she remember to contact his family in Baltimore? Would they believe her, if she did? God, his parents! How could they deal with losing another son?

Grinding the heels of his palms into his eyes, he couldn't stop the shudders from taking hold of his body. He was abandoned, sent to a time that wasn't his; leaving behind the woman who had captured his love, gave meaning to his life.

Trying desperately to open the window, he knew without her there was no meaning.

Chapter Thirty-eight

The steam from the hot water rose up and gathered on her forehead, shoulders, and arms, anything exposed above the water. The heat was almost overwhelming, yet she continued to lie in the tub, feeling the moistness enter through her pores, purging her body. If it could only do the same for her mind.

It seemed to her her hand lifted from the water in slow motion, and again, she stared at the gold band. She was losing her mind. That was it. If she just lay here in the tub, never got out, maybe it would all go away; maybe everyone beyond this room would retreat and leave her alone.

"Jenna?"

Turning her head slowly toward the heavy haze of steam that hung in the air, she glanced at the woman coming closer to her. Identifying her, she looked back to the water as her left hand disappeared beneath it.

"My God, you can barely breathe in here! I'm going to leave the door open."

Coming closer to Jenna, she sat on the tub's narrow ledge and offered her a long-stemmed fragile glass. "Here, Claire said, "I've brought you chilled wine."

It was only politeness that made Jenna accept.

"Are you ready to talk about it yet?"

Sipping the cold white wine, Jenna didn't answer. There were no words to explain what was in her heart, and she didn't dare reveal the thoughts that tormented her brain. It must be kept secret, never told. No one would believe her anyway, and she couldn't blame them.

Looking down at her daughter, Claire Weldon unconsciously grasped the front of her skirt with her hand. Her expression was that of a worried mother. Something had happened to Jenna on this last trip, something that had changed her, robbed her of her laughter, her happiness, her zest for life. "Won't you please tell me? Maybe I could help."

Hearing the concern in her mother's voice, she turned her head and smiled sadly. "I'll be all right," she said slowly. "I just need a little time."

Pushing wet strands of blond hair away from Jenna's forehead, Claire tried again. "You can take your hand out of the water, dear. I've seen the ring. Why don't we start with that?"

Seeing her mother's imploring look, she straightened her back and sat higher in the tub. Leaning her elbow on its ledge, she balanced the glass with a shaking hand.

"Are you married? It is a wedding ring, isn't it?"

She brought her left hand up from the water to cover her eyes and, pressing her fingertips into her forehead, she nodded.

She heard Claire's quick intake of breath. "Who?"

Jenna breathed deeply, several times. Without bringing her hand down, she murmured, "His name's

Morgan Trahern." Just hearing his name aloud made her body convulse with sobs. Hiding her face in the crook of her arm, she continued to cry. It was what she had done in private for days now. She vaguely felt her mother take the wine away and begin to gently rub her back.

"What happened, Jenna? Where is he?"

She shook her head. "He's gone." Lifting her chin, she turned red-rimmed eyes to her mother. "I don't know where he is. He just . . . disappeared!"

"Disappeared?"

Nodding, Jenna took hold of her mother's hand and crushed it between her own. *"I've lost him!"* she moaned in anguish.

Afraid of what she was seeing in her daughter, Claire rose to her feet while still holding Jenna's hand. "Come, get dry. You can't stay in here forever."

Almost like a child, Jenna allowed her mother to help her out of the tub and dry her off. Wrapped in a fluffy terry-cloth robe, she followed Claire from the bathroom and stood at the side of her bed.

Turning down the sheets, her mother looked at her and asked gently, "You know how long it's been since we slept together?"

Not waiting for an answer, she patted the mattress and watched as Jenna obediently lay down. Kicking off her shoes, and pulling her blouse out from the waistband of her skirt, Claire climbed in behind her. Automatically, she moved closer to her daughter's back and brought the comforter up over them. Over the satin-covered down, her arm encircled her child.

Snuggling closer, she brushed back the damp tendrils from Jenna's ear and whispered, "Do you remember when you'd climb into bed with us?"

Staring straight ahead into the blur of her room, Jenna sniffled and nodded.

"Your father and I loved that. We had some of the best talks then, didn't we?"

Again, the silent nod.

Claire waited almost a full minute before she continued. "You can't go on like this. You know that, don't you?" Not getting a reply, she took a deep breath and added, "I love you, Jenna. I hate to see you unhappy like this. You're ruining your health. You don't go out. You haven't even called the plant since you got back."

Silence.

"Will you please see Alan? Let him give you a checkup?" she asked the back of her daughter's head.

There was no sound in the room, save Jenna's erratic breathing. Trying to be patient, she kissed the damp hair in front of her, tightened her embrace and whispered, "Think about it. Please."

Think about it? That was all she could do! Her mind was reeling from thinking. Even aspirin couldn't help the constant headache brought on by days and sleepless nights of constant thinking. Knowing even her mother's comforting presence wouldn't stop the tormenting memories, she let them again come, hoping this time she might find some answer, some reason why her whole life was turned inside out, leaving her with only the pain and heartache.

I grabbed for him—I know I did! she thought with conviction. *Only he wasn't there.*

The next thing she remembered was being surrounded by a group of men and women, one holding her arm, asking if she was all right. Looking up into their faces, she didn't want to believe she was back in the present and had frantically searched for Morgan. Letting them help her to her feet, she had called out his name, and it was only when a conductor, a man the exact opposite of Bullmason, had rushed up to her that she knew her husband was lost. The people around her told the conductor she had entered the car and stumbled. Falling to the floor, they said she must have hit her head because she didn't answer them for a few seconds.

Then the conductor explained that it must have been when the train going in the opposite direction passed. Even he admitted it was going too fast for the close tracks. She hadn't said a word then, only nodded and took a seat. Several times the conductor came back to her, telling her there was no sign of her purse or briefcase and advising her to report them stolen when they reached Sacramento.

She remembered wanting to scream at him that they weren't stolen, that they were in a small room in Verdi that existed a hundred and sixteen years ago. In Sacramento, she stayed closeted in her hotel room, never leaving to join in the convention, unable to think of anything except Morgan. It was then the tears started, and they hadn't stopped.

Blinking away the moisture at her eyes, Jenna looked about her modern bedroom. She'd spent perhaps thirty seconds in Sacramento thinking she was going through a nervous breakdown, wondering when she had bought the wedding ring for herself. Only thirty seconds, half a minute, to doubt the love she had found in the past—and then never again. *He was real! They* were real, all of them: Morgan, Jace, Willow, Gray Wolf. Never again would she desert their memory.

But her mother was right to be worried. While she firmly believed in the love and friendship she had found in the past, she also found that she could not function in the present. It was as if she was supposed to be a widow, without the release of grieving. And she refused to grieve—not for Morgan. Her mind would not accept the possibility that he no longer existed. She found herself held prisoner by the deep, spreading ache within her heart. It was heartache, the overwhelming need to touch him again, to feel his mouth on hers, to be loved by him—just once more.

Closing her eyes, she felt the tears move more quickly down her cheeks and soak into her pillow. Maybe it was happening now. Maybe this was what a nervous breakdown was. Surely her nervous system could stand no more. Yet, she must go on, until she could find a way back.

Alan Friedman had brought her into this world, smacked her bottom and watched her grow into a beautiful, fine woman. Seated across from her now, he closed his eyes briefly and knew his retirement couldn't come soon enough. He wasn't just Jenna's doctor, he was her friend. His practice had included all of the Weldons, and since Keene's death, he'd visited the house more often than in the past for Claire.

Now, her daughter sat on the other side of his desk, almost uninterested in the outcome of his examination. Rearranging his prescription tablet, he leaned closer to her. "Jenna, I'm going to be honest. You look terrible." Not getting the fiery response he had expected, he added, "Of course that might be excused, considering . . ."

Leaving the word hanging had gotten her attention. "Considering what?" she asked softly. "Is something wrong?"

Pushing his black horned-rimmed glasses further up his nose, Dr. Friedman said, "It's not my place to say whether it's right or wrong. Only you can decide that."

Seeing her confusion, he added, "Your blood tes[t] and urine sample show that you're pregnant. Yo[u] should have an internal, or I can recommend a . . ."

Her mouth hung open, shock clearly written on he[r] face. "You didn't know?" he asked. "Look, if it's [a] problem, you have options. Isn't Marty Tabor you[r] gynecologist?"

Jenna stood up, her hands gripping the front of th[e] oak desk. *"I'm pregnant?"* she asked, a look a pur[e] joy transforming her face.

Alan couldn't help but smile and nod to the hand that showed a gold band. "Yes. Frankly, I'm sur[-] prised. Your mother never even mentioned you wer[e] seeing anyone."

"I'm pregnant," Jenna stated in a whisper fille[d] with awe.

Standing up, the doctor laughed and came aroun[d] to the front of the desk. Prying her fingers away from the wood, he held them in his hand. "Yes, Jenna, you are. But I want you to see Marty soon. I may hav[e] delivered you, young lady, but I'm too old to delive[r] your child."

She started laughing and crying at the same time. "It's real!" she cried. "Don't you see? I have proof!" She kissed the dear man's cheek and walked towar[d] his office door. Turning around, she smiled brilliantl[y] at her confused old friend. "I have his child . . ."

Waiting in the outer office, Claire stood up when Jenna came sailing down the hall. The smile on he[r] face was ecstatic as she wrapped an arm around Claire's shoulders and whisked her out of the recep[-] tion room.

"What's going on?" Claire asked, her curiosity killing her. Whatever Alan had said to her had brought back the familiar, happy Jenna.

Tightening her grip on her mother, Jenna used he[r]

486

ther hand to push the elevator button. "You're not going to believe it! Oh, God!" She shook her head, till trying to absorb it herself. When the elevator topped and opened its door, Jenna saw it contained wo women, and she looked down at her mother. "Let's wait for an empty one."

"Jenna, *will* you tell me what has happened?"

Within moments, the second elevator opened, and ogether, they breathed a sigh of relief when they saw t was empty. Hurrying in, Jenna and Claire both ushed the button to close the door at the same time, gnoring the surprised look of a young delivery boy vho was about to join them.

Waiting until the elevator began its descent, Claire urned to her daughter and demanded, "Now . . . vhat *is* it?"

Pulling back her shoulders, she smiled into her nother's anxious face and asked, "Do you remember, before I left for Sacramento, you were nagging me bout settling down?"

Claire raised her chin. "I never nagged."

Jenna laughed. "I know—and I never snore."

"What? What does snoring have to do with anything?"

"Remember I asked if you would be happy if I ound some handsome stud of a man and came back regnant?"

Claire didn't answer her. She couldn't. Whether it vas the speed at which they were traveling or the unnatural amount of saliva that had entered her nouth, causing her to swallow convulsively, she didn't know. All she could think about was what was coming next.

"Are you trying to say . . ."

Jenna nodded, a look of happiness causing her face o look beautiful again. Claire wanted to share her

487

daughter's mood, yet too many questions bombarded her brain.

"How can it be possible, Jenna? That was only last week!"

Throwing back her head, Jenna laughed uproariously. "They said when I fell I was unconscious for only a second!" Looking back at her mother, she found it hard to contain her joy as she tightly gripped the smaller woman's shoulders. Her eyes held a look of tenderness as she asked, "Do you know how wonderfully long a second can be, Mother?"

Leaning back against the trunk of a tree, Jenna watched Cassie and her father practice batting. In her hands were booklets given to her by Marty Tabor, telling her of the changes that would take place inside her body. Breathing deeply, she brought the clean air into her lungs. It was important now that she remain healthy. Her arms hugged her abdomen as she watched the improvement in Cassie's swing.

"Great!" she shouted to the happy young girl. Waving back at Cassie, she smiled when she thought how a week had changed them all. Jake seemed to have finally put his wife's desertion behind him and realize what she had left behind. Now Cassie and her father looked to be inseparable.

We've all changed, she thought as she absently watched a distant cab make its way up the long entrance drive to the estate. Looking back to her young friend listening intently to her father's instructions, she silently wished that her child be a boy. She wanted a smaller version of Morgan, someone whom she could watch grow into as fine a man as his father. How she would love him! She would make sure he knew how strong, brave, tender, and loving Morgan

Trahern was. *Is* she mentally corrected himself. Is. He's still alive, somewhere, in some time.

Morgan was almost out of breath as he ran across the vast lawns. He stopped at a tree and grabbed hold of a branch as he looked at her. Gasping for air, he wanted to shout her name, but his throat had constricted with emotion. My God! She was here! All along, she was here. In the flash of an instant, he cursed himself for not thinking of coming until he had again looked through her wallet. All these days of thinking he had lost her.

Looking at her back, he tried to calm down, to slow the frantic beat of his heart. He knew if he rushed up behind her, she would be frightened. Only a few feet away from her, his hand ached to reach out and caress her beautiful hair, to turn her around and gather her into his arms. Yet, he knew to do so would be too much of a shock. A small shred of sanity held him back, knowing what she must also have gone through in the last week.

Regaining his breath, he slowly walked up behind her.

"Who are you waiting for, *desperada*?"

Looking out to Cassie and her father, Jenna stopped breathing for a second, thinking her mind was playing tricks on her. Not now, she prayed. Not now when she was trying to put her life back together. Please God, please make the voices go away.

But a tingling had started at the back of her neck, spreading across her shoulders and up into her scalp. Afraid, yet unable to stop herself, she slowly turned around.

The books dropped from her hands, her knees buckled, and she cried out in a soft, helpless moan.

"Morgan?"

He ran to her then, crossing the short distance, and gathered her into his arms. "Jenna . . . Jenna . . . Thank God . . ."

Clinging to him, she tried to separate fantasy and reality as in between her sobs she kept repeating, "Are you real? Please tell me. Are you real?"

He held her face tightly and looked into her eyes. "I'm here, Jenna. I'm here! Oh, God . . ."

They kissed quickly, then held each other with a ferociousness, their bodies needing the same reassurances as the mind. Slowly, they sank to the ground. Touching his face, running her fingers over his eyes, his nose, his mustache, she asked in a small voice, *"How?* How did you do it?"

He shook his head slowly, never taking his eyes from hers. "I don't know. One second I was in the train with you and in the next . . . I was on a modern train heading for Reno."

"You were on that train? We were both taken back, but in different directions?"

Again, he shook his head. "I don't know how it happened. I thought I had lost you, Jenna! I never thought I'd see you again!"

She held him close. "I know . . ." Quickly pulling back from him, she widened her eyes so she could see beyond the film of tears gathering at her lids. Searching his beloved face, she spoke hesitantly, desperately trying to force her voice through the tightness of her throat. "I thought I was losing my mind, Morgan. But I knew you were real . . . I knew it! And now I have the proof."

Gently he ran his thumbs over her cheekbones to wipe away her tears. "It was our love that brought me here. Nothing can separate us again. Not anything . . ." His gaze was intense. "Thank God, I found you.

Our love never needed proof, though, Jenna. You know that."

She nodded and smiled for the first time. "But I have it anyway, Morgan. I have it! You gave it to me . . ." His hands continued to hold her face, and she grasped his wrists. "I'm carrying our child."

Shaken, he looked down at her body, then back into her incredible blue-gray eyes. "A baby?" he asked in a cracked voice. When she nodded, his features went through a series of transformations: first shock, then joy, and finally, a release as his eyes filled with tears. His lower lip slightly trembled. "A baby, Jenna!" he stated with wonder. "You're sure?"

When she again nodded, he inhaled deeply and slowly brought her mouth closer to his. It was sweet, tender, and soon, overpowering. They claimed each other with a possessive passion, emptying their souls of the desperation, heartache, and grief that had taken hold since their separation. When they parted, Jenna felt she couldn't get enough of him and kissed his cheeks, his mustache, his neck, swallowing his tears with her own.

Grateful, so very grateful, she silently thanked God for His generosity in granting them yet another chance. Holding her husband close, Jenna raised her head and looked up beyond the trees. Quietly, she remembered that day, so very long ago, when she had sat with Jace in a forest. How she missed him! How she missed them all. But she would remember her friends always. Always! Sniffling, she watched the clouds slowly move, and as a serene peacefulness entered her heart, she included Jace's Mother Earth and Father Sky in her gratitude because they, too, were instrumental in bringing Morgan back to her.

"Who'd believe it, Jenna?" he whispered into her hair as he kissed his way to her face.

491

Looking down at him, she gazed deep into his eyes and murmured, "We believe it, Morgan. That's all that matters," right before her lips sealed their love.

And someday, someday they'd tell their son together. Tell him everything. For theirs was a story only the innocence of a child could accept—and believe.

ROMANCE FROM HANNAH HOWELL

MY VALIANT KNIGHT (0-8217-5186-7, $5.50/$6.50)
In 13th-century Scotland, a knight had to prove his loyalty to the King. Sir Gabel de Amalville sets out to crush the rebellious Mac-Nairn clan. To do so, he plans to seize Ainslee of Kengarvey, the daughter of Duggan MacNairn. It is not long before he realizes that she is more warrior than maid . . . and that he is passionately drawn to her sensual beauty.

ONLY FOR YOU (0-8217-4993-5, $4.99/$5.99)
The Scottish beauty, Saxan Honey Todd, gallops across the English countryside after Botolf, Earl of Regenford, whom she believes killed her twin brother. But when an enemy stalks him, they both flee and Botolf takes her to his castle feigning as his bride. They fight side by side to face the danger surrounding them and to establish a true love.

UNCONQUERED (0-8217-5417-3, $5.99/$7.50)
Eada of Pevensey gains possession of a mysterious box that leaves her with the gift of second sight. Now she can "see" the Norman invader coming to annex her lands. The reluctant soldier for William the Conqueror, Drogo de Toulon, is to seize the Pevensey lands, but is met with resistance by a woman who sets him afire. As war rages across England they find a bond that joins them body and soul.

WILD ROSES (0-8217-5677-X, $5.99/$7.50)
Ella Carson is sought by her vile uncle to return to Philadelphia so that he may swindle her inheritance. Harrigan Mahoney is the hired help determined to drag her from Wyoming. To dissuade him from leading them to her grudging relatives, Ella's last resort is to seduce him. When her scheme affects her own emotions, wild passion erupts between the two.

A TASTE OF FIRE (0-8217-5804-7, $5.99/$7.50)
A deathbed vow sends Antonie Ramirez to Texas searching for cattle rancher Royal Bancroft, to repay him for saving her family's life. Immediately, Royal saw that she had a wild, free spirit. He would have to let her ride with him and fight at his side for his land . . . as well as accept her as his flaming beloved.

Available wherever paperbacks are sold, or order direct from the Publisher. Send cover price plus 50¢ per copy for mailing and handling to Kensington Publishing Corp., Consumer Orders, or call (toll free) 888-345-BOOK, to place your order using Mastercard or Visa. Residents of New York and Tennessee must include sales tax. DO NOT SEND CASH.

TANTALIZING ROMANCE
FROM STELLA CAMERON

PURE DELIGHTS   (0-8217-4798-3, $5.99/$6.99)
Tobias Quinn is Seattle's sexiest divorced man, and he needs artistic rebel Paris Delight to save his fortune and his life. Tension, unraveling secrets and bursting chemistry between the two is sure to end in hot, passionate love.

SHEER PLEASURES   (0-8217-5093-3, $5.99/$6.99)
Set out to find an old and dear friend who disappeared from a private club in Washington State's Cascade Mountains, attorney Wilhelmina Phoenix meets the sexy Roman Wilde, an ex-Navy SEAL working undercover. Treading dangerous waters they find the truth and blazing desire.

TRUE BLISS   (0-8217-5369-X, $5.99/$6.99)
Bliss Winters and rebel Sebastian Plato were teenage sweethearts, until a jealous rival's deceit tore them apart. Fifteen years have passed and Sebastian has returned to his hometown as a bad boy made good. He is set on revenge and has no intention of leaving the woman he has always loved.

GUILTY PLEASURES   (0-8217-5624-9, $5.99/$7.50)
When television personality Polly Crow and ex-Navy SEAL Nasty Ferrito meet, love ensues from the magnetism between them. But Polly has a past she must conceal at all costs and when it creeps closer to home, Polly must trust that Nasty will discover how far a man will go to protect true love.

ROMANCE FROM ROSANNE BITTNER

CARESS   (0-8217-3791-0, $5.99)

FULL CIRCLE   (0-8217-4711-8, $5.99)

SHAMELESS   (0-8217-4056-3, $5.99)

SIOUX SPLENDOR   (0-8217-5157-3, $4.99)

UNFORGETTABLE   (0-8217-4423-2, $5.50)

TEXAS EMBRACE   (0-8217-5625-7, $5.99)

UNTIL TOMORROW   (0-8217-5064-X, $5.99)

New York Times bestselling author
Constance O'Day-Flannery has touched millions of
readers' hearts with her magical romances that enchant
and stir the imagination. Now, she gives us the story
of a woman from the present and a man from the past
who discover that only the most passionate
kind of love can transcend time...

TIMESWEPT LOVERS

*As a corporate executive in her family-owned railroad company,
Jenna Weldon was always on the go. So when she had the
opportunity to take a cross-country train ride as part of a
promotional gimmick, she gloried in the idea of such old-fashioned
luxurious travel. She even found the costumed actors in the parlor
car amusing, for they were dressed in clothing from the last century.
But all too quickly, Jenna realized that the joke was on her...
somewhere along the line she had fallen backward in time—and
into the arms of a dashing government spy named Morgan Trahern.*

*Dressed in a short skirt and puffing away on a cigarette, Jenna
enraged the passengers who were ready to throw her off the train,
except for Morgan Trahern, who was fascinated by the sight of the
reckless beauty. Now, if Jenna could only convince this rugged,
good-looking cowboy that she really was from the twentieth
century—and that she was his best chance in his undercover
investigation of a railroad scandal. But when an unrelenting
passion sparks between them, Jenna is torn between returning to
the future and staying in the past where the
love of a lifetime awaits her...*

"A warm and wondrous tale. Superb. Spellbinding. Sensational!"
—*Rave Reviews*

"A beautifully done work of art."—*Romantic Times*

"Delightful. A sure winner."—*Affaire de Coeur*

05961>

UPC

0 71268 00599 1

ISBN 0-8217-5961-2

ZEBRA
U.S.$5.99
CAN.$7.50